Be Mine

Cupid's Kiss

PATRICIA HAGAN, BOBBY HUTCHINSON, LINDA MADL, BOBBI SMITH

An Angel's Touch

In this heartwarming collection, four heavenly beings are certain to work a few miracles through the power of love—and leave more than one couple blessed by the touch of...

Cupid's Kiss

PATRICIA HAGAN

"A Marriage Made In Heaven"

"Ms. Hagan weaves a tale of true love!"
—*Romantic Times*

BOBBY HUTCHINSON

"Heaven On Earth"

"Ms. Hutchinson portrays the often heartrending travails of the human spirit with skill."

—*Romantic Times*

LINDA MADL

"Heaven In His Touch"

"Linda Madl weaves an irresistible spell!"
—*Rendezvous*

BOBBI SMITH

"A Gift From Heaven"

"Spectacular storytelling, romance, and adventure!"
—*Romantic Times*

Other Holiday Specials From *Leisure Books*
and *Love Spell*:
THEIR FIRST NOEL
CHRISTMAS ANGELS
AN OLD-FASHIONED SOUTHERN
  CHRISTMAS
CHRISTMAS CAROL
A WILDERNESS CHRISTMAS
A TIME-TRAVEL CHRISTMAS
A FRONTIER CHRISTMAS
AN OLD-FASHIONED VALENTINE
A VALENTINE SAMPLER

Patricia Hagan, Bobby Hutchinson, Linda Madl, Bobbi Smith

Cupid's Kiss

LOVE SPELL ⬦ NEW YORK CITY

LOVE SPELL®

February 1996

Published by special arrangement with Sutton Press, Inc.

Dorchester Publishing Co., Inc.
276 Fifth Avenue
New York, NY 10001

If you purchased this book without a cover you should be aware that this book is stolen property. It was reported as "unsold and destroyed" to the publisher and neither the author nor the publisher has received any payment for this "stripped book."

CUPID'S KISS Copyright © 1996 by Sutton Press, Inc.

The publisher acknowledges the copyright holders of the individual works as follows:

"A Marriage Made In Heaven" Copyright © 1996 by Sutton Press, Inc., and Patricia Hagan
"Heaven On Earth" Copyright © 1996 by Sutton Press, Inc.; special thanks and acknowledgment to Bobby Hutchinson for her contribution to the anthology
"Heaven In His Touch" Copyright © 1996 by Sutton Press, Inc., and Linda Madl
"A Gift From Heaven" Copyright © 1996 by Sutton Press, Inc., and Bobbi Smith

All rights reserved. No part of this book may be reproduced or transmitted in any form or by any electronic or mechanical means, including photocopying, recording or by any information storage and retrieval system, without the written permission of the Publisher, except where permitted by law.

For further information contact: Sutton Press, Inc., 6 Tristam Place, Pine Brook, NJ 07058-9445

The name "Love Spell" and its logo are trademarks of Dorchester Publishing Co., Inc.

Printed in the United States of America.

Sutton Press, Inc., dedicates this book to
Ronald and Victor

PATRICIA HAGAN
"A Marriage Made In Heaven"

"An angel! or if not, an earthly paragon!"
—Shakespeare, Cymbeline

Chapter One

Pennsylvania, 1850

Susannah gazed up at her portrait thoughtfully, her lips pursed. Without conceit, she thought the artist had indeed painted her true likeness, and she was proud. Her coppery-blond hair complemented her sea-green eyes, her best feature, and he had captured the high cheekbones she'd inherited from her grandmother, once considered the most beautiful woman in Philadelphia.

For the sitting, she had chosen to wear an emerald-green velvet gown, its bodice not terribly low. Not gifted with enviable cleavage, she

11

was a nice size overall, though a bit on the petite side.

Sitting for the portrait had required many tedious hours of remaining perfectly still. It had been grueling, and many times she had been tempted to tell the artist not to continue. But she was the only Tutweiler not in the collection of paintings in her mansion's great circular foyer—and also the last Tutweiler.

That was one reason she had agreed to marry Phillip Jernigan—to continue the bloodline. The other was that she was lonely. When her enormous eighteen-room house, including a ballroom, teemed with the people who attended her many socials, it was a gala place. But at twenty years old, she was already tired of her frivolous lifestyle, and her vast wealth was little comfort. She wanted, needed, a family of her own.

Orphaned at fourteen when her parents were killed in a buggy mishap, she had been sent by the administrators of her parents' estate to a boarding school until she came of age. In the two years since she had finished school, hopeful young men had flocked to her door, but she had found no one suitable. She was either put off from the start for various reasons, or, after a while, either sensed, or discovered, that their prime motivation in courting her was her money.

She hadn't worried about her unmarried state until six months ago on her twentieth birthday when Mr. Grierly, her banker and head administrator of her estate, had paid her what he called a "fatherly" visit. Offering advice about her future, he had proposed that since she was having difficulty finding a mate, it might actually be fate's way of telling her she was not meant to be a wife and mother. Perhaps, instead, she was better suited to enter a convent and give her fortune to charity. He, of course, would be glad to administer the funds.

She had not been at all receptive to his idea. Although she considered herself a spiritual person—she had special reason to be—she had never felt a calling to the religious life. But Mr. Grierly had provoked thoughts that perhaps she was destined to be a spinster, and she sensed that very prediction was being whispered in her social circle and among her friends behind her back.

Now, however, she no longer had to concern herself with what anyone thought, because Phillip had proposed, and she had accepted. He would be the father of her children, and their portraits would one day be displayed with hers and her ancestors'. And it did not matter that she did not love Phillip. She would be a good and dutiful wife to him in all ways, and perhaps one day her heart would open to him. All that mattered was that he loved her. She knew his motive for wanting to marry her was not to get his hands on her fortune, since he had his own wealth.

They had met a month ago at a social; Susannah had almost missed the occasion due to her reluctance to accept Runella Jernigan's invitation. Runella's husband, Gordon, was a gambler and forever in debt. Susannah had felt Runella should not be hosting an expensive tea dance merely to introduce her nephew, Phillip, who was visiting from New York. The bank where Susannah kept much of her fortune was one of Gordon's creditors trying to collect from him. She had changed her mind, however, when she heard gossip that the purpose of Phillip's visit was to help his aunt and uncle financially.

Lonely and always eager for something to do, she had gone to the party, and Phillip had confessed later that his heart had been hers to command from the first instant they met. Likewise, she had been immediately attracted to him.

He had stayed by her side the entire evening. Apologizing to his aunt for not mingling with the other guests, he had claimed he was completely captivated by Susannah, and by the time the party ended, he had boldly declared his intention to win her hand.

Thus had begun their whirlwind courtship. Phillip had extended his visit, saying he would not return to New York without Susannah as his bride. Her candid response was that she would never think of leaving Philadelphia. She loved the estate and all its heritage and wanted to raise her family there. He had not hesitated to say he was willing to move from New York; he had no responsibilities beyond overseeing his inheritance.

He had showered her with small gifts, but nothing extravagant. "You have so much already, my dear, and besides, there are no jewels grand enough to compete with your beauty," he had explained.

Susannah preferred that he spend his money in other ways—like helping his aunt and uncle. She had always liked the couple and was sorry that Gordon had money worries. But so far, she had noted from papers Mr. Grierly had sent to her, Gordon was still indebted to the bank for a goodly sum. However, she had said nothing to Phillip about it. After all, it was none of her business, she thought, as the light scent of lilacs whirled around her.

"The portrait turned out rather well, didn't it?"

She turned at the sound of the familiar voice. Standing in the midst of a swirling golden light was Joshua . . . her guardian angel.

As always, her heart was instantly warmed by his presence. "Oh, Joshua, where have you been for so long? I've been praying you would come. I've wanted to tell you about Phillip."

The light changed to a warm glow that gently faded as he walked to her. Putting his hands on her shoulders, he brushed her cheeks with his

15

lips, and she felt loved and protected within his embrace.

"I know about him," he said quietly.

She had always been fascinated by Joshua's gold-specked hazel eyes, which changed colors depending on his mood. When he was happy, they sparkled a brilliant blue. Now, however, they were lackluster and a shadowed brown.

"You don't sound pleased," she said, worried.

"I'm not. And quite frankly, I had hoped you would be wise enough to see things as they are without my having to show you."

She felt an uneasy quiver dance along her spine. "What are you talking about? Phillip isn't like the others. He loves me for me, not my money. He has his own fortune and doesn't need mine."

"How can you be sure of that?"

The quiver was becoming stronger. But surely Joshua was being unnecessarily skeptical, and she wondered if he was being overly protective of her. "It's obvious he has wealth. He's helping his aunt and uncle, and—"

"He hasn't helped them yet, has he?"

She shrugged. "No, but I'm sure he has his reasons. Maybe I've taken up so much of his time that he's been unable to transfer his funds. Who knows? But I'm certain he's not after my money, Joshua. He hasn't said one word about it."

"Very clever," he said, sniffing in disdain and stepping away from her.

"Joshua . . ." She placed her hands on her hips and looked him straight in the eye. "You are wrong this time. I would have suspected something by now if he only wanted to marry me for my money. I've certainly been able to tell with other men."

"With help from me," he reminded her. "As I said, I thought I'd leave you alone this time to see if you've learned anything. Obviously, you haven't, but he's shrewder than I thought, and you can't see it."

She shook her head.

He shook his head. "How long does it take to pay off someone's debts if the money is there? Think about it, Susannah. Think about it carefully, because you've always had a problem seeing things you don't want to see. That's why I have to manifest myself to you in human form when I need to counsel you. You ignore me when I speak inside you."

"Well, I'm glad I can see you. I like to look at the person I'm talking to."

"But that doesn't mean you listen, and you aren't listening now," he insisted.

"Sometimes I don't think you want me to get married."

"I want you to be happy."

"Well, Phillip makes me happy, and I wish you wouldn't be so suspicious. I want you to like him. It's important to me that you do."

Joshua smiled mysteriously. "Then perhaps

you should take me to see him so I can have a better look."

Her hand flew to her throat. "But I thought no one could see you but me. You said that's because you're my angel."

"I didn't say I wanted him to see me, Susannah. I said I wanted to see him. He won't know I'm there. Come along." He gestured for her to follow him as he moved to the door.

"But Phillip isn't expecting me, and besides, he said his cousin Bonita was visiting from New York," she protested, following him.

"How interesting. And is Runella having a party for her as she did for Phillip?"

"No, but—"

"Then is he arranging for the two of you to meet? After all, if she's family, it would seem he would want to introduce you."

"He said she was only passing through for a day and a night, and there wasn't time."

"Well, you can introduce yourself. Let's be on our way."

"Joshua, I can't just walk up and knock on the door. That would be rude."

"You won't have to. It will be nearly dark by the time we get there."

"I don't understand," she said, frustrated. She did not want to go, but Joshua meant so much to her. True, she might be stubborn sometimes. But nonetheless she was eternally grateful to him for his love and devotion to her since she was a child, and since this all seemed to mean so much to him, she could not refuse. Too, she told herself, once he was proved wrong about Phillip, he would be happy for her and pleased about their union.

Even though the hour was growing late, Lyle, the buggy driver, had not asked questions when Susannah told him to hitch up a team and take her to Philadelphia.

Once in the city, she directed him to the fashionable neighborhood where the Jernigan house, an impressive two-story building, was set back from the street and surrounded by thick shrubs and trees. Susannah walked up the cobblestone walkway.

Light streamed through the windows and spilled onto the front porch that ran the width the house. Hearing angry voices inside, she slowed. "Joshua, are you here?" she whispered uneasily. He had been beside her in the carriage for a while, then faded from sight without warning.

When he did not answer, she cursed under her breath to think he had abandoned her. But she was immediately chastised by a light thump on her head that let her know he was still there.

"This was your idea," she all but growled under her breath. "Now you can see you've led me on a wild-goose chase. They're obviously having a family argument, so let's go."

He chuckled softly. "They're fighting, all right. I thought you said this was a family reunion. It certainly doesn't sound like one to me."

"Whatever it is, it's none of our business. You've wasted my time in making me come here, and I want to leave before someone sees me. I'd be absolutely mortified, because I would never be able to come up with a convincing reason for prowling around in the dark eavesdropping."

She turned to go but at that moment heard her name mentioned—and not in a pleasant tone of voice.

"If you're going to marry Susannah Tutweiler, then do it and be done with it."

The woman's voice was unfamiliar to Susannah. She quietly moved up the steps and stood in the shadows of the porch to listen.

"I've told you a hundred times, Bonita, I can't appear too eager. She might get suspicious. All I can do is try to make her think I'm so in love with her that I can't wait any longer. But it's up to her to set the wedding date."

Susannah sagged against the porch railing and probably would have toppled over had it not been for Joshua supporting her.

"He's right, Bonita." Recognizing Runella's voice, Susannah was further shaken but she forced herself to listen. "You have to think about our situation. If Phillip doesn't hurry and marry her and get his hands on all that money, we're going to lose everything. So be patient."

"Patient," Bonita snorted. "It's bad enough to have to think of the man I love marrying another woman. At least I should start enjoying some of the booty."

"You will, darling, I promise," Phillip was quick to assure her.

Hearing that, Susannah feared she was going to be sick to her stomach.

"And you mustn't worry," Phillip continued. "I'll not only see to it that you live like a queen, but after the wedding I'll slip away to be with you every chance I get. And sooner or later, when I've gotten as much money as I can out of her, I'll arrange for her to discover I'm unfaithful, giving her cause for divorce. Then you and I will be free to marry and live the rest of our lives in luxury."

"You know," Runella said, "I really dislike doing this to Susannah. She's a sweet girl, and I've always liked her, but there's just no other way. Besides, it's not as if she doesn't have plenty of money. She won't be left destitute, by any means."

Joshua guided Susannah down the steps and back to the buggy.

"At least it's only your pride that is hurt," he said as Lyle helped her up, "and not your heart. You didn't love him, Susannah. Remember that and be glad you found out in time."

"Thanks to you," she murmured, forgetting

about Lyle. "Maybe next time I'll be smarter."

Looking at her strangely, Lyle responded politely, "Yes, ma'am. Folks get smarter as they go along."

Dumbfounded and embarrassed, she realized he had heard her talking to Joshua. Sometimes she forgot that no one else could see or hear him, but thank goodness Lyle seemed to think she was speaking to him.

Settling against the smooth leather seat, she was careful to speak low so that Lyle couldn't hear. "Damn you, Phillip Jernigan," she cursed. "Damn you and every scoundrel after my money."

This time there was no thump on the head from Joshua to admonish her for her profanity. Well, she thought, at least he felt the same way.

Chapter Two

It had been six months since Susannah's tragic experience with Phillip, and now she sat staring at broken pieces of a flowerpot on the gazebo floor. "It's happened again. I've let a man make a fool of me—again," she said, crying and trembling.

Dirt and remnants of the chrysanthemums were scattered over the floor. She hadn't remembered the pot being there on the railing. No doubt, Joshua must have placed it there just in the nick of time for her to reach for it and bring it smashing down on Windham Bishop's head. That had quickly stopped his attempt to ravish her.

Windham Bishop. She clenched her fists, enraged, tears running down her face. She hadn't seriously injured him and he had quickly left, but she wished she had smashed his head in. How dare he touch her!

He was another scoundrel who had pretended to love her so he could get his hands on her money. Not only had he swindled her out of five thousand dollars, but he had the audacity to lie about it, even after she'd confronted him with the absolute proof of his crime.

She tried to compose herself and stop the tremors racing through her. Calmer now, she thought about their first meeting at a formal dinner given by her old family friends, Mallory and Katie O'Donnell. Mallory, in making the introductions, had explained that Windham was a horse dealer and had just brought Mallory a prize stallion from Spain.

Susannah had been intrigued by Windham's fascinating tales of his European travels. She had clung to his every word, delighting in his stories and descriptions of lands she longed to visit.

From that night on, they had been almost inseparable. On his arm, Susannah had made the rounds of Philadelphia society, and it was not long after that people began speculating as to when their betrothal would be announced.

Susannah had begun to wonder as well, for Windham's intentions certainly seemed honorable. He had appeared to be a man of means who dressed well and enjoyed high living. Not once had he mentioned his financial situation, but she had assumed he made a comfortable living.

Then one night he had confessed that he could not ask her to marry him because he was not financially worthy. But, he had added, if she would trust him and help him, he had a chance to improve his wealth.

He had then told her of a man in Texas who wanted to buy some prize breeding stock, and Windham knew where to buy the horses in Virginia at a bargain price—if he had the money. Then he would take them to Texas, sell them, repay Susannah, and make a tidy profit. It would be the beginning of his own business. No longer would he merely be paid for his time delivering horses.

So she had loaned him the money. When Mr. Grierly had later asked her about the large bank withdrawal, she had confided her investment in Windham's business venture.

At the time, Mr. Grierly had not said anything. A few weeks later, however, he reluctantly informed her that he'd had Windham investigated and was distressed by what he had learned. Windham had a history of gambling losses, and, in fact, had used much of her money to pay a long overdue debt.

Susannah had not believed Mr. Grierly at first. But then he had told her he had hired a detective to follow Windham and had trailed him to New York, where he was gambling with what was left of the money Susannah had lent him.

So, when Windham had finally returned a short while ago and come to see her, she had confronted him with what she knew. He had promptly denied everything and accused Mr. Grierly of wanting to make trouble because he didn't want her to marry anyone, not ever, for a husband would take control of her fortune.

Susannah had asked him to leave, and that was when he had gone berserk. She had smelled the whiskey on his breath too late as he grabbed her and wrestled her to the floor, swearing that once he made love to her she would want to marry him.

Shivering again, she thanked God she had managed to get him off her. Tears trickled down her cheeks, and she furiously brushed them away. She would not cry. And if fate decreed that no man would ever want her except for her money, then she would live her life alone. After all, she had always been independent.

Despite her self-reliance, she did value Joshua's opinion, and when she had called on him in the beginning of her relationship with Windham to ask his advice, his reply had been, "Go slowly. Things are not always what they seem."

Now, for perhaps the thousandth time, she wished she had listened to him.

She remembered the first time she was aware

of her guardian angel. She had just turned six, and her father had given her a pony, along with specific warnings against attempting to jump the rails in the training circle until she'd been properly instructed.

But she had a wild, reckless streak, even at such a young age, and one day she disobediently began jumping the pony over the lower rails. Gradually, she worked higher, and just as she approached the highest hurdle yet, sure she would make it, her father came out onto the upstairs balcony. He screamed at the top of his lungs, and that threw her off balance. Just as the pony's hooves left the ground, she felt herself falling to one side.

Her father cried out in horror. Terrified, Susannah dropped the reins. But then she felt strong hands on her shoulders pulling her up and holding her firmly in the saddle as the pony cleared the railing.

She looked around to see who had helped her, but saw no one—except her relieved father, who hugged her one instant and scolded her the next. So she told herself she had only imagined that someone had saved her, that she had actually managed to save herself. How proud she had been, in her childish innocence, to believe it had happened that way.

Then, when she was ten, she had been stricken with a fever and the doctor feared for her life. But once again, she felt a strange sense that someone besides her parents and the doctor was with her through the long night when her illness reached its peak.

Finally, as she felt herself slipping away into blackness, which now she knew had to be death, something, someone, pulled her back. When dawn came, her fever had broken, and the doctor declared her recovery a miracle.

She did not tell anyone what had happened, for that night a tiny voice had whispered in her ear that it was their secret. "But who are you?" she had asked.

"Your guardian angel, and I will always be near when you need me."

She decided it had only been a dream, but then, a short time after that, she entered a jumping contest and wanted desperately to win to show up Rosa Perryman, her arch rival. She prayed for divine intervention to ensure her triumph, and the night before the contest, her bedroom filled with the scent of lilacs and Joshua appeared.

At first she was terrified and wanted to scream. But he held up his hand and suddenly her throat was paralyzed and she could not make a sound.

"Do not be afraid, Susannah. I am Joshua. Your guardian angel."

She shook her head wildly from side to side in bewilderment. Then, as he lowered his hand, she found she could speak. "But . . . but you

28

can't be an angel. You . . . you look human."

He laughed. "No, I don't have a halo and wings. I look like a man and can appear as one whenever I wish."

"But why haven't I been able to see you before?"

"There was no real need till now."

He frowned and she knew he was annoyed. She did not have to ask why, for he was quick to explain. "I decided it was time we had a talk, face to face, so you will understand the seriousness of your situation."

She braced herself for admonishment, wondering what in the world she had done that was so awful.

"I cannot answer your prayers, Susannah. My job is to protect you, guide you, and advise you. In fact, you cannot summon me at will. I will know when I am truly needed, and only then will I come.

"And you should be ashamed," he added, pointing his finger at her, "for asking God to let you win that jumping contest so you could best your rival. You should want to win for yourself and for no other reason. If you ask Him for anything, it should only be to help you be the best you can be—not to make someone else fail."

She nodded and knew she had to ask God to forgive her. She just hadn't thought of praying in the way Joshua explained it.

"Something else I want you to understand," he

continued, "is that I cannot force you to do anything. God gave you free will, Susannah. All I can do is try to influence you to make the right choice."

"I'll—I'll remember," she stammered, awed by everything he had said.

Then he had smiled, the most beautiful smile she had ever seen. His face had shone, and his strange hazel eyes with their tiny flecks of gold had sparkled radiantly with love and devotion.

"If only I could meet a mortal man like Joshua," she now whispered longingly. "So strong and intelligent. Sympathetic and kind. Then I would have no doubts, no reservations."

And he was so handsome, too. His soft, light brown hair curled about his ears and neck, and he had a wonderful physique, tall and muscular. To her, he was everything she could ever want . . . the perfect man, the perfect mate.

A sudden breeze whipped through the gazebo, making her shiver. Then she noticed that the sun had begun to set. The days were getting shorter. Soon autumn would fade into winter, and the bleakness of the cold weather would make her feel even more alone.

"And now," she said aloud, "I've ruined a beautiful afternoon sitting here thinking what a fool I am. Oh, Joshua, please, please come to me. I need you so badly."

The sweet fragrance of lilacs filled the air and she saw a swirl of rich, radiant light. She felt his gentle touch on her shoulder, and then he sat down next to her.

"Thank you for coming," she said, tears of gratitude springing to her eyes.

"You sounded desperate."

"Don't you know what just happened in the gazebo? You did leave that pot of chrysanthemums on the railing for me to use as a weapon, didn't you?"

"Yes, but only because I was able to sense you were in danger. I was not watching, if that's what you think. I've told you before, I would never embarrass you by hovering, unseen, when you are in an intimate situation."

"Thank you again," she murmured, then squeezed her eyes tightly shut in painful remembrance. "It was awful. Oh, Joshua, I'm such a fool. Why did I waste my time in school? I certainly didn't learn anything."

"Unfortunately, your education did not include lessons in human nature, Susannah, nor did it teach you that sometimes you can be too kind and compassionate. People take advantage of you, particularly fortune-hunting men who see you as a woman in desperate need of a husband to look after her money."

"Maybe Mr. Grierly's right. I should enter a convent," she mumbled, more to herself than him.

"Entering a convent for the wrong reasons

31

would be a mistake, and you don't mean it, anyway."

"Then what am I supposed to do? And why can't you help me find a suitable man rather than merely warn me against those who are unsuitable? You're so wise, Joshua, and you have the power to see inside a person and know his true nature, so why don't you point me in the direction of the right man for me?"

He grinned. "Well, you've never specifically asked me to do that for you, have you? You've only wanted my help once you were already involved with someone."

"Well, I'm asking you now," she snapped impatiently. "Help me, Joshua, please." She reached out to him, wanting his embrace, and was glad when he allowed her to touch him. Sometimes he did not.

"Very well," he said. "I will do what I can. Now don't you need to get ready for the church supper tonight?"

"I don't feel like going, not after what's just happened."

"Well, I think you should. Remember, it's being given to introduce the new teacher and to raise money for a schoolhouse, books, and materials."

She knew all about that. Everyone was talking about Trent Newman, who was starting a school for the poor rural folk who lived in Bent Creek. They all thought he was crazy. He was not going to be paid for his services unless his pupils' parents offered something, and everyone knew they were barely able to scrape by themselves. So it was Ruth Barnaby's idea for the church to have the supper to help him.

"I'll just give Mrs. Barnaby a donation," she said with a lazy shrug. "I really don't feel like being around people just now, especially not until I can forgive myself for letting Windham make such a fool of me."

"I want you to go, Susannah."

She looked at him and could see he was quite serious. No doubt he had a reason, but if she asked, he probably would not reveal it to her. That was Joshua's way. He could be so mysterious, but eventually his motive became clear—and always turned out to have been justified and reasonable.

"Oh, all right," she said finally, "I'll go. But I want you to remember I'm depending on you now to find the man I was meant to love, and who was meant to love me."

When he did not speak, she turned to see only drifting shards of light that disappeared as quickly as he had.

He would help her, she knew, but she prayed he would hurry, for both her heart and her life were so very, very lonely.

Chapter Three

Susannah had attended St. Mary's Catholic Church all her life. Small and quaint, nestled in the country away from bustling Philadelphia, it was where she wanted to be married one day. She envisioned herself walking down the red-carpeted aisle in a flowing gown of white satin and Brussels lace.

She could picture the entire ceremony, from the lighting of the cream-colored candles at the altar to taking communion from Father Dimitri as she and her new husband knelt before him.

And there would be lots of red flowers, for red was her favorite color. Only they would have to be hothouse flowers, because another part of her dream was to be wed on Valentine's Day, and no flowers would be blooming outdoors then. Still, she longed for the romantically sentimental day to also become her wedding anniversary.

But for now, her visit to the church was for a different occasion. The basement, used as a social hall, had been decorated with gold and yellow marigolds and chrysanthemums. The table centerpieces were corn shuck dolls, and delicious smells filled the air—pumpkin and sweet potato pies, roasted duck and chicken, and bowls of sweet corn and peas. Hot apple cider, spiced with cinnamon, complemented the bountiful array of food.

Mrs. Barnaby, seated behind a table inside the door to take donations, greeted Susannah effusively. "We're just so glad you came, dear, and I can't wait for you to meet our guest of honor." She grinned and lowered her voice. "He's quite handsome, you know, and not married."

"Well, I only came to help his cause," Susannah said, hoping she had not actually begun to *look* desperate to find a husband.

Mrs. Barnaby giggled. "Oh, I didn't mean anything like that, dear. But you would make a nice pair. Everyone knows you are a woman of independent means, and he hasn't got a cent and probably never will have, if he thinks those poor folk in Bent Creek will help him out."

"Then he should get a job here in the city. Teachers don't get rich on their salaries, but they manage to live comfortably, I understand."

"But he was determined to go to Bent Creek, and you know those people don't have a pot to pee in or a window to throw it out of, as the saying goes."

"Well, I suppose he has his reasons," Susannah remarked indifferently.

"Yes, I'm sure he does, but from what I've heard, Professor Newman could have had plenty of money." There was no one else coming in, so Mrs. Barnaby shared her gossip. "It's said his family lives in a wealthy section of New York, and his father is a prominent attorney who expected Professor Newman to go into practice with him. His father wanted Professor Newman to pursue a law degree at Harvard, but when Professor Newman didn't do that, his father disinherited him. Isn't that terrible?"

"It's sad that a father would do such a thing merely because his son didn't live his life the way his father wanted him to. I feel sorry for both of them," Susannah said.

"But what is so ridiculous is that Professor Newman would choose to do what he's doing— work for nothing. No one in his right mind does that."

"Maybe if he believes in something strongly enough, money doesn't matter," Susannah said.

"Easy for you to say." Mrs. Barnaby laughed, then continued, "You know, I'm not the only one who thinks the two of you would make a perfect match. . . . " She paused as she glanced down at the table. "I'm sure he'll be impressed with you for many reasons."

Susannah stiffened. She had just placed a sizable donation on the table, but seeing the smug look Mrs. Barnaby was giving her, she wished she had not been so generous. It appeared as if she wanted to be noticed.

Mrs. Barnaby picked up the money and rose. "Come along. I will introduce you to him myself."

Susannah held back, embarrassed. "Actually, I hadn't planned on staying," she said in a rush, drawing her arm from Mrs. Barnaby's grasp. "I wasn't feeling well to start with . . . a slight headache . . . Now it's worse. I'm going home. Another time, perhaps."

"Nonsense. You can stay long enough to meet him. You can't just go running off."

"But I really don't—"

"Is there a problem, Mrs. Barnaby?"

They turned to see Father Dimitri standing behind them.

Mrs. Barnaby shook her head. "No, Susannah is just being shy. She says she has a headache and wants to leave, but—"

"Well, she knows best," he said with a kind nod to Susannah. "We don't want to make her stay if she isn't feeling well, and her face does look a bit flushed. Is your buggy outside, Susannah, or shall I have someone see you home?"

She shook her head. "No, I don't need a ride.

My driver always waits for me. And I'll be fine, really. Give my regrets to everyone, won't you?"

"See how generous she is, Father?" Mrs. Barnaby asked.

Father Dimitri raised his brows at the thick wad of bills Mrs. Barnaby still held. "My goodness, Susannah, is that your contribution for Mr. Newman's school?"

"Most generous, isn't she? That's why I want her to meet him. He'll want to thank her personally," Mrs. Barnaby chirped.

Susannah knew that Father Dimitri was used to her regular large donations to the church, but he probably was surprised at her generosity toward a complete stranger. But he could not know it was her way of putting Windham Bishop and all the men just like him behind her.

She turned to go, but this time Father Dimitri caught her arm. "Mrs. Barnaby is right. You must stay long enough for Professor Newman to thank you properly. He'd never forgive us if we let you run away."

Susannah groaned inwardly. Father Dimitri probably also thought she had an ulterior motive for her donation. She knew why he'd said her face looked flushed, because she could feel her cheeks flaming. Oh, why had she been so foolish?

Glancing about wildly, she longed to disappear as Joshua did, and not in a dramatic swirl of golden light, either. Right now she wouldn't have cared if the earth just opened up and swallowed her whole, and she wished with all her heart that it would.

"Let us through, please," Father Dimitri called amiably to the women gathered around someone Susannah could not see. "I want Professor Newman to meet his most generous benefactress."

The women, all of whom she recognized as being young and single or hopeless spinsters, reluctantly stepped back for her. But she did not miss their narrowed eyes or their disapproving faces.

Taking a deep breath, she braced herself to meet a man who would surely think she was as eager and as desperate as all the other women fawning over him.

She silently asked Joshua to perform a miracle and take her away. Make her disappear, fall into a faint, anything, she implored, for never in her life had she dreaded such an encounter. She had not known Professor Newman was a bachelor, and if she had, she certainly would have been more discreet with her money.

"Professor Newman," Father Dimitri said, a bit too loudly, "I would like you to meet a lovely and extremely altruistic young lady—Miss Susannah Tutweiler." Then, to her, "Susannah, may I present Professor Trent Newman."

She had closed her eyes in apprehension, but when she felt a warm, gentle touch as he clasped

39

her hand, she forced herself to look. She could not help herself and laughed out loud with delight.

Everyone was staring at her, and Trent Newman looked stunned by her outburst.

She had been so happy to open her eyes and see Joshua holding her hand. For a fleeting instant, she thought he had, by some miracle, manifested himself as Professor Newman—to be the man she would want to marry. But how foolish that notion was! After all, Joshua had once told her that although angels could engage in human activities and behavior, they could not experience human intimacy, such as marriage.

And as she stared at the mirror image of her guardian angel, Susannah knew that had she taken a better look, she would have seen that it was not Joshua. Professor Newman had blue eyes, heavenly blue eyes, but certainly not hazel.

Also, at that moment, Joshua stood beside Professor Newman, looking smug and pleased with himself.

"That wasn't very nice," she declared.

"Excuse me?" Trent Newman said, bewildered.

She blinked, horrified at her blunder.

"Uh—" She swallowed hard, then, as Joshua grinned, which only infuriated her further, she found her voice. "I meant to say, Professor Newman, that it wasn't nice to think I'd be meeting

40

an old man, only to find someone so young and charming."

Then, hearing gasps explode around her, she was embarrassed again. She had made herself appear coquettish, for heaven's sake. Now she didn't know what to do and could only stand there and feel her cheeks burn even hotter.

"Well, I'm glad you aren't disappointed, Miss Tutweiler," Professor Newman said. "I'm certainly not." He smiled.

She was so undone by her own outlandish behavior that she mumbled some inanity about her pleasure in meeting him and having to leave because of a headache. Then, lifting her hand to her forehead in a gesture of anguish, she fled before anything else could be said.

Chapter Four

Dressed in a red velvet riding outfit and wearing white leather gloves but no hat, Susannah was in the stable, waiting for Pegasus to be saddled, when one of the house servants came to announce a gentleman caller. He had neglected to get the name.

Impatient to ride after several days of foul weather, and not expecting anyone, she did not hesitate to dismiss the visitor. "Take his name and extend my regrets."

Finally mounted, she was about to leave the stable when she was startled to see a man standing in the doorway. She was even more surprised when she realized it was Professor Newman.

"Hello," he called jovially. "I apologize for dropping by uninvited, but I saw your servant come this way to find you, so I followed him. I came by to ask how you're doing and whether you've had any more headaches. I know it's been two weeks, but this is the first chance I've had. Bent Creek isn't exactly close by, you know."

Susannah knew where Bent Creek was—nearly an hour's ride to the west. And she also knew exactly how long it had been since the night of the church supper, because she had been unable to put him out of her mind no matter how hard she tried. Adding to her frustration had been Joshua's ignoring her when she asked him why he had played such a cruel trick on her.

"Well, that was extremely thoughtful of you, Professor Newman," she replied, trying to keep her voice even. The way he was smiling up at her had her insides doing cartwheels. "And, thank you, I'm fine. No more headaches."

There was an awkward silence. Then they both spoke at once and laughed. Professor Newman bowed slightly. "I'm sorry. Go ahead."

"I was just going to say that had I known you were coming, I would have been a good hostess and offered tea. As you can see, I'm about to go riding." She patted the horse's neck. "Pegasus needs some exercise."

"Well, so do I," he said boldly, glancing at the stalls. "What if I join you? I came by buggy, of course, and I'm afraid Molly, my horse, would be offended if I unhitched her and put a saddle on her back. She considers it beneath her to do anything except pull a buggy."

Pleased, Susannah told the stable boy to saddle Victory, a strong but well-behaved gelding. "It will be nice to have company," she said, not divulging that it was his company in particular that she wanted.

They walked the horses slowly as Susannah showed him the estate. She pointed out the sleepy stream and the windmill that supplied their water, and the herd of prize cattle from stock brought to America from Europe by her grandfather before the turn of the century. She took Professor Newman to the apple grove, almost bare after the fall harvest, and indicated the dense forest in the distance with its winding trails.

"Don't you sometimes feel overwhelmed by all this?" he asked. "I mean, wouldn't you be more comfortable living in the city rather than here with just your servants?"

"I was born here, Professor Newman, and—"

"Please. Call me Trent. Professor sounds so formal, anyway, and I plan to tell my students to call me Mister Newman."

"Very well. Trent it is." Merely speaking his name made her shiver. Dear Lord, what was wrong with her? Why did he have such an unnerving effect on her?

"I love it here," she went on. "This is my home.

I can't imagine ever living anywhere else."

"I suppose I can understand that. I felt that way about New York at one time. Couldn't imagine myself ever living anywhere else, much less in such a completely rustic area like Bent Creek."

"So why don't you teach in the city?"

"Well, I could, but that's not the kind of teaching I want to do."

"I don't understand."

"It's simple, really. At least to me. You see, children in the city have schools, teachers. They have the opportunity to learn. But children in the country don't. It would be too far for them to travel, so I want to bring education to them that they wouldn't otherwise have."

"Even if it means being as poor as they are?" She was not being sarcastic. It was just the way she saw it.

"I'll be paid in other ways besides money. I've been promised livestock—horses, cows. Some chickens. . . . But I am already getting paid in a way. The men are helping to build the school, as well as my cabin, and the women feed me. If they didn't, I'd probably starve." He laughed. "I'm a terrible cook."

Even though Mrs. Barnaby had told her the gossip about his having been disinherited, she wanted to hear it from him. "Won't your parents help you get established? People do talk, Trent, and I've heard you come from a family of means.

You could have a nice school built, a nice house, and—"

"That's not possible," he said, cutting her off, then gave a rueful laugh. "They aren't happy with what I'm doing at all. My father had this dream of wanting me to be an important, influential lawyer like him, but I didn't want that. In fact, my parents refused to pay for my education since I wasn't going to study law, so to pay for it I worked for one of my professors as his assistant.

"If you want to know the truth, I came to hate living in the city. This is what I've longed for— the country with all its peace and beauty—and now I have it.

"But most of all," he continued, "I want to help these people, and I can do it in other ways besides teaching their children. I can improve their lives, for example, by getting them to understand that some of their folk remedies can do them more harm than good. They have to learn to trust people from outside their close-knit community, like doctors."

She could not help being impressed, even though it still seemed strange he would give up so much. "I think it's terribly noble of you, Trent."

"Well, I'm not trying to be noble. I just feel it's my calling, but it's not going to be easy. First I've got to gain their trust as well as their acceptance. They'd never have any faith in a fancy-dressed teacher living in a big house and riding around in a dandy carriage. I've got to make them think I'm one of them.

"And," he hastened to add, "I want you to know I didn't solicit help from the ladies of the parish. It was their idea. Your donation was extremely appreciated, by the way."

His expression as he looked at her was not altogether one of gratitude but one of attraction and desire. Once more, she felt her stomach flutter. "I was glad to do it," she said shakily. "I can give you more if you need it. I'm always giving to charities, and—"

"No."

He spoke so sharply that she winced. "I'm sorry," he said instantly. "I didn't mean to snap. It's just that I don't want charity. Not for me, and not for my students. If they are to respect me, they must first respect themselves, and they can't do that if they're made to feel everything must be given to them in order for them to survive."

Now she was truly astounded. "But they're as poor as church mice, Trent. Bent Creek was set up by a group of farmers from around Philadelphia years ago so that the workers would have a place to live when they weren't working the crops. That way they wouldn't leave and be away when they were needed. I've ridden to Bent Creek, and I've seen the shacks. They're hardly more than a pile of boards leaning against each other. If the churches didn't collect food and clothes in the winter, those people would starve or freeze to death."

"I know, and I'm hoping once my place is finished that I can rally the men together to do something about their living conditions. We can all work to build better houses for everyone. There's just so much to be done, and I'm looking forward to every bit of it.

"And though I don't have everyone's trust yet, it's happening slowly. The way I treat them is changing their way of thinking. Two of the men have told me they aren't going to sit around this winter and drink home-brew whiskey by the fire the way they've always done. They're taking jobs at the docks, and I expect others to follow suit."

Susannah smiled. "You sound more like a missionary than a schoolteacher."

"Oh, I wouldn't say that. I'm just trying to help them. That's all. Things will get easier as time goes by."

Susannah thought that perhaps once he had met the challenge he would grow bored with his impoverished lifestyle and want to return to the kind of life he'd known, a life of luxury and conveniences. Right now it was just an adventure, perhaps a rebellion against his parents who wanted to dictate his life.

She hoped it would ultimately turn out that way and that he would change his mind. If Trent Newman was the man Joshua had chosen for her, she could not imagine herself living the kind of life Trent had mapped out for himself.

Sensing he was watching her, she wondered if maybe her perplexity was obvious. Wanting to dispel the somber mood, she suddenly dug her heel into Pegasus's side. "Race you to the woods."

"You're on."

They took off, and side by side the horses galloped across the meadow. Pegasus finally pulled ahead down a path and into the cool, green forest.

"I let you win, you know," Trent needled her good-naturedly as Victory fell in behind her.

"Ha. I know better, because I know both horses, and Pegasus is the best." She turned to flash him a grin, marveling at how good it felt just to be with him.

They rode in silence for a time. Susannah enjoyed the sweet smell of the foliage after the rains of recent days, and quietly watched the wildlife—rabbits, squirrels, a few deer.

When they reached a pond, they dismounted to allow the horses to take a drink.

Without word or warning, Trent pulled her into his arms and kissed her tenderly, passionately. His heated gaze devoured her when he lifted his head. "I don't know what's happening to me, Susannah. I haven't been able to get you out of my mind since the night we met. I've thought of nothing else, and I'll never know another moment's peace unless you allow me to call on you. Please give me a chance to get to know you better . . . for you to know me," he said, his breath soft against her skin.

"I'd like that, Trent. I've been thinking about you, too."

"I'm afraid I won't have a lot of time. There's plenty of hard work ahead of me, but if you'll be patient, I'll be with you as much as I can."

"I have all the time in the world," she whispered, and tilted her face to his, inviting another kiss.

Chapter Five

Though it was nearing the end of fall, the day was warm, and Trent's shirt was wet with perspiration. He had been wielding a hammer all morning setting logs, and it was backbreaking work. But he was struggling to finish the cabin before winter set in. Usually, he had plenty of help from the men, but Seth Hollowell, a farmer south of Philadelphia, had sent word he had a late crop of sweet potatoes and needed workers. So every able-bodied man had accepted Hollowell's offer in order to make a few last dollars for the season.

Trent did not really mind the hard work, since it distracted him from his thoughts about Susannah and how much he had grown to care for her. In the past weeks he had visited her as often as possible, which was usually only one evening during the week and every Sunday afternoon. And the more he was with her, the more he wanted to be. Not only was she beautiful, but she was fun to be with as well. Witty, playful, full of mischief, she made him feel like a child again.

Every time they were together, he discovered a new reason to adore her. But then, when they were apart, he had to ask himself if they really had a future together. After all, his heart bore scars from making the mistake of thinking another woman could share his way of life.

His arms ached as he pounded yet another nail, and he paused to rub his lower back before reaching for the bucket and the dipper. He drank the cool water, grateful the men had been available to help at the time he was digging his well.

Needing to rest, he sank to the ground and leaned back against the pile of hewn logs. Because he was so weary, it was easy to let his mind drift back to thoughts of Amanda. Golden hair, eyes the color of the sea, skin like the finest honey. . . . He had worshipped her, and she had sworn she loved him.

His parents and Amanda's were close friends, and it had delighted both families that they planned to be married one day.

They had been sweethearts since Trent was

sixteen and Amanda two years younger. He had shared his dream with her of wanting a different career from his father's, but it was only later that he realized she had never really taken him seriously.

Now he allowed his thoughts to drift to one of the incidents that had set him on his new course. He was fifteen, and at the time, his father had not yet opened his office in the fancy building uptown but had maintained his practice at home.

One night their day maid, Matilda Durning, and her little daughter had come to his father begging for help. Her husband was in jail, she said, charged with a robbery he swore he had not committed. She had no money for a lawyer, but if someone didn't defend him and prove his innocence, he would surely be sent to prison for a long time. She begged his father to take the case.

Trent would never forget how horrified he had been when his father had turned them away. Not only did his father refuse to defend Mr. Durning, but he also said he felt it would be best if she did not return to work.

Trent watched the little girl as she walked away, crying and clinging to her mother's arm, and his heart went out to her.

He asked his father why he wouldn't help them.

"Well, now, how would they pay me for my

services?" his father countered with a smirk. "True, it would be nice of me to represent Mr. Durning for free, but the food on our table isn't free, Trent. And this house was not given to us for free, either. Everything costs money. That is why people work. If they did not need money, they would not have to work, now would they?"

"But that's why you should defend Mr. Durning. If you keep him from going to jail, he can work to support his family," Trent argued. "And wouldn't it make you feel good that you helped him and his family? Money can't always be the reason for doing something. I mean, you can afford to just be kind once in a while, can't you?"

His father leaned back in his chair and lit a cigar, smiling, obviously enjoying the debate. "I understand what you're trying to say, son, and of course it's nice to help people—people who count, that is."

Trent shook his head, more confused than ever.

"Listen," his father had continued, "Mrs. Durning is an ignorant woman. Her husband is an ignorant man. That is why they are poor, because they don't have an education that will ever enable them to get jobs that will make them rich. They will always be ignorant. They will always be poor. That is their lot in life. That's the way it is."

"But it doesn't have to be that way," Trent insisted.

His father began to grow weary of the conversation. "Well, that's the way life is for some people."

"But why? You are educated. You want me to be educated. So why can't they get an education, too? Then they won't be ignorant and poor, and Mr. Durning wouldn't have to go to jail, because he could afford to pay someone to prove he's innocent."

"Oh, for heaven's sake, Trent!" His father lost all patience then. "They can't afford to get an education. It's just the way it is. Now stop wasting your time worrying about people like that, because they aren't important."

But they were to Trent, and he thought about it years later when he saw Matilda Durning's daughter on the street one day. He hadn't recognized her dressed in rags, but she had called to him, begging for a few coins for her and the fatherless baby she held in her skinny arms. Her father had died in prison, she told him, and her mother had worked herself to death trying to keep the family from starving.

He emptied his pockets, giving everything to her, somehow feeling responsible for her plight. Had his father kept her father from going to prison, perhaps her life would have turned out differently.

Other things had also happened along the way to make Trent ultimately decide on a teaching career, but the experience with the Durning family was undoubtedly what had set him in that direction. He wanted to teach those who were otherwise unable to get an education. Maybe they would not ultimately become rich, but at least they would have a fighting chance to survive in a world that could be terribly cruel.

He had never said a word about his decision to anyone except Amanda, and every time he had spoken of it, she would nod and smile. She had never indicated in any way that she did not support him.

So he had gone off to Harvard, supposedly to study medicine but instead focused on becoming a teacher. Professor Hanes, for whom Trent had worked, came from Philadelphia and had told him about the needy seasonal workers who lived in that area. Trent had even accompanied him on one of his visits, without telling anyone, and witnessed, firsthand, the workers' desperation.

Professor Hanes had also told Trent of their deep-seated distrust of strangers, and that unless Trent lived among them and gained their acceptance, he could have no influence in their lives.

But Trent had not foreseen a problem. He loved the country and wished he had grown up on a farm. And although he had been unsure of Amanda's feelings about country life, he was certain she loved him so much she would follow him anywhere.

She was the first person he had told of his plans to move to Pennsylvania. He had wanted her with him when he finally had to tell his parents he was not going to medical school.

Initially she had been excited, for she had heard there was an elite social class in Philadelphia, responsible for glittering parties and balls. Actually, she had not been concerned with his not wanting to be a doctor, knowing their families had so much money they would never want for anything. But when he had told her they would be living in a rural area so he could build a school for poor children, she had told him he was out of his mind.

His parents, as well as hers, had shared her opinion. His firm conviction to follow his dream had resulted in estrangement from his family and the end of his engagement to Amanda.

Now he wondered if he was getting himself into a similar situation with Susannah. From everything he had heard about her, she, too, was socially inclined, and he could not imagine her wanting to live with him in Bent Creek. However, his heart refused to listen to his head, which told him to retreat.

What truly needled, however, was knowing he would face real anguish if he was disappointed this time. After he had left home and Amanda, he realized he had never loved her the way he wanted to love the woman he married. Theirs had been a relationship encouraged by their families, and he had never thought about marrying anyone else.

Enjoying another dipper of cool water, Trent surveyed the world around him and knew he really didn't want to live anywhere else. Maybe the theory that he had to be around his students and their families had actually been an excuse. Here, he had room to build and grow and dream. In the city, he would feel stifled. And, later, when he was completely established, he could build a larger house, a finer house, where his children could grow up and be happy . . . children he wanted to have with Susannah.

Susannah sat on the front porch steps, her elbows on her knees, her chin propped on her hands. Lonely and depressed, she looked out at the sprawling land and wondered what good it was to have so much wealth when she was so miserable.

She was tired of fancy teas and the meaningless chatter that went along with them. The same was true of parties and dances, and God forgive her, she was even bored with going to church when all her life she had been so devout.

None of it meant anything when she was so alone, and since meeting Trent, she had never felt so forlorn as she did when she was not with him.

And Joshua was no help. He had not appeared since the night he coaxed her into going to the church supper, and she was anxious to talk to him about Trent and to find out if he was the one Joshua had found for her.

"Damn it, Joshua!" she said out loud, stamping both her feet on the steps. "Where are you?"

Instantly, the scent of lilacs enveloped her as she felt the familiar chiding thump on her head. "You know better than to swear, Susannah."

"I'll do it again if it will bring you to me," she replied defiantly. "Oh, Joshua, where have you been, and why haven't you come before now?"

"I thought it best to let you follow your heart."

She gave him a feeble smile when she turned and saw he was sitting beside her. "I'm afraid my heart is at Bent Creek."

"Are you sure that's where you want it to be? After all, if ever a man needed your money, it's Trent Newman."

"He hasn't indicated he wants any of it," she said.

"In the beginning, neither did the others."

"I've offered him donations several times, but he always turns me down. For instance, with his cabin. He's cut down trees for wood, but I've offered to pay for windows and furniture, only he won't hear of it. He says I've done enough. Then I remind him I have plenty of money and can spend it any way I choose. He says he wouldn't feel right taking money from a woman all the time. He insists he can make it on his own because that's what he set out to do and nothing is going to make him change his mind."

"Have you offered to lend him money?" Joshua asked.

"Yes, but he won't hear of that, either, because he says he could never repay it. His salary will be in pigs and chickens, not dollars."

"Then maybe his intentions where you are concerned are honorable."

"I wonder if I want them to be," she admitted.

He cocked his eyebrow. "What do you mean?"

She moaned. "I think I've been hoping he would take my money or borrow it so he'd feel beholden to me," she confessed, ashamed. "Joshua, the more I'm with him, the more I care about him. He just seems to be everything I could ever want in a mate."

"That's why I found him for you."

"Then you did plan for us to meet."

He beamed. "Of course I did. He's perfect for you."

"I'm not so sure. All he talks about when we're together is the school and his students. He thinks of nothing else. It's his dream, and I don't know if I can be a part of it."

"You wouldn't want to be married to a teacher? It's certainly a noble profession and quite rewarding. And you know he's given up a lot to pursue it. It can't be easy to have to stand up to your family for something you believe in and then have them turn against you."

"I know all that, and I agree with you, but why

does he want to live in the middle of all that poverty? Why can't he live here?" She gestured about her.

"I think the real question might be, do you want to live there?"

She frowned, annoyed. "Joshua, you aren't answering my question."

"It's not my job to answer your questions. I'm merely here to give you advice and offer you encouragement."

"Then advise me," she snapped irritably. "Encourage me. Tell me what I should do. I've never felt this way about a man before in my life, and I'm afraid I never will again, but I can't come right out and ask him if he loves me enough to live in my world."

"No," he said soberly, "but you can find out if you love him enough to live in his."

"And how am I supposed to do that?"

"If I told you, I would be in trouble, and when you discover the answer for yourself, you'll know why."

And with that, he was gone.

Chapter Six

It was late afternoon when Trent heard the sound of approaching hoofbeats. Shading his eyes against the setting sun, he could see a black horse but was unable to identify the rider. Then, recognizing Susannah, he felt a jolt of pleasure. She was a beautiful sight with her long coppery hair whipping about her face, the setting sun framing her in an almost ethereal glow.

He dropped his tools and hurried to meet her. Lifting her down, he could not resist kissing her even before her feet touched the ground.

She patted her hair, smoothed her skirt, then straightened her short-waisted jacket. "I was afraid I wouldn't find you. I had to stop and ask directions to your cabin."

"I'm glad to see you, but you shouldn't ride so far by yourself. What if your horse got spooked and you fell off and got hurt? There might even be thieves around. It's not safe, Susannah," he finished, frowning.

"Thieves, indeed," she scoffed. "There's never been any trouble around here that I know of. As for Pegasus, he'd sooner die than see any harm come to me."

She gave the horse an affectionate pat, then glanced about. "So this is where you're building."

He smiled, feeling proud. "It's wonderful, isn't it? Rolling hills, valleys, grass green and thick, lots of trees for timber and shade. I've even got a stream running through my property."

"Your property? You mean you bought it?"

"Yes, I had some money saved up. Remember I told you I worked for a professor while I was in college? Well, he gave me all the work I could handle, so I managed to put away a tidy sum."

Holding her hand, he led her to the spot where he planned to put up a barn. "So far, all I've got is a buggy and one horse. The father of one of my students says he's got a mare about to foal, and I can have it, so that will give me two. I do a lot of bartering." He smiled.

"So where do you live now?"

He led her to the shed situated behind a clump of bushes. The ramshackle hut, its only furnishings a bed against one wall, a desk, and two chairs, was only a temporary dwelling, and from the look on Susannah's face, he thought he'd better reassure her of that.

"I know it's not much, but in a few more weeks my cabin will be finished, and then I'll have more room. Two of the men are even building me some nice furniture."

He pointed to a grassy knoll. "We'll wait till spring to really get going on the school. Till then, my students will just have to crowd into my cabin.

"You should have waited and come Sunday," he continued. "We're having a work party. The men are going to put up the roof on my cabin, and the women are bringing food."

"But you visit me on Sundays," she protested, then quickly said, "I mean, I didn't know you weren't planning to come this week."

"I didn't know it myself. The men offered to help me just yesterday. But why don't you join us? I'm sure the women would welcome an extra hand with the food."

"I don't know whether they would accept me. Frankly, everybody in the county and beyond knows the Tutweiler name. If the folks here are reluctant to accept a teacher of means, they'll be even less anxious to have a Tutweiler in their midst."

"I disagree. Be friendly to them, and they'll accept you as you are. It's a bit more difficult for me because I'm asking them to trust their children to me."

"I can understand that, but do you really have to live here? If you lived in town, it wouldn't be so terribly far for you to travel to work."

"Yes, it would. Besides, I like living in the country."

She gave a playful toss of her head. "Well, then, you need to marry a rich country woman," she said with an impish smile.

"I'm afraid these folks would wonder why a man living in a mansion would want to waste his time teaching their children," he said softly.

Seeing the hurt in her eyes, he wished he had not been so curt. If only she could understand he had to move slowly with these people. He was confident that once they knew him, trusted him, and understood he only wanted to educate their children so they would have a chance at a better life, then things would be different. Then he could live anywhere—with her. But until the workers accepted him, he could not risk jeopardizing what he was trying so desperately to build.

He took her hand, wanting to end the sudden tension between them. "Come on. There's a field of wildflowers on the other side of that ridge that will take your breath away. And there are other things I want to show you, too. I found an owl's nest, and a beaver dam."

They walked, lost in each other, until evening

began to descend. Trent suddenly realized how late it was. "I totally forgot about the time. I'll hitch up my buggy and take you home. You can't ride by yourself," he said, worried for her safety.

"I guess not," she said feebly.

Her buggy was behind the shack, her horse tethered nearby. "We'll tie Pegasus to the back," he said as he tried to find the harness in the scant light remaining. "And there's a coach light around here somewhere so I can see the road."

Abruptly, he turned, bumping into her. For a moment, neither moved, as their gazes locked and held. He cupped her face, then claimed her mouth, his tongue melding with hers. Then, trembling, he broke the kiss. "You can't know how glad I am you came here today, Susannah. I think of you night and day and count the hours till I can see you again."

"I've missed you, too."

Tenderly, he trailed his finger down her cheek. "I felt something very special for you, Susannah, from the first time we met. You're so lovely, so sweet, kind and giving. I've never known a woman like you."

She caressed his shoulders. "I felt it for you, too, and I was so glad when you came to see me that day. I couldn't stop thinking about you. And I didn't want to," she added with a shy smile. She rained kisses on his face.

"If you stay with me tonight, will anyone become alarmed and send out a search party?" he asked gently.

"I didn't want anyone to know I was coming to see you alone, so I said I was going to retire early and did not want to be disturbed. I even saddled Pegasus myself and rode away without anyone seeing me. It isn't proper for a lady to visit a gentleman this way, but—"

He scooped her up in his arms. "I think you want me as much as I want you, Susannah. I know it. I can see it in your eyes. But if I'm wrong, tell me, because I would never do anything to hurt you. If you want to go home, just say so."

"I do want you, Trent," she whispered raggedly, clinging to him. "I've never wanted anything more than I want you at this moment."

"Lord, woman, if you only knew how I've longed to hear you say that."

Swiftly, he carried her into the shack and placed her gently on the bed.

"I don't want to frighten you, darling, and I don't want to hurt you. I'll be slow and gentle. I promise you." He had no doubt that it was her first time and wanted to reassure her.

She tried to help him as he undressed her, but he was in no hurry, wanting to savor each and every part of her as her body was revealed to him.

He slipped off her jacket, then found the fastening for her blouse and peeled it away to marvel at the rapid rise and fall of her breasts. Pressing his face to her cleavage, he drank of her scent as her fingers entwined in his hair, holding him tight against her.

He untied the strings of her chemise, allowing her breasts to spring forth. Cupping one, he squeezed it, and her nipple sprang to instant tautness. He sucked, then licked, circling it, feeling her stomach undulate. He moved to her other breast, while he removed her skirt and undergarments. When she was completely naked, he pulled away to gaze at her. "So lovely," he murmured, claiming her mouth once more, pleased that she parted her lips eagerly for him.

He discarded his own clothing and was pleasantly surprised when she began to caress his manhood. He had dared hope she might be passionate and uninhibited in his arms. In the past weeks when they had been together, their bodies had seemed to transmit silent messages of longing . . . and promises of eventual fulfillment.

He moved his fingers between her legs and caressed her. Rolling to his side, he slipped his knee between hers to force her legs gently apart. His fingers stroked her in that magic place while he watched her face, so lovely in the peach and golden hues of twilight. Her eyes were half-closed, and she made tiny sounds of pleasure deep in her throat.

Her hand stroked him, and his tongue played across her face, slowly, deliciously. He savored each and every second as he felt her move against his hand.

He thought he would explode but wanted the sweet anguish to continue. He could tell that her own moment of rapture was dangerously close, and that she, too, was striving to prolong her pleasure . . . but they were both losing the battle.

He looped his hands behind her, his palms cupping her buttocks to draw her to him. Then he rolled to position himself above her. He hesitated, then moved slowly, feeling her close about him, reaching out to him with velvet promise. Then she thrust herself against him with a little cry of pain that quickly melted to sighs of pleasure as he pushed deep inside her.

He held her, his hands on her bottom, as he continued to thrust into her. Her whimpers of joy became cries of happiness, and wrapping her legs tightly around his waist, she drew them closer, bringing him yet deeper inside her.

He felt as though his very soul was being sucked from his body and drawn into hers. They were one, their bodies fused together in ecstasy. They clung together, swathed in love.

Suddenly, he withdrew from her halfway, hovering, caught by her pulsating heat. His eyes met hers in the golden light, and neither moved nor spoke, lest the intensity of the moment be lessened, weakened, destroyed.

Then grasping her tiny waist, he thrust deeper inside her, unleashing himself at the moment he felt her body shudder. In that unbridled moment, their world changed forever in the awareness of their desire . . . of their love.

Once more he rolled to his side, taking her with him, cradling her head on his shoulder as he held her close.

He was too shaken to speak, but after a few moments he found his voice. "Dear God, Susannah, I didn't think I could love someone so much. You've completely stolen my heart."

"And you mine. I love you, Trent. I always will."

Darkness fell, and for a while they slept, their arms around each other, their legs entwined. Then he awoke, stirred, and felt Susannah snuggle closer to him. He drew her to him as the smoldering embers of his passion ignited once again.

Chapter Seven

Susannah tried not to stare at the food, fearing someone watching her might be able to see that she thought it was a pitiful sight. And watching her they were, for she had found herself the center of attention from the moment she had arrived.

She had accepted Trent's invitation to the Sunday work party because she wanted to be with him. But she was also curious about what their life would be like if they married. He had not proposed, but she had a feeling it was just a matter of time until he did—and not just because they had shared such wondrous passion. It was more, so much more. She had never had such a feeling in her heart for any man.

She had longed to share her emotions with Joshua, but when he had not responded, she supposed he wanted her to make her own decisions. Still, she would have liked to tell him that one of the reasons she was falling so helplessly in love with Trent was because of his resemblance to her guardian angel, which she was sure would please Joshua.

She turned her attention again to the food. Her cook, Beulah, had complied generously with Susannah's request to fill a wagon with food, and she watched as Lyle began to unload the boxes. There were hams and roast chickens and a variety of vegetables from the root cellar. The aroma of fresh-baked bread and fresh-churned butter wafted through the air, as did the sweet smells of apple and peach pies, and chocolate and lemon pound cakes. Big jugs of tea and lemonade had also been packed, along with milk for the children.

Susannah could not tell what the women were thinking. But they made no move to assist Lyle as he placed the food among their offerings of watery potato soup, dried beans, and a kettle of some kind of boiled meat that she hoped was not horse meat. The bread looked old and stale, and there were only two pies offered, made of crows, she had overheard someone say. It all looked so unappetizing, she was glad Beulah had fixed so much food. No doubt everyone would pounce on what she had brought.

72

It had been nearly noon when she arrived, and she saw that Trent and the men were still hard at work on the cabin walls. She marveled at how much they had accomplished. If they continued at their present pace, Trent's cabin would be finished by day's end.

Trent was stripped to the waist, and his firm, corded muscles glistened as the sun beat down on his bare back. His hard, lean thighs strained against his trousers, and Susannah wondered if her cheeks flushed as the memories of their lovemaking came rushing back, thrilling her. They had made love too many times to count that night, finally surrendering to exhaustion. When she had awakened at dawn, they were still coupled, and even before his eyes had opened, she had felt him grow hard inside her.

They had bathed together in the stream, and she had feasted on his masculine beauty. They had played and splashed in the cool mountain water and finally caught fire again, eventually making love on the ground wildly, uninhibitedly.

Later in the day, when she returned home, she had been surprised that there were no raised eyebrows among her servants. She had assumed they thought she returned from an early-morning ride.

Trent saw her now and waved, grinning broadly. Telling the others it was time to eat, he grabbed up his shirt, buttoning it as he came toward her.

She was standing near the wagon, not knowing what to do, because none of the women had spoken to her yet. She had offered a smile and a nod to several, but they continued to stare mutely, so she had given up and now felt terribly ill at ease.

Reaching her side, Trent said in a low voice, "I wish I could just take you in my arms and carry you to the stream and make love to you until you begged me to stop."

The shimmering lust in his eyes matched her own desire, and her fingers ached to touch him while every nerve in her body became taut, eager. Even her lips began to burn with sweet anticipation of his kiss.

"I'd like that, too," she replied without guile, "but actually I'd settle for you just getting me out of here. I feel so out of place."

"You shouldn't."

"But the women haven't said a word to me."

"I've told you they're leery of strangers. Once we fill our plates, we can mingle, and I'll introduce you to everyone. They'll warm to you, you'll see. . . . " His voice trailed off as his eyes swept the tables, which consisted of planks set across nail barrels. "Did you bring all that food?" he asked, his voice strained.

"Yes, and it's a good thing I did, because there's hardly enough to go around, and what's there looks hardly palatable."

"I wish you hadn't, but it's my fault. I should have made sure you understood."

"I don't know what you mean. You said I could help the women with the food."

"But I didn't mean you should bring anything. I meant you could help them serve and clean up. I'm afraid they won't eat what you've brought, Susannah."

"But that's absurd."

"I know. It's just the way they are. They're wary of anything a stranger has to offer."

She was astonished. "Well, good heavens, Trent, they take food and clothes from the church all winter long. I told you that. They certainly aren't particular then, so why should they be offended by my food?"

"When the church gives them things, that is charity, and it doesn't matter whether it comes from a stranger or not. But I'm not offering them charity, and I don't want you to, either. To become a part of them and their community, I have to behave as they do, and so do you when you're here with me. Otherwise, they will question my motives for being here."

"Well, a lot of people do, Trent, because it's very unusual for someone to choose to live in destitution."

His mouth spread in the grin that always warmed her to the tips of her toes. "I'm like a missionary, remember?" Then, becoming serious, he caught her hand in the folds of her skirt so no one would notice. "I thought you understood all this, Susannah. If not, we'll talk about it again later, but please be patient. It means so much to me, darling, just as you do, and it's important that you know my feelings."

Just then a dilapidated wagon, pulled by a worn-out mule, rumbled into the clearing to stop right next to where she and Trent stood.

Susannah watched as a hugely pregnant young girl awkwardly climbed down. None of the men offered to assist her. "Why aren't they helping her?" Susannah whispered. "And why aren't you?" she added a bit sharply.

"I wish I could, but I don't dare. That's Lucy Graham, and she's being shunned because she's unmarried and pregnant. But don't worry, if she stumbles, I'll catch her."

Susannah's heart went out to the girl. She looked absolutely wretched. There were dark circles under her eyes, and she was pale and drawn. Dressed in rags, she was skin and bones except for the huge mound that showed she was in the last stages of her pregnancy. Once out of the wagon, she reached back for a basket, then went to join the women, but not one of them so much as nodded to acknowledge her presence.

"So why is she here?" Susannah demanded. "Why doesn't she stay at home and not subject herself to such humiliation?"

"Her parents probably made her come. It's

sad, but that's the way it is, and if I had helped her, I would have made some enemies."

Susannah bit her tongue to keep from speaking her mind. She was having a difficult time understanding why Trent wanted to be with these cruel, ignorant people.

As she watched the men move along the tables to be served, it was as Trent had predicted. The women passed over Susannah's food and dished up only what they had prepared.

"Maybe now you can see a little of what it's been like for me. But don't worry"—he slipped his arm about her waist as he attempted to cheer her—"your food won't go to waste. It will feed me for a week, and I'm grateful."

Hand in hand, they walked to a secluded spot beside the stream and sat down on the grassy, sloping bank. They talked about when the cabin would be finished and about Trent's holding classes there until the school building was completed.

The grass was browning, and their conversation turned to winter and Christmas, which was only a few weeks away. Susannah asked if he'd be going home to New York for the holidays, but he shook his head and said he would not be welcome there. Her heart went out to him.

"Then you will spend Christmas with me," she said brightly. "I'll have a party Christmas Eve, and we'll have stuffed goose and all the trimmings. You can stay in one of the guest rooms, and I'll have a friend from town stay, too, so it will be all very proper."

"But what about later, after your friend has gone to bed?" He pretended to leer at her. "What if I walk in my sleep and find my way to your room? Would you turn me away?"

She giggled. "You'll probably bump into me on the way to yours. Do you honestly think I could spend the night under the same roof with you and not be in your arms?"

Their eyes met and held, and their humorous bantering melted into longing. They reached for each other at the same instant, even though there was a chance someone might happen along and see them, and their lips met.

When they finally drew apart, Trent's gaze was still locked with hers. "I like the idea of sleeping under the same roof with you, Susannah, and I'd like it every night for the rest of my life. I want to be in the same room with you, the same bed, and I want my arms about you all night long. I want to fall asleep inside you and awaken inside you, and make love to you day and night forever and ever."

They kissed again, and then Susannah felt tears in her eyes. "I want that, too, Trent. It"— she swallowed hard, drew a deep breath, and let it out slowly—"sounds like a marriage proposal."

He threw his head back and laughed before grabbing her and crushing her against him. "Oh, darling, it is. Say you feel the same way, please."

"I do, only—"

He kissed her, cutting off her words, and she allowed him to. It was not the moment to discuss her doubts and fears. Surely, she told herself, as much as they loved each other, nothing could come between them.

Reluctantly, he drew back. "I wish we had more time, but we've got to get back to the others or they'll start gossiping. I've also got to get back to work. I'll come to see you very soon so we can make plans to be married as soon as possible."

Still dizzy with wonder over all that was happening, Susannah shook her head. "Not until Valentine's Day."

He laughed. "You can't mean that you don't want to talk about it till then. That's February. Months away. I can't wait that long, and I'll be hurt if you're able to."

"Of course not. What I meant is that we can't be married until Valentine's Day, because I've always dreamed of having my wedding then. It means everything to me, Trent, and it's not so terribly far off."

"No, it isn't," he agreed. "Whatever you want."

"We can have our engagement party on Christmas Eve. Won't that be wonderful?"

"As I said, my sweet, anything you want. Now we've got to get back."

She held his hand tightly as they walked

along, her heart pounding with joy, thinking that she had never known such happiness.

It was only later, when she was alone, that her doubts came creeping back. Where would they live? Surely not in his cabin among the squalor of Bent Creek. He would never expect her to leave the luxury of her palatial estate. It wasn't even worth worrying about, so she would not. She would begin planning their engagement party and be content believing that Trent would do everything in his power to make her happy.

She would not, could not, allow herself to think otherwise.

Chapter Eight

From the dining room came the mouthwatering smells of roast turkeys, honey-baked hams, pumpkin and sweet potato pies, and fresh baked breads. The aromas mingled with the pungent fragrance of the pine garlands decorating the curving staircase.

In the great foyer stood the towering Christmas tree, shining with balls and tinsel. The dainty cedar limbs were tipped with ivory candles that glowed in the festive air.

The ballroom, with its parquet floor and mirrored walls, was a shimmering display of color. Ladies in elaborate gowns flaunted precious jewels that sparkled in the light of the crystal chandeliers, and white-gloved servants in red velvet coats and black velvet trousers offered champagne from their trays as they passed through the crowd of guests. In a corner, positioned on a raised stand, a string ensemble played holiday carols.

It was Christmas Eve. Susannah, poised at the top of the stairs to make her grand entrance, thought how she had been waiting for this night her entire life—the night she would announce her engagement.

She could see Trent now, so dashing and handsome in formal attire. Even on the occasion of his engagement, the young, unmarried ladies of Philadelphia swarmed about him, vying for his attention. It did not concern her. She knew that even after she and Trent were married, women would probably still flirt with him, but his heart belonged to her. He had sworn it was true, and she believed him.

There had, however, been some tense conversations regarding their future. Trent had argued that they should live in his crude little cabin. It was necessary, he repeated for perhaps the hundredth time, so that he would be accepted. But she had countered that there had been ample time for the people of Bent Creek to conclude that he had only their best interests at heart.

What she did not say was that it made no difference if his school was unsuccessful. If he never worked again, they could enjoy a life of luxury and never want for anything. But she kept silent about that, for she knew Trent was proud and would never be comfortable living off her money.

Because he loved her, he finally yielded to living on her estate. Yet, she had not missed the wistfulness in his voice when he said he supposed he could understand that a lady of her background would never be content living in Bent Creek.

Susannah would not allow herself to feel even the slightest bit guilty. She intended to make sure he would never regret giving in to her wishes.

She drew a deep breath, her hand tightening nervously on the banister. She nodded to the servant awaiting her signal, and he, in turn, gestured to the musicians who abruptly stopped playing to give her a loud fanfare.

Everyone crowded into the foyer, all eyes on her in her red satin gown with its low-cut bodice and off-the-shoulder sleeves. At her waist, the skirt billowed in ruffles and tucks held by clusters of tiny seed pearls. Her hair was pulled high atop her head, where a cascade of curls was held by a diamond and ruby tiara which matched her earbobs.

Daintily, she held the hem of her skirt as she slowly began her descent.

Taking the steps two at a time, Trent bolted to meet her. Then, tucking her hand in the crook of his arm, he looked down at their guests. "I just

Patricia Hagan

can't wait a second longer to tell all of you. This is the woman I am going to marry."

Everyone broke into gales of laughter and applause, and Susannah squeezed his arm. "That wasn't proper, Trent. We were supposed to wait for Mr. Grierly to formally make the announcement," she scolded, but kept smiling.

"I couldn't help it, and everybody knows the reason for the party, anyway. Besides, it was all I could do to keep from shouting it to the whole world."

"Isn't that what you just did?" she bantered.

He turned to face her, speaking so low she could barely hear. "I don't care about decorum and propriety, darling. I only know I love you more than anything in this world, and I can't wait to make you my wife. If I had my way, we'd get married here and now and not wait another day."

"I know, but the time will pass quickly, and afterwards, before you know it, you'll be tired of me," she teased.

"Believe me, that will never happen. I want to be with you every day and night for the rest of my life."

They descended to the foyer, where they were at once surrounded by well-wishers.

Mr. Grierly stepped forward to give Trent a pat on the back. "You stole my moment, son. I was supposed to be the one to tell everyone the wonderful news, but I forgive you, because I know how happy you are."

Trent laughed. "Then let's allow you to do your job and make it official. I'll get champagne for the three of us, and then we can stand by the tree as Susannah wanted."

As he turned, Susannah caught his arm and smiled. "Our guests still don't know when the wedding will be, Trent, so please don't say anything. At least let Mr. Grierly be the one to tell them it's Valentine's Day."

"Don't worry." With a wink, he walked away.

"He's quite a man, Susannah, and it's obvious he adores you," Mr. Grierly said as they watched Trent, stopping to chat with their guests as he maneuvered through the crowd. "I'm just relieved you were able to convince him to live here. I couldn't imagine you living in that wilderness in a log cabin, for heaven's sake."

"The cabin is actually quite cozy, and it's not exactly a wilderness. There are people around, and—" She fell silent, smelling lilacs, and saw Joshua standing just behind Mr. Grierly. Resplendent in formal attire, he lifted his glass of champagne to her in salute.

"What are you doing here? I mean, I'm glad that you are, but I didn't expect you," she said, delighted.

Mr. Grierly quickly glanced around and turned back to her. "My dear, are you all right?"

But she did not respond, her attention solely on Joshua.

"Did you think your guardian angel would miss your engagement party, Susannah? Not likely. After all, I've been praying this night would come."

"Then you knew—"

"Stop." He frowned. "I know you're excited, and that's understandable, but you have to remember no one can see me but you, and people will hear you and think you're tetched. See how Mr. Grierly is looking at you now?"

Her eyes darted to Mr. Grierly. She swallowed hard. "Forgive me. I was thinking of something else. It's such a thrilling night, and—"

"Here, sweetheart." Trent appeared with a servant who held a tray bearing three glasses of bubbling champagne. "Now we can toast and make it official."

Mr. Grierly took his glass and stepped to take his position in front of the tree, but the front doors opened.

Sam Becker and his wife breezed in, apologizing for being late. Sam explained that one of his workers had taken ill while baling a late crop of hay.

"Who was it?" Trent asked.

"Lyman Sauls, I think his name is," Sam replied.

Trent groaned. "Oh, no. I've been really worried about him lately. What happened?"

Sam was looking beyond Trent at the food. "Oh, don't worry. He'll be fine. Somebody said he was sick to his stomach, and then he fainted. His wife was there working, too, and she had some of the men load him in a wagon. She said she was taking him to a doctor."

Trent snorted. "Doctor, indeed. She'll take him to Granny Albritton, who is just a root doctor with old-fashioned potions. Lyman needs to be treated by a real doctor. I tried to tell his wife that one day last week, but she wouldn't listen. The Sauls family is one of the last clans to give up the old ways, and—"

"Now you listen to me, boy." Sam put his hand on Trent's shoulder. "Those people have got by for years without you, so don't get yourself all riled up. They'll do fine. Lyman Sauls will do fine. Now enjoy your night with your fiancee."

Sam steered his wife past Trent and Susannah and headed for the food.

Susannah watched Trent nervously. Something told her he was not going to be able to get Lyman Sauls out of his mind.

"Are we ready?" Mr. Grierly asked impatiently.

She nodded, but Trent sighed. "I'm sorry. I'm going to have to leave. Lena Sauls will take her husband to Granny Albritton, and I've got to try and head her off. I've got to convince her to let me take him to a city hospital."

"You can't be serious, Trent. You can't leave now. This is our engagement party," Susannah objected, stunned.

"I can stay long enough for the announcement, but then I really must go."

"But you can't be sure it's even serious. You heard Sam. He said he didn't think there was anything to worry about."

"But he doesn't care," Trent argued. "I do. And as I said, I've been concerned about Lyman. He hasn't looked or felt well. So I've got to get to him before Granny Albritton does. Believe me, she'll run every step of the way to try and beat me to him. I've had to fight that crazy old woman since I got to Bent Creek. God only knows what she'll do to Lyman with her crazy spells and potions. Why, *I* know more about medicine than that old witch."

He turned to Mr. Grierly. "If you want to go ahead—"

"No," she protested. "There won't be any announcement. Not tonight. I can't stop you from leaving, Trent, but I won't have our engagement party ruined by your rushing out the door the minute the announcement is made. Sam will tell everyone that he assured you it wasn't serious, and they'll laugh at me for not being more important to you on such a special night. I'd rather tell everyone I suddenly became ill and asked that our announcement be postponed."

She turned to Mr. Grierly. "Will you please do that for me? Say I'm ill and offer my apologies? And also tell everyone that I want them to stay and enjoy the food and music."

Tears brimming in her eyes, she turned to the stairs, not wanting to cry in front of Trent, but he caught her arm.

"Don't be this way. Please try and understand. I've dedicated myself to helping these people, and you knew that when you fell in love with me, when you agreed to marry me."

She tried to pull away from him, but he held tight. "Please let me go. People are staring," she hissed between clenched teeth.

"But you have to try and understand—"

"I understand only that you don't put me first in your life, Trent. It's not as though this man you're so concerned about is dying. So what if he does go to Granny whatever-her-name-is? Is that so terrible?"

"Yes," he said tightly. "It just might be. She could make him sicker than he already is. I told you I have to be there for these people if they need me. You have to understand that."

"Well, I don't." She yanked free of him, and they faced each other warily.

Finally, he drew a deep breath. "All right. If that's the way you want it, that's the way it will have to be for now. I'll come and see you tomorrow, and we'll talk."

Susannah thought of her friend from town, Lissa Mebane, who was spending the night as her chaperon, even though her servants were in the house. She had dreamed of the hours later, after everyone had gone, when he would come to her room, where they would make beautiful, tender love into the wee hours of Christmas morning. It was to have been one of her holiday gifts to him—joy and pleasure in the luxury and privacy of her bed. Only now, because others meant more to him than she did, the entire night was ruined.

"No, don't come tomorrow," she said, backing toward the stairs and holding up her hands. "I need time to think, so I can decide if I can live the rest of my life with you putting other people before me and our marriage."

"Don't wait too long, Susannah. I have feelings, too," he warned. Turning, he crossed the foyer and walked out.

She rushed up the stairs, where Joshua was waiting on the landing. "That was not very wise of you. It also was not very nice."

"Leave me alone." She rushed past him. "This is something I have to cope with myself, and I don't need your scolding to confuse me."

She hurried down the hall, waiting until she was in the sanctity of her room with the door locked before she allowed her tears to fall.

Chapter Nine

Days later, Susannah was still miserable, but her pride would not let her send word to Trent to come and discuss the situation. After all, he had walked out on their engagement party, causing her to flee to her room, too embarrassed to face their guests.

Mr. Grierly had returned the next day—Christmas Day—bringing a gift and some friendly advice. "Please don't be angry with me for saying so, dear, but I think you should reconsider marrying Professor Newman. He is so fanatical about helping those people at Bent Creek that I fear your marriage would suffer greatly. You'd never be happy."

But even in her hurt and disappointment with

Trent, she felt the need to defend him. "I wouldn't go so far as to call him a fanatic, Mr. Grierly. He's simply too devoted, but we shouldn't judge him so harshly. He means well, and perhaps I need to be more tolerant of his needs and ambitions."

"That speaks well of you, Susannah, but what about him? He's obviously not concerned with *your* needs and ambitions."

"The only ambition I have is to be a good wife and mother."

"But can you do that without his cooperation? Think about it. This is only the beginning. He will always put what he wants ahead of you. And if you really think about it, I'm confident you'll realize he is not the right man for you."

Then why does my heart tell me otherwise? she had wanted to cry. Instead she had kept her anguish to herself as she thanked him politely for his concern, as well as for his gift.

Even though she was drowning in her wretchedness, she had not asked Joshua for his help. She knew he would say she should have been more understanding, and the more she thought about it, the more she realized she should have been. After all, Trent had never made a secret of the fact that he was so dedicated. Yet he had made the concession to live in her home after they were married, even though she knew he would have preferred to live at Bent Creek. Didn't that prove his desire to please her and his willingness to make compromises?

After all, she knew there was only so much he could do without abandoning his dream completely.

All she had done these past few days was sit by the parlor window, hoping to see Trent's buggy coming up the road. The nights found her rambling through the house, thinking it had never seemed so large, or her life so lonely. Fond memories of the times they had shared made her ache to the depths of her tortured soul. Love had blossomed so sweetly, but then the petals had fallen, and she was left with only the sweet fragrance of precious memories.

Invitations had come to holiday socials, but she had declined each and every one. She had no desire to celebrate the season.

New Year's Eve dawned clear and crisp with a hint of snow in the air, and Susannah stared out at the thick, gray clouds and thought of the dismal evening ahead. Before the quarrel with Trent, she had looked forward to being with him at the stroke of twelve, toasting each other with champagne as they greeted the new year—the year they would begin their lives together as husband and wife.

Suddenly she could stand it no longer. Rushing to her desk, she took out paper and quill and wrote a hasty note of apology. She begged him to come for dinner so she could tell him she had changed her mind and was now willing to share his life in every way.

She hurried to find Lyle and told him to deliver the note as quickly as possible. Then she instructed Beulah to prepare a sumptuous dinner.

It was almost noon when Lyle returned to say that he had been unable to deliver the note. He reported that Professor Newman was not at home, and someone passing by had said he was out visiting some of his students.

As instructed, Lyle had brought the note back. She had not wanted it left tacked to the cabin door for anyone to read.

So now it appeared that she and Trent would spend New Year's Eve apart, and she could not bear the thought.

She rushed to the kitchen, situated behind the house. Beulah stared at her in wide-eyed surprise when she told her to pack up the roast duck and all the trimmings and the wine and champagne Susannah had selected earlier.

"I've decided I want to spend the evening with friends in the city, and I'll surprise them by bringing such a lovely dinner. And I'll probably stay the night," she added, so there would be no concern when she did not return. If all went as she hoped, she would be sleeping in Trent's bed, wrapped in his loving arms.

Finally, dressed in a white riding outfit, a fur blanket draped across her lap, she waited as her servants loaded the food in her buggy.

"Sure you don't want me to take you?" Lyle asked.

She assured him she preferred to go alone. "You can enjoy the evening with your family. I'll be fine," she added.

Glancing warily at the threatening snow clouds banked on the horizon, she surmised two hours of daylight were left. Since it was only an hour's ride to Trent's cabin, she was sure she could make it before the snowfall.

Keeping the horses at a steady gait, she arrived in Bent Creek in good time, but to her dismay, Trent was still not there.

Confident he would return soon, she unloaded the food and took it inside the cabin. Then, wrapping the fur blanket around her against the chill, she sat down at the table to wait.

The wind began to intensify, howling and screaming. She wished for a fire but saw that the fireplace needed wood and cleaning. She would have to carry in the wood from the pile outside— and she was wearing white.

Grimacing, she took a deep breath and got up. It was either get dirty or freeze. Seeing that the snow had begun to fall, she knew there was no time to waste making up her mind, and there was really no debate, anyway.

As she worked, she tried not to think of the threatening storm. If Trent did not return soon, she was going to be marooned in the cabin alone in a blizzard. She realized then that she might very well have made a terribly foolish mistake in coming. She wasn't expected, and perhaps worse, she had lied about where she was going, so no one would know where to look for her.

A half-hour later, her clothes were mussed and grimy, but she was rewarded by the warmth of the cozy fire she had made.

She found a kettle already filled with water and hung it over the flames to boil for tea. There was plenty of food, thanks to what she had brought, so she would not starve. Neither would she freeze to death, at least not for a while, because she had brought in plenty of wood and stacked it near the hearth.

Darkness fell and she lit the lanterns. In the mellow glow, she decided perhaps the cabin was not so bad a place to live after all. Besides, she felt a warm tremor when she thought that being with Trent in such a small place might be nice.

Tears sprang to her eyes as she thought of how much she wanted to be with him. She then promised herself that if she ever felt his arms around her again, she would beg him never to let her go.

A sound outside sent her running to the door to fling it open, and Trent's name, about to burst from her lips, was swallowed in disappointment. It was a girl straddling a mule, a blanket wrapped about her.

She seemed vaguely familiar, but there was no

time to wonder who she was as she began to topple from the mule.

Susannah rushed forward in time to keep her from falling and helped her down. Then, as the blanket fell away, she could see the girl's swollen belly and realized it was Lucy Graham.

Slumping against her, Lucy cried, "Professor Newman. Get him for me, please. My baby is coming, and he has to help me."

"Lucy, how did you ever make it here on your own?" Susannah asked as she took her inside the cabin.

"I ran away. I had to. My family sent for Granny Albritton, and I can't let her deliver my baby. She'll let it die. I know she will. It's happened before to other girls when it was a shameful birth. She swears she doesn't do it on purpose, but I know it's true, and I want my baby. I don't care if it is shamed, I—" Her words dissolved into a scream of anguish.

Susannah watched in fright as Lucy's stomach suddenly tightened.

Long moments passed, and then Lucy gasped. "I think it's getting ready to come. Please, please get Professor Newman. He's been so good to me. He's been letting me come to classes here. I'm one of his students now," she said proudly. "And I know he'll help me. He knows about Granny Albritton, you see, and how she'll kill my baby, and he'll see to it that I get to a real doctor if I need to—" She grimaced as another pain gripped her.

Her hands shaking and her heart pounding so hard she was afraid it was going to leap right out of her chest, Susannah waited for Lucy's contraction to pass, then helped her to lie on the bed. She had never seen a baby born and had no idea what she was supposed to do, but figured the first thing was to get Lucy undressed.

"Where is he?" Lucy wailed.

"He isn't here, and I don't know where he is or when he'll be back. There's only me, and I don't know how to help you, Lucy. I'm sorry."

"But you must." Lucy clutched the front of her coat. "There's no one else, and my baby has to live. I told you I don't care if he is shamed—"

Hearing Lucy repeat the word "shamed," Susannah became angry. "Stop saying that. There is nothing shameful about the birth of a baby, no matter how it was conceived. Now, my name is Susannah, and I'll do what I can to help you, Lucy, but Joshua . . ." She blinked as she realized that he would come to assist her and tell her what to do. Dear God, he just had to.

Susannah pulled away from Lucy's grasp, bent her head, and closed her eyes. "If you're ever going to help me, Joshua, help me now, please," she beseeched.

"Who . . . who is Joshua?" Lucy asked in a frightened voice. "I don't see anyone else here. Who are you talking to? Are you all right?"

"Joshua . . ."

"You want me to name my baby Joshua if it's a boy?" Lucy laughed nervously. "Is that what you mean?"

Susannah did not answer. Thrilled at the scent of lilacs, she saw Joshua standing at the foot of the bed. "Thank God you came," she said, breathing a sigh of relief.

"I'll always come when you truly need me, Susannah. You know that." He caressed her cheek with his fingertips, and she was glad for his comforting touch.

"Now do as I say," he commanded. "First, you were right. You must get Lucy undressed and then find scissors and string so you can cut the umbilical cord after the baby is born. But don't worry. I'll tell you what to do every step of the way. I'll be right beside you.

"It's good that you already have water boiling," he continued, "and now you need to warm some blankets by the fire to wrap the baby in. But please relax," he added with a smile. "Together we're going to do just fine."

Susannah proceeded to follow his instructions.

As Lucy's contractions became stronger and closer together, Susannah continued to talk to Joshua, and was quickly caught up in the miracle of birth. She cried and laughed as the baby crowned, and she could finally see the downy fuzz of its tiny head.

"Here come the shoulders," Joshua said. "Now tell Lucy to push as hard as she can."

Susannah relayed the order. Lucy obeyed, and soon the baby was sliding into Susannah's waiting hands. "It's a girl, Lucy. You have a daughter, and she seems perfect to me, thank God."

"And thank you, Miss Susannah," Lucy said breathlessly as she held out her arms for her newborn infant.

"And Joshua," Susannah responded, without thinking, as she quickly wrapped the baby in a warm blanket before handing her to Lucy.

Lucy laughed. "No. I'll not name my daughter Joshua. I'm going to name her Susannah, after you for saving her life."

Susannah did not know what to say for a moment. "Well—well, I'm truly honored, Lucy," she finally stammered.

Later, when Lucy and her baby were both asleep, Susannah and Joshua sat side by side in chairs before the fire, and she thanked him once more for coming so quickly.

"As I've told you often through the years, Susannah, I'll always come when you truly need me."

"I've needed you desperately in the past few days, but I was too stubborn to call you."

"I knew that, so I left you alone. You were trying to come to terms with your heart, and I couldn't help you there. You had to do that yourself."

"But I don't think I realized what I truly wanted until I helped Lucy deliver her baby, Joshua. I can see now what it means to Trent to help these people. Maybe I knew that all along but just couldn't accept it. I wanted him to be just like you in every way."

"But that's not possible. He's a human being, like you, but I think he has shown you by his unselfishness that he is both human and divine. Susannah, you have to realize that no man can possibly fulfill all your ideals of what a perfect mate should be. So if you can accept Trent for who he is, what he is, then you can have a marriage truly made in heaven.

"And never forget," he added, leaning to give her a hug, "I will never leave you. I will always be with you."

Impulsively, she kissed his cheek in gratitude, and he touched the spot and whispered, "Thank you, Susannah."

They sat in silence for a few moments, and then Susannah remembered something strange that had happened at the very instant Lucy's baby had come into the world. "It was as though a light was hovering over her. It startled me, but then there wasn't time to think about it, because I was having to struggle to keep from dropping her."

Joshua closed his eyes and nodded, a pleased, peaceful look on his face. "That was her guardian angel, making sure everything was all right."

"You mean . . ." Susannah stopped rocking and stared at him in wonder. "The baby has a guardian angel, too?"

But he was gone, and the door burst open. Trent rushed into the cabin and crossed the small room in quick strides. He grabbed Susannah and held her tight.

"I saw the smoke from my chimney and thought something was wrong. You don't know how glad I am to see you. Are you all right?" He fell silent as his eyes went to the bed.

"They're both fine," Susannah proudly declared.

He shook his head, bewildered. "I don't understand."

Quickly she told him everything, leaving out the very important part that Joshua had played, of course, then explained her reason for being there. "I came to tell you I love you and want to marry you, but now it's different. Now I understand, and if you want us to live here, we will. I want to work beside you, Trent. I want to know the same kind of satisfaction you get from your life, your work."

He lowered his head, pressing his cheek against her neck. "I love you, darling, and between the two of us, we can face anything."

Behind him, Joshua suddenly appeared, beaming. "Actually"—he grinned—"the three of us can face anything, but he can never know that. It's our secret, Susannah. Yours and mine."

And with a wink, he disappeared.

Chapter Ten

Susannah peered out from behind the dressing screen as Mrs. Barnaby scrutinized the six bridesmaids and their gowns.

The young women looked anxious and seemed to be holding their breath. Mrs. Barnaby, whom Susannah had asked to take charge of the wedding, had made no secret of her opinion that the style of the bridesmaids' gowns was inappropriate for a wedding.

Now, her mouth pinched tightly, her hands on her hips, she walked among the young women and studied them with narrowed eyes.

Susannah thought the pink satin gowns, overlaid with delicate pink lace, were beautiful and in good taste. The heart-shaped bodices dipped discreetly, and the puffed sleeves at the shoulders tapered to fingertip lengths. Wide sashes tied with large bows trailed to the floor, and the cascading skirts were caught and held by clusters of crocheted white roses. She thought her bridesmaids looked exquisite.

"I think . . ." Mrs. Barnaby said, and paused to tap her finger against her chin, "that you are the most stunning bridesmaids I have ever seen."

Susannah sighed in relief, withdrawing behind the screen, and she heard the other women gasp with joy.

"Now, now." Mrs. Barnaby laughed and clapped her hands. "Father Dimitri hasn't given his approval."

"Yes, he has—years ago," Susannah called from behind the screen. Mr. Grierly's wife, Anna, was helping her with her gown, and she was bending for it to be pulled over her head. "He's heard me say all my life that I intended to be married on Valentine's Day with my bridesmaids in pink and the church decorated in red and white."

"Oh, it's decorated, all right," Mrs. Barnaby was quick to assure her. "I've never seen so many paper flowers."

"That's thanks to Trent's students," Susannah said proudly. "They've been making them all winter."

The bridesmaids began to babble happily among themselves. Then one of them called,

"He's here, Susannah. Trent's here, and—oh, he looks so elegant. He's wearing a—"

"Don't tell me," Susannah quickly interrupted. "He can't know what I look like until he sees me coming down the aisle, and I want his attire to be a surprise to me, too."

There was a knock on the door, and Susannah heard Mr. Grierly's voice. "It's time, Susannah. The guests are all seated. The groom has arrived, and I'm ready to give the bride away.

"Goodness knows," he added, laughing, "it's time another man took over and tried to rein you in. I've certainly had my hands full all these years."

She heard the women giggle, but they immediately fell silent when she stepped from behind the screen.

"Susannah, I only wish your mother and father could see how lovely you are," Mr. Grierly whispered.

She was overjoyed with his compliment. Her white satin gown, overlaid with Brussels lace trimmed with satin ribbon in the palest shade of pink, had turned out exactly as she had envisioned. And so had her veil. Fixed to her hair with a circlet of white silk roses, it fell down her back, and the tiniest pink rosebuds had been embroidered into the netting and interspersed in her billowing skirt.

She had decided to wear the same pearl-and-diamond earbobs her mother had worn on her wedding day, and the matching necklace graced her bare skin above her modest cleavage displayed by the same sweetheart neckline as on her bridesmaids' gowns. In her hands she held a white prayer book, a family heirloom.

Mrs. Barnaby pulled a hanky from inside the cuff of her sleeve and dabbed at her eyes. "Beautiful. Just beautiful. A true fairy princess if ever there was one."

Her bridesmaids were even blinking back tears, and Susannah swallowed around the lump in her throat. "Stop it. All of you. We can't walk down the aisle crying, for heaven's sake," she said gently.

Hearing the music, she tucked her hand in Mr. Grierly's arm and they followed her bridesmaids into the foyer. They walked in single file down the aisle, and then it was time for her entrance.

Everyone stood, turning to watch as she moved slowly down the long, white carpet, clinging to Mr. Grierly's arm. But she saw only Trent, waiting at the altar . . . waiting to become her beloved husband.

Someone caught her hand, and she glanced down. Lucy Graham, holding her baby, tears in her eyes, whispered, "Bless you, Susannah, on your wedding day. Bless you now and always."

Susannah blew her a kiss and noticed that one side of the church was filled with the people from Bent Creek. They were not dressed in the finery of those seated on her side—the bride's side—but it made no difference. She was glad they were there. It meant they had accepted her as they had accepted Trent.

As she walked, it was as if her feet were not even touching the floor. Ecstatic, she felt as if she were actually floating.

As Mrs. Barnaby had said, red and white paper blossoms were everywhere. The altar was banked, and the panels of the pews were covered.

Heaven had sent a perfect day. The sun shone through the stained-glass windows and their colors danced amidst the gently burning candles positioned around the church.

Finally she reached the altar and was moved by how strikingly handsome Trent was in his white formal suit.

His love for her was mirrored on his face, and she could see that his eyes were moist with tears.

The familiar scent of lilacs pervaded her senses and she smiled. Joshua stood beside Trent, resplendent in his own ceremonial attire.

He gave her a mock frown. "Now don't you dare speak to me. You knew I'd be here. I'll always be here. But today, of all days, I don't want anyone thinking you're tetched."

She bit back a laugh of delight and nodded slightly. Then she turned her full attention to Father Dimitri as he began the ceremony of her marriage made in heaven.

About the Author

Patricia Hagan, the *New York Times* bestselling author of thirty books, cannot remember a time in her life when she did not want to be a writer.

An avid reader, she found that the words of Whittier in *Written in A Lady's Album* made a lasting impression:

> "Our lives are albums written through,
> with good or ill,
> with false or true . . .
> And as the blessed angels turn the pages
> of our years,
> God grant they read the good with
> smiles . . .
> and blot the ill with tears."

A Marriage Made in Heaven

Patricia believes that angels, like romance, are in each of our souls, and that all we have to do is open our hearts to our guardian angels . . . as well as to love, to romance, and to joy.

Patricia lives in the western North Carolina mountains with her husband, Erik, and her very special wire-haired fox terrier, Krystal.

BOBBY HUTCHINSON
"Heaven On Earth"

*"Behold, I send an Angel before thee,
to keep thee in the way."*

—Exodus

Chapter One

Indiana, 1889

"Lillie, you have exquisite taste. Which would you say is the better choice?" Myrtle Thorsen held the two fabrics up, one on either side of her florid face, and Lillie pretended to study them, wondering how in the world to dissuade Myrtle from purchasing either.

The fiery red serge and Myrtle's unfortunate carrot-colored hair clashed like cymbals. On the other hand, the bright yellow alpaca emphasized the millions of freckles that dotted the young woman's wide face, and Lillie knew the tiny checks would look as if they went on into eternity encompassing Myrtle's more-than-ample hips.

"Both are striking," Lillie declared, which was no less than the truth. Near Myrtle, they definitely walloped one in the eye. She just couldn't allow the poor woman to create yet another fashion disaster—and then announce that she'd bought the fabric in Lillie's store.

"Before you decide, I've a new shipment of goods in the back that I haven't had time to display. I just know one of the fabrics would be perfect for you."

Lillie hurried through the beaded curtain and into the back, sighing with regret as she snatched up the bolt of sky-blue Liberty print she'd intended as a dress for herself. That particular blue complemented her dark brown eyes and brought out the highlights in her blond hair.

Never mind, she thought. Next week would bring another shipment, perhaps another fabric just as lovely, and Myrtle might actually look pretty in this.

"Oh, Lillie, it's so wonderful to have someone my own age running this store," Myrtle gushed.

She knew for a fact Myrtle was at least six years older than her own twenty-four, but she murmured a thank you anyway.

"Old Mr. Freeman, God rest his soul, would never have ordered fabric this scrumptious," Myrtle crowed as Lillie draped the soft material across her shoulder. She peered into the mirror

Lillie had mounted on the wall near the fabrics and turned her head this way and that. "It does bring out my coloring, doesn't it? I'll take it, and thread to match, of course, and oh my goodness, I nearly forgot the pound of sugar and the block of yeast I came for in the first place. Mama would skin me alive if I forgot them."

Lillie stacked the goods on the counter and was adding them up when the bell over the door tinkled its merry little tune.

"Morning, Dr. Dennison." Lillie smiled at the tall, broad-shouldered young man, and he nodded back at her and immediately stumbled over the iron doorstop. She pretended she didn't notice as he recovered his balance and shoved his round glasses back into place on his patrician nose.

Dr. Dennison was both clumsy and endearingly shy. His handsome face turned as red as the serge Myrtle had been considering, and he headed blindly down a side aisle, pretending to study the array of pots and pans Lillie had hung on hooks from a post, while he recovered his aplomb.

Lillie counted out Myrtle's change as the doctor approached the counter, fingering his smudged shopping list.

"Oh, Dr. Dennison, good morning," Myrtle simpered, patting the carrot curls peeking out under her warm bonnet.

"Miss Thorsen," he said with a courtly nod and

115

a tip of his brown fedora. "And how is your grandmother today?"

"Oh, she's much better, thanks to that rheumatism potion you gave her. We're all ever so grateful. She's a trifle, um, difficult, when she's ailing." Myrtle blinked furiously, giggled, and searched for something else to say to the eligible bachelor. "Will we see you at the church social on Thursday, then, Doctor?" she cooed in an arch tone. "Mother's making her mile-high lemon pie, and I'm bringing my special scones."

"I'm afraid not."

"Oh. Oh, I see. How unfortunate." Myrtle blinked her pink-rimmed eyes rapidly, waiting for an explanation. When none was forthcoming, she dithered for another long moment and at last gathered her parcels and headed for the door.

The doctor hurried over and politely held it open, but Lillie thought she heard him breathe a relieved sigh when he closed it again. She smothered a grin, although she felt a pang of sympathy for Myrtle. Alexander Dennison wasn't an easy man to chat with, and as for flirting . . . Well, she could have told Myrtle it was entirely wasted on the doctor.

In the three months since she'd purchased the General Store, she had served him two or three times a week, depending on how many items he forgot to add to his list each time.

He tended to be absentminded, which she

knew very well. She knew other intriguing things about him too. Running the only general store in town provided insight into its inhabitants, probably far more than they ever suspected.

But as for *really* knowing Doctor Dennison, the way she knew almost every other single man in town, she was no closer than she'd been the first time he came in to buy baking soda. Not, as she'd quickly learned, to make biscuits, but to ease old Mr. Hammeker's indigestion.

"Can I help you find anything, Doctor?" These shopping trips followed a set pattern, and she adhered to the routine because it amused her and so did he.

"I can't seem to locate the molasses, Miss O'Neal."

"How much do you require?" The molasses was in a barrel that might have bowled him over if he moved a scant two feet. It had been in that spot goodness knew how long. It was one of the few things she hadn't rearranged since she'd taken over the store.

"Enough to make beans," he said in the vague manner she was now familiar with. "And I need some of those as well. Beans, I mean. The small white ones for baking."

It amazed her that a man who dispensed medications every day of his life could be so vague when it came to foodstuffs.

She got him the molasses and then moved easily from one aisle to the next, collecting his other supplies as he called them out to her, wondering again why he didn't hire a housekeeper to cook and clean for him. She knew the good women of Greenwood kept a steady supply of bread, biscuits, and even pies flowing to his door, but his daily meals seemed to consist of far more baked beans and fried bacon than she considered palatable or even healthy. And as preoccupied as he was, she suspected he probably forgot to eat more often than not.

Oh, he wasn't thin, she thought as she piled the groceries on the counter and sneaked a sideways glance at him. He was dressed in a bulky brown overcoat on this cold January day. But she knew from warmer days that under it his shoulders were broad, his arms and chest well muscled. He was lean, long-legged, and slim-hipped. In fact, he had a physique quite as good as any of the town's young swains, and better than most. She liked the fact he was clean-shaven. He had an interesting face, a strongly carved nose, high, prominent cheekbones, and a determined chin with a definite cleft. There was something elegant, even aristocratic, about Alexander Dennison.

And he'd probably turn purple if she called him just plain Alexander. Heavens, he was formal—and shy.

"Flannel, Miss O'Neal. Sheets, flannel sheets, the heaviest you have." He peered around as if

118

the items might leap out at him.

Lillie frowned and tipped her head to one side. "I don't have ready-made flannel sheets, Doctor. Most people hereabouts sew their own. I do have wide fabric, of a good thickness."

"Give me that, then."

"And what size is your bed, Doctor?" She went to the table where the fabric was and looked at him from under her lashes, flirting outrageously even as she smothered a grin. Now there was a personal question if ever there was one. He'd likely turn scarlet and stammer. She did enjoy teasing him just a little now and then. He became so deliciously undone.

But he didn't turn a hair this time. "They're not for me. They're for Mrs. Liposke. She keeps catching the grippe, and I'm sure it's because she's chilled at night." He frowned, and Lillie noted the tiny frown line etched between his eyebrows. He was far too serious for his own good, this attractive fellow.

"I think her bed's about this wide." He held his arms apart, and she measured and cut, amused again by his vagueness and touched by his thoughtfulness.

A cranky, opinionated woman, the ancient Mrs. Liposke lived alone in a tiny house by the livery stable. Very few people knew or cared that she was virtually penniless, but Lillie knew, and always managed to slip a few extras into the old woman's bag when she came into the store.

Bobby Hutchinson

"I know there are fine seamstresses in town, but who would you recommend I hire to sew the sheets, Miss O'Neal?"

"The Misses Semple," she said as they walked back to the counter. "And they could use the business. You'll need thread." She smiled at him, her open, sunny smile that usually charmed any male from six months old and up, then turned to the display behind her.

"And why not call me Lillie?" she added on impulse. She'd wanted to suggest it before, but there were usually other customers around, and the right moment hadn't arrived until now. "It seems silly, doesn't it, being so formal when we see each other all the time?" She turned around, holding the thread and smiling at him.

He nodded, but he didn't return her smile, and neither did he say her name. "Put in whatever is required, and wrap it separately. I'll take it to the Semples directly. And I need oatmeal, and some salt. And vinegar."

He suddenly sounded impatient, and she quickly filled his order. He always sounded that way long before they finished his list, however short. It was obvious he disliked shopping—except for the purchase of sweets. He definitely had a sweet tooth.

"I'll take a half-pound of that taffy, and some of those sugar drops."

The bell rang as she was measuring the candy, and Bill Evans swaggered in the door, along with a blast of icy air. "It's snowin' again," he announced in a cheerful tone, removing his hat and slapping the moisture from it. His boots made a great deal of noise on the wooden floor. Bill was a young man who didn't do anything quietly. "Howdy, Lillie. You're lookin' mighty pretty today." He gave her his crooked grin and winked at her with bold black eyes.

"Why, thank you, Bill." Lillie wrinkled her nose and smiled up at the tall farmhand as she wrapped and tied the flannel and thread in one bundle and put the rest of the doctor's purchases in the canvas sack he'd brought for that purpose.

"So, Doc, how's things?" Bill smoothed his thick dark hair and replaced his hat. He lounged against the counter, watching Lillie as she tallied the bill.

"Fine, thank you, Bill. Your arm has mended well, I see."

"Good as new. Aches a little in this cold, but nothin' serious." He flexed his left arm like a boxer. "Wagon slipped and fell on me last spring when I was fixin' the axle, Lillie, just before you and your pa came to town, and the Doc here patched me up." He winked at her again. "Good thing, too. A man needs two good arms around the ladies."

Lillie rolled her eyes. Bill was an incorrigible tease.

"What do I owe you, Miss O'Neal?" The doctor looked both disapproving and ill at ease. He searched his pockets and finally located his money, peeling off bills in a heedless manner and setting them on the counter.

"Thank you, Doctor." Lillie sorted them out and handed him his change, noting that he and Bill were the same height, several inches over six feet. She barely came to their shoulders, which in her opinion was perfect. She was partial to tall men. They made her feel fragile, which she wasn't in the slightest. She was sturdily built, and hefting kegs and boxes had put muscles in her arms. But it was nice to pretend she couldn't lift a handkerchief if she dropped it.

Doctor Dennison gathered up his purchases, solemnly nodded at her, and hurried out the door.

"Oh, dear. He's forgotten his gloves again." Lillie raced after him, gasping at the icy blast of cold air when she opened the door.

"Doctor. Dr. Dennison, wait." She ran, and he turned just as she slipped on the ice. She would have fallen, but he reached out and grabbed her arms, steadying her. She recovered her balance quickly and he instantly let her go. He was incredibly strong. He'd almost lifted her off her feet.

"Oh, thank you, Doctor. I nearly took a tumble." She had to smile at the way he looked. His glasses had frosted over and he'd slid them to the end of his nose and was peering at her over them like an owlish professor. He must have realized what she was smiling at because he snatched them off and tucked them into his jacket pocket. His eyes, the color of sherry, were long-lashed, intense. Their startling beauty almost made her forget her errand. "Uh, you left your gloves." She held them out. "Brrrr, you'll need them. It's absolutely freezing out here."

"Thank you, uh, Lillie." Her name came awkwardly to his lips. "Hurry back inside now. You'll catch pneumonia."

He guided her back to the store, held the door for her, gave a little bow, and at last he smiled. She stared, because the lack of glasses and the smile quite transformed his face. He looked young and vulnerable and unbearably handsome. In spite of the bitter cold, her heart lurched and hammered against the tiny pleats on the front of her pink handkerchief-linen blouse.

She was shivering as she hurried back inside, but there was a warm tingling in her stomach. She enjoyed a challenge, and from now on she would make much more of an effort to get Dr. Alexander Dennison to take an interest in her.

Chapter Two

Inside the store, Bill clasped her hand in his huge callused one and led her along the aisles to the back of the store where the pot-bellied stove emitted welcoming waves of heat. "Poor little thing, you're freezing cold. Come and warm up. I've put more wood on."

Dear, smitten man. Why was it Bill Evans adored her with no effort whatsoever on her part, while Alexander Dennison remained impervious to her charms? Lillie sank into one of the high-backed chairs that surrounded the stove, grateful that apart from Bill, there were no customers.

She looked around at the woven baskets displaying bright yarn, and at the little oaken dresser with its drawers ajar, adroitly showing buttons, lace, and edgings. The changes she'd made in the three months she'd been the proprietor never ceased to please her. The General Store had gone from dreary and utilitarian to bright and welcoming, and if a large percentage of the bodies that regularly occupied these comfortable chairs were now young males of marriageable age, so much the better. She enjoyed their attention. She liked to laugh—and she was the first to admit she also liked to flirt a little. She enjoyed feeling like a queen bee with dozens of drones buzzing around her.

If the prudish and sour elements in town were gossiping about her, then, as her daddy had always said, they were leaving some other poor soul alone.

She remembered a pair of sherry-colored eyes and decided to do a bit of gossiping herself. "Bill, has Dr. Dennison lived here very long?"

Bill was slumped in the chair next to hers, one booted foot resting on his denim-covered knee. "Yup, sure has. He was born here, same as me, only he's about four years older. Must be thirty-two, thirty-three by now. We went to the same grade school, 'cept he went through faster than most. Everybody knew Alexander was smart."

"Were his parents well-to-do?"

He snorted. "Hell, no." His neck reddened. "Sorry, Lillie. Heck, no, they was farming people, same as mine. Older, quiet, hard-workin',

125

not two beans to rub together. Alexander was their only kid. He stayed on the farm after he finished school, cuz his folks needed him. Farmed for quite a spell, maybe six or seven years. Then they both up and died within a single week. It was that influenza that rampaged through here. Musta been in seventy-nine. He'd a been twenty-one, twenty-two."

She nodded. It wasn't difficult to form a picture of a studious, intelligent young man, tied to farming that he probably hated because of loyalty to his aging parents. It was a familiar scenario in towns like this.

The bell announced a customer, and reluctantly Lillie rose. Smoothing her gray wool worsted skirt down over her hips, she was aware that Bill was admiring her figure while pretending to check the stove for fuel.

"How did he ever become a doctor, then?"

She waited for Bill's answer, her eyebrows raised, giving him a stern look when at last his eyes snapped from her chest to her face.

He looked appropriately shamefaced and guilty. "Who? Oh, Dennison. Well, he sold the farm and livestock to old Barnaby Clapmore and lit out of here right after the funeral. Went to some fancy school back East. Harvest or somethin' like that."

"Harvard." Well, well. Alexander must have been bright indeed, to qualify for Harvard.

She hurried to the front of the store, her professional smile already in place, her mind still on the doctor.

"Good morning, Mrs. Dahl. I have those new butter molds that you ordered." It would take time, Lillie reflected, but she'd learn all there was to know about Alexander Dennison. He was different, good-looking, and intelligent, and he intrigued her. Truth to tell, he also annoyed her. He was the only single man in town of marriageable age who never once even seemed to notice her figure at all.

Miss O'Neal really was an incorrigible flirt, Alexander concluded as he hurried down the street toward home, absently responding to the greetings from the few townspeople out on this cold January morning. It was all too evident she had poor Bill Evans wrapped around her little finger, and no wonder, batting her long eyelashes and cooing at him the way she had.

He made polite noises to a few more passersby while his mind conjured the intriguing curves under Miss O'Neal's blouse and at the same time censored her for being far too forward.

And that scent she wore—lavender—always lured him into leaning a little closer to her. It probably had the same effect on other men, which really could be quite dangerous. He hoped she was aware of men's baser instincts.

"G'day, Doc. Filthy weather we's havin', ain't it?" The town drunk, Milton Goslin, was un-

doubtedly on his way to the tavern to begin his
daily drinking ritual. Alexander despaired for
Milton's liver, but there was nothing he could
do. He'd tried everything short of locking the
poor man up. Drunkenness was a malady for
which he could devise no cure.

Was flirting just as irreversible?

"Morning, Doctor. Watch your step. It's icy."
Peter Rapson, the town barber, was out with his
shovel, ineffectually clearing his patch of
wooden sidewalk. Peter had asthma, but Alexander had it under control. He'd concocted a
remedy of elecampane, angelica, and comfrey
steeped in honey, and Peter hadn't had an attack
in months.

On the bench outside the barber shop, bun-
dled against the cold, sat the four old codgers
Alexander privately called the barber shop quartet. Walter, Vernon, Frank, and Lars were the
town's eyes, ears, and conscience. They
watched, judged, criticized, and castigated
everyone and everything that occurred in Greenwood. For years they'd been in the habit of sitting around the stove in the General Store. But
when old Freeman died and Miss O'Neal—Lillie,
Alexander corrected—when Lillie took over and
made changes, they moved to Peter's barber
shop, grumbling about upstarts, highfalutin no-
tions, and dire predictions of bankruptcy. Lillie
had proven them wrong, though.

"Mornin', Doc," they mumbled now, one after the other.

Alexander nodded. "Gentlemen."

"Oh, Dr. Dennison, what a coincidence! I was just on my way to your office." The peevish female voice sounded from behind him, and Alexander's heart sank. "Wait up, I'll walk with you," she panted.

A bossy, idle woman, Mrs. Martz tried his patience. She developed one symptom after another, never quite recovering and never becoming seriously ill, either. Yet she seemed to blame him for both conditions. In his opinion, a large part of her problem was her weight, and he'd diplomatically tried to tell her to reduce, but to no avail.

"Of course I can't walk quickly," she whined now. "My legs are acting up again, it's my veins, and my neck's been sore . . ."

At a snail's pace that made him want to bolt, they made their way along the town's main street and at last turned into the front yard of his white clapboard house.

His office door was always unlocked, and the Gothic-scripted sign on it read "Dr. Alexander Dennison, Family Physician." Underneath it, another sign said, "The Doctor is Out" on one side, with the opposite message on the back.

He turned it around now, and said, "Go in and make yourself comfortable, Mrs. Martz. I'll just take these things into the kitchen. I'll be with you in a moment."

He was in a thoroughly bad mood as he went through the waiting room and headed to the kitchen in the rear of the house. He upended the canvas sack on the kitchen table and remembered, too late, about the flannel sheets. Now he'd have to go out again to see the Misses Semple. Not anticipating many patients in this weather, he'd planned on spending a quiet day studying the latest medical journals.

Sighing, he went through the connecting door and into his office where Mrs. Martz waited impatiently to regale him with her latest list of incurable symptoms.

Alexander was wrong about the number of patients who ended up in his office that day. After Mrs. Martz, a steady stream appeared with assorted ailments peculiar to the season—sore throats, ague, catarrh, severe chapping, and chilblains. As always, he devoted himself wholly to his work, doing his best to alleviate his patients' pain and discomfort.

At last, the waiting room was empty. He glanced out the window, amazed to find it already dark. His growling stomach reminded him he'd forgotten lunch, and although the fire in the small stove blazed, the kitchen cookstove was out. Patients were very cooperative about stoking the stove. They'd learned he tended to forget.

In the kitchen, he used shavings to light the stove, wondering what was in the larder for a quick supper. Bacon . . . He was certain he'd purchased bacon that morning, and there were always eggs because many of his patients paid him with eggs, or milk, or even bread.

As he placed the bacon in the skillet, a child's frantic screaming startled him. He quickly left the kitchen and hurried down the hallway, and as he entered the waiting room the office door burst open. Carl Patterson, a farmer Alexander knew well, strode in holding his small son in his arms. The boy was shrieking in agony. The woolen blanket around him had fallen away and his right arm lay across his chest, bent at a grotesque angle. Blood had stained his long-sleeved flannel shirt and the blanket.

"Zeb fell out of the loft. He was pitchin' hay down to the cattle," Carl said above his son's cries. "Broke his arm bad." The man's usually ruddy complexion was waxy, his eyes glassy with shock and anxiety.

"Bring him into the surgery." Carl followed him and Alexander pointed to the table. "Lay him down over here." Alexander quickly assessed the break, trying to reassure the little boy. "I know it hurts, Zeb, but we'll get you fixed up in a jiffy, I promise."

The break was compound, the bone protruding from the flesh just above the elbow. The boy's wild shrieks continued unabated.

Alexander knew the break was quite serious, the kind that often resulted in the loss of a limb or even death, not from the break itself but from sepsis. The accompanying shock was also dangerous.

"Carl, I'm better off dealing with him alone. Go to the kitchen and fix us a pot of coffee. Fire's just started in the cookstove, and there's more kindling out back. Heat some water in case I need it." Giving the father something to do would distract him.

As soon as Carl left the room, Alexander said in a soft, urgent tone, "Stephen, I need your help."

As always, the moment the words were spoken, Alexander felt a presence infiltrate the room. He knew from experience that the small boy on the table, whose cries had now dulled to a nerve-rending, agonized moaning, would be unable to see the tall, slender young man who materialized at the head of the table. Alexander had learned long ago that Stephen was visible only to him, a phenomenon he found amazing, because Stephen seemed so very solid and robust whenever he appeared.

His hair was silver blond, and his eyes, too, were silver, like shimmering, brilliant moonlight reflecting on water. His features were striking, with a mesmerizing beauty, and his aura of strength was both physical and emotional, quiet and clear. Without a word, he laid his graceful, long-fingered hands on either side of Zeb's head. The little boy sighed and, between one groan and the next, fell into a deep sleep.

Alexander immediately snipped lengths of sutures from a spool, dipping them into a carbolic bath.

"Is there nerve damage?" he asked. "The arm was undoubtedly jolted," he said. He had worked with Stephen often and relied on his ability to diagnose conditions that were beyond modern medicine's scope.

"None." Stephen's voice was deep and resonant, and always had a calming effect on Alexander, no matter how dire the emergency. "He's weakening, however. We'll just control the bleeding . . ."

Stephen extended his hand and held it, palm down, over the seeping wound. In a moment, the blood coagulated, and Alexander was able to see the vessels that needed to be tied off.

For an hour, Alexander sat on a high stool, bending over the table, meticulously cleaning the wound, scarifying the edges and suturing. Stephen made quiet suggestions and helped set the bone. When the arm was encased at last in bandages and wooden splints, he cast a blue-violet light from his hand toward the injured limb.

Alexander, familiar with this powerful healing

technique, nevertheless felt chills run up his spine. He watched in awed silence until the powerful light faded and then slowly disappeared.

"Zeb will heal quickly now," Stephen predicted with a gentle smile. "Healing energy always works best on children. They have no barriers. He'll sleep long and well, and when he awakens, the worst of the pain will be over."

Alexander drew a soft blanket over the sleeping child and tucked it in. Then heaving a deep breath, he flexed his aching shoulder muscles. He looked deep into his friend's eyes, and the joyful peace and reassurance in them wiped away his weariness and exhaustion.

"Thanks, Stephen," he said with heartfelt gratitude. "As usual, I could never have done it without you."

Stephen smiled, punching him affectionately on the shoulder. "Of course you could. We're going to have to work on your self-confidence. What I do, you can do, too. All you need is faith in yourself."

For some obscure reason, Lillie O'Neal's beautiful, animated face suddenly appeared in Alexander's mind, vivid and smiling.

Stephen's laughter was low. "You need to have confidence in that part of your life, too. Your life is incomplete."

Alexander scowled and swallowed hard. He might rely on Stephen and be grateful to him, but he didn't always have to agree with him. "I hardly think there's anything lacking in—" he began, but he was aware suddenly that he was alone in the room. "My life," he finished in a whisper.

Stephen had a disconcerting habit of disappearing before Alexander could disagree with him.

"Is—is Zeb gonna be okay?" Carl knocked and then stuck his head in the door of the surgery, his huge, gnarled farmer's hands clasping and unclasping, his weathered face lined with fatigue and anxiety. "I got a washtub o' water boilin' on the range, and I chopped a pile o' wood out back. There's a pot o' coffee brewin'."

Alexander removed his glasses, rubbed the bridge of his nose, and smiled at the man. "Zeb's going to be just fine," he said. "He needs to be kept quiet for a while, until that arm has a chance to heal some, but there won't be any complications, I can assure you of that. I'm going to keep him here tonight, and you can pick him up tomorrow about noon."

"Oh, thank God. Thank you, Doc." Carl's voice was thick with emotion. "Ellie and me, we can't thank you enough. Zeb's our youngest, he's her baby, see, and we was so scared . . ." His eyes filled with tears and he ducked his head and swiped at them with the back of his hand.

"Let's go sample that coffee, and I'll fry some bacon and eggs for us. Bet you missed your supper just like I did, Carl."

Bobby Hutchinson

At times like this, Alexander felt humble, embarrassed by the gratitude his patients heaped upon him. It was Stephen who deserved their thanks far more than he, but how did one explain that an angel had assisted with their healing?

Chapter Three

Long after Carl had harnessed his horse to his buggy and gone home, Alexander sat by the fire, chewing taffy and holding a mug of the truly awful coffee Carl had brewed. He pondered, for the millionth time, the presence of Stephen in his life.

He knew if he tried to explain about Stephen, the kind and simple folks of Greenwood would shake their heads and whisper that poor Doc Dennison was more than a little tetched in the head, and that would be the end of his practice.

But knowing how they would react didn't stop the feeling that he was taking credit for something he didn't deserve. He'd finally discussed the problem with Stephen, and his friend had laughed uproariously.

"Stop worrying about my ego, Alexander. I haven't got one. And if I may say so, you haven't got much of one, either." He sobered then and added, "You're here on earth to learn lessons, and one of those is about yourself and your self-worth. My task here is to help you, nothing more, nothing less. I'm here for you, whenever you call. I'm not going to get insulted and disappear because I feel I'm not getting my fair share of glory. I would leave only if you asked me to." He grinned in a decidedly mischievous manner. "Besides, I get quite enough of Glory."

Alexander remembered in vivid detail the first time he had been aware of Stephen's existence. He was nearing the end of his difficult third year at Johns Hopkins University in Baltimore. Exhausted by the prestigious medical school's academic demands, and drained by a severe lingering bout of influenza, he tried to study and couldn't. His brain refused to absorb the complicated information, and at last he gave up, despairing of ever passing his courses. More than anything else in the world, he'd dreamed of becoming a doctor, but now that dream was shattered and he lost hope.

That time he felt Stephen's presence in the form of optimism, an indefinable feeling that everything would work out in spite of his difficulties. He slept soundly for several hours, and afterwards the formerly incomprehensible material seemed logical and crystal-clear in his mind.

But later, during his final examinations, he once again fell into despair. Alone in his room, late at night, he tried to study for the final examination in his most difficult course, pharmacology.

Hours passed, and the chemical symbols made less and less sense, and giving up at last, he threw his books on the floor. He'd never pass the examination, never attain his dream of becoming a doctor, and furthermore, he no longer cared. Having already written three examinations, anatomy, botany, and chemistry, he was now certain he'd failed them as well.

Disgusted, he began tossing his clothing into his trunk. There was no sense staying here. He'd catch the early train. But where would he go? He'd sold his parents' farm to finance his education, so there was no home to return to, and there wasn't a living soul who cared if he lived or died. Maybe death was the answer. . . .

At that moment, when there seemed nothing left to live for, he felt someone reach over his shoulder and pluck the key to his trunk out of his hand.

Startled and shocked, for his door was bolted, he whirled around and stared at a man standing a few feet away.

"Who—who are you? How did you get in here?"

The tall young man looked at him, gazing into his eyes with the most compassionate and loving expression Alexander had ever seen. Before the man said a single word, Alexander felt an all-encompassing peace and sense of well-being flow through him.

"My name is Stephen." The man's voice reverberated through every nerve in Alexander's body. "I've come to help you. I'm your friend, Alexander, your soul's companion." He smiled, a joyous, light-hearted smile, and retrieved a paper Alexander had tossed into the wastebasket. "Let's see what we can do with this list of symbols, shall we? You have a great future as a healer, so let me help you with this last small obstacle."

With Stephen's help, Alexander easily mastered the material. He not only passed his examinations, but placed third in his class.

When he returned to Greenwood to set up his practice, Alexander once asked the question he'd puzzled over often and long.

"Why did you choose to help me, Stephen? That first time you came to me at the university. Why me?"

Stephen had shrugged. "Why not you? You're my responsibility, you know." His voice had softened, becoming infinitely caring. "You always have been. You always will be."

And he had always been there for Alexander, just as he'd been tonight with Zeb. They were a team, and until tonight, Alexander had assumed that Stephen was concerned only with the medical problems they addressed together.

Your life is incomplete ... Stephen's gentle reprimand echoed in Alexander's head, and again the image of lovely Lillie O'Neal flashed in his mind.

Flirtatious, his head warned.

Warm, his heart answered.

Frivolous, his mind insisted.

Desirable, his body responded.

Out of the question, he told himself. However attractive, Lillie O'Neal was a coquette who toyed with every man in sight. He'd witnessed it himself on numerous occasions in the store. In one jerky movement he got to his feet, slopping cold coffee over his trousers.

Chalk and cheese, his mother used to say when two things absolutely didn't go together. Well, he and Lillie O'Neal were chalk and cheese.

Old Granny Trone, the ancient midwife who'd delivered half the town before she finally retired, came hobbling into the store early that Monday, leaning on her cane.

Lillie was pleased the store was empty. She loved serving Granny, and she knew the old woman enjoyed the cup of tea Lillie always brewed if business permitted. The eccentric old

141

woman was a garden of information about Greenwood's residents.

It helped Lillie, for instance, to know that pompous, impossible-to-please Mrs. Lindsay had once been the poorest little girl in town. She had been forced to accept hand-me-downs from more fortunate children who then teased her for wearing their old clothes. Whenever she sailed into the store and treated Lillie like a serving maid, all Lillie had to do to keep from losing her temper was to imagine Mrs. Lindsay as that miserable, beleaguered, little child.

In the same way, knowing that cantankerous, dour Mr. Bakken's beloved only son drowned in Mirabel Lake, and that his wife had committed suicide shortly after, made it easier for her to deal with him.

So when the old woman's order was completed, Lillie decided that if anyone could tell her about Alexander Dennison, it was Granny. It took only a cup of peppermint tea and Lillie's few subtle questions to learn that Granny had brought Alexander into the world. He'd been born on January 30, during the worst snow storm ever to hit Greenwood, Granny recalled, and he had weighed over ten pounds.

"He was a special child from the very first. I said he'd have powers, and he does—healin' powers. Came late in life, Alexander did. His mama, Thelma, was forty-four, Phineas nigh on fifty. Given up any hope fer a family long since,"

Granny reminisced. "My, and were they proud o' that boy, and rightly so. Smart as a whip, and a good son to 'em, right up to the end." She shook her head. "Never saw a boy so tore up over losin' his folks. Looked at death's door hisself there fer a time. Thought we'd seen the last o' him when he sold up and left, but lo and behold, didn't he come back here to do his doctorin'? And he came and visited me right off, never forgot old Granny in spite of all his book larnin'," she confided proudly.

"Him bein' one o' my own, o' course, I got a special soft spot fer Alexander. Told him lots about birthin' he'd never learn in those fancy schools, too. Why, right to this day, he comes and visits with me. We sit and jaw and have a cuppa," she said with a self-satisfied nod.

So Alexander was a perceptive and wise man, Lillie thought. Greenwood women trusted Granny, and would probably have shunned the young doctor if Granny had gone against him. By currying the old woman's friendship, he had avoided the competition and bad feelings that often existed between a formally trained doctor and the local midwife in a small town. And not least of all, he had bolstered the old woman's ego.

"You heard from yer pa lately?" Granny had a habit of changing the subject whenever it suited her.

"I had a letter just last week. He's heading up

to Canada," Lillie answered. "He asked to be remembered to you."

Her father had hit it off with Granny the moment he and Lillie first drove their wagon into Greenwood last July. Lillie remembered every detail of that day that had marked the beginning of a new life for her. She thought of that day now with nostalgia and pride in her father's kindness and wisdom.

An itinerant handyman, Patrick was able to repair almost anything with the odds and ends he kept in the back of his wagon, and when they had passed Granny's cottage, they saw that half of her roof had been torn off. They watched as the old woman climbed a rickety ladder, holding a hammer and several shingles.

"Faith, would you look at that now, and the woman's seventy if she's a day," Patrick exclaimed, pulling the team to a halt. He asked Granny what had happened to the roof and she told him a storm the day before had destroyed it. He insisted that Granny let him fix the roof for her. He refused payment when she offered, accepting instead a hearty meal for himself and Lillie.

Her stomach ached even now at the memory of the heaping platefuls of food Granny set in front of them, and the warning glance her father shot her. They'd eaten dinner not half an hour before arriving in Greenwood, and Lillie almost burst before she managed to force down Granny's food as well.

She mused now on how well her father understood pride. He'd also understood that an old-timer like Granny could tell them more about the town and its inhabitants than he and Lillie could learn on their own in two weeks. How she missed him.

Granny's voice cut into her thoughts. "You ever regretted stayin' on here whilst he went wanderin', child?"

She hesitated a moment, then shook her head. "I get lonely for him. There was always just the two of us, and we were very close. But honestly, I'd had more than enough of traveling, Granny. I wanted to settle in one place, to have something of my own. We'd lived in more towns than I can remember."

Patrick hadn't objected, though, when she told him she wanted to stay in Greenwood, and he had given her the money to buy the store, more money than she'd known he had. Love and gratitude welled in her heart every time she thought about it.

"It was to be your dowry, darlin'," he'd said, handing her the thick wad of bills. "But I'm thinkin' the lucky man should be payin' me fer the privilege when the time comes, so buy your store and a blessin' on you. You'll make a fortune, what with your mother's beauty and the gift of gab you've inherited from me."

145

She looked at Granny and shook her head. "It finally dawned on me Pa would never settle down," she said sadly.

Granny nodded. "The Irish're funny that way." She held her cup out in her gnarled fingers for Lillie to refill. "Mighta been different, had yer ma lived."

"I don't remember her at all. I was only two when she died."

"Hard fer a girl-child, growin' up without a ma to guide her. Hard fer her to learn womanly ways, though seems you did right fine that way, Lillie." Granny cackled. "Never saw any young bucks loiterin' round here when old Freeman had the place, and now a body can hardly get near this stove most days, what with the crowd of duded-up fellers vyin' fer yer attentions."

She gave Lillie a shrewd look from under her bushy eyebrows. "Sumthin' tells me you ain't really got eyes fer any o' that crowd, though. You got yer sights set elsewhere, am I right, child?"

Lillie fidgeted uncomfortably and wondered where her customers were when she needed them.

Granny nodded. "Alexander's a fine man, none finer, but he's a hard one to corral. Most o' the mamas with gals of marriageable age has tried everythin' they know and then some to catch him, with no luck." She leaned closer to Lillie. "I'm right fond o' you, gal. Seems to me you'd be good fer him, and him fer you. I'll make ye a potion to wear round yer pretty neck. It'll draw him like a possum to molasses."

Granny left at last, and Lillie had to giggle when she thought about the foul-smelling "potion" Granny would undoubtedly produce. The old woman's idea wasn't too far off, though, she decided. But she had her own notion of the type of elixir that might make Alexander unbend a tiny bit.

"Why, Dr. Dennison, what a delightful surprise! Do come right in." Miss Amelia Semple smiled a warm welcome when Alexander appeared at the door, holding his bundle of flannel for Mrs. Liposke's sheets. "Let me take your coat and hat. Is it snowing again? Come into the parlor. This chair's quite comfortable. Sheila and I were just having our late-afternoon glass of sherry. You will join us, won't you?"

He'd planned just to hand over his package and leave. But somehow he found himself ensconced in an armchair in front of the fireplace, a glass of sherry in his hand. Amelia and Sheila sat side by side on a sofa a few feet away, a large tabby cat curled between them.

The Semple sisters were in their mid-twenties, dark, exotic-looking women who, he knew, had arrived in town two years ago and set up shop as seamstresses. Where they'd come from originally, or why they'd chosen Greenwood as a place to settle, remained a mystery. They'd never been his patients, so he didn't really know them well.

"How delicious, having a handsome gentleman drop in on us like this," Sheila said in her husky voice, smiling at him and toying with the lace at the rather low neckline of her dress. "These long winter evenings can be so tedious, don't you think so, Doctor? Here, let me pour you just a little bit more sherry."

She leaned forward, brushing his arm with hers, steadying his hand with her warm fingers as she poured the golden liquid into his glass.

Amelia was stroking the cat, slowly, sensuously, and looking up at him from under sooty lashes. "Now that you've braved the snowstorm to get here, Doctor, you really must stay for dinner. We have a rather nice leg of lamb roasting, much too large for just the two of us, and I've made an apple tart. Do say you'll stay."

Sheila nodded with enthusiasm. "Oh, yes, you absolutely must! We won't take no for an answer."

He was becoming more uncomfortable by the second. "That's most kind of you, but no, thank you. I really must be getting back. I often have patients in the evening," he fibbed, trying not to spill the sherry as he reached for the paper-wrapped bundle he'd put on the floor beside his chair. "I came because I wondered if you'd sew some sheets for me?"

"We'd be delighted," Amelia cooed. "And if

you need shirts, Doctor, we're very good at shirts." Her liquid dark eyes seemed to measure his chest.

It was another twenty minutes before he managed to escape. Out on the street again, where the snow was falling in huge soft flakes, he stomped along, vexed by the coquettish Semple sisters. They were women in business, he thought irritably, and their behavior had been most improper and undignified.

Lillie O'Neal flashed in his mind. She certainly wasn't as blatantly flirtatious as the Semples, he assured himself. But he couldn't deny that she was a very forward young woman—and that he thought of her far, far too often these days for his liking.

Chapter Four

Just after eight on Wednesday morning, Lillie climbed the back stairs to Alexander's house, her basket over her arm. Though her store opened at nine, she had no idea what time Alexander began seeing patients, so she'd decided to come early.

Her heart was hammering. Maybe this wasn't such a good idea after all. Part of her wanted to turn tail and run. *You've come this far, Lillie O'Neal*, she chided herself. *You might as well go through with it.*

Trembling slightly, she knocked, waited, knocked again, but there was no answer. He might be in the front, where his office was located, she thought.

She rounded the house, smiling when she saw his sign on the door. "Dr. Alexander Dennison. Family Physician." It was so like him, formal and slightly aloof. She would have written "Phamily Fysician," just to make everyone smile. The sign underneath announced simply, "The Doctor Is In," with no office hours.

She shook her head at this folly. She knew well the wisdom of opening a business at one set time and closing at another. When she'd first taken over the store, people expected her to be there from dawn until midnight. She'd set rigid hours and adhered to them. Otherwise, she'd never have a single minute to herself.

What in heaven's name was Alexander doing in at eight in the morning? And on his birthday, no less?

The answer was soon obvious when she entered the waiting room and heard the murmur of voices through the surgery's closed door. Lillie sat down, waiting for him to finish with his patient, and took stock of the uninviting room.

Though there was a nice little pot-bellied stove sending out waves of heat, the room sadly lacked character. The walls were papered in a drab beige stripe, the dun-colored sofa screamed out for a bright throw, the pictures of someone's ancestors were dismal, and the dusty brown curtains were atrocious.

In her mind, she had the room stripped and entirely renovated by the time the surgery door opened. A farmer with his hand thickly bandaged and copious amounts of blood on his coveralls came out. Behind him was Alexander, who saw the man to the door.

Her breath caught in her throat. Every time she had seen Alexander, he was always dressed formally in a suit jacket, vest, and tie firmly in place. This morning he'd obviously been interrupted in the midst of dressing. His white starched shirt was open at his throat, revealing soft, curly golden-brown hair. His shirt sleeves were turned back at the cuffs, baring strong, muscular forearms, also dusted with tawny hair. His suspenders rested on his wide, strong shoulders, and his pleated gray trousers hung low on his narrow hips, revealing his long, powerful legs.

Best of all, to her way of thinking, was that his narrow feet were bare.

She'd slipped out of her long woolen cape, and she knew she looked fetching in her rose alpaca shirtwaist dress, its lacy frill clinging to her throat. She'd taken special pains with her hair, coaxing it into a frothy mass of curls under her beguiling little black felt fedora.

"Good morning, Dr. Dennison." Her voice was less than steady, but she gave him a wide smile.

"Miss O'Neal." He was visibly taken aback for a moment. He used his thumb and forefinger to shove his glasses up his nose, and he'd obviously forgotten they'd progressed to first names.

"Lillie," she reminded him.

"Lillie. Of course, Lillie. Won't you come in?"

Here in his office, he was different than in her store, she noted, more relaxed, more confident. Not as clumsy. Not as self-conscious. But just as absentminded, she decided, suppressing a giggle. She'd bet money that he'd forgotten he was only half-dressed and barefooted.

"You're at work early this morning," she said, trying not to choke at the sharp smell of carbolic and the coppery tang of blood that pervaded the surgery. Whew! It could do with a dose of potpourri.

"Yes, Mr. Hanson had a mishap with an axe. I had to stitch his wrist and fingers."

She breathed through her mouth and looked around with avid curiosity, noting the tidy rolls of bandages, the shining array of rather frightening instruments, the precise rows of medicine bottles, pills, mortars, and pestles arranged on the shelves. His neatness impressed her. She knew the value of order in business, and so, it seemed, did the doctor.

Alexander motioned to the plain wooden chair in the corner.

"Be seated, while I just clean this up," he said, whisking blood-stained dressings, scissors, and a basin of pinkish water out of the room.

He returned quickly, drying his hands on a white towel, flashing her a smile that tugged at her heartstrings. "Now, what can I do for you?"

She'd planned on taking out her surprise and then singing a rousing chorus of "For He's A Jolly Good Fellow," but mischief beckoned. Perhaps this was a perfect opportunity to command his attention.

"I seem to have this strange sensation in the region of my heart, Doctor," she said in a throaty tone, using her eyelashes to good advantage.

"I see." To her amazement, he wasn't discomfited in the slightest by her teasing. "And how long have you had these symptoms, Lillie?" His deep voice was filled with concern, and she realized he thought she was serious.

She couldn't resist baiting him further. "For several weeks now. They come and go."

"Would you describe it as a sharp pain, or more of an ache?"

"Oh, an ache, to be sure." It amazed her to find she was actually telling the truth. She did have a peculiar sensation, like an ache, in her chest when he was near her.

"If you would just open the buttons of your bodice . . ." He reached for a stethoscope and waited.

The joke had gone much too far. She felt her face become warm as she reached into her basket. "Actually, Alexander, all I planned to uncover was this." She withdrew the concoction, a devil's food cake with a frothy white boiled icing that had taken her forever to whip.

He stared at her, his forehead wrinkled in puzzlement. "I'm afraid I don't understand. What does this have to do with the pain in your chest?"

Oh, dear. He really was impossible. Had he no sense of humor?

"Alexander, it's your birthday." She held on to her smile, but it was becoming a bit forced. She carefully set the cake on his examination table. It looked incongruous beside the stethoscope.

"Birthday?" He sounded as if he'd never heard the word before this moment.

"Birthday." Her voice was rising. "The day you were born, the day most people celebrate having lived another year of their lives."

He simply stared at her as if it were a strange concept.

She lost her patience and her temper. "Honestly, Alexander, haven't you ever celebrated your birthday! My goodness, you make me feel like a—a frivolous—nincompoop! I baked you a cake, I teased you a little about the ache in my chest, and I was about to sing you a song, but so help me, you're impossible! Why, any other man would have appreciated my trying to get him to have a little fun. But you! You can't even crack a smile." She snatched up her basket and stormed out, the door slamming behind her.

When Alexander recovered his wits enough to follow her, a quiet, familiar voice stopped him. "Put some shoes and stockings on first. There's snow out there. It's below zero."

He stared first at Stephen and then down at his bare feet. "Damnation! I totally forgot I hadn't finished dressing. What must she think of me?"

Stephen's smile was whimsical. "I doubt it was your feet that sent her running, Alexander." He studied the cake. "It looks delicious. Personally, I've always had a weakness for devil's food. Why not put your stockings and shoes on and go after her, invite her back to have some?"

Alexander's shoulders slumped. "She'll never come back now. I acted like an idiot. I had no idea it was my birthday. I stopped paying attention to that nonsense when . . ." He swallowed and didn't finish the sentence.

"When your parents died," Stephen supplied in a gentle tone. "I know. You closed off so much of yourself after that. Don't you think it's time you began to feel again?"

Alexander scowled. "I don't have any idea what you're talking about."

"Yes, I know that, too." Stephen sighed. "Look, why don't you go after Lillie and see if a simple apology will help? You certainly owe her one. She must have worked very hard on this cake."

"What if she slams the door in my face?"

Stephen rolled his eyes. "Put your foot in it and go right on being abjectly humble. For goodness sake, Alexander, you'll never know unless you try. Now go, go."

It was the truth. Much as he dreaded trying to

explain his stupidity, Alexander hurried off to
find his coat and shoes, his lips moving in silence as he tried to formulate a suitable apology.

The store was locked, a simple "Closed" sign
hanging in plain view. Wanting to give up and
go home, but knowing Stephen would probably
accuse him of being a coward, Alexander went
around to the back of the building, to the steep
flight of stairs that led up to Lillie's living quar-
ters.

He climbed as if he were going to the gallows
and knocked as softly as he could. His hand was
still on the door when it flew open.

Lillie, her soft curls dishevelled, her brown
eyes stormy, her pert little chin lifted high, stood
with her hand on the doorknob and her other
hand on the frame.

"What do you want?" She glared at him, her
eyes shooting sparks. "Haven't you done enough
for one day?" Her voice trembled. "You must be
quite pleased with yourself. You've succeeded in
making me feel like an utter fool."

He was taken aback by the force of her anger,
so ashamed that his carefully prepared apology
went straight out of his head.

"I . . . Please, Miss—Lillie, I can't . . . You see,
I thought you were ill . . . You did say your
heart—"

"Oh, you—you—idiot!" She stamped her foot,
rage making her almost incoherent. "Go away.

157

This instant. You're the most—most—" Her chest heaved. "I never—ever—want to see you again!"

The door slammed with such force he jerked back, very nearly losing his balance and tumbling down the stairs.

He walked home, his hands shoved deep into his overcoat pockets, his shoulders hunched against the humiliation that rolled through him in waves.

He was aware that Stephen was beside him, but he had no desire to talk, and Stephen, too, was silent.

At last, when they were nearly home, Stephen spoke. "Maybe that wasn't the best idea I've ever had. I'm sorry I pushed you into it."

"I deserved it," Alexander said, thoroughly miserable. "I truly believed she was having heart problems. All I could think of was examining her to find out the cause."

"Of course you did and that's the problem," Stephen said in a sympathetic tone. "You've fallen into the habit of seeing people only as medical cases. Hearts aren't only physical organs that pump blood. They're also the center of people's emotions. You've got to learn there's so much more to life than sickness and death. There's happiness, peace, and love. Lillie opened her heart to you, and you rejected her. No wonder she's in a rage." He shook his head. "I think we're going to have to devise something special to make up for this."

Alexander was despondent. "It's hopeless. She'll never speak to me again."

"There you go, admitting defeat before we've even begun to fight. Courage, man, courage. There is always a solution when it comes to matters of the heart."

"What can I do?"

Stephen thought for a long moment and then snapped his elegant fingers. "Valentine's Day. The celebration of love. Start thinking about a truly unique gift you can give her for Valentine's Day."

"Valentine's Day? But I've never given a woman anything for Valentine's Day. Besides, I'd have to buy it at her store, which is ridiculous. I have no idea—"

"You have over two weeks to figure it out."

"But—"

But Stephen was gone, and Alexander was left with the problem.

Chapter Five

On February 14th Alexander had an unending flow of patients all day, and it wasn't until after six in the evening when it was already dark that he was able to wash and put on a fresh shirt. He walked to Lillie's house, carrying the gift he'd agonized over and the card he'd spent hours making. He climbed her back stairs and hesitated, his fist poised to knock.

From inside came the sound of laughter, a woman's high voice saying something, a man's low tones in reply, and another chorus of light-hearted laughter.

Damnation! She had company. He stood, torn between the urgent need to see her and to apologize and his reluctance to face her in front of other people.

He'd rather face a firing squad than go through this. But the memory of her anger had haunted him and he had to somehow win her forgiveness. If that meant making a fool of himself before half the town, he'd just have to suffer through it.

He ran a finger under his shirt collar, straightened his hat, cleared his throat, and knocked, his heart hammering.

Just as it had at his last visit, the door flew open and Lillie stood there. But this time, there was no anger. Instead, she smiled quizzically at him, absolutely radiant in a low-cut red satin gown that clung to her generous curves and set off her blond beauty to perfection. She was so lovely she took his breath away.

"Alexander? What brings you here?" The words were gently spoken, but wary, and her smile faded.

He was stricken dumb. He opened his mouth, but not a sound emerged.

"Say something, or the door will close again." Stephen's urgent voice inside his head brought him out of his trance.

"You brought me a delicious cake on my birthday," he finally managed to croak, holding out the card. "So I've brought you this for Valentine's Day, along with my deepest apologies. Please say you forgive me, Lillie."

She looked uncertain for an instant, and cold fear suffused him. But then she was smiling again, a wide, generous smile that seemed to reach out and warm him.

"Of course I do, Alexander. Come in, won't you? I'm having a small Valentine's Day get-together."

He stepped inside. The room, bright and cheerful, filled with winsome decorations, seemed to glow with sunshine even on this dark, cold night. It was overflowing with young and old people alike, faces and bodies Alexander recognized intimately. Over the past two years, he'd treated most of them for one illness or another, but because he shunned social gatherings, he'd never encountered them as a group. Most were sending curious glances his way, obviously wondering what he was doing there.

Anxiety gnawed at his gut and he felt horribly self-conscious and exposed as Lillie reached for his card and opened the envelope. What if she didn't understand his attempt at humor? What if Stephen, with all his heavenly wisdom, had been wrong? "Make her laugh," he'd counselled, and Alexander had tried his best.

On the front of the hand-drawn card, he'd sketched a remorseful and quite demented-looking doctor, his huge feet bare, a stethoscope stuck in his ears, his glasses crooked and low on his nose, and tears dripping off his chin. He was holding in his large clumsy hands a heart jag-

162

gedly broken into two pieces. "Please forgive me," the lettering read. "If you don't, you'll break my heart." Inside the card, the message read, "I've been a proper horse's—" and an arrow led down to a cross-eyed horse's rounded backside, drawn in the shape of a valentine.

Lillie read it and looked up at him, her brown eyes dancing with glee. "Why, Alexander, I'm shocked. This is quite wicked." She pressed a palm over her mouth and giggled.

"Accurate, however," he said with a remorseful grin.

"Not at all." She laughed, her eyes filled with mischief. "You're much better looking—than the horse."

Alexander laughed with her, relieved beyond belief that the card had been a success.

A plate heaped with food was thrust into his hand. "Here y'go, young feller. Take that coat off and bide a spell. You could use some plumpin' up. Yer downright skinny in places," Granny said.

As he removed his heavy coat, Granny gave him several irreverent prods in the ribs and grinned up at him, baring her toothless gums in delight.

He smiled affectionately at his old friend. "It's good to see you, Granny."

"And you. I been sayin' it's 'bout time ye took some jollification. Ain't that a fact, missy?" She winked at Lillie, who blushed scarlet and fingered a small locket she wore on a leather thong around her neck.

"You certainly did say that, Granny, and you were right." Alexander noticed that for some reason Lillie was suddenly ill at ease, shooting Granny a reproachful look.

Granny chortled, and Lillie blushed even more. She took his hand and whisked him into the room. "Come and say hello to everyone. You know Myrtle, of course."

Myrtle Thorsen, her freckled face as red as her hair, looked up at him from under her sparse lashes. "Why, Dr. Dennison, I can hardly believe my eyes. Does this mean we might see you at the next church social?"

Alexander greeted her politely but didn't commit himself.

"And here's Benjamin and Prudence Irvine," Lillie went on.

"Happy Valentine's Day, Doctor." Prudence, too, looked surprised but pleased as well to see him. Her young husband, Benjamin, stood up and shook his hand, smiling a friendly welcome.

Alexander liked the young couple, whom he knew well. They'd married the year before, and Prudence was now his patient because they were expecting their first child in early May.

He scrutinized the young woman anxiously. Her pregnancy had been difficult from the very beginning, but tonight she seemed well and happy, and Benjamin's arm twined protectively around his fragile wife's shoulders. Alexander noted the loving glances that passed between them, and something like envy stirred in his heart.

Some of the guests were more welcoming than others, like Bill Evans who wasn't his usual exuberant self. "Thought you wasn't much fer social occasions, Doc," he remarked.

"Alexander's turning over a new leaf," Lillie said, squeezing his hand. "He's decided to become a social butterfly, haven't you, Alex?" Her smile and her glance were only for him, and the affectionate shortening of his name lightened his heart.

There were far more men than women present, and several of them seemed less than enthusiastic when Lillie drew him over to say hello. She still held his hand, and the men gave him cool, assessing glances. Something basic and primitive that he'd never suspected in himself stirred, deep and possessive, and now he enfolded Lillie's hand more firmly in his.

"Gentlemen," he said with cool aplomb, knowing full well that battle lines were being established, and that as far as Lillie's attentions were concerned, it was every man for himself. The competition didn't bother him. Instead, it evoked a fighting instinct he'd never known he had.

During the next hour, he relaxed, joining in and enjoying the playful banter. Someone played the fiddle and everyone sang, first "Jeanie With the Light Brown Hair," and then the romantic "Lorena."

"Sing us that Irish ballad your father used to sing, Lillie," Prudence urged.

With the fiddle playing softly in the background, Lillie, in a husky, true contralto, sang "I'll Take You Home Again, Kathleen."

Alexander watched and listened, downing several glasses of the pink-tinted punch. He also made short work of the plates of food Granny kept handing him. Every moment, he was aware of Lillie, flitting from one group to the next like a crimson firefly, shining in the soft lamplight.

Gradually, the older people left the party, and soon there was only a small group of young people.

"Blind man's bluff," someone suggested, and everyone shouted approval.

"Blind man has to kiss the one he captures," Bill Evans declared, his dark, knowing eyes on Lillie.

But when the blindfold was around his head and he groped his way toward her, Lillie slipped behind Myrtle. It was that giggling young woman Bill seized and, after an instant's hesitation, gallantly kissed while the others whistled and cheered.

"Alexander's turn," Lillie said.

He wanted to refuse, but Lillie's look challenged him. He removed his glasses and bent

166

low so she could tie the bandanna around his head. Then he was spun around and around. Dizzy, he took a moment to orient himself, but then his nose told him exactly where Lillie was—her evocative lavender perfume was like a beacon. He touched others and they laughed and slipped from his grasp, and then his hands were on her satin-covered shoulders. She didn't resist or move away. He felt tension in her softness, a quivering in her body, but when he took her in his arms, she came willingly.

Catcalls and teasing voices rose around them, but he hardly heard them. He dipped his head, searching blindly for her lips, finding instead the velvety softness of her cheek. His nose bumped hers, and then, like a miracle, his lips met hers.

His heart hammered as if it were going to burst inside his chest. Her lips were sweet, parting the slightest bit beneath the pressure of his. For the moment that propriety allowed, he gave himself up entirely to the kiss, feeling elated at the shudder that rippled through her.

He was astounded at the depths of his own reaction. One short kiss wasn't nearly enough. He longed to enfold her tightly in his arms, feel her breasts crushed against his chest, her body close to his. Instead, he released her, and the blindfold was snatched from his head by Bill.

"Hey, Doc, you're hoggin' the show. Give one of us other fellas a turn."

Alexander blinked, nearsighted without his

spectacles. The only face he could see clearly was Lillie's, her skin golden in the lamplight, her cheeks flaming, as her startled gaze met his and then fluttered away.

The rest of the evening passed in a rosy haze for him, until one of the women yawned delicately and said it was time to leave. The other guests rose, but when he got to his feet to accompany them, Lillie restrained him, her hand on his arm.

"I haven't opened your gift yet, Alex. Please stay a moment, won't you?"

So with Bill shooting murderous glances his way, he sat back down on the sofa until the others were gone.

"Phew." Lillie leaned back against the closed door, feigning exhaustion, the back of her hand pressed against her forehead, laughing.

Alexander fantasized that if she were really his and alone with him at last, they would have the whole, delicious night for loving. . . .

Lillie retrieved his gift from the table by the door and sat down beside him. He watched her unfold the clumsily wrapped package. He was nervous all over again as she untied his crooked attempt at a bow, and relieved beyond measure that the others were gone.

He'd thought long and hard about what to give her, wondering what would be both meaningful and not readily available in her store.

"Oh, Alex, how lovely." The wrappings had

fallen away, revealing the soft shawl, and he saw her eyes widen with delight and pleasure.

Crocheted in soft, fragile woolen yarn, the shawl was a huge triangle with elaborate fringed edges. The color had always pleased him, variegated shades of bronze and gold and a particular rich chocolate that he now realized was the exact shade of Lillie's eyes.

"It was my mother's. I hope you don't mind."

She clasped it to her chest, her eyes shining. "Oh, no, indeed I don't. I'm honored, Alex. That makes it very special to me. Thank you."

She shook it out and placed it around her shoulders, and when it caught on the sofa back, he reached out to help her. As naturally as breathing, she was in his arms. This time, there was no clumsiness as he bent his head to kiss her.

Her arms encircled his neck, and her head tilted like a flower to the sun. His hands ached to cup her breasts, and desire raged through him as her lips parted beneath his, fully this time.

His spectacles got in the way and he stripped them off, aware of the curve of her cheek, the length of her sooty lashes, the contrasting creaminess of her skin against the crimson satin. He groaned and kissed her, enveloped by heat and passion.

His hands slid up to cup her half-exposed breasts, his thumbs gently rubbing her nipples. She gasped and then slowly pulled away, her breathing making the bodice of her dress rise and fall sharply. She looked mussed, her lips swollen, her brown eyes smoldering with the same desire that coursed through him.

He leaned back, aware they were progressing too far, too fast. He held her hands, raising them, turning them so he could plant a lingering kiss in each palm.

"I must go." His voice was unsteady as he got to his feet, found his glasses, and put them on his nose. He reached down and drew her up, succumbing to temptation one last time. His arms around her, he kissed her soundly, tasting the delicious echo of his own passion in the shy probing of her tongue with his. This kiss was meant as good-bye, but it felt like hello instead, and it went on until once again he could hardly tear himself away.

At last, with great reluctance, he held her at arm's length, his hands on her shoulders. "Thank you, Lillie, for a wonderful evening," he said with a catch in his voice. "This is the best Valentine's Day I've ever had."

She laughed softly. "I'll bet you don't usually even remember it. A man who forgets his birthday isn't likely to remember Valentine's Day."

He laughed, too, because she was right. Resisting the overwhelming urge to hold her again and kiss her senseless, he opened the door instead.

"Good night, Lillie."

"Sweet dreams." Her words floated out as he closed the door behind him.

Outside, the frosty night's sky was awash with distant stars. As he strolled, he whistled the lilting ballad Lillie had sung with such poignancy.

He felt an arm around his shoulders and grinned like a fool at Stephen.

"Pipe down. You'll wake up the whole town."

"I don't care. I never knew I could feel this way."

Stephen smiled and shook his head. "That's because you've never let yourself feel this way. It's like opening a door. It's simple once you find the doorknob."

Chapter Six

During the weeks that followed, Lillie was certain Granny was indeed part sorceress, because Alex's courting of Lillie had begun Valentine's night. The charm, containing a lock of Alex's baby hair and goodness knew what else, that Granny had slipped around Lillie's neck that night had worked. Alex had appeared almost every day since then at the store, inviting her for a walk, a sleigh ride, a church supper.

At first shy, often clumsy, and at times inarticulate, he was always endearing, and he gradually relaxed with her, allowing her to discover how wonderful he was. He had a quirky, droll sense of humor, often making himself and his absentminded behavior the brunt of his funny stories. He was intelligent, and their conversations encompassed politics, literature, and religion. But it wasn't their discussions that made her heart hammer and her body burn for him. It was his kisses.

Lillie had realized that the first time his lips met hers in front of everyone in her parlor on Valentine's Day. Her knees had very nearly given way, and she'd longed to wrap her arms around him and further explore the delicious sensations he had created.

She'd done exactly that later whenever they were alone, and she continued to, each and every time they were together—with Alex's ardent participation, of course. But now their kissing was no longer enough to satisfy the hunger he stirred in her. She wanted more, and it irked her that Alex continued to be a gallant gentleman, stopping their loveplay before it reached the point where there was no turning back.

Sometimes, early in the March evenings, she accompanied him as he visited patients in the country, and it was on these visits that she came to know another side of him.

She watched and listened, intrigued by the change that came over him when he was with someone who was ill. Gone was the captivating clumsiness that made her smile, the shyness that touched her. With his patients he was confident, gentle, wise. He paid attention to their complaints, and at times seemed to listen even after they finished speaking, nodding his head and murmuring in a peculiar, distracted fashion.

Almost everyone liked and respected him, but Lillie noticed it was the older people in the community who absolutely adored him. He was unfailingly patient with them, listening to their long-winded stories and enjoying them. In many instances his elderly patients were painfully poor, living on the grudging charity of relatives, or eking out a bare existence in dismal cottages.

She learned that whenever and wherever he could, Alex quietly supplied food, clothing, and fuel, always in a way that allowed the recipients to retain their pride. She was with him when he delivered the sheets to Mrs. Liposke, and Lillie marvelled at his tact.

She soon took great delight in helping him. From the store she packed food that was a little past its peak, clothing that hadn't sold but was serviceable and warm, lengths of fabric that were flawed and wouldn't sell, and quietly left them wherever they were needed.

One warm, cloudy evening in late March, they were heading home in Alex's open buggy. They'd been to visit a sick old man and taken him a basket crammed with food when suddenly it began to rain, a few drops at first, and then within minutes a downpour. Alex urged the horse to a trot and then a gallop, but by the time they arrived at her store a half-hour later, they were soaked to the skin and laughing uproariously.

Still laughing, they pounded through the deluge up her steps and burst in the door. She lit a lamp and giggled even harder when she looked at Alex. "Oh, my, you should see yourself. You look like a drowned rat."

His hair was flat, splayed across his forehead and neck in dripping strands, and drops of water trickled off his chin. His rain-spattered spectacles perched uselessly on the tip of his nose. He'd taken his suit coat off and draped it around her shoulders to try to protect her, and his white cotton shirt clung to him like a second skin. Water ran from his shoes and pooled on the scatter rug.

"A drowned rat, huh?" He reached out a lightning-quick hand and tugged her into his arms. "Come close, Miss O'Neal, where this nearsighted drowned rat can see you." He held her tight, studying her with frowning intensity. "Yup, you look the very same," he growled. "Your hair is all down your back, and it's soaked . . ." He took a handful of the curling strands, gently tipped her head back, and then kissed her, a teasing, half-rough kiss that predictably set her on fire.

"Lillie . . . Oh my God, Lillie, you're so beautiful."

He lifted his hand to pull his glasses off, dropping them heedlessly on the nearby table, and then slanted his head so his mouth fit hers at a more intimate angle. Their tongues danced, and need flared inside her. Moving even closer to him, she twined her arms around his neck, shivering.

With a strangled groan, he shoved the wet coat from her shoulders and cupped her swelling breasts. Pressed against him, her wet skirts and petticoats clinging to her legs, she could feel him grow hard. With innocent hunger, she rubbed against him.

"Lillie, my dearest Lillie, we must stop." His breath was hot in her ear, his tone urgent, but even as he spoke, his hands were stroking her breasts, his body even closer to hers. "You're innocent, I mustn't—"

"I'm a woman, Alex, and I care for you and want you," she said in a breathless whisper. Every inch of her body felt flushed.

He grew still.

"Please," she mouthed against his ear, and exultation swept over her as she sensed his defenses crumbling.

Turning her around, he undid the buttons at the back of her dress, her petticoat ties, and the small pearl fastenings of her damp chemise. As she breathed a long sigh, he stripped off her pantaloons, garters, and stockings in one efficient movement.

Then his own wet clothing lay beside hers on the rug. In the flickering lamplight, her breath caught as she stared at the strong, clear-cut beauty of his body. Tall and muscular, he was everything she'd ever dreamed her lover might be.

"Oh, Alex." She slid hesitant fingers through the silky hair on his chest. He was holding her, naked skin to naked skin, and she could hardly breathe for the sensations in her belly.

"I love you, Lillie."

The earnest words curled around her heart and soul.

He slid his hand under her thighs and swept her into his arms. Without his glasses he misjudged the doorway and she banged her head a little, but she hardly felt it at all.

He put her down on the soft feather bed in her dark bedroom. She felt him lie down at her side, his weight on one elbow, his free hand gliding down her body as if he were memorizing, by touch alone, the shape and feel of her.

She rested her hand on his chest, and felt his wildly beating heart. Her own was pounding so hard she trembled. Everywhere his fingers stroked, her skin seemed to catch fire.

"You are ravishing, Lillie." His voice was rough, raw-edged, filled with desire, and it thrilled her. "So very, very lovely . . ."

She could feel his rapid breathing on her skin, and then at last he kissed her, long, lingeringly, passionately, while his hands roamed ceaselessly across her breasts. He teased her aching nipples, then his hand moved with maddening slowness down her abdomen, gently easing her

177

thighs apart, sliding his fingers inside her.

She could feel his manhood, hot, throbbing, urgent, pressed against her thigh, and for a moment she stiffened, both shy and frightened. She wasn't certain exactly what came next.

"You're certain you want to do this, darling?"

She nodded, her hair imprisoned beneath his shoulder. The query was gentle, allowing her to reconfirm all she felt and wanted—or, if she so desired, to change her mind. "I'm certain."

He took her nipple in his mouth, his tongue and teeth making her cry out with frustration and pleasure. His fingers stroked her, causing her to move involuntarily, thrusting up against the delicious pressure of his hand with desperate need, seeking a fulfillment she hadn't dreamed existed.

Then she arched and screamed his name, and groaning, he straddled her. With one long, sure movement, they were joined. The shock of his entry coming on the crest of such pleasure made her tense and cry out again, but the fierce pain lasted only for a moment.

Then her body opened, hungry for him, and the ecstasy returned, and she learned his capacity for gentleness as well as the ferocity of his strength.

When at last she lay, sated and limp, marvelling at the power of this exquisite dance and how wonderfully talented he was at it, she realized that she could echo his words back to him. "I love you, too, Alex." Then she sighed, utterly content, as happy as she'd ever been in her life.

Alexander smiled as he began to prepare his breakfast. He was eating much more frequently now and taking better care of himself. And he had wonderful, desirable Lillie to thank for that. He'd made love to other women, of course. He was a young, virile man. He'd just never made love to the same woman repeatedly. For him, lovemaking had been a matter of physical release, and it had no similarity to what he shared now with Lillie.

She was like a drug. The more time he spent with her, the more he longed to spend. In the enchanted days that had followed their first magical night together, all Alexander could think of was the curve of her back, her delicate throat, while he ostensibly listened to his patients' litany of symptoms. Intoxicated with her, he couldn't stop smiling at inappropriate moments, whistling cheerfully while he lanced boils and stitched wounds, and he'd never before noticed how green the new leaves were and how sweetly the birds sang in the spring.

To his dismay though, he also noticed how many men still seemed to hang around Lillie's store. The stove was unlit now that spring had arrived, but in his opinion, the high-backed chairs were all too often occupied by young men who ought to have better things to do than loiter.

Surely there were fields to clear, crops to plant, stock to tend to? He'd said as much to Lillie, his voice testy, and she'd shrugged, holding out her hands in a helpless gesture, smiling at him with studied innocence. "The store's a public place, Alex, and I'm certainly not their mother," she'd said.

Don't act like their sweetheart, either! he had wanted to roar at her, but of course he hadn't. He shrugged as he turned the bacon and then put two eggs on the counter.

He had started dropping by the store whenever his surgery emptied to see Lillie and exchange a few words. At least, he told himself that was his only reason for hurrying over every chance he got.

But at four separate times in the space of one week, Bill Evans had been there, lounging at the counter or sprawled in a chair in the back, watching Lillie's every move with his hot, dark eyes, teasing her and making idiotic jokes. But what disturbed Alexander was that Lillie had giggled at Bill's foolishness, tossing her head and looking up at him through her eyelashes.

John Miller, Greenwood's young, single schoolteacher, had also been in the store most afternoons. Alexander had ignored the shy, quiet John until one day he found him reading to Lillie from a book of poetry. Some ridiculous jingle had her laughing until tears came and she dabbed at her eyes with an absurd scrap of pink lace. When the reading was over, she had put her hand on John's arm in an affectionate gesture that Alexander still thought had been entirely inappropriate.

"Thank you so much for sharing that with me, John," she'd said in a pleased tone, smiling into his eyes. "I do so love nonsense rhymes."

Alexander cracked the eggs against the side of the skillet and dropped them next to the bacon. He had wanted to shake her that day. Didn't she recognize the naked adoration in John's face? It was wrong of her to encourage the poor man.

He had wrestled with the alarming emotions these encounters roused in him, trying to subdue the anger he felt about her flirtatious ways, but each day seemed to bring some new evidence that Lillie was irresponsible with her affections.

Just the other day, he had watched, filled with outrage, as she allowed a pathetic widower, who was fifty at least, to present her with a bouquet of wildflowers. She had smiled at the man with the same wide, affectionate smile she'd given Alexander just moments before.

Then the memory of one afternoon when he was getting his hair cut almost caused him to break the eggs' yolks as he flipped them. He'd never forget seeing her walking down the street with a tall young stranger, talking with animation and tilting her head back, laughing. The gentleman had appeared mesmerized by her,

181

and Alexander had watched the four old men in front of the barbershop exchange knowing glances as she passed by on the stranger's arm.

His insides had knotted, but he never mentioned that he'd seen her, waiting for her to bring it up. But she never had, and when he'd finally asked her about it, she'd answered offhandedly that the man was a salesman for a dry goods company she dealt with.

He placed the bacon and eggs on a plate and sat at the table. As he ate, he realized that though he had never spoken to Lillie about his feelings, if her behavior didn't change, he would just have to show her the error of her ways.

Chapter Seven

In mid-April, Alexander escorted Lillie to the church social. Her dress was as blue as the sky, with enormous sleeves and an intriguing ruffle of white lace not quite covering the tops of her full breasts. Her curly blond hair was drawn up into a high knot, her cheeks were a delicate pink, and her brown eyes sparkled. Alexander felt as if his chest would burst with pride when he walked into the crowded hall with her clinging to his arm.

The band, two fiddles and an ancient piano, tuned up and then burst into a spirited polka. Alexander hesitated, aware he wasn't much of a dancer, and before he could gather his nerve and figure out the steps, Bill Evans had whirled Lillie away.

Alexander swallowed hard and tried not to notice her skirts flaring high around her shapely legs as she twirled, or Bill's hand clutching her narrow waist.

She went straight from Bill's arms to Lucas Fowler, a pot-bellied old patient of Alexander's, and from there to John Miller, who held her much too close. She didn't seem to object, and then Bill was whirling her around in a waltz, and her face was tilted up to his, her smile bold and inviting.

Alexander seethed. Lillie was at it again, he thought as he made his way onto the dance floor and cut in, furious at her and Bill. He stepped on her toes twice and knew he was doing a miserable job of waltzing, but she pretended not to notice, gazing at him with a misty smile.

"I do love dancing, Alex." She tilted her head so her mouth was close to his ear. "And I love you, too," she whispered.

Slightly mollified, he tried a dip and swirl and even managed a smile, but his smile faded because almost before the waltz ended, she was swept away again. He made his way to the refreshment table, wishing there were something stronger than grape juice in the punch. He didn't know how much more of this he could take.

What seemed like eons passed. By the time the musicians laid down their instruments and everyone bid each other a cheerful good night, he had watched Lillie dance with every man in the room, single, married, old, young. She'd beamed up at each one, chattering away, giggling, tossing her curls, showing off her ankles, flirting, laughing, teasing.

She'd danced with him exactly twice, and his simmering anger was ready to explode at Lillie—and the entire male population of Greenwood. She hadn't stopped her flirtatious behavior in the least and she was toying with his affections. She was the woman he loved, and tonight she had forced him to feel an emotion he'd never had cause to feel, and resented feeling now—burning, torturous jealousy.

Alexander escorted Lillie home, barely responding to her giddy chatter. He climbed the steps behind her, politely took her key and opened the door, and then stood aside for her to enter. She lit the lamp and then looked at him.

"Come in, Alex. You are staying, aren't you?"

"I think not." His tone was formal and very cool.

She frowned. "You're angry, aren't you?"

He didn't answer.

"Why are you angry?" She sounded confused and hurt. "Didn't you have a good time at the dance?"

"If being forced to watch you dance and flirt with every man in the room is having a good time, then I had a perfectly wonderful time." His tone was scathing.

"Those men happen to be my customers and my friends, Alex." Her voice trembled with emotion. "So are their wives and sweethearts. Refusing to dance with them would have been an insult."

"So all that merriment was simply good customer relations, is that it, Lillie?" he said in a caustic tone. "You seem to be on rather intimate terms with some of those men." His anger was making him say things he knew he shouldn't, but he couldn't stop the cruel words from pouring out. "In fact, I began to wonder if I'm the only man in town enjoying your favors."

She stared at him, her dark eyes wide and wounded. The color in her cheeks faded. "You should know better than anyone that there is nothing between me and those men but friendship, Alex," she whispered.

"When I made love to you the first time, I did know. But how would I know now? Since the day I came into your store, I've watched you give your attentions freely to everyone. Flirting with the men in there, on the street. In fact, wherever you go. And after your performance tonight, what am I supposed to think, Lillie? Perhaps I'm just a flirtation, too. Something to amuse you."

She gaped at him, speechless. Tears glimmered in her eyes. "You—you stuffed shirt! How like you not to understand simple friendship and warmth. You—you're nothing but a hypocrite, Alexander, a holier-than-thou hypocrite, not saying anything to me about how you felt all this time, acting as if you loved me." Her entire body was trembling visibly. "How—how dare you make what we have together dirty! If that's what you think, then get out."

She lifted her shaking hand and pointed at the door. "Leave now! And don't ever come back!"

Rage carried him out the door and down the steps, down the quiet, sleeping streets to his own door. He threw it open and slammed it as hard as he could. In his bedroom, he tore off his suit, heedless of flying buttons and ripped collars, throwing the garments on the floor.

"You may need to wear these again, Alexander." Stephen picked up his vest and hung it on a hanger in the cupboard. He sat down on the side of the bed and looked at Alexander, shaking his head. "Now why did you act like that, just when things were going so well?"

"Don't you start on me," Alexander roared. He, who'd hardly ever raised his voice to anyone, now felt as if a bottomless pit of anger had opened up inside him. He curled his fists, longing to smash something, to destroy someone, but there was only Stephen.

"I don't need or want any more of your—your sanctimonious claptrap. I've had all I can take from you and Lillie." He pointed a trembling finger at Stephen. "What do you really know about men and women? You don't have any idea what it feels like to be hurt and betrayed."

Stephen rose, his handsome face sad. "You're right," he said softly. "There are human emotions I can never experience firsthand. But I do know how *you* feel. I see your pain, and I'm sorry for you." His voice held endless compassion, but it also held inexorable truth. "But, Alexander, you have only yourself to blame."

Some distant, honest part of him recognized the truth, but admission would be more than he could bear. Instead, he summoned up the fury that drove him like a painful whip. "I don't need you, Stephen." His awful words spewed like lava, and yet he couldn't stop them. "I never asked you to come into my life. All you've done is make a mess of things, urging me into this relationship with Lillie, mewling that my life was incomplete."

He snorted and flung a shoe against the wall. "Incomplete be damned. I was perfectly happy the way I was. I want you to leave me alone, so I can go back to being content." He flung the other shoe, and it hit the daguerreotype of his parents that he kept on his bedside table. The glass shattered, and the prized likeness tumbled to the floor.

"Get out, Stephen." The terrible dictum rang like a death knell, but he was too enraged to call it back. "Get out of my life, and stay out."

His eyes sorrowful, Stephen looked at him for

what seemed a long time. "If that's what you want, then so be it."

In an instant, Alexander was alone, more alone than he'd been since the death of his parents so long ago.

With a cry of anguish and utter despair, he picked up the crystal water pitcher from the table and sent it flying across the room, straight at the spot where Stephen had been only a moment before.

The pitcher crashed against the wall and shattered into millions of fragments, and to him they seemed to represent the broken shards of his life.

Lillie had hardly slept last night, and for the first time since Valentine's Day, she left Granny's magic locket on her dresser when she finished putting on her clothes. Her eyes were heavy from crying, and she hated to go downstairs and open the store.

Unfortunately, when she did, one of her first customers was Bill, and his mindless, cheerful chatter about the dance grated on her raw nerves.

"For gracious sakes, haven't you anything else to do but hang around here?" she finally snapped at him. "Some of us have work to do."

His face fell. "Sorry, Lillie," he mumbled, and headed for the door, his shoulders slumped.

The next customer, always slow at making up

her mind, made Lillie purse her lips and tap her foot impatiently. The transaction was made in strained silence, and there were no cheerful good-byes exchanged when the door finally closed.

As the morning progressed, each and every customer was a strain, and of course, her mood didn't go unnoticed. One woman remarked on it, and Lillie mumbled something about feeling unwell, only to be told she ought to visit Dr. Dennison for a tonic.

John Miller came in just past noon, a wide smile on his face and a book clutched in his hand. "I ordered this volume of limericks and it just arrived. You simply must hear this. It's hilarious." He began to read aloud, something about a young woman named Lillie.

"Oh, John, not now, for pity's sake." She knew she sounded like a witch, but she just didn't care. "Look at this disgusting mess. You'd think people could be a little more careful."

She grabbed a broom and began to sweep up oatmeal someone had spilled, and John swallowed hard, his Adam's apple bobbing. He turned scarlet, closed the book, and hurried out without another word.

She knew she'd hurt him and she was too miserable to care. She closed early and stumbled upstairs, feeling wretched. Alex had become the center of her life, and now he was gone, and she didn't know what to do.

She knew she loved him with all her heart and soul, but how could she stay with a man who doubted her, didn't trust her? Who had accused her so vilely of wantonness? She had never been with any man but Alex and now she understood that he wanted to isolate her and rob her of her spirit. It hurt that he hadn't ever discussed with her his feelings, but instead had lashed out at her, hurling cruel, terrible accusations.

Tears coursed down her face, and she felt sick to her stomach. Difficult as it would be, she would rather be alone than suffer his suspicions and insults. She didn't want a man who treated her as if she were his property. She picked up Granny's charm and dropped it in the drawer under her handkerchiefs. She'd get through this, get over him, and somehow go on with her life. The trouble was, she thought as she went to bed, that she couldn't quite see how. She cried herself to sleep.

The next morning, she forced herself to go to church. Alex wasn't there, which was both a relief and a disappointment. Perversely, she longed to see him at the same time she dreaded it.

After the service, Myrtle invited her over to see the fashion plates in her latest issue of *Godey's Lady's Book*, and Lillie went, grateful for Myrtle's empty-headed chatter. It was a distraction from her agony, and it filled the long, dismal afternoon.

Monday, she began a major stocktaking. With frantic energy, she moved goods, rearranged shelves, and counted everything in the store. It took an entire week and exhausted her so that at least she could sleep.

With the warmer weather and longer days, she opened the store earlier and closed it later, and slowly the anguish inside of her dulled a little, enough so that she could once again smile at her customers. It seemed, however, that her natural, inborn gaiety, her joy in life, was gone forever.

May arrived, a wet and dismal May that seemed to mirror the pain in Lillie's heart. She and Alex gave each other a wide berth, though it was impossible to avoid each other totally in the small town. Alexander had stopped coming to the store, and when he needed supplies he sent a young boy for them. She would fill his order and have the boy deliver them. At church, she made certain to sit far away from Alex. In the street, she ducked into a shop if she saw him coming. It seemed childish, but she simply couldn't face him. Her hurt was too deep.

Alexander tried to bury himself in his work, but for the first time, medicine failed to either occupy his mind or bring him satisfaction. Worse still, he couldn't summon up the patience and forbearance that had been an integral part of his nature.

When Milton finally took one drink too many and went quite mad one night in the tavern, Alexander heard himself lecturing the other patrons on the evils of drink like some puritanical fanatic, even though he knew full well most of them were honest, hard-working farmers enjoying a rare and well-deserved pint.

In his office, he was curt and preoccupied. He no longer had the tolerance to sit and listen to long, involved stories from his elderly patients. He cut them off and hurried them out.

He told Vernon, one of the barber shop quartet, that his piles would be much improved if he found something more worthwhile to do than sit on his backside ten hours a day.

"Yer gettin' a mite big fer yer britches, ain't ya?" Vernon grabbed his decrepit old hat and plunked it on his head, glaring at him. "I knew yer daddy well, young Dennison, and he'd be mortified if'n he heard ye talkin' to yer elders this way." He stomped out of the office. "Young whippersnapper. Call yerself a doctor, humph."

The mention of his father brought a rush of agonizing memories. Lillie had asked him once about his parents, but he'd told her only about the happy days of his childhood.

Damn Lillie, for worming her way into his heart. Damn himself, for allowing it to happen.

The day after Vernon's visit, Alexander was surprised that his first patient was Granny.

"Well, Granny, good morning." He tried to in-

ject enthusiasm into his voice and muster up a
smile for the old woman, but he knew his efforts
were futile. "What brings you here?" Granny had
always prided herself on her own remedies, so
he wondered why she was in his waiting room.

She peered around with open curiosity, examining the rows of bottles and jars on his
shelves, poking a wary finger at his stethoscope.
"Newfangled frippery," she snorted, then turned
and peered up at him from under her black bonnet, her shoe-button eyes seeming to see into his
very soul.

"What's amiss 'tween you and Lillie is why I'm
here, lad." She settled herself in a chair and
folded her wrinkled hands in her lap. "She's a
fine lass. I'm right fond of her, and I was the first
to shake yer hand when ye came into the world,
so I reckon that gives me leeway to poke and
prod a bit, don't it?" She smiled at him, a caring
smile.

"Yer not yerself, Alexander. Folks is sayin' yer
losin' yer healin' touch, that yer right cranky and
outta sorts. What's ailin' ye, lad?"

He liked the old woman, but at this moment
irritation at her prying welled in him. The last
thing he needed right now was Granny lecturing
him about his life. "I assure you, I'm quite well,
Granny," he snapped.

"Humph. Ye don't sound it. Don't look it, neither. Mebbe ye oughta get down offen yer high

horse and go speak to Lillie, talk things over, like."

Each repetition of her name was like a spear in his heart. It was all he could do to force himself to speak about her. "Miss O'Neal was the one to sever our relationship, so perhaps it's she you ought to speak to instead of me." He wasn't about to admit to Granny that it was his fault Lillie had thrown him out, and he was relieved beyond measure to hear the outer door to the office open and close. "Now, I have someone else waiting to consult me, Granny, so if there's nothing I can do for you medically . . ."

She gave him a long, measuring look before she struggled to her feet. "Pride's cold comfort in bed, Alexander." There was resignation and sadness in her voice. She walked out slowly, leaning on her cane. For an instant he wanted to go after her, but the young mother in his waiting room had a child with a bad nosebleed, and he hurried them inside.

During the days that followed, his patience was nonexistent, his temper volatile. When he found Mrs. Martz in his office for the third time in one week, he rudely interrupted her latest complaint of aches and pains.

"Mrs. Martz, your only problem is you eat too much and do too little. Lose forty pounds and find a worthwhile endeavor to fill your idle hours, and don't come to my office again until you do."

Her mouth, half-buried in flesh, opened and closed like a fish, and her small eyes seemed about to pop out of her head.

"How dare you . . ." she managed to gasp. "How dare you speak to me in such a fashion, and me not a well woman." She heaved herself to her feet and stood glaring at him out of spiteful beady eyes. "I assure you, the entire town will hear of this insult. As you well know, Mr. Martz is on the town council, and he will most definitely hear about this."

He watched as she huffed her way out the door, and all he felt was indifference. He didn't care if he lost his practice. Lillie was gone. Stephen was gone, and there was a dark and empty space inside of him as massive as the gray Indiana sky.

Chapter Eight

Several days after the scene with Mrs. Martz, Alexander was summoned at dusk to Granny's tiny cottage. A neighbor had noticed there'd been no smoke from the chimney all day, and inside she'd found Granny on the stone floor, unconscious.

When he saw Granny, he was almost paralyzed, because he knew it was already too late to do anything to save her. A hard lump formed in his chest, a lump of despair.

Knowing it was fruitless, still he worked with frantic determination over the frail, barely breathing birdlike body, doing everything in his power to restore the life that was ebbing away. But Granny had suffered a massive stroke and there was nothing he could do.

Just before midnight, the old woman died without regaining consciousness, and he held her, tears coursing down his cheeks. He leaned down and kissed her wrinkled cheek and stroked her knotted hand.

"I was the first to shake yer hand when ye came into the world," she'd said the last time he'd seen her. Now, he was the last to hold hers, and the memory of her visit to his office haunted him.

"Forgive me, Granny," he whispered, grief and remorse mingling like bitter gall inside him. "I'm so sorry for the way I acted. You were a good friend, and I'll miss you."

His chest ached with sorrow when he left her cottage that night, and he cursed himself for the way he'd treated her. How could he have been so callous, so cold, when she'd come to him wanting to help? What kind of man was he to treat an old woman that way?

He'd miss Granny, and so would Lillie. They'd often talked of the eccentric old woman, exchanging amusing bits of her folk wisdom. If only he could go to Lillie now, share with her his terrible feelings of sadness, shame, and loss, and tell her he regretted the horrible way he had treated her, too.

He detoured through the village so he could walk slowly past the closed door of the General Store. It was long past midnight, and there was no light in Lillie's rooms. He stood and stared up at her bedroom, and he thought of all the glorious nights he'd lain there with her clasped in his arms.

He wanted so much to see her tonight, to tell her of Granny's death, to apologize, and he moved toward the stairs. Halfway up, he stopped. He'd lost the right to go to Lillie for comfort. He'd said unforgivable things, and he couldn't take them back, any more than he could change the way he'd acted toward Granny at his office. How could he expect Lillie ever to forgive him? He went down the steps again and back to his lonely house.

At dawn, he lay on his bed, fully clothed and wide awake, staring blankly at the gray light seeping in his window. Then he heard someone run into the office and on through the house to the bottom of the stairs.

"Dr. Dennison," Benjamin Irvine hollered. "It—it's Prudence," he stammered when Alexander appeared. "The baby . . . Come quick, Doc."

"When did the pains begin?" He didn't bother tying his shoes. Holding his medical bag, he leaped down the stairs and hoisted himself into the buggy.

"Three hours ago, but Ma's there and she says something's wrong. We have to hurry, she says," Benjamin repeated, his handsome face stark-white with fear. "There's blood everywhere, Doc.

There shouldn't be so much blood, should there?"

Alexander did his best to reassure Benjamin, but an overwhelming sense of doom overcame him the moment he rushed into the farmhouse. He ran up the stairs to the small bedroom where Prudence lay.

Benjamin had spoken the truth. There was blood everywhere, soaking the bedsheets, dripping to the floor. For a moment, as experienced as he was, Alexander had to quell his instinctive horror at the sight of so much blood.

"Dr. Dennison, thank God you're here. I've done everything I could think of." Benjamin's mother, Letitia, was a level-headed farm woman, and she'd tried unsuccessfully to staunch the flow by packing towels around Prudence and raising the end of the bed on stout wooden blocks.

It was all too obvious her valiant attempts had failed. Prudence moaned feebly as each new pain racked her, and she was becoming progressively weaker. The labor was precipitate, the birth already near, but she no longer had the strength to expel the child. It was imperative that the baby be delivered as rapidly as possible, and the flow of blood halted.

Alexander sent Benjamin running for a basin of hot water, and when it came, he rolled his sleeves past his elbows, scrubbed his hands with carbolic soap, and set to work.

He showed Letitia how to drip chloroform on the gauze covering Prudence's nose. The moment the young woman slipped into unconsciousness, he ruthlessly delivered the child, a large, well-formed boy. He hurriedly clamped and cut the cord. The baby didn't cry, but there was no time for him to tend it. Prudence was still bleeding.

"Clean out his nose and mouth. Breathe into him if you have to." He shoved the child's limp body at Letitia, and turned to minister to the young woman lying lifelessly on the bed.

As he worked, he was aware of the baby's first, weak cry from somewhere behind him—and of the fact that he was losing Prudence. Despite his every frantic effort, her life's blood gushed from her in a stream nothing could stop.

He knew it was over, and still he kept on. Then Letitia touched his arm and said in a broken whisper, "She's gone, Doctor. The baby's fine, but she's gone."

The next hour was a nightmare for him as he explained to Benjamin why his beloved wife had died. Alexander also tried to comfort him, saying his newborn son needed him now.

The young man's sobs and curses echoed in Alexander's ears long after he left the little farmhouse and stumbled up his own steps.

Inside, he slumped into a kitchen chair, aware of the awful blood stains that covered his clothing, but unable to make himself get up and wash them away. A terrible weariness made his limbs feel like stone. The kitchen was icy cold, the fire long dead, the house empty and still.

Intolerable longing rose up in him as he envisioned Lillie's warm rooms, filled with color, overflowing with the same exuberant life force she herself exuded.

Lillie. His stomach clenched, and for the second time in only a few hours he longed for her comfort, her strength. But again he reminded himself harshly that he was the one who'd severed the bond between them.

Two deaths in less than a day, and he had been unable to prevent either one. And he called himself a doctor? He'd wanted nothing more than to save lives, ever since his parents' illness, when he had stood by helplessly and watched first one and then the other die an agonizing death.

Helpless, lonely, feeling abandoned, he'd pledged from that moment on to devote himself to healing. He'd also pledged never to allow anyone to get that emotionally close to him again. If he kept the world at bay, he'd never risk the terrible pain of loss. He'd managed it, until Stephen came into his life. And Stephen had been the one to urge him to lower his defenses, to fall in love with Lillie.

Stephen. Lillie. Alexander's mind went from one to the other. They were the only two he'd ever allowed inside his barriers, but he'd driven them away. Now he was truly alone.

His chest seemed to knot with pain, and his hands doubled into fists as waves of agony rolled over him.

"Stephen," he gasped. He drew a shuddering breath, and the whisper became an agonized roar that echoed through the empty house. "Stephen—Stephen—Stephen—"

Could the angel have prevented Granny's and Prudence's deaths? He didn't know for sure. He knew from experience that certain medical situations were beyond even his friend's help. Stephen had explained that in some cases, a greater power was at work, and passing into the next world was the choice of the spirit. He thought that both Granny and Prudence had been beyond medical aid even before he reached them. But he couldn't be entirely certain. Had Stephen been right? Had they been ready to die?

He needed the comfort of Stephen's presence, his reassurance that he had done all that was humanly possible. But he had pushed him out of his life, just as he'd done with Lillie.

In his head, he reviewed the two cases repeatedly, trying to imagine what else he might have done, berating himself for omissions he now felt he'd made.

He was a failure. He'd lost two patients and driven away those he loved. He was alone, and he deserved to be, because he had no idea how even to begin to remedy the situation he'd created.

"Physician, heal thyself," he whispered with a bitter laugh, and then he laid his head on the wooden table and wept.

"Ashes to ashes, dust to dust . . ."

Lillie heard the preacher's words, but it still seemed incomprehensible that her friend, Prudence, could be in the pine box being lowered into the earth this sunny May morning, or that a short distance away and a scant hour before, Granny had also been laid to rest.

Two funerals in one day. It seemed the entire town had turned out, and most of them were weeping for both the old and the young woman.

Benjamin stood near the edge of the open grave, his head lowered, his strong face ravaged with grief, and beside him his mother held his swaddled newborn son. The baby cried piteously all during the burial, as if he, too, grieved for the young mother he'd never know.

Lillie smothered a sob and dabbed at her eyes, her glance going to Alex. This was the first time she'd seen him in weeks, and she could hardly believe the change in him. He'd lost so much weight his dark suit hung on him. His eyes, when they met hers, were sunken and hollow, as if he hadn't slept in days. His burning glance lingered for a long moment on her and then slid away.

He looked lost and abandoned, and in spite of her resolve, her heart went out to him. She knew he must be devastated by the deaths of women who'd been both friends and patients, and to make matters worse, there was the gossip. Some were saying he'd become derelict in his duties as a physician, a charge that made her furious.

She recalled the conversation that had taken place at the counter in her store just yesterday morning. One of her customers, a neighbor of the Irvines, had tearfully related to her friend gruesome details Letitia had given her of the baby's birth.

Mrs. Martz, also in the store, eavesdropped shamelessly, then waddled to the counter. "I couldn't help but overhear, and I have to say I blame Dr. Dennison for the death of the Irvine girl," she said in a loud, peevish voice. "It's common knowledge he's taken to imbibing spirits. Why, when I went to see him, he was downright insulting. They say he didn't even get to Granny until it was too late. She lay there on the floor for hours, poor old soul. If dear little Prudence had only had a decent doctor, this tragedy wouldn't have happened, either, and that poor dear baby would have his mother."

The other women didn't openly agree with her, but Lillie sensed the seeds of doubt growing in their minds. She'd always made it a point to ignore any gossip she overheard, but she didn't this time.

"Mrs. Martz, I do believe you've been misinformed," she said in a sweet tone as she added up the other women's purchases. "Dr. Dennison never touches spirits, and his medical qualifications are impeccable. Everyone knows he did the very best anyone could do for dear Prudence, and Granny's neighbor told me he came immediately, but there was nothing he could do there either. Granny was very old, you know."

The two other women nodded agreement, and Mrs. Martz's face grew scarlet. Giving Lillie a nasty look, she brayed, "Well, dear, it's noble of you to defend him, especially when the entire town knows how he took advantage of you. Why, I saw him myself, coming down your back stairs in the early morning."

Lillie had felt her face flame. The other women had shot avid glances her way, and Mrs. Martz had smirked and then huffed out of the store.

Lillie's anger rose even now at the memory, and she fervently hoped that vicious old thing never came near her store again.

"We commit the soul of Thy servant, Prudence Irvine . . ."

Lillie closed her aching eyes and made up her mind that when this final prayer was ended, she would march straight over and speak to Alex. But when she looked up again, he was gone.

Chapter Nine

Lillie hurried home and changed her black silk dress for a workaday cotton, thinking of Alex the entire time. Instead of lessening, her feelings for him were just as powerful as ever, and it broke her heart to see him so alone and desolate. She opened her handkerchief drawer, found Granny's charm, and looped it over her head.

"Oh, Granny, I have to try to help him," she whispered. He might reject her—he likely would—but at least she had to make the effort.

As she ran down the back stairs, she heard someone pounding on the store's door, demanding service, but she ignored the summons. She hurried down the street and raced up the front steps of Alex's house to the office door that was always open.

She turned the knob and then rattled it. The door was locked, although the sign, hanging lopsided, announced "The Doctor Is In."

She knocked and knocked, but there was no answer. She ran to the back and up the stairs to the porch. This door was locked, too, but she was certain she heard movement inside. She lifted her fist and banged until her knuckles were sore, and still there was no response.

"Alexander, open this door. I know you're in there," she called. "I want to speak to you." She waited, her temper fraying. "What on earth's the matter with you?" She moved to the window. The curtains were drawn and she couldn't see inside. She banged on the glass and called again and again, but there was no answer.

At last she lost her temper and shrieked at the top of her lungs. "Damn you, Alexander Dennison!" She stamped her foot on the wooden boards and rested her hands on her hips, panting with exertion, tears of frustration running down her face. She sniffed loudly and rubbed her cheek. "So help me, this is the last time I'll come running after you, Alexander. Stay here and rot, if that's what you want, you stubborn—egotistical—idiot!"

Alexander heard her stomp down the stairs, the back gate squeak open and slam shut, and then silence. He climbed the staircase and went into his bedroom. He lay on the bed, staring up at the ceiling and seeing only a bright pool of blood.

Several times that day and the next, he heard patients mount the front steps, try the office door, linger a few moments, and then leave. When it grew dark the second night, he roused himself to go down to the kitchen and eat some cheese and bread. Near midnight, he went out the back door and down the street, following the road that led out of town.

He walked for miles in the darkness, knowing he had nowhere to go. The silence mocked him, reminding him he was totally alone. He'd cut himself off from people, pushing them away. The love he'd felt for Lillie had given him direction in life. He'd even begun to think of marriage, to dream of a son, of a daughter who looked like Lillie. Now there was an empty void where those dreams had once lived.

Even medicine was lost to him now. The two women's deaths had stripped away his self-confidence. He couldn't treat anyone when he doubted himself.

You have only yourself to blame, the darkness mocked. His feet kept time to the words that drummed endlessly in his head.

Eventually he turned and retraced his steps, arriving home just as the first streaks of dawn lightened the eastern sky.

He locked the doors, washed himself, and went up to his bedroom. He slept a few hours and then listened again to the footsteps that came and went, the buggies that passed on the street, the children's voices as they played. When darkness fell, he got up and walked again, and somehow the days and nights fell into a new routine.

"Have you heard what they're saying about Dr. Dennison, Lillie?"

She ignored Myrtle's question, pretending to be engrossed in dusting the shelves behind the counter.

"It's such a tragedy for a gifted doctor."

Myrtle was obviously taking a great deal of pleasure in repeating what Lillie had heard a dozen times already, in church last Sunday, on the street, and in her store. Her hand tightened around the duster and she vigorously attacked the stack of canned goods she'd already dusted twice today and three times yesterday.

"Hardly a soul has seen him since the funeral two weeks ago, you know," Myrtle continued with relish. "He's locked himself in that house. They say the only time he comes out is at night. Mr. Wellington saw him walking on the road, miles out of town."

Myrtle's voice vibrated with excitement. "Mr. Wellington said the doctor looked quite demented. He had no hat or coat and no necktie, either, and you know how meticulous he always was about his dress." Her voice dropped to a conspiratorial whisper. "They say Granny's and Prudence's deaths have quite unhinged his mind, and he's given up doctoring."

"Poppycock!" The word exploded from Lillie's mouth, and she turned and brandished the duster at Myrtle so that the other woman leaped back and pressed her hand over her bodice.

"That's nothing but rubbish," she exclaimed, smashing the duster down on the counter and glaring at Myrtle. "You should be ashamed of yourself for spreading such idle gossip. I heard you myself not so long ago saying what excellent care he'd given your grandmother. Why, the poor man probably has the—the grippe. For all anyone cares, he could die in that house."

"But—but why would he be wandering the back roads at night if he's ill?" Myrtle tried to sound chastened, but the effort failed.

"I have no idea, but then, neither do you, Myrtle." Her tone was scathing. "Do you?"

Myrtle's face turned red, and she hastily paid for her purchases and scurried out the door.

Probably never to return, Lillie fumed. She was losing customers and friends at a rapid rate, and all because of Alex. "This is ridiculous," she said out loud.

Vernon and Lars were rooting through the nail barrels. She knew they'd been listening with interest to what she and Myrtle had been saying.

"I'm closing the store," she announced.

They turned and stared at her. "I'm sorry, but you'll have to leave and come back another time," she told them.

"Can't close the store in the middle of the day, it ain't fittin'," Vernon grumbled.

She ignored him. "I have an errand to run."

It was time someone did something other than gossip about Alex. Someone had to try to shake him out of his isolation and despair—and she was the one to do it, she decided with grim determination. She knew all about despair, thanks to him. She'd had more than her share since their breakup. And the days hadn't grown any easier. If anything, she missed him more instead of less as time went by.

"It's gonna storm right smart out there, missy," Lars remarked, thumping his collection of nails down on the counter and reaching in his pants pocket for the dime to pay her. "Wind's gettin' up. It might hail. Seen 'em come down the size of goose eggs when there's clouds like those."

She ushered the muttering old men out the door and locked it. She turned her sign around. Rain was beginning to pelt against the window by the time she threw her apron off and grabbed her cape.

The wind whirled her cape around her when she dashed out the door, and the driving rain half-blinded her as she ran down the street, past the barber shop where Vernon and Lars were watching from the window.

Go ahead and stare, she raged silently. *Go ahead and gossip, too. It's going to take more than words or insults or hail or even a locked door to keep me out of Dr. Alexander Dennison's house this time.*

She was out of breath by the time she reached Alex's house and ran up the front stairs. The wind had blown her hair loose from its knot and it hung around her shoulders, soaked from the rain. She thrust it back and hammered on the door. All the shades were down, and the house looked as if no one lived there.

"Alexander!" she shouted. "I know you're in there. Now open this door, or so help me, I'll break it down!"

No answer.

"Fine, I'll break it down," she muttered, going back down the steps.

Around the corner of the house she found a long, stout stick. She picked it up in both hands and went back up the steps. Taking a deep breath, she lifted it high and smashed the window that formed the top half of the office door.

The glass shattered, and with trembling hands she reached inside and undid the hook that secured the door.

"Alexander?" The house had a stale, musty smell. She went through the office and down the hall to the kitchen, calling his name. The stove was unlit and a neat stack of dirty dishes stood on a counter. There was no sign of him, and the silence was so complete she became frightened.

"Alexander." Her voice echoed as she ran down the corridor and up the stairs. The bedroom doors were open except for one—his. She burst through it, terrified now at what she would find.

The room was dark and stuffy, the curtains drawn, the windows closed. It took a moment for her eyes to adjust, and at first all she could see was his form on the bed.

"Alexander, what on earth is the matter with you?" She moved to the window and drew the curtains aside, shoving the window up to let in fresh air. Rain came pelting in and the stormy light was faint, but it was enough so that she could see him clearly when she turned.

She gasped. He lay on his back, wearing wrinkled trousers and what had once been a starched white dress shirt. His feet were bare. He turned to look at her but didn't say anything, and for a moment she couldn't speak, she was so shocked.

He looked ravaged, his cheekbones standing out in stark relief. He hadn't shaved in days and his eyes were sunken and haunted. His spectacles were on the bedside table, and he made no effort to put them on.

His despair was obvious, like a thick cloud that almost crumpled her with its weight. She struggled for composure.

214

"Alexander, you look terrible. Are you ill? Can I get you anything?" She moved closer to the bed, longing to throw herself down beside him, to hold him in her arms, to comfort him.

He sat up and swung his feet to the floor. He looked at her, his eyes flat and blank, as if she were a stranger. "What are you doing here?" There was no warmth, no recognition in his tone, and she fought against the pain piercing her.

"I'm worried about you. No one's seen you in weeks." She tried for a light note, forced a smile. "Gossip has it you've become a ghost, haunting the country roads at night."

"Go home, Lillie. I don't need your pity." His angry, scathing tone told her that her effort had been futile.

"Contrary to what you might think, I can manage quite well on my own. Unlike you, I don't need crowds of people around me all the time."

Hurt to the depths of her being, she persisted. Her voice quivered, but she maintained the light tone. "It looks as if you could at least use a cook, Alex. You've lost weight, you can't have eaten, I'll go down and—"

"Get out!" He rose, standing beside the bed, and his roar penetrated her very pores. "Get the hell out of my house, out of my life! I don't need you. I don't need anyone!"

Chapter Ten

Alexander saw the awful hurt on her face, but he was frozen inside; he couldn't allow himself to feel. He heard the sound that came from her throat, the sound of a woman in mortal pain, but he couldn't respond. He watched as she shuddered, her wonderful brown eyes wide, spilling over with anguish, her vivid features mirroring the wound he'd made in her heart. But he was no longer a healer. He was poison.

He watched as she whirled and ran, her bright blue cape wet-stained, her yellow curls damp and soft around her shoulders. Against his will he remembered how soft those curls were to his touch, how they wound around his fingers the way her love had wound around his heart.

He stood rooted as he listened to her feet pounding down the stairs. He heard the front door open and slam behind her, and he knew it was the end, the last time she would ever come to him.

At that terrible realization, his despair and fear crumbled. Unless he went after her, he would surely die.

"Lillie!" The agonized cry tore from his throat. He moved, one step and then another, forgetting his spectacles and having to turn back and grope for them. Then he stumbled down the stairs, raced along the hall, heedless of broken glass under his bare feet. "Lillie, come back!"

When he went out the back door and down the steps, the force of the storm took his breath away. The rain obscured his lenses and everything was a blur—puddles of water, a flash of blue cape, a small figure running into the field behind his house.

"Lillie!"

He pounded after her, ignoring the stones that bruised his feet, the wind that tried to push him back.

He caught her in the middle of the field.

"Let—me—go—" She fought him like a wild thing with her fists and elbows and knees. Her face contorted, her sobs rattled in her throat, but he held on until at last she quieted in his embrace, her heart hammering against his chest like a trapped bird.

"Lillie, forgive me."

The rain poured down on them, a cloudburst now. He did his best to shield her from it as he wondered how he could ever explain what he didn't fully understand himself.

But somehow the words were there. "I've been alone too long." He squinted through the wet, unable to see, but it was as if a light went on inside him and all at once he saw clearly what had made him the way he was.

"I was an only child, Lillie. I had the best parents a boy could have. They were everything to me, and when they died, it hurt so much I vowed never to let anyone get that close to me again."

She was quiet in his arms, and he knew she was listening. He wrapped her still closer, locking his arms around her.

"I became a doctor to fight death, but Granny died, and then Prudence." He had to swallow hard, the pain was still that acute. "I felt I was a failure." He shut his eyes tight, and self-loathing overcame him. "I *was* a failure, not with Granny, perhaps, but with Prudence." He shook his head. "I should have been able to save her."

"Oh, Alex." She touched his cheek.

He opened his eyes, and hers were filled with compassion and glistening with unshed tears. "You can't control life or death, Alex. You can't control people, either, the way you tried to control me. You have to learn to trust me and learn to trust yourself." The tears overflowed and trickled down her cheeks.

He drew a shuddering breath. "I know . . . I know . . . I had a friend, Lillie, the dearest friend anyone could have, and I drove him away, just as I did you. I've destroyed all the things I cared for." He'd tell her all about Stephen, but not now. "I'm so sorry for all the awful things I said to you, Lillie, and for the abominable way I've acted. I was stupid and foolish and I didn't mean any of it." He took his thumb and swabbed at her wet cheeks, at rain and tears alike. "Do you think you can ever forgive me?"

She was looking up at him, squinting through the raindrops.

"Yes, but there's one important thing you haven't said, Alex." Her voice held a challenge. "You used to tell me you loved me. Do you still?"

He cupped her chin and shoved his smudged glasses up to rest on his tousled hair. He looked into her eyes for a long moment, feeling everything shift and melt and re-form inside him.

"I love you, Lillie," he said simply, from the depths of his being. "I'll love you until I die, and afterwards I'll go right on loving you. You're my heaven on earth."

She sighed, a huge, satisfied sigh. "And you're mine, and nothing else matters, does it?"

He bent and kissed her, deep and long and passionate, and wondrous joy filled his heart.

When he lifted his head, he peered in near-sighted awe. The rain had stopped, and the sun blazed in the sky. Then at the edge of the field, he saw Stephen smiling at them, and behind him a radiant rainbow cast a spectrum of breathtaking unearthly light.

Holding Lillie closer to him, Alexander knew that for now and all eternity, he would never be alone again.

About the Author

What makes two very different people fall in love?

Bobby Hutchinson believes there are no accidents in the universe, and that special angels are in charge of bringing men and women together. She's convinced those heavenly matchmakers often take great delight in uniting the most disparate of personalities because such relationships provide the best opportunity for learning.

The author of twenty-five romances, Bobby not only believes in angels, she relies on them for inspiration, encouragement, and the touch of whimsy that makes her love stories unique. Stephen, the guardian angel in "Heaven on Earth," has a droll sense of humor, and Bobby, too, thinks humor is an essential ingredient in a relationship. She believes along with G. K. Chesterton that angels can fly because they take themselves lightly, and she's certain Stephen agrees wholeheartedly.

LINDA MADL
"Heaven In His Touch"

"In this theater of man's life, it is reserved only for God and angels to be lookers on."
—*Francis Bacon,* The Advancement of Learning

Chapter One

Colorado, 1885

Emily longed to wipe the condescending smirk off Zach Dunwoody's face. She also itched to remind the overdressed attorney that she remembered when he'd operated out of a shabby boardinghouse parlor, soliciting cases from Oro City miners. They had paid him in gold dust rather than the fresh greenbacks he now received from his cattlemen clients. He'd grown too fat for his own good, she thought, looking around his opulent storefront office.

"As I said, the answer is no, Miss Holt, or Captain Holt, or . . . whatever," Mr. Dunwoody said in a patronizing tone.

225

"It's Captain Holt, sir, and I heard you the first time," Emily snapped, then bit back the words she'd regret blurting in front of the children. Zach Dunwoody wasn't the problem, she reminded herself.

"Here's my message for Mr. Yager, who never seems to be available to meet with me. Tell him that since he won't rent Holt House to the Mission Army for my homeless children, I want to know why . . . Oh, never mind, I'll tell him myself."

Before Dunwoody could mutter another inanity, she herded the children out of his office and shut the door soundly.

She took a deep breath to still her angry trembling. Wade Yager was in for a big shock if he expected her to accept his refusal from his hireling again. The baby squirmed in Emily's arms, and the children gathered around her dark blue skirts, their eyes wary, their usually noisy good spirits subdued for once.

Emily breathed deeply again, trying to calm herself for their sakes. Her anger would accomplish nothing. The baby coughed and Emily stroked Nina's black hair away from her cherubic face.

"Everything will be all right," she said, wanting to reassure her orphans in as steady a voice as she could manage. But she didn't believe her own words. She'd been trying to find them adequate housing for a month now, and only Holt

House offered the space she needed for the orphanage. But Wade Yager refused to cooperate.

Oh Lord, she prayed silently, just send me a little luck and some help. The children need a good roof over their heads. Another rain like last week's storm and we'll all catch pneumonia.

Miraculously, a weight lifted from Emily's heart, a weight she hadn't realized she was carrying. Looking up at the wide blue sky, she almost expected to see a dark cloud floating away with her burdens wrapped up in it. But the sky was clear. She blinked and smiled down at the children. Strange that such a little prayer made her feel so certain all would be well.

"You'll see," she said more confidently now. "Soon we'll have a place without a leaky roof or a smoky stove."

"Why won't Mr. Yager rent Holt House to us?" twelve-year-old Billy, the oldest of her orphans, asked with a frown. "Why won't he help us?"

"I don't know." Emily shook her head, afraid she knew more than she wanted to admit. Two months ago when she'd returned to Oro City, she'd hoped that Wade had put the past behind him as she had, and that his refusal had nothing to do with what had happened between them so long ago.

"I hear Mr. Yager is rich." Agnes looked up at her solemnly. The little girl, whose entire family had died less than a year ago—her father in a mine cave-in and her mother and little brother from the measles—had lost so much, and Emily knew having a home meant everything to her.

Nine-year-old tow-headed Toby with the loud mouth was silent for once, and eleven-year-old Susan remained pensive.

"That's what I hear," Emily said, preoccupied with the thought of hiring a rig to drive to the Flying Y, where she could confront Wade. She had yet to meet him in town, which seemed odd, since she'd heard that "Mister Yager" rode in every day or so. The "Mister" had been uttered with great respect, and that had pleased her, because there had been a time when the town had known him only as the son of a drunken miner.

"When I knew Mr. Yager nine years ago, he was a hard-working but generous man," she added.

"Did he own a big ranch then?" Susan asked, looking up at Emily with almond-shaped eyes that reflected her Chinese heritage.

"No, not in those days," Emily said. She was still a little overwhelmed by the magnitude of Wade's success. At twenty-seven, he was being touted as the youngest and most successful rancher on the eastern slope of the Rockies. "He didn't own much of anything when I knew him."

Looking up and down the nearly deserted Main Street, bright in the midday sun, Emily heard the steam engines' chugging and the crushers' thundering noise drifting down the mountain. She knew that one reason the town was so still was that it was the afternoon shift at the Lucky Belle—the only working mine left of the many that had brought prosperity to Oro City.

Though most of the stores were vacant, several others like Smithers' General Store and the print shop wore fresh paint and displayed new merchandise. All but one of the bordellos, Sally's Cat Emporium, were gone, and at the end of the street, the opera house stood silent and shuttered. But the Hadley Hotel still flourished, catering to the prosperous cattlemen, and on Second Street the old bakery still filled the morning air with the aroma of fresh bread each day.

Maybe Oro City wasn't the glittering boom town of Emily's girlhood memories, but it hadn't become a ghost town like so many other Colorado mining towns. For that she was thankful.

Billy touched her arm. "Look." He pointed toward the new red brick post office. "It's spring roundup time," he explained, his eyes growing wide. Emily knew the boy had dreams of being a cowboy, and that he would drop his job at the print shop at the flick of a lariat if he thought a rancher would hire him. "The Flying Y is hiring cowhands. The notice was in the newspaper and hanging in the post office, too."

Billy was right. A group of cowboys stood in front of the building, and as Emily watched,

Wade came out of the post office with Clive, the postmaster.

She stared at the man she hadn't seen in nine years. He was taller, sturdier, and broader than she remembered. The gangly awkward youth had matured into a strong, powerfully built man.

Her stomach fluttered. Even after all these years he could still make butterflies tickle her insides.

She could hardly take her eyes off him, and swallowed hard. She recalled clearly his broad, long-fingered hands, making her weak with the softest touch.

His Stetson was tipped back so she could see his chestnut-brown hair on his forehead, and the image of his deep, probing teal eyes flashed through her mind.

She shook her head, willing away all the unexpected tender, vulnerable feelings seeing him had caused. Nine years was a long time, time enough for emotions to die or at least wither. Yet they suddenly threatened like a storm on the horizon. She simply couldn't allow Wade's and her past to keep the children from having a good home. She had to keep her wits about her for them.

She watched as Wade and Clive set a table between them on the boardwalk in front of the post office, and the cowboys moved closer to it.

This wasn't exactly the right time or place for

her to confront Wade. But she knew that if she didn't speak to him now, before roundup, it could be weeks before he was in town again.

"Well, children, come along." Emily settled Nina on her hip and took Agnes's hand. Squaring her shoulders, she prepared herself to face Wade again after all these years.

Her lips pressed together in grim resolve, she and her orphans struck off down the middle of Main Street to have a showdown with Wade Yager.

Wade's instincts went on alert the moment he caught sight of Emily with a gaggle of children marching down the street toward him. Instantly he knew from her determined gait that she was ready to do battle.

He cursed silently. He should have known that was what his refusal would lead to. Emily had never been one to give up easily, especially not when she had a cause, and today she had five of them, one a baby.

Resolutely, he concentrated on hiring for his roundup. During the mild winter the cattle had ranged far, and he needed a good-size crew to cover a lot of ground. He thumped his ledger down on the table he'd borrowed from Clive, then looked up the street again.

As Emily passed the saloon, the barkeeper and his patrons peered over the batwing doors, and as she hurried along, the spring breeze blew off her plain bonnet. Wade got his first real glimpse of her in nine years. Her auburn hair gleamed like fire in the sunlight, and the wind plastered her dark skirts against her long legs, revealing her slim body. His dreams constantly reminded him that her slenderness belied a voluptuous nature he knew he'd never discover in another woman. He'd already tried.

He wanted to look away but couldn't. He tried to see her face, but she was too far away. She had to be twenty-five years old now, and the years had made a difference, judging by her serene, confident air, which captured Wade despite his cold anger.

In Emily's dusty trail scurried the four orphans to whom she'd given a home in the name of the Mission Army. Where had they all come from, those homeless youngsters?

Didn't that little slant-eyed girl look like the child he'd seen stealing coal from behind the Hadley Hotel?

The dark-skinned baby in Emily's arms must be the Indian baby—the foundling left on the Mission doorstep who had become the talk of the town.

He shook his head imperceptibly. He would have bet anything there weren't a half-dozen orphans in Oro City, but there they were, gathered around Emily's skirts. She'd always come to the rescue of stray dogs or lost kittens, and not even nips and scratches discouraged her. She'd always taken whatever—whoever—she found into her home and into her heart. When they were hers, she fought for them, and with that baby in her arms, she already carried the best weapon to use against him in front of the town.

Grimacing, he turned back to the scruffy cowboys. Pretending not to notice Emily bearing down on him, he counted twelve men. They were a meager lot, too few range-proven hands to make up the large crew he needed. He studied them. Half the men were familiar to him, hands he'd hired in the past. Three others looked like experienced cowpunchers judging from the worn condition of their gear, and two looked like trouble-making kids. One appeared to be a miner turned cowboy for the wages.

Still ignoring Emily's progress toward him, he said, "So you want work?"

Sweat-stained hats bobbed in response.

"Okay, I need all the hands I can get, but I've got rules," Wade began. He always believed in putting everything on the table. He hadn't built a successful spread by making foolish deals or hiring undependable help. "I don't tolerate any tomfoolery at the Flying Y. Spring roundup is a big job, and I expect every man to do his part from sunup to sundown."

A few of the cowboys nodded, the ones with familiar faces.

He went on. "No drinking or gambling till roundup is over. I pay cash, prompt, when the job is done. If you don't think you can do your part, don't sign on."

He took a moment to glance over the men's heads. Emily had just passed Smithers' General Store, where two ladies with parcels stopped to watch her.

He cursed silently. Though it was unlike Emily to make a scene, it was also unlike her to let go of something she wanted. Apparently, she was going to fight for Holt House. This little scene would keep the town gossips' tongues wagging for days.

Emily and her orphans halted at the edge of the group of cowboys. "Mr. Yager, I'd like to speak to you."

The men turned and gawked at her. The polite cowboys tipped their hats while the troublemakers leered. Wade wished she'd put her bonnet on again to hide her shining, caressable hair.

He maintained an attitude of nonchalance. "Not now, Miss Holt. I'm signing on a roundup crew."

"Yes, so I see." She shifted the Indian baby from one hip to the other. "When is a good time, Mr. Yager? I've been put off each time I've called at your lawyer's office. If I didn't know better, I'd think you were avoiding me."

"I'm a busy man, Miss Holt," he said, rankled by her accusation. "And I have nothing to add to what Zach Dunwoody has told you."

Pulling a pencil from his vest pocket, he

turned his back on her and tapped the open ledger on the postmaster's table. "If you're signing on, boys, make your mark here."

The men hastily lined up in front of the table.

"Mr. Yager, your lawyer has given me your answer, but I find it unsatisfactory," Emily called over the heads of the cowboys. "I think you and I should discuss it face to face."

"There is nothing more to discuss, Miss Holt," he said, shaking the hand of each man as he signed on. "I have no intention of renting Holt House to the Mission Army or anyone else."

"Then why did you purchase the place, Mr. Yager?"

He paused, thinking surely she knew the answer to that. Did she expect him to say it in front of the whole danged town? "Because I wanted it, Miss Holt. For business reasons." He turned to look at her.

"I'm not asking for charity, Mr. Yager. Nor am I pleased at having to ask to rent my own family's home from you." An uncharacteristic expression of distaste crossed her face. "But I can assure you the Mission will pay a fair price."

Her eyes bored into his. "The storefront we're living in is next to Sally's Cat Emporium. Hardly a suitable place for children," she said, her voice low.

He chuckled unkindly. "Don't you and the Mission approve of Sally and her girls?"

He caught the cowboys exchanging looks.

"On the contrary, Miss Sally and her ladies have been kind and generous to us." Emily's tone was haughty, cool. "It's her ill-behaved clientele I don't care to have the children associate with."

A few cowboys shuffled uncomfortably.

"Naturally, I would never be so indiscreet as to mention names." She demurely tilted her head.

Looking horrified, Clive leaned across the table. "You ain't making them kids live next to the bordello are you, Wade?"

"I'm not forcing them to do anything!" Emily wasn't fighting fair, he fumed. "What about the Hansen place? It's for rent."

"It's a two-room cabin, Mr. Yager. Hardly larger than where we're living now."

"Well, Holt House is hardly a good place, either," he countered. "No one has lived there since your father died six years ago. The front door is almost off its hinges and the well pump doesn't work. I'm not inclined to invest money in repairs, and I doubt you have the money or the help to do it, either."

"I'll help Miss Holt make the repairs," a tall blond cowboy called from the crowd.

Wade squinted at the man. He'd have sworn the cowpoke dressed in the blue-and-white checked shirt and white felt hat hadn't been standing there before.

The cowboy had the long, loose-jointed, rangy look of a good wrangler. His face was young, though suntanned and weathered, like a man used to working in the sun. Yet his shirt looked store-bought bright, as if it had never seen the light of day or the surface of a washboard. The Stetson on the back of his head was so new it didn't even boast a sweat stain.

"It's roundup time." Wade searched the ledger for the man's name. "And I need every cowhand. Did you just sign on?"

"Yep. My name is Nathaniel, but most folks call me Nat."

"Yeah, I see it." Wade was still puzzled that he hadn't spotted the cowboy among the other men. "You've signed on to work cattle, not to nursemaid a bunch of orphans."

"Why can't I do both?" Nat's remarkable slate-gray eyes innocently questioned Wade. "I'll ride roundup during the day and help Miss Holt in the evening."

"That would be very kind of you," Emily said, weaving her way through the crowd toward Nat and Wade. The children followed. When she drew near, she smelled of lilacs as she always had, a scent that unsettled Wade and almost made him forget all about cattle, roundups, and orphans.

"What about when it's your turn to ride night herd?" Wade objected, trying to remain unaffected by Emily's nearness. A cowhand working more than one job was unheard of.

"I'll be there," Nat said with complete confidence. "Before sunup like you said. Don't worry,

Mr. Yager. I can do my part during roundup and help Miss Holt, too."

"Thank you, Nat." Emily's grateful smile at the cowboy annoyed the heck out of Wade. She added, "I can't pay you. But I can feed you and put you up in the carriage house."

"That'd be fine, miss." Nat removed his hat and his fair hair glowed golden in the sunlight.

"Hold on," Wade protested, bent on putting a stop to this nonsense. "I didn't say you could rent Holt House."

"You mean you're going to let those kids keep living next door to a cat house?" Clive asked, astonishment in his voice.

The tall cowboy frown and shook his head in disapproval, as did some of the other cowboys. Wade couldn't believe he was being railroaded in front of the whole town.

Only Emily seemed unruffled. "What's your price, Wade?"

He named one as high as possible without getting himself tarred and feathered by the cowboys. But Clive gasped and Nat's frown deepened.

Emily's brow furrowed slightly as she appeared to consider it. Her sweet feminine demeanor, her fair, heart-shaped face, and her delicate features masked the shrewd business woman beneath the uniform. She'd learned business from the best, from her banker father, and Wade knew it.

Finally she said, "I'll pay you half that amount plus the clean-up and any improvements we make on the place."

"Half!" Now Wade frowned.

"It's a fair offer." Nat turned his unnerving but soothing gray gaze on him.

"I'll be the judge of that," Wade snapped, waiting for inspiration, for one solid irrefutable argument against renting the house to Emily. He knew all the dark reasons why he savored keeping the mansion to himself, but they seemed of no use now.

Then Emily smiled at him for the first time and his heart lightened some. He'd been a fool to think he ever had a chance against her and the children.

"Okay. It's a deal, Emily. You and your Mission Army can rent Holt House. But don't get too comfortable there. I can't guarantee how long you can stay. I might find a buyer and then you'd have to leave."

He paused, wanting to be sure he had her full attention. "And understand, I expect my rent paid in cash and on time. I operate a business, not a charity."

"Done." Emily offered her hand to seal the agreement.

Wade stared at it, so deceptively small and delicate. In these parts a handshake was binding. Bitterness curdled in his belly. If he shook her hand, he was committed to a relationship he

239

didn't want. Despite the daintiness of her hand, he knew she wasn't the sweet young girl he'd fallen in love with years ago. Maybe she never had been. Over the years he'd convinced himself he'd loved a fantasy, believed in an apparition.

Now he wanted to believe he was hardened against the appeal of that fantasy. What did it matter if he let her use the house for a while? It was only a business deal.

Reluctantly, he took her hand, her fragile fingers disappearing in his grasp, yet she returned his grip with firmness and purpose. She smiled at him, and his heart lurched.

"You won't be sorry," Nat said, a light of encouragement gleaming in his eyes.

"That remains to be seen." Wade quickly withdrew his hand. "I'll send word to Dunwoody to give you the key to the house." Then he turned to Nat, aware of a new anger growing inside of him. Who the hell was this cowpuncher to offer aid to Emily and to stick his nose in his business? "And you, cowboy, I expect to see you at the Flying Y ready to ride at sunup Monday."

Nat smiled. "Yes, sir, Mr. Yager, I'll be there ready for anything."

Chapter Two

The next day, as she packed her few belongings, Emily could hardly believe her good fortune. Granted, Wade had rented Holt House to her reluctantly, but rent it he had. And her good fortune hadn't stopped there. She'd found someone to help her and the children move, all in one afternoon.

When she had stopped at Dunwoody's office this morning, he'd handed her the key without comment, and when she had returned to the storefront with Nat and the children, they had found boxes and started packing their meager possessions. Miss Sally had offered her redfringed surrey to transport them to their new home, and Emily had gratefully accepted. Hav-

ing very little help for the move, she was in no
position to refuse any contribution, whatever its
origin. The spirit of giving was what counted,
she had reminded herself. If only Wade could
have been as generous.

Carrying her box to the surrey, she watched
Nat help the children into the conveyance. At
first the children had been awed by the tall, en-
ergetic cowboy, but his casual chattiness
seemed to reassure them, and he had remembered their names and treated them with a teasing good humor, as an uncle might.

Climbing into the carriage beside Nat, Emily
listened to the children's laughter as Nat joked
with them. During the trip it seemed as if they
had accepted him as part of their little family.

Finally they arrived at Holt House. As she
turned the key in the lock, Emily felt a moment's
panic, fearing that painful memories would
come flooding back to ruin the pleasure of moving the children into their new home. But when
she entered the empty front hall, there was only
the smell of mildew and dust instead of her father's cigars. The parquet floors were bare, the
royal-blue furniture and draperies she
remembered were gone, and the imported wall-
paper was stained. It was hardly the grand house
she had grown up in.

The boys thundered past her and up the stairs,
claiming the rear bedroom for themselves. The
girls chose the upstairs room in the front, and

Emily decided on the room between the children's. Nat would sleep in the carriage house bunk room.

That evening Emily cooked their first meal in the house, which filled the kitchen with light, sweet smells of vanilla custard and skillet-fried chicken—the fryer a donation from Clive. During the meal, the children seemed elated, and when they finished eating they charged outside for another hour of play before bedtime.

"How does it feel to live in your old home again?" Nat asked.

Surprised by his question, Emily thought for a moment, pausing in scooping up a spoonful of mashed potatoes for the baby. She'd never returned to her hometown after she went East to school. Shortly after her graduation from the ladies' academy, her father's bank, The Oro City Bank and Trust, had begun to fail. Her father had written her often during her school years, encouraging her to marry—for security, of course, security being his word for money. She'd refused, and instead had joined the Mission Army.

"It's fine," she answered at last. "Walking through the house wasn't nearly as difficult as I thought it might be. And it's such a relief to have the rooms and porches and the yard for the children."

She had no intention of telling Nat, a virtual stranger, that the most difficult moment had come when she'd cleaned the bunk room for him. She and Wade had stolen their last hours together there. Did Wade remember those precious moments as clearly as she did?

Nat smiled, bringing her back from her sad memories.

"We still have a lot of work to do around here," Emily went on, marveling that she already felt so comfortable with this man. "But the front door is back on its hinges, swinging like new, and the well outside is working, and the broken parlor window is fixed. Why, you've performed miracles, accomplishing so much just this afternoon. I'm grateful to you."

Nat looked at Emily, admiring the ruby lights of her hair and her sweet gratitude. He liked this exceptional woman, a fascinating blend of courage, generosity, and good humor. He wasn't entirely certain Wade Yager deserved the place he held in her heart.

"We need to get the kitchen pump working, too." He went to the sink and worked the squeaky handle. Not a drop of water fell from the metal lip.

"Do you think you can fix it?" Emily asked, letting Nina guide the spoon to her own mouth.

"I'm not sure. Maybe it just needs adjusting."

"Can I help?" Agnes's freckled face peered around the back door.

Nat frowned. He didn't need the sharp-eyed

eight-year-old looking over his shoulder. "I think I saw a wrench hanging from a hook in the basement stairwell. Will you get it for me?"

Agnes headed for the basement stairs, her braids flopping down her back.

Nat turned his back to Emily so she couldn't see his hands. He gave the pump a meaningful tap and began to work the handle again. The metal monster choked, gurgled, and groaned once, then began to spit out brown water.

"There we go." He continued to work the handle. "All we have to do is pump the old water out."

"Wonderful," Emily said. "What a luxury it is to live here after that cramped storefront."

Nat heard the patter of Agnes's feet.

"Aw," she cried, "you fixed it without me."

"It wasn't as hard as I thought it would be," he explained, dragging a chair to the sink. "Here, I could use your help to get the bad water out of the pipes. Keep pumping."

Delighted to help, Agnes climbed up on the chair and took over the job.

Nat sat down as Emily poured him a cup of fresh coffee.

"I hope this isn't going to be too much for you, Nat." Emily put the coffeepot back on the iron stove. "I mean working for the Flying Y, and working here at night."

"I'll be fine. Besides, when my shift's done at the ranch, I'll enjoy spending my time here."

"Mr. Yager spends his time at the McKee ranch with Miss Madeline," Agnes said, still at the sink.

Emily frowned. "Agnes, where'd you hear that? You shouldn't be repeating gossip."

"It's not gossip," Agnes said confidently. "Miss Sally said it was true. Mr. Yager's been courting Miss Madeline since Christmas."

Surprise and alarm played across Emily's face. She put another spoonful of mashed potatoes into Nina's mouth. "Sounds serious."

Madeline McKee is no match for you, Nat wanted to whisper across the table, but he suspected that Emily wouldn't believe him.

"All the bad water is out." Agnes climbed down.

"Good, it's bedtime. Call the others in," Emily said.

Agnes disappeared out the back door without protest.

"You know, I've been thinking," Nat said. "Your father must have been angry when you joined the Mission Army, since he had bigger plans for his only daughter."

"My goodness, have I told you my life story in just a few hours?" Emily asked with a soft, self-conscious laugh. "I guess I've been babbling. But now that you mention it, I'm afraid I was rather dramatic about my decision, too," she admitted with a forlorn smile.

"By then Papa was having trouble using

money to hold onto me or anything else in his life, and he didn't know what to do. He died lost and alone, surrounded by his ledgers and proposals for new investors, still trying to keep his bank alive. How often I've wished it could have been different."

Nat nodded, hearing the regret and sadness in Emily's voice. "Isn't it curious that in all the time you've been gone Wade never married?"

Her astonished gaze sought his. "You think I have something to do with that?"

He shrugged. "The way you two talked, it seems as if you know each other pretty well. And I thought I glimpsed a look in Wade's eye—and in yours."

"Hardly anything to keep Wade from marrying if he's ready." She scraped the last of the potatoes from the bowl. "I can see his grand plan right now. If he marries Madeline McKee, he'll be able to merge the Flying Y and the Diamond K into one big spread."

"Seems like he could have done that before now," Nat said, wondering how well she understood Wade Yager.

"Wade's ambitious, but he's no fool. Madeline can't be more than nineteen, and he's probably just giving her time to get used to the idea of having the responsibility of running such a huge operation."

"And you disapprove of his wanting more land?"

"My father always wanted more of everything." She rose. "He measured himself by how much he owned. But it never brought him happiness."

"Or you either?"

"No." She set Nina's empty bowl in the sink. "I've chosen a different road. Maybe it was out of rebellion at first, but I've found it's right for me."

She turned to the baby and smiled, putting her fingers to her lips. Nina sat with her head resting on the chair tray, sound asleep. Nat and Emily exchanged a smile.

"I'm very happy with my life," she whispered.

Monday morning, Wade sipped his second cup of steaming coffee while standing on the cook house porch, watching his hired hands near the corral. Nat was among the men, just as he'd promised. His white hat fairly gleamed in the sunlight, and his checkered shirt sported hardly a crease.

Yet Wade's sources in town reported that Nat had worked plenty hard settling Emily and the children into Holt House. That didn't make Wade think any better of the stranger. Something about the man just didn't sit right with him, something he couldn't quite put his finger on. Nathaniel Whoever-he-was just didn't seem to be a cowboy.

Losing interest in his coffee, Wade threw it on

the dusty ground. Truth was he would have been real happy if Miss Emily Holt had never shown her face in Oro City again. But she was here, and try as he might, he couldn't ignore that. Nor could he ignore the fact that some strange cowboy was hanging around her offering her smiles and a helping hand.

If Emily needed help, then Wade would find her the perfect man—some half-blind, toothless old codger who could wield a hammer, harness a horse, and mind his manners on Saturday night. Wade settled his hat low on his brow, pulled on his doeskin gloves, and started for the corral. The sooner Nat hightailed it out of town, the better, and he knew just how to accomplish that.

Wade's regular hands roosted on the fence rails, drinking coffee from tin cups, rolling cigarettes, and inspecting the horses. Across from them, Nat sat with Ben, one of Wade's regular hands, who blew on a harmonica. The sour notes screeched through the crisp morning air.

A cowboy hollered to Ben to put the harmonica away and the other men muttered in agreement, but Ben ignored them and continued his sorrowful serenade. The horses rolled their eyes and twitched their ears. Dust rose from their hooves as they pressed against the fence, away from the music. Ben had won the harmonica in a poker game last week, and he'd been torturing the men and the animals with his musical attempts ever since. Wade had considered confiscating the danged thing until roundup was over, for the sake of their ears and the herd's.

"May I try it?" Nat asked.

"Help yourself." Ben handed him the harmonica. "I cain't seem to make much music on it."

Reverently, Nat polished the wooden object against his jeans, then cupped it to his lips and blew softly.

Sweet, melodic notes floated over the corral. The men stopped talking and listened. The horses quieted. Wade halted in his tracks, struck by the tranquil song.

"Hey, that's purdy good," a cowboy marveled when Nat paused. Though Wade agreed, he wasn't about to say so.

Nat played on, and the music soared, soothing men and horses alike.

Wade frowned as he resumed his steps. "Yeah, it's good if I'd hired musicians. What can you boys do on horseback?"

Nat's gaze challenged Wade's across the corral. Then the cowboy returned the harmonica to Ben.

Wade started issuing orders, and by midmorning the regular hands had chosen the best mounts from the herd. Then Wade turned to Nat. Judging from the look of resignation on the cowboy's face, Wade figured Nat knew what was coming. "Randy, cut Biscuit out for our new hand."

The cowboys waited in silence as Randy roped a bay gelding from the herd. The mustang nickered with rage and reared, nearly striking the second cowboy trying to put a rope over its head. As soon as the bronc was boxed in, a third cowboy ventured close enough to throw a saddle on him.

Even roped, Biscuit snorted, mean as a bull, and stomped his forefeet, raising a cloud of dust. The horse was in rare form today, Wade thought with satisfaction.

"Tell you what, Nat," Ben said loudly. "You ride that bronc around the corral once, and I'll give you this mouth organ. Deal?"

Nat grinned, clearly delighted with the prospect. "Deal."

"Ready, Nat?" Wade called across the corral.

The cowpoke tipped his hat cockily and climbed off the fence. As he approached the mustang, Biscuit twitched his tail, but Nat ignored the menace and stroked the horse's nose. The animal quieted some, but continued to tremble as Nat swung up into the saddle.

Randy and the other cowboys dashed for safety.

Nat waited, not using his spurs or the reins, letting Biscuit take his measure. Like a man who knew horses, Wade noted warily. The horse's ears twitched, then flattened, and his eyes were wall-eyed.

Wade thought the gelding was preparing for

his famous great surging buck—head down, all four feet clearing the earth, forelegs stiff, rump thrust high—and in midair he would add an exquisite twist to his spine. Hardly a cowboy in Colorado could hang onto Biscuit when he performed that stunt. Before long the spotless Nat would be dusting off the seat of his breeches, Wade mused with grim pleasure.

Nat gently stroked Biscuit's neck and spoke softly. The horse snorted and shuddered again. Nat spoke once more, then brushed his spurs lightly along Biscuit's sides.

Softly snorting and sidesaddle trotting, polite as an old maid's mare, Biscuit minced around the corral. He bowed his neck prettily, his dark eyes as dewy soft as a milk cow with a new calf. Wade stared. He'd never seen anything like it, a range pony prancing through his paces like a show horse.

As Nat and Biscuit circled the corral a second time, Ben tossed him the harmonica.

Nat pocketed the mouth organ and brought Biscuit to a halt in front of Wade. "This is a nice ole hoss. Don't you have something really mean for me to ride?"

Wade felt the other hands cast uneasy glances in his direction, waiting for his reaction. He studied Nat for a long moment, torn between admiring the man's skill and wanting him out of Colorado. Nat grinned, flashing the open, good-natured expression of a cowboy who could take a joke as well as play one.

Wade gave a short, dry laugh. "I'm afraid Biscuit is the best I've got. He's stomped more than a few good bronc riders into the corral droppings. He's yours if you want him."

The regular hands chuckled at last.

Wade looked at Nat with renewed interest. The man had a talent with horses too rare to let go when good wranglers were scarce. "Where'd you say you worked before?"

"Around Tombstone last year, and before that in Dodge City."

"Figures. If you'd been wrangling around here, I'd have heard of you." Though satisfied with the answer, Wade was still convinced that more was at stake than the success of his roundup. He climbed off the fence. "Is Miss Holt settled in the house?"

Nat dismounted. "Yes, sir. Miss Emily is as pleased as a hen with a new coop."

Wade gazed off toward the rise where his three-room, log-cabin-style ranch house sat surrounded by pines. He tried to picture Emily in Holt House again—after all its years of being empty. "You're living in the carriage house?"

"Yep. It has a comfortable bunk room with a south window to catch the breeze."

"Yeah, I know." Wade decided to be frank. "Miss Emily is a respectable lady. I wouldn't want to see any gossip get started."

"There won't be," Nat promised, shaking his

head. "No, sir, I'm a sworn bachelor. I'm just helping out until some good man comes to his senses and lends her a hand."

"Good." Wade was relieved at Nat's loyalty to the unmarried state, but annoyed at the thought of another man in Emily's life. "Anyone angling for Emily Holt had better be able to put up with her orphans and strays."

"Yep," the cowboy said. "But there're worse faults in a woman than generosity."

The cowboy's defense of Emily rekindled Wade's anger. Lord, he wished she'd never come back. It had taken him a long time to get his life on track. Now the very sound of her voice tore at old wounds he'd thought had long since healed. Even her face disturbed his sleep and tantalized his dreams with bittersweet memories. "Sure, there are worse faults in a woman. Fickleness, for one. Well, let's get going. We've got lots of work to do."

"Yes, sir," Nat said as the angry ranch owner turned away and strode toward the barn. "Plenty of work to do here. Maybe even more than I thought."

Troubled with Wade's reactions, Nat pulled the harmonica from his pocket. Admiring it once more, he put it to his lips. With just a little coaxing, a melody drifted up and around him, and the music crystallized the quandary facing him.

Neither Wade nor Emily understood that they belonged together. Emily might pray for help, but she insisted she was happy with her life the way it was, and Wade's pain had festered so deeply it blinded him to the truth.

Emily had a compassionate heart, so she wasn't going to be too difficult to bring around, Nat thought.

Sadly, he stopped playing and tucked the harmonica into his pocket. But Wade . . . Now, there was a hard man. No, this wasn't going to be as simple as he had thought.

Chapter Three

At the end of the month, Wade rode into town to ask Zach Dunwoody to collect the rent on Holt House. After all, Wade paid the man a healthy monthly retainer to handle the Flying Y's legal affairs.

Entering Zach's office, Wade stated his request bluntly, but Zach kept shifting his eyes, looking decidedly uncomfortable.

"I'm not facing Captain Emily Holt again," Dunwoody finally said, hunching behind his desk as if it were the last refuge in town. "No, siree. That's final, Mr. Yager. Maybe her daddy's bank failed and she isn't a rich lady anymore, but she's something else. I hear she wheedled a month's worth of flour from Smithers at the general store and finagled two cords of firewood from Ira Johnson."

She was probably expecting him to donate the rent on Holt House, too, Wade concluded. If so, she had a surprise coming. He was going to have his rent, and no wheedling or finagling would change his mind.

As he rode back to the ranch, he considered another approach. Maybe Nat would collect the rent for him. Wade hated to admit it, but the rangy wrangler was a darned good cowpuncher. He never shrank from any task, and Wade had given him some tough duty, too, like riding drag whenever they moved the herd and bulldogging the calves during branding.

After Wade arrived and put his horse in the barn stall, Nat rode into the barn. As the cowboy dismounted, Wade walked over to him.

"Ah, Nat, I need you to do something for me. When you see Miss Emily this evening, I'd like you to ask her for my rent."

"Ask Miss Emily for money?" Nat pulled the saddle off Biscuit and shook his head. "Ask me anything else, Mr. Yager, and I'll do it. But a cowboy don't go collecting rent from a lady with five orphans to feed."

Wade felt about an inch tall. But a business deal was a business deal, and Emily had agreed to his terms in front of a dozen witnesses. She'd even shaken hands on it, and he would hold her to it, even if it meant collecting the money himself.

That evening after Wade had changed his clothes, he saddled his horse and rode to Holt House.

Thunder clouds gathered on the horizon as he climbed the porch steps, and the sticky evening darkness rapidly closed around him. At first the house seemed deserted, and wondering where Emily and the children were, he lingered at the front door. He felt uncomfortable and awkward, as he had so often as a boy. Given the social order of the town nine years ago, a miner would never have called at Holt House. If he had business with James Holt, he went to the bank and cooled his heels until he was shown into the banker's office. As Holt's daughter, Emily had never mingled with the dirty miners or their sons, except at town gatherings. Everyone knew this class structure and accepted it.

So Wade had gone along with keeping their romance a secret. Their meetings were usually hidden in the shadows, in the dark, often in the carriage house. But every moment had been precious and sweet. In Emily's arms, he had discovered there was light in the world, a flame so much more dazzling and fierce than the flicker of a miner's carbide lamp. He'd loved her and she'd said she loved him, too.

He shook his head and turned away, unwilling to remember any more of his painful past. But vivid images of James Holt finding him and Emily together flashed unrelentingly through his mind—the screeching hinges of the carriage house door; Holt's glaring bloodshot eyes and contorted face; his ugly, angry shouting; Emily's embarrassment as she clutched her bodice against her bare breasts, pleading for peace between them; and Wade's own helpless surprise, possessiveness, and desire to protect her.

Holt had never spoken to Wade—before the discovery or after. Though Wade had understood and respected a father's right to disapprove of a daughter's suitor, the indignity of being ignored had infuriated him.

But sweet vengeance had been his the day he bought James Holt's house at the bankruptcy auction years later. Even though Holt had died by then, Wade still felt he had won a victory over the banker. He was proud to call the grandest house in Oro City his, and he still didn't feel like sharing that conquest with anyone—least of all Emily.

Angry now, he turned to the door again. Peering through the beveled glass, he spotted a glowing light at the end of the front hall. He figured it came from the kitchen.

As he started to ring the doorbell, he heard the distant melodic sound of Nat's harmonica. He paused, listening to the strains of a familiar song, and then the children began to sing. What a happy little home Emily had made for them all, he thought, envious of Nat and the children wrapped in warm domesticity in *his* house.

He headed toward the back of the house, in the direction of the music. As he passed the side of the house, he noticed that flowers had been planted in the old window boxes and that the shutters had been repaired. A swing had been hung in the old cottonwood tree.

The minute he appeared at the corner of the house, the music stopped, and Emily, dressed in a flower-sprinkled muslin gown, rose from her place next to Nat on the porch steps. Wade was surprised at the absence of her drab uniform, and drew a deep breath of unexpected pleasure at the sight of her, looking soft, round, and womanly.

Nat pocketed his harmonica. "Hello, Mr. Yager."

All of the children turned to Wade, their small, innocent faces pale in the summer darkness.

"Good evening, Mr. Yager," Emily echoed, wariness clouding her expression.

"Good evening, Miss Holt." He did not remove his hat. "I'm here on business."

"Oh, of course," Emily said. "Agnes, will you and Susan put the baby to bed, please. Boys, you wash and get ready for bed. I'll be up to hear your prayers. Mr. Yager and I won't be long."

The girl with the braids picked up the baby from the basket at Emily's feet, and she and the rest of the brood glanced at him cautiously as they clambered up the porch steps into the house. Nat remained.

"This is about the rent, isn't it?" Emily asked.

"It is part of our agreement."

"Yes, it is." Emily started into the house. "Please, won't you come into my office so we can discuss it?"

At the door, Wade took off his hat and stepped into the kitchen. The lamplight revealed a huge round table surrounded by mismatched chairs, two of which he recognized from Sally's Cat Emporium, and the others he assumed had been donated. But despite the ugly furniture, the room was warm and homey, filled with the smell of fresh baked bread and cinnamon baked apples.

The spacious hallway was bare, except for a worn rug on the parquet floor. A glimpse into the dark front parlor revealed that it was also empty, just as Wade had left it when he locked the place up. He had sold off the house's furnishings separately, and apparently the Mission Army hadn't replaced them.

"This way." Emily led him across the hall from the parlor into a small front room where a desk was stacked with papers and ledgers. She moved behind the desk.

"Please sit." She gestured to a hard, straight-backed chair.

"I don't think this will take that long," he said. "I'll just take the rent money and go."

261

Linda Madl

"Well, that's what we need to talk about." Emily held his gaze and clasped her hands over her muslin skirts. "I don't have enough cash to pay the rent just now."

"You what?" He stared at her, astonished. It wasn't like Emily to play games. "That's not what you said when you agreed to this arrangement in front of a dozen witnesses."

"I know, but you see, Sergeant Sara, the lady who came here with me to set up the orphanage, was called back to the Denver Mission office last month," Emily began. "She will be so relieved to see that we've moved away from the Emporium. Anyway, she needed funds to travel, and that's why I'm here alone and operating on a small budget."

"Alone with the children and Nat."

She acknowledged his addition with a nod. "When Sergeant Sara returns, she will bring funds for Holt House."

"Just when will she be returning?"

"Well, I can't say for certain." She looked away. "That depends on how much work the Denver Mission has for her. In the meantime, I propose giving you an IOU. As soon as Sergeant Sara returns, we will make it good."

"Wait." He could hardly believe it. She had hoodwinked him and finagled the house out of him, just as Dunwoody had said she'd done to the town's other businessmen. "I doubt your father would have accepted an IOU under similar circumstances. Would he?"

She scowled and fingered a pencil. "I'll be the first to admit that my father did not have a generous heart. Believe me, Wade, I don't like asking this of you any more than you like being asked. But I simply don't have the money."

"That's not good enough, Emily, especially when you knew you didn't have it when I agreed to rent to you." He was frustrated and annoyed. "Dang it, a business deal is a business deal."

In the silence, thunder rumbled.

Emily raised her head, and her amber eyes flashed molten gold. "What's happened to you, Wade? My father measured the world in dollar signs. Coming from a banking family, he was raised that way and didn't know any better. But you . . . Once you had so much heart. I really expected more compassion from you."

His smoldering anger flared. "Compassion? You expected *me* to have compassion?"

"Look, maybe there's a compromise."

Nat appeared in the office doorway, a forbidding frown on his face, but Wade was too angry to heed it. "This is private, cowboy."

"You can say anything you have to say in front of Nat," Emily said, holding her head high and her lips pressed into a thin line.

Wade glared at the wrangler. So she had adopted Nat, too, just like she had the children. They all lived together in this house and took care of one another. Now, wasn't that nice? he thought, his anger blazing into full flame. "All right. Here's what I've got to say to you, Emily Holt. You've got a heck of a lot of nerve expecting help from me. Nine years ago you left m— town. Remember? You didn't even have the decency to say good-bye. You just packed all your promises, all your soft-eyed declarations of love and loyalty, boarded the train for Philadelphia and left."

He stopped, almost unable to go on. The passage of years had done little to dull his desolation and pain. The boy he was then had loved Emily—trusted her. Now he just ached to know why she had deserted him.

When he spoke again, his voice was low, husky with anger and emotion. "Now *you* have the gall to talk to me about compassion. I received none from your father or from you. You were just gone, Emily. You said nothing. *Nothing!*"

To his bitter satisfaction, Emily paled and looked away.

"Now you expect an open heart and an open pocketbook from me? Am I supposed to just forget—"

"That's enough." Nat stepped between them. "As I recall, Mr. Yager, when you and Miss Emily agreed to the rental price, part of the compensation would be made in repairs and clean-up of the house and the property."

Wade nodded, glancing across at Emily. She

stood frozen, still refusing to look at him.

"Miss Emily and the children have fulfilled that part of the agreement." Nat folded his arms across his chest, and his eyes narrowed. "The house has been cleaned, the windows washed, the garden tilled, the grass mowed. Surely you can accept Miss Emily's IOU for the remainder of the agreed amount."

Emily spoke without looking up from her desk. "We are *grateful* to you, Wade, for allowing us to move into the house."

"Gratitude does not pay the rent," he answered.

Nat frowned. Thunder rumbled louder this time.

"I know that work has been done," Wade admitted. Emily's obvious pain troubled him, and his taste for fighting with her faded. He watched and waited for her to throw his heated words back in his face, but she remained silent. He'd voiced his long-burning anger, and he'd hinted at the question that remained unanswered for him. As he watched the silent Emily toy with the pencil on her desk, he cursed silently.

"Write me the IOU," he muttered. "I want to get home before the storm breaks."

Emily flicked a relieved glance in his direction and seized her pen. The only sounds were the ticking of the clock and the scratching of the nib across the paper.

"Here you are, Wade." She handed him the paper with a trembling hand and a hesitant, apologetic smile. Rich red lights gleamed in her hair.

When he leaned across the desk to take the IOU, he caught her lilac perfume. The old longing seized him. He wanted to touch her hair to rediscover its silkiness and to taste her sweet, soft skin—pleasures still vivid in his dreams.

She moved away. "I truly appreciate your willingness to do this for the Mission."

His longing vanished. He jammed his hat on his head. "I'm not doing this for the Mission. I'm doing this because I have no other choice."

He didn't bother saying good-bye, slamming out the front door. He flung himself on his horse and headed for the Flying Y—riding hell-bent for leather into a heavy wind laden with the scent of rain and the tingle of lightning.

Wade's angry outburst had disappointed Nat, but he wasn't entirely surprised by it. Wade longed for an explanation of Emily's desertion. But she hadn't given it, even though Nat could see that Wade's anger had upset her.

What troubled Nat most was that Wade's resentment toward Emily was unfair. She'd made incredible sacrifices, and though it was a mistake for her not to confess to Wade her reason for leaving, she didn't deserve his lingering ill will.

Emily looked so sad and disheartened that Nat couldn't bring himself to question her.

The children filed in from the kitchen where they'd been washing for bed. They had surely heard more of the angry exchange than Emily would have liked, Nat thought. In somber silence, the pink, fresh-scrubbed orphans stared up at him and Emily.

"He's going to let us stay, isn't he?" Toby asked. "Mr. Yager, I mean."

"Yes, of course he's going to let us stay." Taking the fretful Nina from Agnes, Emily offered them all a weak smile.

"I don't like Mr. Yager," Billy growled.

"He's not a bad man, Billy," Emily said, "and you mustn't think of him as being mean or anything like that. He and I made a business deal and he has the right to expect me to uphold my end of it."

Billy looked doubtful, and the other children frowned, apparently equally unconvinced.

Nat touched Emily's arm, lending comfort. She rewarded him with a wistful smile, a real expression of gratitude that made him glad he'd come to Oro City. "Now, *compadres*, Miss Emily said it's time for you to hit the sack. I have a tale to tell you."

The children giggled, the drama of Yager's visit fading already, then ran up the stairs.

Chapter Four

The crash and boom of thunder woke Emily from a deep sleep. The house shuddered and the window panes rattled. In her cradle, Nina fussed. Emily staggered out of bed and carried the baby back to bed with her.

More flashes, then more thunder rumbled across the sky. In the darkness a floorboard creaked and her bedroom door opened. A shadowy figure appeared in the doorway.

Emily pulled up the bed covers. "Nat, what's wrong?"

"Nothing, but I think I should get to the Flying Y and see if they need help keeping the herd from stampeding."

Emily nodded and he was gone. She heard

him run down the stairs and the front door close.

Settling the baby closer to her, she listened to the wind tear at the eaves and howl down the chimney. Fearing for the roof and knowing there was nothing she could do, she fell asleep.

In the morning, she and the children, chattering about the night's storm, scuttled downstairs to peer out the kitchen window at the damage the wind had wreaked.

The storm had passed, but gray clouds still hung low in the sky. A few shingles lay scattered in the yard and a huge splintered cottonwood branch blocked the walk to the carriage house. If it had fallen on the house, it would have damaged the roof badly. They'd been lucky, Emily thought, breathing a deep sigh of relief.

At noon Billy returned from the print shop to report that there'd been little destruction around town, but there were rumors about damage and a cattle stampede at the Flying Y. Despite her absolute faith in Wade's ability to take care of himself, Emily was worried.

By supper time, when she'd heard nothing from Nat, she was contemplating hiring a rig to drive out to the ranch. But within moments, through the kitchen window, she saw Nat ride up with Wade.

Nat entered the kitchen first, and the children crowded around him, exclaiming their pleasure in seeing him and plying him with numerous questions about the storm damage and the exciting stampede.

Wade followed, his shoulders slumped and defeat written on his face. He pulled off his hat and greeted Emily with a humble nod. She returned the silent salutation, suppressing an urge to comfort him.

She'd heard Nat telling the children that Wade's ranch had been hit pretty bad, and looking at Wade, she felt cold fear pool in her stomach. "Was anyone hurt?" she asked.

"Ben has a broken arm," Wade answered, bewilderment in his eyes. "We just brought him into town to see Doc Finley. Are all of you all right?"

"Yes, we're fine," she said, certain there was more she should know. "We lost a few shingles. . . . How bad is the damage at the ranch?"

"A pine tree fell through the roof of the house," Wade said.

"The log walls are still standing, of course," Nat explained, "but the heavy rains made the place pretty much unlivable."

Emily stared at Wade, her heart aching for him. She of all people knew how much that ranch meant to him.

Nat tossed his hat onto one of the wall pegs behind the door. "The bunkhouse is damaged and overflowing with men. Some of the roundup cowboys are sleeping in the barn."

"Then, Mr. Yager, you don't have any place to

sleep," Agnes concluded.

"You could stay here," Emily offered, ignoring the consequences of her invitation.

None of the children moved or spoke as they stared at Wade. Dismayed, Emily realized they still thought of him as a heartless villain, despite her attempts to convince them otherwise.

"That's a good idea." Nat grinned as if her suggestion deserved a prize. "We already checked the Hadley Hotel but it's full, and Ingersoll's boardinghouse shut down last month."

"Well, then it's settled," Emily said, mindful of the children's continued silence. But what else could she do? Wade was homeless. "After all, this is your house, and the entire third floor is vacant."

"I wouldn't be around much," Wade said. "There's so much to be done at the ranch. I'll just be here to sleep."

Still the children said nothing, glaring at Wade, and Emily knew if she put the question to a vote, as she sometimes did with household decisions, the verdict to Wade's staying with them would be no. Powerless, she glanced at Nat for help.

"Come on in here with me, all of you." Nat led the group toward the front parlor. "I have lots more to tell you about the storm."

"Maybe it's not such a good idea," Wade said when they had filed out of the kitchen. "The children—"

"Of course, you must stay and have your breakfast and supper with us," Emily insisted, unwilling to go back on her invitation.

"Naw, Cookie and his chuck wagon will do me just fine." Wade paused as if he were sniffing the air. "Well, I'd take supper tonight, if it was offered. Smells mighty good."

Emily gestured toward the kitchen table. "Hang up your hat and sit. I was just about to serve it."

She turned to the stove to begin ladling the potato soup into her chipped, secondhand soup tureen. To be able to help Wade pleased her. She owed him, and she quickly decided that the sunny front room on the third floor would be perfect for him. As she served the thick, steaming soup, she made a mental list of what she needed to prepare the room.

"We can call it even, then."

Emily hesitated, her ladle poised in midair. She turned from the stove. "Call what even?"

"The rent and all." He shrugged indifferently as he settled himself in Nat's favorite chair. "If I'm going to be living and eating here, we should call it even, don't you think?"

"That would be fine." His offer surprised her. This man believed a business deal was a business deal. But the truth was, she hadn't given the rent a thought, what with all the excitement caused by the storm. Just perhaps Wade's unexpected losses had awakened his generosity.

She smiled to herself, pleased with the prospect.

"Good." He unfolded his napkin in his lap. "Besides, your IOU is lost in the shambles. I'd be hard put to produce it now."

So that was it. The IOU was lost. Generosity, indeed, she fumed. Her ladle trembled. The only thing the windstorm had changed was the condition of Wade's home, not of his heart. And thanks to her own thoughtless generosity, she'd invited her landlord to live under the same roof with her and the children.

Disgusted, she returned to the stove, splashing the ladle into the kettle and serving the soup with noisy vigor.

Having slept like a log, Wade spent the next day assessing the storm damage to his house and herd.

The cattle had suffered little despite a minor stampede, but because of the water damage, the house was nearly a complete loss. Still, once the rubble was cleared away, a new roof could be built, the chimney replaced, and the windows reglazed. By autumn, nobody would know a pine tree had fallen through the front-room roof.

The worst part was that the construction work would take his time and attention from his ranching operations, and would delay his asking Madeline to marry him. That didn't trouble him too much, despite his desire to expand the Flying Y. He just wasn't in any hurry to get tied down.

By the end of the second day when he and Nat rode back to Holt House, Wade was looking forward to a good meal and the pleasure of Emily's company, even if he had to share her with the kids and Nat. But the sight of Madeline's shiny little horse and buggy in front of the house startled him, almost making him haul back on the reins.

"Looks like you've got a caller." Nat smiled at him. "I'll take care of your horse."

Wade swung down from his saddle, wondering what the heck she was doing here. He'd already sent her a note about where he was staying and his intention to call on her Saturday night as usual.

Immediately, Madeline came flying out the front door. Her blond curls bounced on her shoulders, excitement blushed in her fair cheeks, and green gingham and white lace fluttered around her ankles. "Wade! I'm so glad to see you," she cried. "Daddy and I were stunned to hear the news about the ranch. I had to come see for myself that you were all right."

"Well, now you can see." He held his arms out from his sides so she could inspect him. What'd she expect? Before he realized it, she threw herself against his chest and he staggered as he caught her in his arms. She smelled of rosewater.

At that moment Emily came out onto the porch. "I'm glad you're back. Madeline's been so very anxious about you."

Wade released Madeline.

"Indeed, I have, dear." She beamed up at him. "You're sure you're not hurt?"

"I'm fine, just like I wrote you. You did get my note?"

"Yes, of course," she said, clinging to his arm. "But I couldn't wait until Saturday to see you. Besides, Emily and I have been getting acquainted, dear. She's shown me the house. What a grand place it was, in its day."

"I really wish you'd waited until I came to the Diamond K on Saturday." Wade put Madeline at arm's length. When he looked up at the house, he saw that Emily had gone inside. "I'm filthy and I don't like you seeing me like this."

"I don't mind." Madeline smiled at him, and a twinge of guilt tickled his conscience. "And did you really think that I'd wait three days to see if you were really all right? You should have come and stayed with us at the Diamond K."

He had thought of asking Madeline's father for help but had dismissed the idea. He didn't want to be beholden to Henry McKee or his daughter, not before everything was arranged and final. "Holt House is mine, Madeline. And it's closer to the Flying Y than the Diamond K."

"Oh, maybe a little." Madeline pouted. "Daddy was almost insulted that you didn't come to him for help. But I reminded him how independent you are."

"I'm fine here, and I've already started plans to repair my house, so I shouldn't be here too long." He had no intention of being swayed.

He heard the front door squeak, and he and Madeline turned to see Emily standing there again, her white apron flapping ever so slightly in the evening breeze. The scent of chicken and noodles drifted past him.

"Won't you join us for supper, Madeline?" Emily asked, her smile pleasant, but her manner a little too polite to be truly cordial, he thought.

"How thoughtful." A society-miss smile touched Madeline's lips. "I really can't stay. But thank you for the invitation."

When the door closed behind Emily, Madeline's smile vanished. "As if she thinks I'd eat at the same table with all those unmannerly children!"

He stared at the door, suddenly aware of how much he'd enjoyed eating at Emily's table with "those unmannerly children"—though they did glare at him a bit—and with Emily. Sharing a meal together was a luxury they'd never been allowed when they were secret sweethearts.

"Do what you like, dear. You always do," Madeline said off-handedly, sounding miffed. "If Miss Emily weren't so obviously a confirmed old maid of twenty-five, I'd be jealous."

He silently thanked fate that Madeline was too

young to have heard the rumors that had cir-
culated about him and Emily.

"There's no need for you to be jealous." He
looked back at the door where Emily had disappeared.

Madeline kissed him on the cheek. "Well,
don't work too hard. I'm looking forward to a
charming dinner partner on Saturday, and Father is expecting a sharp card game from you."

"I'll be there."

He helped her into the stylish buggy, and
when Madeline had driven out of sight, he
pulled off his bandanna and wiped as much of
the trail dust off his face as he could.

He stared at the inviting house once more.
The enticing glow of the kitchen lamp warmed
the front hall and illuminated the doorway, and
the aroma of chicken and noodles still wafted
around him.

Though he knew there could never be anything between them again, that needn't keep
him from savoring whatever Emily was willing
to share under Holt House's roof. And he had
the storm to thank for that strange bit of luck.
He tucked his bandanna in his back pocket and
walked up the steps to the front door as if he
belonged there.

During the next two weeks, Wade discovered
that living at Holt House wasn't nearly as simple
or delightful as he'd expected. Though his room

was on the third floor, he still heard all of the children's clamor—squeals, giggles, shouts, whispers, sobs, and tantrums.

Having had no brothers or sisters, he hardly knew what to make of the sounds. The only family he'd ever had was his morose father with whom he had lived in the one-room mine shack on the mountain above the town. And his relationship with his father had consisted of nothing more than trying not to provoke the old man's bad temper and of ducking the whiskey bottles hurled at him when he failed.

That seemed an uncomplicated existence compared to managing four noisy children and a baby day after day. How Emily did it without losing a wisp of hair from her smoothed-back coil of curls amazed him.

She seemed to accept him into the household without much fuss, either. For her, his presence seemed to mean nothing more than an extra plate at the supper table and an additional "Good morning" at breakfast. But, much as he hated to admit it—glaring children aside—he felt like a starving man invited to a feast. Every morning he relished the sight of Emily frying bacon and scrambling eggs, her braid hanging down her back and biscuit flour smudged on her cheek. Flour never looked that good on any Flying Y grub cook. But he especially enjoyed sitting on the back porch near her in the summer darkness while Nat played his harmonica.

But despite Emily's acceptance and his efforts, the children, each in his own way, showed their disapproval of him.

At the end of Wade's first week in the house, he had tried to help Billy, who was practicing lariat roping in the backyard without hitting his mark. Wade's suggestion that Billy try another hold had earned him a disgusted look.

Toby and Susan hardly spoke to him beyond a sullen "Good morning" and "Pass the bread, please," and Agnes just stared at him across the table.

And the baby. Why, the one time he had held her while Emily and Susan washed the dishes, she threw a tantrum. Quickly thrusting Nina into Emily's arms, Wade had beaten a fast retreat.

No, he was not doing well with the children, but that wasn't going to weaken his determination to stay.

Chapter Five

Emily paused at her bedroom door to listen for the children, but she heard nothing except the creaking and groaning of the old house. All was quiet and dark except for the lamp in her hand and the light she'd glimpsed beneath Wade's door. He was often up late, poring over ranch records and his future plans, she supposed.

Satisfied that the children—and Wade, too—were settled for the night, Emily set down the lamp on her dressing table and began to undress for bed.

She'd been up before sunrise and was ready to collapse onto her feather mattress to enjoy a long restful night of dreamless sleep. Every night for the last three weeks, since Wade had moved in, she had come to bed exhausted. She'd finally figured out it wasn't the children who wore her out. It was being near Wade so much, covering her true feelings, hiding her pride in his success and respectability, hiding her irritation when he left for his weekly Saturday call on Madeline.

To her relief, the pretty, stylish young woman had made no more visits to Holt House. Wade's courting Madeline right under Emily's nose would have been unbearable.

But, she reminded herself as she hung up her blue calico dress, she'd made her decision years ago, and she'd known then exactly what the outcome would be. And she'd been right, almost too right, she thought, stepping out of her camisole and petticoats, and pulling her muslin nightgown over her head. But there was no reason for regrets now. Wade had been angry because of her departure, and that was understandable. Yet he seemed happy enough now, and she was glad.

Still, it hurt to be so close to him every day and to be unable to share their thoughts and their dreams as they once had so naturally and easily.

She shrugged into her dressing gown and sat down in front of the mirror to brush and braid her hair for the night. She picked up her brush and pulled out one hair comb easily, but the other one clung, snarled in her unruly curls. She tugged at it again, but it refused to budge.

Behind her a floor board creaked. She looked up into the mirror to meet Wade's gaze.

"Oh!" Startled, she dropped her brush.

Standing in the doorway, he watched her, the expression in his eyes hidden by the flickering shadows cast by the kerosene lamp.

She turned to him. "What are . . ."

"I'm sorry." Wade stepped into the room and in a swift graceful movement scooped up her hair brush from the floor. "I couldn't help . . . I mean, your door was open."

"I always leave it open so I can hear the children, in case they're sick or have a nightmare," she said, wanting him to understand that her open door was not an invitation to intrude.

"Sure. I was just going down to the kitchen for a drink of water. . . . " His voice trailed off into an awkward silence.

"There's some cool water in the stoneware crock by the door." She reached for her brush, but he made no effort to return it.

"Maybe I can help. I noticed you were having trouble with your hair comb."

"Thank you, but I can manage." She held out her hand for her brush, annoyed and embarrassed that he had watched her prepare for bed.

A small knowing smile touched his lips. Slipping her brush into his back pocket, he fell to one knee at her side and reached for the comb. "I'll have it out quicker than a maverick can stray. I've had some practice at this. Remember?"

"I remember," she murmured, heat creeping into her cheeks as she recalled how, long ago, Wade had liked to lace his fingers through her hair. She turned back to the mirror to hide her uneasiness.

His knuckles brushed against her jaw as he gently worked the comb free. His light touch tickled, then burned, stirring a deep longing inside her.

"Are you about finished?" she demanded, panicked by her sudden awareness of him, of his body and his strength.

Her own body seemed to remember too well the pleasure he had once given her. The heat of his touch still burned along her jaw, and his scent of fresh soap and cigarette smoke lingered in the air. He and Nat always smoked on the porch before they came in each evening.

"Yep, finished." He tossed the comb onto her dressing table and reached for her brush in his back pocket. "Now to get rid of those tangles."

"Wade, really," she protested, terrified of the aching flutters that swirled in her belly. He'd always had this unsettling effect on her, with a touch or even a look, leaving her weak and mindless and ready to follow him anywhere.

But she wasn't going to let anything happen between them again. Wade was a rich rancher, and she had a Mission orphanage to run. She tried to retrieve her brush once more. "Wade, I can brush my own hair, thank you."

"I'll just brush the straw out," he whispered, leaning close so his breath tickled her ear. "You know, like in the old days. You liked it then."

"That was different." She was surprised at the cool steadiness of her voice. "Besides, there is no straw in my hair now."

"Then let me do it just for old times' sake."

He moved behind her and stroked the brush through her hair. She closed her eyes as the tingling in her scalp sent small shivers down her spine, robbing her of the desire to protest. His brush strokes were slow and languid, easing away her fear, soothing her panic.

"Remember when you had a maid? Someone to brush your hair, to dress and undress you. To prepare your bath. Just think of me as your maid." His voice was husky.

A riot of tantalizing, erotic images swirled through her mind. She opened her eyes. "You're being wicked."

He smiled at her in the mirror. "You wear your hair in one long braid at night, right?"

"Yes. I'll do it."

He laid her brush on her dressing table, but never released his hold on her tresses. His large hands moving with surprising skill, he began to braid her hair so gently at first that she hardly realized what he was doing. She closed her eyes again and enjoyed feeling his hands in her hair.

"Do you tie it with a ribbon?"

She handed him a piece of blue yarn.

"No ribbons?" he asked, surprise in his voice. "I'll get you some ribbons."

The magic of the moment evaporated. "I don't want any ribbons, Wade." She caught his gaze in the mirror. "Yarn works fine. I like yarn."

"Sure." He stood up behind her, disappointment on his face. Lightly, he placed his hands on her shoulders, his thumbs brushing along her nape, the heat of his palms penetrating her muslin wrapper.

The warmth and pressure of his hands startled her, and she fought an urge to press her cheek against the back of his broad hand. "No ribbons," she whispered.

"No ribbons," he repeated softly, then bent and kissed her on the top of her head. "Good night, Em."

The familiar nickname fell so easily and carelessly from his lips that tears sprang into her eyes. When she'd regained her composure and looked up into the mirror again, he was gone. Coolness settled on her shoulders where his hands had been.

She rose from her dressing table and got into bed, but she was unable to fall asleep. Her mind was filled with the memory of Wade's breath tingling against her ear, her heart filled with the sorrowful weight of regret.

*   *   *

The next day began with Agnes in tears. Almost grateful for the diversion, Emily pushed the memory of the encounter with Wade from her mind. She was too busy—and just a little too bewildered—to deal with all the feelings that threatened her peace of mind.

Agnes had been moping around the house for days since Billy had broken her doll. Emily had hoped the repaired doll would restore the child's natural, even disposition, but it hadn't. The only other possibility was that, though she didn't realize it, Agnes still grieved for her family, and Emily knew that only kindness and time would heal that wound.

At dusk as Emily moved a skillet of gravy off the fire, Wade and Nat arrived home. Through the kitchen window, she saw them smiling at each other as if they shared some amusing secret. Without going to the carriage house to clean up first, Wade and Nat dismounted and strode up to the porch, beaming like two mischievous schoolboys.

Curious, Emily wiped her hands on a towel, picked up Nina, and followed Agnes out onto the back porch. Billy ran out to help with the horses as he always did. Toby and Susan appeared from the side of the house where they'd been playing on the swing.

Wade moved strangely, in a protective way as if he carried something tucked inside his vest.

"C'mon, Billy," Nat called the boy from the

barn. "We've got something for all of you."

As soon as everyone gathered around, Wade pulled a black-and-white mixed-breed pup from inside his vest.

The dog yapped and wagged its tail, undaunted by the squeals and by the childish hands that grabbed for him. Toby laughed and took the pup from Wade, and the children jumped off the porch and put the animal through his paces on the grass. Only Agnes stood back and watched, her face empty of expression. Emily's heart went out to the forlorn little girl. Nothing seemed to delight the child these days.

"Come here, Agnes." Wade sat down on the porch step. "Don't you want to see what else is inside my vest?"

Agnes appeared hesitant.

Emily peered over Wade's shoulder and into his vest, then stood back and drew the girl closer. "You'd better have a look, Agnes."

Her pigtails dangling over Wade's shoulder, Agnes peeked inside his vest, gasped, then giggled. She reached for the white kitten that Wade fished out for her.

"She's—she's beautiful," Agnes stammered.

"She's for you." Wade gently placed the kitten in Agnes's hands. "She's one of Kitty's litter. Kitty is the friendliest cat at the Flying Y. And a good mouser, too, so this kitten'll make a good pet."

Agnes held the kitten up, nose to nose. It gave

287

a pink-tongued mew and blinked clear blue eyes at the child. The shining light in Agnes's eyes assured Emily that Wade had hit on exactly what the orphaned girl needed. He had known, as they all had, of Agnes's unhappiness. Emily studied him, looking for the gentle boy she remembered. He was still there after all, lurking inside the arrogant, successful rancher.

Agnes clutched the furry ball to her chest and threw one thin arm around Wade's neck, hugging him tightly.

Wade's face softened and he caressed the top of Agnes's head, the tender loving touch Emily remembered so well.

She smiled at him, her heart full. She could kiss him for thinking of the kitten. He'd won her heart years ago with just this kind of spontaneous, selfless generosity.

Suddenly Wade looked up and caught her staring at him. She glanced away and cleared her throat. "Well, supper's ready." She nervously wiped her hands on her apron. "You can play with your pets after we've eaten."

As they sat down to eat, Nat noticed that Emily seemed to take little interest in her food, and her gaze strayed toward Wade again and again. Wade could hardly eat for answering all the children's questions about their new pets and the work at the ranch.

Nat perceived that the moment was critical.

Though delighted by Agnes's joy, it was the luster in Emily's eyes as she looked at the rancher that truly heartened Nat. If Wade had won the child's heart with his gift, he had also touched the woman. Maybe the rancher had more compassion than Nat had been willing to give him credit for. There was no time like the present to find out.

"Come on, gang." Nat hoisted Nina out of the high chair and herded the noisy tribe out the door. "There're some old harness pieces in the carriage house. We'll make a collar for the pup, find a toy for the kitten, and think up names for them."

The noisy children followed him out the door, shouting pet names as they ran.

"Aren't you going to join them?" Emily asked Wade, surprised.

"Seeing as I'm the cause of you losing your kitchen help," he said, pleased to have her alone to himself again so soon after last night, "I figure I'd better pitch in."

"Well, Mr. Big Rancher . . ." She looked him up and down as if she doubted he could possibly measure up to her standards. "Do you wash dishes?"

"I never ask my men to do anything I haven't done myself," he said honestly. "Including dishwashing."

"Then pour the hot water in the sink and let's get started."

Effortlessly, they fell into a conversation about the ranch, and Wade admitted that construction was moving more slowly than he'd planned.

"I decided to enlarge the house," he said, polishing a cracked plate. "It was a good solid house, but this seemed like an opportunity to add some luxuries."

"Oh, like what?" Emily asked. The steam from the water had pinkened her cheeks and added a wispy halo of dark curls around her face as she worked.

"A real parlor." The kitchen was filled with the fresh smell of soap and the lamp hanging above the sink cast a golden light around them. He'd never thought washing dishes could be so pleasant. "I was thinking about enlarging the kitchen, too."

"Sounds grand for a ranch house," she said, scrubbing a blackened pot clean.

"The Flying Y is a well-established ranch now," he said, sensing instantly that they'd better move on to another subject. He didn't want anything to spoil the sweet accord between them. "Have you heard about the Fourth of July plans?"

"The Fourth of July?" She looked up from the dishes. "What fun that used to be."

"The circus is coming this year, too."

Emily smiled at him as she handed him the clean gravy bowl. "How I loved the circus."

Neither spoke. He remembered well and wondered if her head was as full of memories as his. They'd risked being seen together one Fourth of July, and they'd set the town gossips' tongues wagging.

Emily turned back to the dishpan and wrung out the dishrag. "Well, that should do it. But there is something I'd like to say to you."

He waited, admiring the slim taper of her back as she hung the rag on the towel peg, while his heart beat a little more rapidly.

She turned to him. "I want to thank you for the kitten. It was so thoughtful of you, and your generosity meant a lot to Agnes."

To his surprise, she pressed her hands on his chest, stood on tiptoe, and kissed his cheek. Though her movement was swift and sweet, he was quick to drop the dish towel and grasp her arms before she could retreat.

"And the puppy." He gazed into her amber eyes, clear and wide with surprise. "I had to bring something for the others, too. Do I get a kiss for the puppy?"

"I suppose," she began, but he cut her off with a kiss, the first since their last night together all those years ago. He kissed her with all the passion, love, longing, and sorrow that had festered inside him through the lonely years.

She tried to resist him but only for a moment,

then yielded, pressing close, giving of herself as she always had. Her sweetness banished his lingering anger and stirred his desire.

He groaned with pleasure—and pain. All the prestige and safety his wealth had brought him fell away. His cattle, his ranch, his respected place in the cattlemen's association, and his standing in the community meant nothing. He was only a man needing the love of a woman, of Emily.

She was soft in his arms, warm and willing, damp from the steamy dishwater, and scented with soap and flowers.

Finally, she broke the kiss and tried to move out of his arms.

"Wait, wait." He refused to release her. He was too hungry for her, needed her too much. "What about the rent? We've settled that, too, haven't we? Do I get a kiss for that?"

Emily stiffened, and the warmth in her eyes vanished. She struggled to free herself. "No, you do not. What are you trying to do, buy yourself into my good graces and the children's, too?"

Abruptly he released her. "No. I don't need to buy anyone's favors." But he knew perfectly well he'd buy her favor any danged way he could.

She retreated from him. "I'm glad to hear that. You know my father wasted his life thinking the world was his for a price. When his bank collapsed and he lost all his money, it killed him. He could never understand how his precious

dollars could desert him. He could never understand that life is so much more than making the
best deal or winning the highest stakes."

"I don't think there's any danger of that happening to me," he said, overwhelmed and confused by her words. His body still ached to hold
her. Everything was so right when she was in
his arms. "I don't like being compared to your
father. I'm not anything like him."

"Good!" She searched his face, peering into
his eyes. "We may have our differences, Wade,
but I don't think I could stand to see the love of
money destroy you, too."

Chapter Six

After the kiss in the kitchen, Emily and Wade's daily exchanges became short and awkward, and Emily tried to tell herself it was for the best. Though she would have liked for them to be friends, perhaps that was impossible.

Nevertheless, today the memory of Wade's kiss crept into her mind, distracting her from her daily chores. Each time she remembered the sensation of his lips on hers, his hands pressing her against him, her stomach fluttered and her body trembled.

All the sweet aching she'd once had for him filled her again—just when she'd been so sure she was immune to him. Goodness knows, if he hadn't brought up the subject of the rent, she probably would have surrendered to him right there in the kitchen. She was stunned at how easily she could have lost her head and her heart to him again. His kiss had shaken her, made her feel as if they were lovers again, when she had found heaven in his touch. Except that Wade kissed better now, more thoroughly, yet with a tenderness she had never expected or experienced. A sweet, tender assault. She wondered what kind of lover he was now. Did Madeline know?

The large book Emily was dusting slipped out of her hand and fell on her toe. She swore softly under her breath, muttering an oath no Mission Army captain should know, then limped out of her office, determined to shut thoughts of Wade out of her mind.

Now every evening the children ran out to meet Wade as eagerly as they greeted Nat. Even Nina smiled at him across the table at supper, and once Emily had glimpsed him playing peek-a-boo with the baby from behind his coffee cup. He obviously basked in the pleasure of the children's affection. She reminded herself that he'd never really had a family, and had now become part of this unorthodox clan, and that thought warmed her heart.

She knew roundup was over at the Flying Y, and that Wade had asked Nat to stay on to train horses. The wrangler had readily accepted the offer. But the work of rebuilding the ranch house was creeping along, and Wade didn't seem to mind that he'd have to stay on at the house. Neither did the children. Their reaction hadn't surprised her. Wade had won their gratitude with the pets.

On Saturday night after supper, they gathered on the back porch steps to sing along with Nat's music, except for Wade, who had already left to visit Madeline.

Tonight Emily didn't feel like singing, content to hold Nina on her lap and listen to the children's lilting voices and Nat's lively music.

When they'd finished singing the last chorus of "She'll Be Comin' 'Round the Mountain," the subject of the circus came up. The Fourth of July was only a week away.

"I saw the circus last time it was in town three years ago," Billy announced importantly, unfolding a circus flyer he'd taken from his pocket. "I helped post these today. See? There are trained lions and ladies dancing on horseback."

"Did it cost a lot to go?" Toby asked.

"Naw, I crawled under the tent flap."

"Billy," Emily scolded, though she was not surprised. She knew the children had sometimes resorted to less-than-honest pursuits to survive, and she remembered she and Wade had also watched the circus by peeking beneath the tent skirt, because Wade had been unable to afford a ticket.

They had laughed at the clowns until their sides ached and later snitched a watermelon from a wash tub of iced melons for the picnic. What fun that Fourth of July had been, even though they'd had to endure the endless gossip afterward.

Well, the children weren't going to have to sneak into the circus, not while they were in her care. "Billy, there won't be any more peeking under the circus tent, because it's not honest. We'll buy tickets."

"I would have worked for a ticket like the other boys," Billy explained, frowning with indignation, "but the roustabout said I was too little."

"Well, what does he know, anyway?" Wade's voice came from the corner of the house. Startled, everyone turned to him. They'd been so intent on their conversation that no one had heard him ride up.

Emily shot Wade a curious look. "We thought you were calling on Miss Madeline this evening."

He smiled, seemingly untroubled. "She wasn't feeling well, so I went to the post office to talk to Clive. Look what I bought from him." He held up a handful of tickets. "Anybody want to go to the circus next week?"

The acceptance was a deafening round of cheers.

"I have tickets for everyone—for the circus,

297

the Fourth of July picnic, the dance, and the fireworks."

"Everyone?" Toby demanded. "Nina, Miss Emily, and Nat?"

"Of course," Wade said, continuing before Emily could object to his gift. "My way of thanking all of you for your kind hospitality. Madeline and I are going, too."

Madeline? Emily's spirits dropped, leaving her hollow and numb. Had Wade forgotten how special the Fourth of July had been to them? Unintentionally, she caught his eye over the heads of the children, and he held her gaze, long and knowingly. With a stab of pain, she realized he hadn't forgotten. He remembered the excitement and the magic of sharing the circus once long ago. Now he intended to share it with Madeline.

Emily looked away, purposely fussing with the baby's gown to cover her hurt and disappointment. The image of Wade escorting the fashionable Miss McKee through the crowd and sitting with her under the big top sullied Emily's precious memories. Depression overwhelmed her.

Tempted by the tickets, the children swarmed around Wade, who was explaining to them that there'd be a parade first, then the side shows before the main event under the big top.

On the steps, Nat leaned back next to Emily. She could feel his eyes on her as she pulled her shawl around Nina against the cool mountain air. "The circus will be fun, won't it? Then there'll be the dance."

"I'm not sure Nina is old enough for all that excitement," she said. She wasn't about to watch Wade with Madeline. It was just too much to ask. "I'll probably come home with her after the picnic. I'll be able to see the fireworks from here."

"Maybe Sergeant Sara will be back by then to watch Nina," Nat suggested, casually polishing his harmonica on his pant leg.

"Well, if Sergeant Sara is here, that might be possible," Emily said, feeling smug and safe. Why would Sara suddenly return from Denver before the Fourth of July after all this time?

"Yoo-hoo! Captain Emily, are you home? It's me—Sergeant Sara."

Nat smiled serenely at Emily, as if the sound of Sara's voice had been expected.

"So you'll be coming to the circus and the dance with us." Nat's smile widened.

"Well, maybe." Emily was puzzled by the odd overpowering conviction that Nat would accept no excuse for her missing the Fourth of July dance.

The circus and the Fourth of July had created more excitement in the children than even Wade's gifts. In fact, Emily thought as she mounted the stairs, the pets were some of the reason for the fuss. Any pet dressed in a costume could join in with the volunteer fire department, the ladies auxiliary, and the circus elephants in the holiday parade tomorrow.

As Emily passed her open bedroom door, she saw Susan and Agnes poking through her wardrobe and figured they were looking for something to dress the kitten in for the parade. Wade and Nat had been helping the boys with the pup's costume last night.

Susan popped out of the nearly empty wardrobe where Emily kept her Mission Army uniform, three cotton day gowns, a worn riding habit, and a few garments from her school days. "What are you wearing to the dance, Miss Emily?"

"Well, I don't know." Emily looked down at her faded green calico as she entered the room. "I hadn't thought about it. What about my yellow gingham? It's not too faded."

Agnes shook her head. "You must wear something *really* pretty. Something special for a dance."

"What about this?" Susan pulled an ivory-colored bodice from the wardrobe.

Emily stared at the shapely, lace-trimmed, decidedly feminine garment. "That was the bodice of my graduation dress." She was reluctant to wear something she associated with unhappy times. Her years at Miss Llewelyn's Academy for Ladies had been full of homesickness, anger, and grief. "Put it away. It's too girlish."

"But it's so pretty. Here, look in the mirror," Agnes prompted, holding the bodice up in front of Emily.

She peered into the mirrored wardrobe door Susan held open for her. The woman who stared back wasn't the determined, uniformed captain, but an attractive creature, confidently mature and feminine, with large eyes edged in dark lashes and framed by winged brows. The ivory lace put a blush in her cheeks and added a rich burnish to her dark auburn curls.

In the mirror a child appeared on each side of her. "See?" the girls chorused.

"Wear your hair pulled back, but loose, and your pearl earrings would look nice, too," Agnes added.

"My pearl earrings?" They had been a graduation gift from her father, the only jewelry she'd kept after she'd left home. How did Agnes know about them? Emily quickly reminded herself that she'd learned early on there was no privacy in an orphanage.

"I found them in the box on your dressing table." Agnes went to the box and removed the earrings. "See? They're perfect." She stood on the dressing table stool to hold the pearls up to Emily's lobes.

"Perfect." A blissful smile appeared on Susan's face. "Mr. Yager won't be able to take his eyes off you."

"What makes you think that's what I want?" Emily felt her face flush and quickly hung the garment in the wardrobe.

"Nat told us. He said you and Mr. Yager have always been in love, since you were very young," Agnes said, putting the earrings on the table.

"What?" Her life seemed to have become an open book to everyone in the house. "I—I don't think Nat quite understands," Emily stammered. "You see, I *used* to, ah, be sweet on Mr. Yager. Then I—I went away."

"You mean you don't love him anymore?" Agnes asked.

Emily shook her head, not daring to admit to any other answer.

"Well, that may be for the best." Susan seemed relieved, but she and Agnes exchanged sorrowful looks. "We wouldn't want you to be disappointed."

"Disappointed? About what?"

"Well, about the engagement," Susan said. "Everyone in town says Mr. Yager is going to announce his engagement to Miss McKee at the Fourth of July dance."

Chapter Seven

Nat disliked seeing Emily take so little pleasure in the circus. Looking lovely in her yellow gingham dress, she wasn't obvious about her misery as she smiled, laughed, applauded, and gasped with the rest of the audience. Nothing she did betrayed her unhappiness to the children, who were open-mouthed and wide-eyed at the wondrous acts.

The tightness around Emily's mouth was hardly noticeable, and the forced quality in her laugh could be heard only by someone who knew her exceptionally well. Nat knew she wished she were anywhere but sitting in the stands directly opposite Wade and Madeline under the circus big top.

He understood her distress. The rancher and the heiress portrayed the perfect couple. Wade played the solicitous suitor, Madeline the adored lady who took great pleasure in her role as everyone looked on with tolerant smiles and speculative whispers.

After the circus, and the spectacle of Wade and Madeline sharing a food basket at the picnic, Nat had expected Emily to make her excuses and disappear. Instead, she said she was going home to freshen up and promised to meet them at the Hadley Hotel.

Nat went ahead with the children and entered the hotel ballroom. Red, white, and blue bunting adorned the walls, and bright lights glowed against the gathering darkness. A cool breeze drifted through the open windows, and the tables and chairs were stacked at one end, creating plenty of dancing space.

At his side, Susan, Agnes, Toby, and Billy oohed and aahed at the bright streamers and the tiny American flags fluttering from the chandeliers. Nat thought the change in the place remarkable. The ladies' dresses were also bright and colorful, adding green, purple, and yellow to the patriotic hues. The gentlemen contributed their own stylish gleam to the festivities with shiny belt buckles and well-polished boots.

Nat fidgeted uncomfortably. He knew that Wade and Madeline planned on announcing their engagement tonight, so if anything was going to stop Wade's commitment to Madeline in front of the whole town, it would have to happen soon.

Now he wasn't certain if anything would, since his hope for Emily and Wade was waning. The reversals in their behavior mystified him. Wade had begun to open his heart and his pocketbook to Emily and the children, then had turned to Madeline, seemingly eager to play her game of appearances and roles. Emily had started to warm to Wade's deeds, then had directed all her attention to the children, ignoring Wade.

Shaking his head, Nat walked to the musicians' stage. He'd been asked to perform because the children had spread the word of his harmonica playing.

"Let's get this hoedown under way," the fiddler and dance caller, Oscar Coen, hollered over the noisy crowd.

Wondering where Emily was, Nat put the harmonica to his lips and joined Oscar and the accordion and guitar players in the tune for the first dance. Music soared through the ballroom, worthy of hand-clapping and toe-tapping, and the dance was off to a rousing start.

Nat saw Emily enter the ballroom alone. Her transformation was so overwhelming he almost forgot about the music. Her ivory lace bodice over her black linen skirt, her upswept burnished curls, and her pearl earrings created a picture of soft elegance. Nat saw the heads of males, young and old, turn in her direction.

He smiled as he continued to play, hope building inside him once again. Wade Yager and Emily Holt still had a chance to find each other.

If Emily didn't know such things weren't done in Oro City, she would have thought Madeline McKee purposely had timed her entrance on Wade's arm after everyone had arrived.

Madeline's gown of pink ruffles and pleats outshone every dress in the room. Her eyes glowed with triumph, and she hung on to Wade's arm as only a girl expecting a marriage proposal would, possessive and assured.

The crowd greeted Madeline and Wade with enthusiasm, teasing them about the benefits and trials of marriage. Wade nodded, his expression pleasant but distant.

As Emily watched them, she had to admit they made an attractive couple. Pretty with a fair complexion, blond hair, and a waspish figure, Madeline was a little young for Wade. But an eight-year disparity in ages was hardly unusual in the West, and Madeline would make Wade the kind of wife and home a successful rancher should have. That was what Wade wanted, and Emily knew she should be happy for him, but she wasn't.

The band struck up another dance, and Emily politely refused several invitations. She was here for only one purpose—to share some last moments with Wade before he belonged to Madeline forever.

"Gather 'round, ladies," Oscar called. "Don't be shy. It's time for you to pick the gent of your choice, so choose your partners now."

A few women headed straight for the men they'd been dancing with earlier. Several others slowly crossed the floor toward the men loitering near the punch bowl.

This was Emily's chance, and she thanked her lucky stars that Madeline had left Wade's side for a moment to speak to a friend. Emily forced a smile and headed toward Wade.

He acknowledged her with a cool hello, and still smiling, she ignored his aloof greeting. Drawing a deep breath to give herself courage, she held out her hand to him. "Wade, may I have one last dance before you are forever forbidden to the ladies of Oro City?"

The men standing beside him chuckled and nudged him in the ribs, urging him to take Emily up on her offer.

From across the room Madeline glared at Emily, but she was too far away to interfere without appearing unladylike.

Wade never glanced in Madeline's direction. He seized Emily's hand in a warm, firm grasp. "My pleasure, Em."

He swung her into his arms and onto the dance floor with a style and confidence that nearly took Emily's breath away.

"You look lovely tonight." He smiled at her with admiration in his teal eyes. "Lace becomes you."

"And your dancing is wonderful. It has improved so much since the last time we danced together," she said, surprised and pleased. "You've been practicing."

His smile broadened. "Yep. I polished up my dancing a long time ago with Sally at the Cat Emporium. You know, the most generous lady in town—next to you, that is."

"Oh." She studied him for a moment, uncertain if he was being kind or wicked, then decided not to ask. "I wanted some time alone with you."

"In the middle of the Fourth of July dance?"

"Well, you know, without the children and Nat around." Couples jostled them, and Emily longed for a quiet place where they could really talk, but she had no choice. "I just wanted to wish you happiness in your future with Madeline."

"Thank you." He frowned and refused to look her in the eye.

"You are happy, aren't you?" she persisted. "Madeline will make you a wonderful wife. She's grown up on a ranch, so she knows what her life will be like at the Flying Y. And you love her and she loves you."

"You're right. She'll make a fine wife." He still avoided her gaze. "We're a good match. Henry

McKee and I will consolidate our ranching operations, and I'll make sure Madeline gets yearly trips to Denver and New York. We'll be happy."

Emily thought he sounded determined rather than enthusiastic, so she decided to speak her mind. "Wade, you have accomplished so much with your life since I left. You've built a prosperous ranch and become a respected citizen. You know you don't need to prove anything more to anyone."

"What are you talking about? I'm not trying to prove anything to anybody."

"Aren't you?" she insisted. "Why did you buy Holt House then leave it sitting empty? To prove to my father who was long dead that you were as good as he was?"

"You give me too much credit, Emily." He expertly led them through the dancers. "I did it out of vengeance, because I knew it would make your father roll over in his grave to know that a down-and-out kid, a loser like me, owned his precious mansion."

She was silent for a moment, considering his words. "Then you've accomplished your revenge. There's no need now for you to acquire more land or more money to get even with my father or me. But it isn't over for you, is it, Wade? Is that why you're marrying Madeline? Do you love her? Really love her?" She had finally said what was really in her heart. "If you don't, is this marriage fair to her—or for that matter, to you? Don't you want love in your life?"

She paused, but he said nothing.

"The man who's been living at Holt House these past two months, the man I remember, wouldn't—" A catch in her voice almost choked her, but she pressed on. "Are you sure this marriage is going to make you happy?"

"Yes, I'm sure, and why do you keep asking me that?" Anger flashed in his eyes and he hesitated in his dance step. "Who do you think you are to tell me what will make me happy? You're a fine one to talk about doing things for love. Was it out of love that you left me on that fine September day nine years ago? What makes you think you know what I want? Who do you think you're kidding? You're just trying to rescue me like one of your needy children. Well, I'm not one of your hopeless causes, and I don't need saving."

He stared at her intently, no trace of warmth in his face.

"What do you know about making a man happy—about love? Look at yourself. Have you ever thought *you* might be making a mistake? Filling your life with orphans and strays when you should be having your own babies? You're an old maid wearing your soul thin and breaking your heart over other people's castoffs. That doesn't seem so smart to me. Don't worry about my future, Miss Sacrifice and Charity. Look to your own."

He released her abruptly. They regarded each other in the middle of the dance floor as dozens of couples whirled around them. Then he turned and disappeared into the crowd.

She was frozen to the spot, stunned and wounded. His anger and cruelty astonished her. He'd caught her with her defenses down and her heart unprotected. She'd been called an old maid before. That accusation did not trouble her. But his words held enough truth about sacrifice, castoffs, and heartbreak to hurt a great deal.

She tried to smile at the dancers spinning around her, but it was a flimsy effort. As quickly as possible, with her head held high, she wove her way off the dance floor and out of the ballroom.

Nat tapped his toe, waiting for his cue to join the band in the chorus. He had watched Wade and Emily gliding across the dance floor, deeply involved in each other, looking so perfectly matched. But then Emily had been left standing in the middle of the dance floor alone, and now she was hurrying out of the ballroom.

He signaled for an end to the dance and left the room. He found her in tears on the hotel kitchen porch. "What happened? What did Wade say?"

"He said my life is a mistake." Emily turned to him with tears streaming down her face.

"That I don't know anything about what makes a man happy and that I'm breaking my heart over other people's castoffs and strays. Oh, Nat, is he right?"

She looked up at him, so young and vulnerable. He realized he longed to take her in his arms and comfort her as any man would. But Emily was off limits, and with great effort he kept his arms at his sides. Only when he was sure of his self-control did he touch her shoulder, offering her solace. "Your life is not a mistake. You give what you want to give honestly and from your heart. And that's never a mistake."

She brushed away her tears with her fingertips. "But it hurts that Wade thinks it is, and he was so angry with me."

"I know." He pulled a clean bandanna from his back pocket and dried her tears. Wade's irate reaction offered more hope. Why would Wade lash out at Emily unless he was in pain himself? Why would he be hurting? Only one reason seemed likely.

Inside, the music resumed, and a lively melody filled the ballroom and drifted outside to them.

Emily smiled. "You know, the band really sounds good tonight."

"They just needed a little inspiration." He peered through the kitchen door. Enough of the ballroom was visible to catch sight of Wade dancing with Madeline.

"Let's go back inside," Nat suggested, eager to get Emily back on the dance floor and under Wade's nose again. She looked especially beautiful this evening, and he hadn't missed the gleam in Wade's eyes when he'd taken her into his arms to dance.

"No, I think I've had enough celebrating. I'd better find the children and go home. But you stay."

"No, we're going back in there and dance."

"Nat, I'm so embarrassed after Wade left me like that. . . . "

"There's no need to be embarrassed. We're going to dance Wade and Madeline right off the ballroom floor." He intended to make Yager well aware of what he was passing up—one way or another. He winked at Emily and took her hand.

Chapter Eight

Nat swung Emily into his arms the way he'd wanted to do before. With worldly abandon, he led her around the ballroom in perfect time to the heavenly music. They danced every jig and reel and waltzed every waltz, and just as he'd thought, the merry activity seemed to be the antidote Emily needed. Soon her smile returned, not as bright as earlier in the evening, but it was back to his satisfaction. He glanced at Madeline and Wade, who glowered at him, and he smiled back.

When Nat went to get a cup of punch for Emily, he overheard Madeline talking to Wade.

"Darling, I've just got to go upstairs and freshen up," she said, and kissed Wade on the cheek. "The dancing has been wonderful, but I have to rest a bit before the fireworks. I'll catch up with you out by the old pine tree in the park."

"Sure." Wade watched her go up the stairs, then strolled outside.

Nat didn't waste any time. He returned to Emily with the punch and steered her to where he knew Wade waited for Madeline to watch the fireworks.

"It's a lot cooler out here," Nat said, hoping that explanation would forestall Emily's asking any questions.

"Yes, it is," Emily said. "Thank you for making me go back and dance."

"Emily," he said, aware of Wade on the other side of the tree where they stood, "don't let Wade's words discourage you. I hope you don't take his anger to heart."

"I can't help it. He isn't the man I remember," she said. "He used to be so open, so willing to take on the world. Life was a challenge and he wanted to face it."

"And now?" he prompted.

"He's possessive and ambitious and thinks only about business and more business." She shook her head in bafflement. "He seems so cold. But I'm not the girl he remembers, either. I have no right to question him about his life."

"You only tried to make him see reason," he said. "Your questions were asked in the right spirit."

"I'm afraid he didn't see it that way."

"Then he's blind." He wondered if Wade would have the courage to remain where he was and hear the truth. "He doesn't see what I see in you."

She laughed as she pressed her hands to her cheeks. "All you see is a woman who is glowing from so much dancing."

He smiled at her resilient good humor. "I see more than that. I see a stunning young woman with lovely hair and warm eyes, who is even more beautiful on the inside than she is on the outside. A generous, giving, passionate woman."

"Oh, Nat, how kind of you, but I'm not so sure I am all those things. And even if I were, it was wrong of me to press Wade about his reason for marrying Madeline." Her smile faded.

"You did that because you care about him, Emily." *Do you hear that, Wade Yager?* Nat asked silently, though he knew his voice had carried to the rancher. "Most importantly, Emily, I see a woman any man would be glad to give his life for—or spend his life with."

This was dangerous ground, but Nat was determined to say what had to be said, what was in his heart.

Emily remained thoughtful and silent.

"You know, being a drifter is a lonely life. Always going where you're needed. Never staying long enough to get to know people. Never long enough to grow fond of them, or long enough to meet a woman you know you could love."

"Nat, please, you don't have to—" She shyly touched his arm. "I appreciate all you've said, but . . . Oh, look, the fireworks are starting."

Nat left the rest unsaid, but he certainly hoped he had lit a firecracker under Yager.

Wade moved away from the shadowy pine tree. He'd just heard the perfect description of Emily—a generous, giving, passionate woman. But Nat's words left him numb. That danged cowboy had said what he'd always longed to say to *his* girl. His beautiful Emily, swathed in ivory lace and pearls, the blush of peaches in her cheeks, the warmth of gold in her eyes.

What was almost as disturbing was that Nat had said to Emily what Wade knew he could never honestly tell Madeline—that he loved her above all else in his life.

Oh, he'd told her he loved her, all right, had whispered it into her ear as a good suitor should. But he'd never meant it. Not in the way he meant it when he'd whispered it to Emily. Not in the way Nat spoke of love.

Sure, Madeline would make a good home for him, furnished with all the trappings a successful rancher should have, but his home wouldn't be heaven—not even close.

Wade headed for the stable. He wasn't fool enough to hang around and torture himself listening to what Emily had to say to Nat.

*   *   *

Emily awoke the next morning to frantic rapping on her bedroom door.

"Captain Emily." The door opened and Sara peered in, Nina balanced on her hip. "The lawyer, Mr. Dunwoody, wants to see us."

Emily squinted at the sun shining through the muslin curtains and heard the summer birds trill. She usually rose in the dark hours of the morning. But this morning she'd overslept. "What on earth does he want?" she asked, sitting up.

"He says he has some important papers for us to look at," Sara answered. "I've served him coffee, but he's mighty restless. Please hurry. I think this is important."

Something important? Like an eviction notice? Emily wondered. But they'd paid the rent soon after Sara had returned, despite Wade's insistence that his room and board made it an even swap. What had Wade decided to nettle them with now? She should have kept her mouth shut last night.

She scrambled out of bed and hobbled to the wardrobe, where her blue calico dress hung. Her feet were still tender from all the dancing. She dressed quickly, her fingers fumbling with buttons and tapes.

Before the mirror she twisted her braid into a neat coil at her nape.

She hurried out of her room and down the

stairs, and at the bottom she stopped for a moment to take a deep breath and gather her wits. She hadn't forgotten about her last encounter with the lawyer. She'd need all her poise to arm herself against his condescension.

"Where are the children?" she asked Sara, who stood outside Emily's office door.

"In the yard, playing."

Emily nodded and opened the door.

"Good morning, Mr. Dunwoody," she said, entering with a pasted-on smile. "Sergeant Sara tells me you have something important for us to see."

At the sight of her and Sara, Dunwoody rose, as humble and respectful as a lady could want. "Good morning, Captain Emily. Mr. Yager told me to come here with these papers as early this morning as possible."

He pulled a document from his satchel and extended it across the desk behind which Emily stood, as if he couldn't be rid of it fast enough.

She frowned at the papers. When she cast Sara a questioning glance, her assistant shrugged, adjusting Nina against her hip. Emily took the document from the lawyer's hand and skimmed the first few lines. It appeared to be an agreement or a contract relating to Holt House.

"Please sit, Mr. Dunwoody. Would you like to give me the short of this?"

"Well, yes." He sat down, clutching his satchel on his lap. "Mr. Yager is offering to apply each of your—I mean the Mission Army's rent dollars against the purchase price of Holt House. When it's paid up, the house will belong to the Mission. You can see the price right there on the next-to-the-last page. Frankly, Captain Emily, the price is the same as what Mr. Yager paid for the house."

Astonished, she sat down heavily behind her desk. She could think of nothing to say.

"You mean Mr. Yager is offering the house for less than the market price?" Sara said, gasping with excitement. "Isn't that wonderful, Captain Emily?"

"He said he couldn't donate the house to the Mission outright," Dunwoody continued. "He asked me to tell you he feels that something purchased is appreciated more."

"Yes, I understand Mr. Yager's feeling," Emily said, astonished. Wade certainly had been busy after the dance. Nevertheless, she was not pleased to receive messages from him through his lawyer again. "I'd like to talk to Mr. Yager about this contract. Where is he?"

Dunwoody shook his head. "He just got me out of bed this morning, told me to draw this up, and informed me that Madeline McKee had called off their engagement. Then he left town."

"Left town? Madeline called off the engagement?" Emily's head was spinning. She recalled that no announcement had been made at the dance last night after all.

320

"He said to give you time to think about the agreement and confer with your superiors in Denver." Dunwoody buckled his satchel. "But he said it's his best offer."

"Well, I'm not accepting any offer without discussing this with him." Emily slapped the agreement down on her desk. He didn't like her meddling in his life. Well, she didn't like messages carried by his lawyer. She wasn't about to accept Holt House just like that. "Where'd he go?"

"To the mountains," Nat said.

Emily looked up at the tall cowboy looming in the doorway, his hat in his hand. His gaze seemed apologetic.

"The mountains?" she repeated. Echoing other people's words seemed the best she could manage this morning. "Why?"

"Well, Captain Emily," Dunwoody said, rising and tucking his satchel under his arm. "You let me know what you decide about the agreement."

"Certainly. Sergeant Sara, please show Mr. Dunwoody out." When the lawyer was gone, Emily turned to Nat. "What's going on?"

Nat shook his head. "The cattle going to market are gone."

"The drive left two weeks ago," Emily said, not understanding.

"The finishing herd has gone to the mountain pastures. This year Wade decided he'd go with them."

"But why? He can send anyone he wants to."

"Emily, he heard us talking last night before the fireworks."

She blinked at him, still not understanding. What had they talked about before the fireworks? What had they said that would have bothered Wade? "You mean when I told you what he used to be like?"

Nat nodded, sitting in the chair vacated by Dunwoody.

"And when you said all those things to make me feel better after I'd made such a fool of myself with Wade? But you didn't say anything a good friend wouldn't, and after the way Wade behaved, why would he care?" She met Nat's honest gaze across her desk.

"I wasn't trying to flatter you, Emily." Nat held her eyes with his remarkable slate-gray ones. "I spoke from my heart."

In that moment Emily glimpsed a bright, powerful being, as ageless and solid as granite. He filled the room and towered over her, yet hovered before her as light and ethereal as the morning mist.

Bewildered, she blinked at Nat, who was the tall, lanky cowboy once more, and sat back in her chair. A chill trickled down her spine. She'd always known in her heart that Nat was more than just another cowpuncher. But the realization of who he was frightened her, yet clarified for her what she had to do. "I want to see Wade.

I want to talk to him myself."

"I think that's a good idea," Nat said, sad approval in his voice. "Put on your riding clothes. Warm ones. It's a long day's ride into the mountains."

Summer snow fell, white and feathery outside the line shack window. Thankful for the quiet, Wade watched it, thinking he'd seen stranger things than a July snowstorm in the Rockies. After last night, he didn't mind being snowed in alone with the cattle.

He could do without company—especially the petticoat-wearing variety. After the dance, when he'd told Madeline their engagement was off, she'd ordered him out of her sight, then thrown herself into his arms in a fit of tears and near hysteria. She'd claimed she would never be able to hold her head high in Oro City again.

Wade knew she'd put a lot of stock in marrying him to please her daddy and impress her friends, so he'd decided that nursemaiding cattle on the summer pasture was the perfect excuse for his staying away for a couple of months while Madeline spread it around town that *she'd* called off the engagement. He figured two months should about cover "never."

But the truth was he'd had his fill of women. If he didn't get sick of his own company, his stay in the mountains might be just the tonic he needed.

Behind him, the fire crackled in the fireplace as he watched the darkness settle as silently as the snowflakes. In the twilight, a movement among the white-laden pines caught his eye. Slowly, he reached for his gun, never taking his gaze off the spot. He didn't expect trouble. Indians hadn't bothered anyone much in this part of the country for a while, but he was prepared for any danger—bears, wolves, rattlers, rustlers.

As he watched, a tall rider emerged from the pine forest, head down against the wind. A smaller rider followed close behind. They appeared to be headed for the cabin. As they drew closer, Wade recognized Biscuit's white-blazed face.

He cursed silently. Nat was among the last people he wanted to see, but he couldn't refuse him shelter from the storm. Setting his rifle aside, he went to the door and opened it.

"Put your horses in the lean-to," he shouted, then went back inside.

Nat opened the shack door, and the other rider followed him in. "Somebody wants to talk to you," Nat said without greeting.

Wade peered beneath the hat and between the edges of the wool scarf pulled close around her face. "Emily?" He rounded on Nat. "What the hell do you think you're doing bringing her out in this weather? You two could have frozen to death."

"I asked him to bring me." Emily shivered and

shook the snow off her hat. "I won't agree to that contract for Holt House without discussing it with you."

Her auburn curls fell loose, wreathing her face. She shrugged out of her coat. The soft green merino of her riding habit felt warm as he grabbed it, but the cold had pinched roses into her cheeks and blued her lips. Her nose glowed red, making him think of warming it with a kiss.

Instead, he took her hat. She had to be the only woman he knew who would brave a blizzard to talk business—on behalf of her orphans, of course.

"It's warm by the fire." He urged her toward the hearth. "You warm up first, then we'll talk. And you, Nat . . ."

The cowboy held up his hand. "I'm leaving, but I have a few things to say before I go."

Wade glanced at Emily and she shook her head, apparently as mystified as he.

"You two belong together. You always have, and you both know it," Nat said. "Why you're having so much trouble figuring it out is beyond me. There's only so much to be done about pure bullheadedness."

"I don't know what you're talking about," Wade said.

"Then listen carefully," Nat said, warning in his voice. "Helping people means a lot to Emily. She has plenty of energy to share and a wealth of love to give. What greater treasure could you want, man? Just because she loves a bunch of orphans doesn't mean she can't love you, too."

"I don't need any lectures from you about what to do or think," Wade began, indignant that the cowboy had the insolence to lay down the Gospel to him. Wade felt a tug on his sleeve and turned to Emily. She was shaking her head.

"As for you, Emily, you've got to accept that Wade is always going to want to make a good living for himself and the people he cares about. It's important to him, and there's nothing wrong with it—as long as he doesn't sell his soul by hurting others or forgetting to share his good fortune with them. That's what he's trying to do with Holt House—share. There are worse goals in life."

Wade waited for Emily to argue, but she said nothing.

Nat walked to the door, then stopped with his hand on the latch. "I'm glad to have known you both. So long."

"But you can't go back out into that storm, Nat," Emily protested. "The nearest place is the Flying Y, and that's a long ride."

Nat smiled mysteriously. "I'll be all right. You both just take care and be happy."

He opened the door and was gone in a gust of wind and a flurry of snowflakes.

Chapter Nine

Wade and Emily rushed to the window, peering into the darkness, but Nat was gone. Only white flakes fell as silently as angel wings around the cabin.

"I'd better go after him," Wade said. "He can't make it back to the ranch tonight in this weather."

Emily shook her head. "You heard what he said. I think we should talk about it."

He leaned back from the window and regarded her in the light of the lamp. "Then you put stock in what he said? About us, about belonging together?"

"I'm not sure." She sat down by the fire. "Are *we* why you called off the engagement? You are the one who called it off, aren't you?"

He hesitated, silently debating whether to admit she'd been right. Madeline wasn't really the one he wanted to spend the rest of his life with. "There were a lot of reasons."

"And the house? Why did you change your mind about it and the Mission Army?"

"I realized I didn't need the place and you did."

"And what about your need for revenge?"

He sat down in the chair opposite her. Her amber eyes were warm and serene in the firelight. She asked honest questions that deserved honest answers. He knew they would never settle anything if they weren't truthful with each other.

"It's gone, and a bitter pill to swallow, too. But I won't deny I got some satisfaction, knowing I had bested the bankrupted, humiliated James Holt. And though his daughter wasn't mine, his house was," Wade admitted. "That great mansion on the hill at the end of Main Street was mine, and everyone in Oro City knew it."

Emily stared into the fire and said nothing. Wade wondered if he'd gone too far, said too much. She'd never been close to James Holt, but he had been her father.

"I never understood what happened, Em," he went on when she remained silent. Now that he had her alone, he needed to press her for answers. "You never hinted that you wanted to go away. You were so eager to climb down the trellis from the third floor every night to meet me that summer."

She shook her head, and he thought he glimpsed tears brimming in her eyes, but he couldn't let tears prevent him from learning what he needed to know.

"I didn't know what to think. After your father caught us in the carriage house, you were gone," he said, better able to hold the old pain at a distance now that Emily sat across from him. "And you never came back. The gold petered out and the foreclosures began as your father closed down mine after mine. As much as he hated me, he spared Pa and me and the ole Senseless Sue mine."

"You might give my father credit for having some honor," she finally said, as if her father had done something noble. Tears still threatened, but to Wade's relief, she wiped them away.

Yet something niggled impatiently at the back of his mind. He reached for her hand. "Emily, do you know why he never foreclosed on us?"

She met his gaze, angry now as tears streamed down her face. His heart hammered and his stomach tightened.

"Because Papa promised me he would never touch the Senseless Sue."

His breath slipped out of him slowly, leaving him as deflated as if he'd just been kicked in the gut. He squeezed her hand so she wouldn't feel the trembling in his fingers. "In exchange for what, Emily?"

Her anger seemed to dissolve into confusion. "Does it matter now?"

"I have a feeling it does," he urged.

She took a deep, weary breath. "Sending me East to school was the only way Papa knew to keep us apart."

"And you went? Without telling me?"

"You think I wanted to go?" Bitterness flashed in her eyes for a moment, then was gone, and she shrugged. "I wanted to tell you, but then what could you have done about it? The only thing I knew to do was refuse to leave town without getting something in return."

"What?" His fear of hearing the truth caused a lump in his throat. Hadn't he always known Emily fought for those she loved?

"I agreed to leave and stay away as long as Papa kept his hands off you, your father, and your mine," she whispered, never lifting her gaze from their hands clasped between them. "I wanted you to have a fair break, Wade. I knew you would know how to make the most of it."

"No!" His mind reeled with the comprehension of so much lost between them, lost *not* because Emily hadn't cared—but *because she had*. He squeezed her hands again. "You should have told me, Em. We could have fought him. I would never have allowed you to do that."

"It's easy to say that now, Wade." She pulled

her hand free to wipe more tears away. "You forget how powerful Papa was. He could have foreclosed on the Senseless Sue in the blink of an eye. Your equipment, your mules, everything would have been lost.

"I was only sixteen, Wade. And you were eighteen. I fought Papa the only way I knew how. The only way he understood. He knew if I ever heard from anyone in Oro City that he'd broken his word, I would come back."

"Emily, why never a message? Never a letter? I would have done anything . . . Surely you knew that."

"I knew you'd be all right." She touched his cheek ever so lightly with the back of her hand. A shaft of pleasure and pain lanced through him, and he closed his eyes. "You were strong and I knew you'd survive."

He shook his head. He didn't want to believe what she was telling him.

She tugged his hand. "I was right, wasn't I? Every time I heard news from Oro City, you were doing better and better. I heard it all, Wade. How you punched cows for a share in the herd. How you sold off the Senseless Sue when your father died in the cave-in. I knew you'd buy land. I knew how much building a ranch like the Flying Y meant to you."

"And you never came back, even after your father died."

Withdrawing her hand from his, she gazed at

the fire again. "After all that time had passed, I had no reason to. You had the life you'd always wanted, and I, despite Papa's vehement disapproval, had found mine with the Mission. You had an empire to build and at that time I had a soup kitchen to run."

"Then why come back now?"

"Because the Mission sent me here. I only agreed because I thought after all these years none of it would matter anymore."

"But it did." Nat's words about bullheadedness were beginning to make sense to Wade.

"Yes, it did." Emily offered him a slight smile. "I knew it the minute I saw you in front of the post office with Clive."

"Then listen to me now." Uncertain, he prayed the right words would come. This moment alone with Emily was hardly time to stand on stubborn pride or stale anger. He took her hand again and knelt on the bear rug in front of her. "Nine years ago we found each other despite the fact that you lived in the big house on the hill and I dug in the mines."

Her smile broadened at the memory. "We met at the Christmas dance in the schoolhouse. The hotel hadn't built on the ballroom yet."

"I asked you to dance."

"Even though you didn't know how."

"I didn't give a damn. I just knew that if you accepted, I'd have you in my arms. That's where you belonged. With me."

She laughed through her tears. "Is that why you were so slow to learn the steps I tried to teach you?"

"I knew as long as I failed, I'd have you." He smiled, the old memory fresh and new again. "You were so patient. I fell in love with you that night, Em."

"And I loved being in your arms," she admitted. "And I didn't care if you ever learned those steps or not. Then you corrupted me."

"What?"

She shook her head. "You know, when you taught me how to sneak into the circus."

He smiled. "That was the *best* Fourth of July."

"Yes, and what we had was right, and you knew it, too. That's why I couldn't understand how you could marry without love. I knew for certain last night that you didn't love Madeline when you spoke of sending her away on trips, and I suspected it when you never invited her to Holt House. Why, you hardly touched her even when you helped her into the buggy the day of her one and only visit."

He cocked an eyebrow at her. "You were watching us?"

"Yes, and as I recall, when we were sweethearts, we could hardly keep our hands off each other in public or in private."

He remembered well, and his hands itched to touch Emily now. He knew what she said about Madeline was true. He'd had a lot more difficulty keeping his hands off Emily while living with her and the children than he'd ever had resisting Madeline—even when they were alone.

Emily leaned forward until only inches separated them. "Promise me you won't marry unless it's for love."

"I promise," he vowed, the reality of everything she'd just confessed to him still too painful to accept. But he shook it off, deciding to forget reality and live his dream. "Marry me, Em? For love, of course."

Her eyes widened in surprise. "I didn't mean—"

Before she could say more, he pulled her from the chair and gently laid her down on the bear rug. She hardly resisted as he bent to kiss her, wanting to show her with his mouth how much he loved her. He laced his fingers through her curls and inhaled her sweet lilac scent.

"I know what you mean," he whispered. "I'm asking anyway."

"Yes," she murmured, her lips against his. "Oh, yes."

Her arms slipped around his neck and she pulled him closer until their bodies were entwined.

He moved away and spread his hand across her stomach. Holding her like this was still too real to believe.

"But I can't imagine how we will manage it," she whispered breathlessly. "What about my

Mission work and your ranch?"

"We'll handle it. For now, *yes* is all I want to hear." He kissed the tip of her nose, which was no longer red. A rosy sensual blush glowed in her cheeks, and her lips glistened moist and full from their kisses.

"But there's so much for both of us to accept," she said, her eyes closing as if she were lost in the sensations of his touch.

"We'll live at Holt House until the ranch house is finished, and you can still run the orphanage while we're there." He bent to kiss her again, sure of himself this time, filling his hand with her tempting breast, the bud firm enough for him to feel through her clothing. "And once we've settled in our new house, wouldn't you like to start thinking about us having our own children?"

"Yes," she said, her eyes still closed, a dreamy look on her face. "And by the time we're ready to leave, Sara will be able to run the orphanage."

When Emily opened her eyes, her smoldering gaze raked over him, heating his blood more than he ever imagined a single look could. He reached for the buttons of her riding habit.

In the silence the fire crackled and only the soft rustling of their clothing being shed could be heard. Wade felt her silky breasts against his chest and her hands caressing his sides and his back.

He kissed her again and again, touching her

335

tenderly. She tasted tangy and sweet, and moved under his hands, inviting more caresses, begging for more kisses. She sucked in her breath when he caressed her most secret place. In the firelight he marveled at the smooth translucency of her skin, at his pleasure at hearing her sighs, at his excitement from her butterfly kisses down his neck and across his shoulder. His burning ache to be inside her grew.

He knew their lovemaking now would be nothing like their first time, when they had succumbed to simple instinct and longing to be one. This time they would come together as a man and a woman more separate than before, but more passionate and needful.

When he covered her, joining their bodies, she wrapped her legs around him and her tongue in his ear tantalized him, almost weakening his self-control. He held himself carefully, wanting her to have her pleasure before he found his.

Once more he moved deep inside her, throwing back his head as he felt her satiny heat, and then she shuddered, her legs tightening around him and her deep spasms exciting him. With one last thrust and a groan of pleasure, he lost himself in her arms.

When their breathing quieted, he rolled over to lie beside her. She stroked his hair from his brow.

"I've never stopped loving you," he said, and smiled at the ceiling, letting himself drift in the contentment of her nearness. She laid her head on his shoulder and he pulled her closer.

"I never stopped loving you, either." She snuggled so near that her breath tickled his collarbone. "I lived to read every issue of the town's newspaper when it arrived in the mail each week. When you bought Holt House, I wondered what you were feeling."

"In my heart I wanted to possess everything of yours I could get my hands on, because I think I secretly hoped it would help me understand why you left—or bring you back to me."

She touched his lips with her finger, then kissed him. "But the true test of our love may be yet to come."

"How's that?" He could think of nothing that could change how he felt about sharing his life with her.

She propped herself up on her elbow. "How do you think you'll adapt to being a father?"

"At least I have a little bit of experience now that I've lived with you and your passel of kids. How do you think you're going to like being a rancher's wife?" he challenged her in return.

She nodded. "Fair enough. Give and take, then?"

"Yep." He laced his fingers through the silken strands of her hair. "But here's the real test."

She glanced at him questioningly.

"If I give you hair ribbons, will you take them? Will you wear them for me?"

Thoughtfully, she laid her head against his shoulder again. He waited for her answer. "Green ones look best in my hair," she said at last, "but nothing too expensive, mind you."

"All right." He kissed the top of her head, thankful for her concession. After all, he had no need to parade his money before the world anymore. He had Emily. That was all the wealth he needed.

The snow had already melted by the next morning when Wade and Emily rode back to the Flying Y. They stayed only long enough for a meal and for Wade to send a cowboy back to the line shack and the cattle. They were surprised to find that Nat hadn't been at the ranch at all, and they began to worry that he might have become lost in the blizzard.

They headed for town to see if Nat had ridden to Holt House. Emily longed to see the children and to share her news with them. And as soon as they found Nat, Wade wanted to talk to the preacher about arranging their wedding.

When they rode up to the carriage house, Sara greeted them from the back porch.

"Is Nat here?" Emily asked.

"I haven't seen him since yesterday when you left with him," Sara said.

More concerned now, Emily hurried into the carriage house, Wade right behind her. Relief flooded through her when she saw Biscuit in his stall munching contentedly on fresh hay.

"Good, he's here," she said, able to smile now.

Wade banged on the door to the bunk room and threw it open without waiting for an invitation.

"Nat!" Emily called. "Nat, we're back. Wade and I are back and . . ."

She stopped in the doorway and surveyed the empty room. It looked as if it had never been lived in, as undisturbed as it had been on that day two months ago when she'd first shown it to Nat. Fresh towels lay folded neatly on the wash stand. The bed clothes lay as smooth and tight as when Emily had first made the bed for Nat.

"It sure doesn't look like anyone's been living here," Wade said, following her into the room.

She stared in disbelief at the kerosene lamp sparkling as clear and bright as if she'd just polished it. "I know I saw the glow of lamplight in the window when Nat retired each night," she said, pointing to the lamp.

"Well, I guess he decided to clean the room before he left. The question is why didn't he say good-bye to us last night." Wade asked, apparently as baffled as she.

Wade gestured toward Nat's harmonica gleaming on the table in the center of the room.

Emily picked up the instrument and turned it over in her hands. Where had Nat gone that he wouldn't take his mouth organ with him? He loved playing it. Or had he left it for her and Wade?

"Oh, Wade, where did he go?" She clutched the harmonica to her chest and closed her eyes. "We have so much to tell him. I wanted to share our good news with him."

The harmonica warmed in her hands as she stood with Wade in the silent, empty room. Suddenly she sensed Nat's presence, almost expecting to see him standing in front of them. She glanced at Wade. "Do you feel it?"

"Yep, like he's here with us," Wade said softly.

"He is. He's an angel, Wade." She looked up at him. "I know he is."

"Angel?" Wade stared at her. "Look, Em, I know Nat's different. Heck, I was sure of it the first time I saw him on Biscuit—but an angel?"

She nodded. "Believe me, Wade. I saw him as he really is yesterday. But even if I hadn't, I'd know it in my heart."

"Well, angel or not, he's gone." Wade sighed.

Saddened, she knew Nat would never return, and realized he had indeed said good-bye to them at the line shack. She and Wade were on their own now.

"Keep the harmonica, Em. I think he wanted you to have it," Wade said.

She put the precious mouth organ in her pocket. It was the only proof that remained of their heavenly visitor, and she knew they would treasure it forever. Whenever life got tough, she would take it out to remind them that their happiness was in being together.

She turned to Wade, and resting her head on his chest, she smiled. She knew that she had found heaven again in his touch, in his arms, and that she had finally come home.

About the Author

Linda Madl is a realistic romantic who believes there is someone for everyone, and that wonderful things do occur. Perhaps they are not miraculous. But they are too good and powerful to have been accomplished by human will alone, such as the fortuitous timing that prevents a fatal car accident, the sudden gift of money just when it is most needed, or a helpful stranger who appears out of nowhere to bring two deserving people together. Such mysterious good deeds, Linda believes, may well be the work of angels.

The author of award-winning short stories, novels, and business magazine articles, Linda enjoys gardening, traveling, and spending time with her family. She currently resides in the Kansas City area with her husband and daughter.

BOBBI SMITH
"A Gift From Heaven"

"Be not forgetful to entertain strangers; for thereby some have entertained angels unawares."
                                                —*Paul to the Hebrews*

Chapter One

Tennessee, 1865

On a late April afternoon, David rode slowly up the tree-lined drive that led to the plantation house. The shady avenue was overgrown with lush spring foliage, and he reined in his mount to savor the peace and solitude. The singing birds and the rustling breeze stirring the trees soothed him. It was a heavenly place, he decided, with a quick, respectful glance upward.

Breathing deeply, he drew on his inner strength, girding himself for the coming days. He kneed his horse, urging him forward. Though the war had ended three weeks ago, he still had work to do here at Riverbend, where sadness lingered so heavily.

His first glimpse of the Randolph plantation was of the pillared two-story house, its white paint peeling, its black shutters missing or askew. It appeared abandoned, lost, lonely. Only the presence of a shabbily dressed, elderly black man working near the front of the house and a few chickens running loose indicated that someone was in residence.

"Now's the time, Harmony," David said softly, and suddenly his horse began to limp badly.

David dismounted, took the reins, and led Harmony toward the old man. "Afternoon, sir. My horse just came up lame, and I wondered if I could camp here for the night."

"You is a Yankee, right?"

David nodded.

"Then it'd be best if you just kept on walkin', mister."

David leveled his gaze at the old man. "Surely you can help me out? My name's David Clark, and I just need a place to stay until my horse's leg heals. It shouldn't be more than a couple of days." His tone was soft yet unwavering.

"Micah?" a woman's voice called from the house.

"Yes, Miz Abbie?"

A young woman appeared on the veranda and came toward the two men. Abbie Randolph was pretty, though thin, with sable hair that was long and wavy, and fair, flawless skin. Her eyes were a brown that could have been warm and beautiful, but when she looked at David, they were hard and wary. She had one hand tucked into the folds of her worn blue cotton dress, and he sensed she might be carrying a gun.

"You having trouble, Micah?" She eyed David suspiciously.

"Afternoon, ma'am," he said cordially, tipping his hat.

"What are you doing here, Yankee?" she demanded. He knew she had heard only his hated Northern accent. He explained Harmony's being lame, concluding, "So I was wondering if I could spend the night?"

"I want you to mount up and get off my land." She started to turn away.

"Believe me, ma'am, there's nothing I'd rather do than move on," he said gently, "but my horse can't go much farther."

She stopped and looked back at him. Their eyes met. She blinked, then stared at him quizzically. "All right. You can camp behind the kitchen, but only for tonight. I expect you to be gone by daybreak."

Micah looked at her in amazement.

"But just remember," she added, "I know how to shoot a gun and I'll use it if I have to."

"You'll get no trouble from me, ma'am. Thank you for your kindness. By the way, my name's David Clark."

"I don't care what your name is. Micah, show him where to camp."

David offered up a silent "hallelujah" that his mission had progressed this far. From what he knew about Abigail Randolph, he had almost expected her to run him off without a thought. It just proved that miracles were possible.

Annoyed with herself, Abbie walked toward the main house. She couldn't imagine what she'd been thinking to let that man stay. Being asked to help a Northerner was more than she should be forced to bear, wasn't it?

In the last four years, everything she'd loved had been destroyed. The Abbie Randolph who'd laughed and danced and flirted, who'd married and planned to bear her husband many children, had died just as surely as if a Yankee had shot her. Now she was angry and bitter and full of hatred for any and all things Northern.

But there had been something in the tall, dark-haired Yankee's blue eyes that had mesmerized her, a look of peace and tranquility that had reached into her very soul. And his soft, soothing voice . . . It had touched her, too, draining away her anger. She shook her head. What had gotten into her . . . thinking about his eyes and voice?

"What is it, Miz Abbie?" Bess stood on the veranda steps, her dark face concerned. "Who is that man and what does he want?"

"A Yankee who needs a place to stay for the

night. His horse is lame."

"You ran him off, didn't you?"

"No."

"No? You lettin' him stay?"

Bess had been with Abbie's family as long as Abbie could remember. Though Bess, her husband Micah, and their six-year-old grandson, Willy, had been freed long ago, they had refused to leave Riverbend. They had witnessed the Yankee army's destruction of the plantation, and shared Abbie's hatred and distrust of them.

"He'll be gone in the morning," Abbie said, staring across the overgrown fields.

"Yes, ma'am."

"You know, Bess, sometimes I think surviving the war was worse than dying in it."

"Miz Abbie! You don't mean that!"

Abbie shrugged. "Look at this place, Bess. The fields are ruined. No matter how hard we work, we can't seem to make any progress. God knows, I've prayed for help, but who is there to help us? Sometimes it all seems so pointless."

Hopelessness and despair overcame her, and she drew a ragged breath. "You know, there are days I can't even remember what Preston looked like." Now, having said those words, she felt as if she'd betrayed her husband, and guilt washed over her.

"Mr. Preston been dead over two years now, Miz Abbie. That's a long time, 'specially with all that's happened 'round here."

"I know. It almost seems as if everything that happened before the war was a dream. That my life then never really existed."

"We gonna be fine, Miz Abbie. I knows it."

"I hope you're right, Bess," Abbie said, but in truth she didn't share her friend's faith in the future. Having to carry her gun whenever a stranger rode up the drive convinced her that nothing would ever be the same. The gentle, gracious life she'd known was gone. Savagery, hunger, and quiet desperation were the war's legacies.

The two women entered the house, and Abbie put Preston's gun on the mantle in the sitting room where she always kept it—close at hand for emergencies, yet high enough to be out of Willy's reach.

David pitched his tent on the spot Micah had shown him, then built a small campfire. As he cooked supper, he thought about the Abbie he'd met today, who bore only a pale physical and emotional resemblance to her former self. This Abbie was filled with anger and nearly consumed by her bitter emotions. He hoped that her allowing him to stay meant that her goodness and generosity were still alive and had only been buried by her pain and heartache.

If Abbie had meant what she'd said about wanting him gone by morning, then he had less than twelve hours to work a miracle. In that brief time, there was no way he could effect the much-needed changes in Abbie's attitude and heart, short of erasing everything that had happened to her during the last four years.

She hated Yankees, believing they were all murderers and thieves. He had to show her that wasn't true and to teach her to forgive, or she would never have any peace or happiness again.

As he ate, he contemplated his next move. Surveying the run-down plantation, he found his answer. Much needed to be done, and here was an opportunity to prove to Abbie the error of her biased judgment of all Yankees.

He worked quietly and efficiently through the night.

Abbie couldn't believe it. That damned Yankee was still there! Hadn't she told him to be gone by morning? Hadn't she told him she didn't want him on her land? Here it was almost eight o'clock and his tent was still pitched!

Furious at his defiance, she stormed from the house, passing the brick outbuilding that housed the kitchen. A basket sat on its doorstep. She stopped, puzzled. Bess would never leave a basket there. Abbie approached it and peered inside. There were five eggs. Where had they come from? The most eggs she and Bess had ever managed to collect were three. She would ask Bess about them later.

Nearing the barn, she stopped again. Beside

the door was a stack of freshly split firewood. Old Micah couldn't have chopped that quantity of wood. What was going on?

Then she heard the sound of an axe and rounded the corner of the barn. A short distance away, the Yankee lifted an axe and brought it down on the log before him, splitting it cleanly in two.

" 'Morning," he called, smiling, and wiped his brow with his forearm.

She stared at him, perplexed. She had wanted to rail at him, to insist that he leave, but his brilliant smile was so disarming that it took her aback. There was no leer in his expression, no threat of any kind. He seemed friendly and warm, and that tempered her fury, confusing her even more.

"I hope you don't mind my doing a few chores," he said. "I wanted to repay you for your gracious hospitality, and this seemed the best way to do it."

"You were supposed to be gone this morning," she pointed out, trying to hold onto her anger.

"Yes, ma'am, but Harmony isn't much better, and I was hoping you wouldn't mind my staying on an extra day or two until he is. If you've got any more work for me, I'll be glad to do it."

Abbie knew that his offer was the answer to her prayers, but this man was a Northerner. He might seem nice enough, but he was probably

just waiting for the chance to steal what little
they had left.

She was struck by the openness in his face as
he returned her regard. She had always considered herself a good judge of character, and at
this moment her instincts told her to trust this
man. Certainly, if he had planned to steal their
few chickens, one cow, and two ancient horses,
he would have done so during the night and
been long gone by now. Instead, he had given
freely of himself, working without being asked,
and that proved he wasn't afraid of hard labor.

She weighed the situation carefully. There
was only so much work she and Micah could do.
Bess was too frail to handle the heavier chores,
and Willy was too young. She scowled. She
hated to admit it, but she needed this man.

"If my being here upsets you, ma'am, I'll go,"
he said, setting the axe aside.

She studied him carefully. "Did you collect
those eggs?"

"Yes, ma'am, I did."

"Where did you get them? Bess and I have
been able to get only two or three a day, and
sometimes not even that." Good Lord, she hoped
he hadn't stolen them during the night from one
of the neighboring plantations.

"I guess we were just blessed this morning to
get so many," he said.

"Blessed? I don't think I'd call us blessed." Her

laugh was short, cynical. "Are you a religious man, Mr. Clark?"

"Of a sort, ma'am. Times like these can turn a person to God."

"Or turn them away," she said. "My name's Mrs. Abigail Randolph. I appreciate what you've done—even if you did steal those eggs. If you need to stay a few more days, you're welcome to." Hardworking or not, it still galled her to be obliging to a Yankee.

"Thank you, ma'am, and just to keep things honest between us, Mrs. Randolph, I don't steal. But I do appreciate your kindness."

She was tempted to tell him she didn't believe him and that she was not being kind, but practical. But she held her tongue.

"Are there any particular jobs you'd like me to do?" he asked.

"I'll have Micah talk to you about it."

Mr. Clark nodded, then picked up the axe and resumed splitting logs. Abbie turned and headed back to the house.

Late that afternoon, dark clouds threatened, and thunder rumbled in the distance. Standing at the kitchen window washing dishes, Abbie saw lightning, and then a heavy rain began to fall. Micah came through the door, already soaked through.

Bess looked up from the vegetables she was peeling. "Where's Willy?"

"He ain't here?"

"No, I thought he was with you. After he brung us this meat for supper"—she gestured to two rabbits on spits over the fire—"he said he was gonna help you and that Yankee with the broken fence."

"He did for a while," Micah answered, "but then he wandered off. I thought he come back here."

Abbie saw worry cloud Bess's face. Micah's brow was furrowed in puzzlement. Now Abbie was worried about the little fellow, too. He had been so excited when he came running into the kitchen, swinging the rabbits Mr. Clark had given him for supper. An adventurous child, he was almost impossible to keep up with some days. She hoped he wasn't lost.

"Well, let's not stand here talking and fretting," she said, hurrying to the door. "Let's go find him."

The storm had worsened, and the torrential rain made it almost impossible to see as Abbie, Bess, and Micah searched the house, the outbuildings, and the barn. But there was no trace of Willy.

Mr. Clark appeared in his rain slicker, hurrying toward them.

"It's Willy," Abbie shouted. "We can't find him. Have you seen him?"

"He was playing in the field near us for a

while," Mr. Clark said. Then he looked off into the distance. "Is there a creek close by?"

"There's one where we was workin'," Micah answered. "Why?"

"Just a hunch. Mrs. Randolph, Bess, you wait here in case he shows up. We'll be back."

With Micah leading the way, they searched the heavily wooded area in the downpour.

Finally, David heard Willy's faint cry for help, and struggling through the slippery undergrowth, he headed in the direction of the little boy's voice. Micah followed close behind him, and they found Willy trapped on the far side of the raging creek, clinging to a tree trunk on the steep, muddy hillside.

"Grampa! David! Help!" Willy screamed, his voice quavering from fear.

"Just hang on, Willy! I'm coming to get you!" David shouted.

Micah put his hand on David's arm. "How you gonna cross that creek? There ain't a man alive who can ford that now."

"Help!" the little boy screamed again, losing his hold on the tree. With nothing to grab onto, he slid down the muddy embankment and into the churning water.

"Willy!" Micah cried.

Unhesitatingly, David charged into the rushing water that pounded at him and Willy, tossing and sweeping them onward. David swam, fighting the current, trying to reach Willy. Though it seemed to take an eternity, he finally snared the boy by the arm and pulled him against his body.

"I could use some help here, Lord," David gasped, struggling to keep his grip on Willy as they were buffeted by the vicious swells.

A bolt of lightning split the sky and exploded as it hit a tree some distance in front of them. As if by heaven's hand, the tree fell into the gushing stream, creating a dam. The water slowed, altering its course long enough for David to grab a branch and propel himself and the boy to dry ground.

"Thanks," David muttered, coughing as he collapsed in exhaustion with the child in his arms. Fighting to catch their breaths, they both shivered.

"Willy?"

"Grampa! We're over here!"

Within minutes Micah was holding the child and hugging him to his heart.

"David saved me, Grampa!" the little boy proclaimed, snuggling in the old man's arms.

"Yes, he did," Micah answered. "David, you all right?"

It was the first time the old man had called him by his name, and David managed a nod as he struggled to sit up. "How's Willy?"

"He's fine." Micah stared at him. "I ain't never gonna forget what you done today. Thank you."

Bobbi Smith

"No, thank God. Well, we'd better hurry and get back. The women must be worried sick."

Abbie and Bess hurried out of the kitchen to meet them.

"What happened?" Bess cried.

"David saved Willy in the creek," Micah told her. "If he hadn't been there, our little fella woulda drowned."

Abbie hustled them into the kitchen to the blazing fire, while Bess hurried to the main house. When she returned with blankets, Abbie helped her drape them over the three drenched males. As they and Bess sat huddled near the fire, Micah related Mr. Clark's incredible rescue.

"Thank you for savin' my grandbaby . . ." Bess said, wiping her eyes. Then she hugged Mr. Clark. "Thank God you was here."

Mr. Clark smiled. "I'm just glad Willy's all right."

Abbie stood quietly in the background, watching the Yankee with Willy, Bess, and Micah. She knew how much the child meant to the elderly couple. After Willy's parents died from fever years ago, Bess and Micah had raised Willy as if he were their own son. He was all they had left in the world.

Suddenly, as if a veil had been lifted from her eyes, she realized she wasn't the only one who had suffered losses during the war, and that Bess and Micah had not allowed their daughter's and their son-in-law's deaths to rob them of joy and happiness. They had gone on—for each other, for Willy, and for her. Had she been self-ish in holding onto her grief, denying her faith-ful friends the best of herself?

She shifted her gaze to Mr. Clark. He had risked his life to save a child he barely knew. A child who meant nothing to him. Why? Why would anyone do something so unselfish? She thought about the kindnesses he had performed during the short time he had been here, and for which he had asked nothing in return. This man was indeed an enigma, and at the first oppor-tunity she was going to learn more about him.

She went to the window and saw that the rain was letting up. David rose and started for the door.

"Where are you going?" she asked.

"The weather's clearing. I thought I'd go back to my tent and change my clothes, then fix something to eat."

"You're not going anywhere," Abbie declared.

"That's right," Bess said. "You stayin' right here by the fire."

"I'll go get your clothes," Micah said. "They in your saddlebag?"

David nodded.

"And then you can eat dinner with us," Abbie added. "I think a celebration is in order tonight."

"Thank you, Mrs. Randolph."

"No, thank *you*, Mr. Clark. If it weren't for

you, life would never have been the same here after today. And please, call me Abbie."

"And I'd be very happy if you'd call me David," he said.

Chapter Two

"Miz Abbie!" Willy's call shattered the quiet afternoon. "Miz Abbie, there's a rider comin' up the drive. It looks like another Yankee!"

Abbie pulled back the red drape of the sitting-room window. A lone blue-uniformed soldier rode toward the house. She swore under her breath. Micah and David were repairing the stretch of damaged fence again, so she was alone. Without hesitation, she went for Preston's gun.

"You think he means trouble?" Bess hurried into the room, nervously rubbing her hands down the sides of her calico skirt.

"You see the color of his uniform, don't you? That alone means trouble," Abbie answered. She stepped onto the veranda, ready to defend herself and her property.

The rider drew near, and she descended the veranda steps. It was one thing to have to deal with David, but to have to endure another Yankee so soon was just too much.

The soldier rode straight up the main path and reined in before her. "Afternoon, ma'am. I wonder if you'd allow me—"

"Get off my land now!" She raised the gun and aimed it straight at his chest.

The soldier stared down at her, then at her weapon, and raised his hands. "Now, ma'am, there's no need for a gun. I'm not here to—"

"There's every need for this gun with men like you wandering around the countryside! Now ride out of here!"

"But all I want—"

"I don't care what you want, Yankee! *I* want you out of here! Get off my property—now!"

When he made no move to leave, she lowered the gun and shot the ground in front of his horse.

The animal reared, throwing the man back and out of his saddle. He landed heavily in the dirt, his hat flying toward her.

She couldn't believe she'd unseated the high-and-mighty Yankee. She stared at him, smiling slightly at her own daring, and waited for him to get up. Her smile faded, though, when he only groaned and then lay still.

Suddenly she realized the soldier was hurt, maybe seriously, and she rushed to his side. She had never deliberately hurt anyone in her entire life, and she was aghast that she might have now—even as angry as she was with this man.

"Lordy, you shot him!" Bess came running up behind her, a stricken look on her face, wringing her hands.

"I didn't shoot him," Abbie said. "He was thrown."

"Is he dead?" Bess asked, staring wide-eyed at the still figure on the ground.

"I hope not. . . . "

They exchanged terrified looks, and at the sound of running feet, Abbie glanced past Bess. David, Micah, and Willy ran toward them.

David reached them first. "Abbie, what happened?"

"I fired and his horse threw him. He's alive, but unconscious. We'd better get him inside so Bess and I can tend to him."

"You gonna let a Yankee in the house?" Micah said. "But you swore on Mr. Preston's grave that no Yankee would ever set foot in the house again."

David looked at her, and his penetrating gaze made her feel she owed him an explanation. It was odd. She had never before felt the need to justify her behavior.

"Two years ago a Yankee captain and his men were quartered here. They took everything we

365

had. And what Micah says is true."

"Who you think he is and where he come from?" Bess asked.

"I have no idea," Abbie replied, thinking it strange that a Yankee soldier had shown up here. Why wasn't he on his way home, wherever that was? She wondered what he was after as she stooped to pick up his blue hat. There was nothing left to steal. Other Yankee soldiers had already stripped the plantation of everything of value.

"This man is also a captain," David said, answering Bess's question and pointing to the soldier's uniform. "I'll take him to my tent and see to him."

Abbie looked into David's kind, compassionate eyes. Well, if he could save Willy, a total stranger to him, then she supposed she could save this man—even if he was a Yankee, and a captain at that.

She squared her shoulders. "That won't be necessary, David. We'll put him in the upstairs front bedroom."

David and Micah carefully lifted the Yankee officer and carried him into the house and up the stairs. Abbie followed, Bess and Willy trailing behind her into the foyer.

"You really tried to shoot him, Miz Abbie?" Willy looked up at her, his eyes wide.

"I didn't shoot him. I just fired a warning shot.

I wanted him to leave. It isn't my fault he can't control his horse," she said, twirling the hat.

"But what if he dies?" Bess asked.

"He might have a bit of a headache when he comes around, but he's not going to die. I'm not that lucky."

"I hope you right." Bess shook her head, frowning. "They might hang you if anythin' happens to him."

Abbie put her hand on Bess's arm. "I'm not going to be hanged, but we'd better see what we can do for him. I want him out of here as soon as possible. Please bring me some water and towels."

Bess hurried off and took Willy with her. Abbie looked up the staircase, dreading facing the stranger. She wanted nothing to do with this man. His very presence brought back all the pain, the loss, the misery, the loneliness. She wished he'd never come here, but wishing didn't change anything. She knew that all too well.

Gripping the banister, she sighed deeply, then started up the stairs. She would endure this, just as she had endured everything else life had thrown her way.

In the front bedroom, the captain lay face-down on the bed, naked to the waist. Abbie stood in the doorway, staring at his broad, heavily muscled back and shoulders. He looked so vulnerable, so harmless, and that disturbed her.

David and Micah stood beside the bed.

David said, "There's a cut on the back of his head and quite a bump forming, but other than that he looks all right. We took his shirt off. It was torn and bloody."

She crossed the room and joined him at the captain's bedside, tossing the hat on the nearby table. "I sent Bess to get what I need to treat him," she said. "I hope he's not out too long. I want him to leave today."

"But he might not be fit to travel."

"I don't care. He's a vile, miserable Yankee, and what happens to him is of no concern to me."

"I see. And what about *this* vile, miserable Yankee?" he asked, pointing to himself. "I suppose you don't want me in your house, either, to help you with the captain when he does wake up?"

When she didn't answer, David looked at her, and she squirmed under his scrutiny.

"So that's the way it is. Well, I'm no different from him, nor are you, nor is anyone else, and the faster you learn that, Abbie, the happier you'll be."

Bess bustled into the room, effectively halting anything Abbie might have said in her defense.

David and Micah headed for the door. "We'll wait downstairs," David said. He turned and glanced back at her. "If you need anything," he added, his tone matter-of-fact, "just call."

Abbie didn't argue. David's voice held such authority that she didn't dare. She dropped a towel in the water basin, wrung it out, and began to wipe the blood from the captain's neck and shoulders.

As she bathed him, she noticed a freshly healed scar on his side and wondered how he'd been wounded. When she cleansed the blood from his head wound, she saw that though it was deep, it was not serious.

"What we gonna do now, Miz Abbie?" Bess asked when they finished doctoring him.

"There's not much we can do but wait for him to wake up." Abbie rested her hand on his back and felt the reassuring slow, steady rhythm of his breathing. Thank God, he would be all right.

"I'll take these things downstairs and throw away his shirt," Bess said. "Then I'll come sit with you." She hurried out, leaving the door open.

Abbie positioned a chair near the window, angling it to face the bed. She tried not to stare at the captain, but her gaze was drawn to the powerful width of his shoulders, to the hard line of his jaw, to his shiny black hair. If she didn't hate him so much, she might have thought him handsome, but this man was her enemy.

She had been forced to suffer the Yankees' presence when they had headquartered at Riverbend for weeks, disrupting her life and terrorizing her. Pregnant at the time, she had lost her baby, and then her husband had died fighting to save a way of life she'd never know again.

Oh, she hated this man all right, and everything he stood for. The war was over now, and she didn't have to tolerate the likes of him ever again!

She didn't realize how deeply she had been engrossed in her thoughts until she felt Bess sit down next to her.

Together they kept a silent vigil, waiting for the Yankee to regain consciousness.

The pounding in his head was enough to set his teeth on edge, and Gage moaned as he struggled to open his eyes.

He lay facedown on the softest bed he'd slept on in years. "What the . . ." he muttered in confusion.

He started to push himself up, but waves of pain and nausea overcame him. He groaned again and sank back on the bed, closing his eyes, trying to remember what had happened to him. The pain made it hard to think straight, but gradually it all came back. He'd reached a plantation; a beautiful woman spoke to him; then there was a damned gun. . . .

He swore violently under his breath and opened his eyes. The room blurred, making him feel even worse, so he quickly shut his eyes again.

"Captain?"

He recognized the sound of the woman's

voice, her soft Southern drawl. "What?" he snapped.

"You're better?"

"Better than what? My head is killing me. What were you trying to do, woman?"

"Please, sir, do not refer to me as 'woman.' My name is Mrs. Abigail Randolph and I do apologize. I did not mean to hurt you. But my being sorry about your accident changes nothing. I still want you gone from Riverbend. You have no right to be here."

He turned his head toward the sound of her voice and opened one eye to focus on her. She sat primly across the room from him, a black slave beside her. Probably her mammy, he thought, disgusted. The young woman was beautiful in her rose dress, her sable hair pulled back with a matching ribbon. But he was in no mood to appreciate anything about this spoiled Southern belle.

"My 'accident'?" he repeated sarcastically. "You think my horse reared by accident?"

"It was unfortunate that you were thrown, sir, but now that you're feeling better, you may leave."

He would have liked nothing more than to do just that. If his company hadn't gotten caught in that skirmish two weeks ago, he'd have been well on his way to St. Louis and then on home to his family in Boston. "You're right. Thanks for your Southern hospitality," he said angrily,

371

swinging his legs over the side of the bed.

He felt a twinge in his side and held it, but he still managed to sit up. But the movement cost him dearly. The pounding in his head intensified, and he was forced to lean forward and rest his head in his hands. But he'd be damned if he would let this hard-hearted woman know just how badly he was hurt.

"Captain." The woman touched his shoulder, pressing him back onto the mattress.

He resisted her effort. He had no desire to be anywhere near this cold, contemptuous woman. Her land, her slaves, her way of life were all she cared about. It was her kind that had started the war, and the farther away from her he got, the better.

"I'm getting out of here," he declared, trying to ignore her hand on his bare skin.

He pushed to his feet. All at once his head felt as if it would split open, and his side ached. The room spun, and nauseating dizziness swept over him. Losing his balance, he staggered.

In the next moment Mrs. Randolph had her arm around his waist and the black woman was on his other side to help support him. Holding him, the women lowered him to the bed.

"It looks like you're staying right here, Captain," Mrs. Randolph said.

"Like hell I am."

"Unfortunately, you're in no condition to ride, so you might as well just accept it."

"I'd rather accept it somewhere my hostess doesn't want to shoot me."

"I didn't shoot you—although I was tempted. I just wanted you to leave."

He closed his eyes against the sharp, unrelenting pain pounding in his head. "You didn't give me time."

"Two seconds would have been too much time. Just who are you, and why are you even here? You know we hate your kind around here."

"I'm Captain Gage Morgan. My company was headed to St. Louis when we got ambushed by some Rebs. I was separated from my men and got lost. I stopped here to ask for some food and to rest for a couple of hours before I continued on my journey."

"Well, you're welcome to what little food we have and you will get as much rest as you need to heal. In a way, I suppose your being delayed is my fault, so it's the least I can do."

"You're right. I would have been well on my way if it hadn't been for you," he snarled, still keeping his eyes shut.

"Well, let me take another look at your head—"

"Just leave me alone. I don't want any Rebel putting her hands on me."

"Then Bess and I will leave you to heal on your own, Captain."

"Good. At least if I'm alone, I'll know no one is trying to shoot me."

"If you need anything—"

"The only thing I need is a new head."

He heard the two women leave the room.

Gage lay in bed, cursing his own idiocy for stopping at Riverbend. He had been a fool to think any Southerner would have greeted him with open arms. But he had been tired, having traveled for two weeks, watching his back, trying to avoid any more confrontations with Rebels who were also returning home. The war might have ended, but hostility and hatred still ran high.

They certainly did in this house. Obviously the war wasn't over for the beautiful Mrs. Randolph, who wore her animosity like armor, and still had slaves working her plantation. Yet he had to admit she was one brave woman. There weren't many females who would pull a gun on a Union officer.

He grimaced, remembering the gun aimed at his chest, and hoped his head injury wouldn't keep him stuck here for any length of time. He couldn't wait to leave.

Chapter Three

David sat outside his tent in the predawn light gazing up at the heavens. Stars twinkled and a sliver of moon hung low on the horizon. It had been a beautiful night, and he'd been awake for most of it, worrying. Abbie had not asked him to stay in the house, and he had left after her assurances that Gage was resting quietly.

David had been disappointed by her rejection, but had consoled himself that at least Abbie and he were now on a first-name basis, and that she had allowed him to stay—small victories, to be sure. And when she had asked him why he had returned to the South, he had hoped his story would show her that all Yankees weren't heartless, destructive warmongers.

So he had told her his relatives in Georgia needed help and that he was headed there when Harmony became lame. She had been amazed at his wanting to help his Southern relatives, and her disbelief made him realize that he had a lot more work to do convincing her that all Yankees weren't "vile" and "miserable." And that Gage Morgan, in particular, was a good man, even if she was determined to shoot him first and ask questions later. It was a positive sign that the captain was still here, but she could easily have killed him yesterday afternoon.

Patience and fortitude were needed, but it wasn't going to be easy helping Abbie learn to forgive. Hatred was a powerful emotion; he could think of only one emotion that was stronger—love. Somehow he had to show her that love could conquer all, that only love could erase the pain of bitterness and hate.

Staring up at the sky, he thought of Gage and wondered if he could also be healed and taught to open his heart and soul again to beauty and love. Well, time would tell.

A falling star streaked across the heavens in a brilliant arc, and he smiled, encouraged.

As the eastern skies brightened, David washed and changed his clothes, then started toward the house. There had been no disturbance during the night, and he was anxious to find out how Gage was. He met Micah near the kitchen.

"Everything all right last night?" he asked the old man.

"It was quiet. I guess Captain Morgan slept a lot. I was just up there helpin' him wash and get dressed, and he was still dizzy."

"Do you think he's strong enough to leave today?"

"I don't know. He seems a mite weak. Bess and Miz Abbie took some food to him. We'll have to see what Miz Abbie thinks when she comes down. Do you want to check on him yourself?"

"I think I will."

As David entered the house, Abbie and Bess were coming down the stairs. Abbie looked unhappy.

"Good morning, David," she greeted him cheerily, her whole demeanor changing when she saw him.

"Good morning," he answered, smiling. "How's the captain today? Is he well enough to talk to me?"

"He's still unsteady on his feet and has a headache, but I don't see any reason why you can't visit with him."

"Fine. I'll only be a few minutes."

David went up to the bedroom and knocked lightly on the open door. He could see Gage sitting in the chair by the window, his saddlebag propped against the wall near him. The captain was no longer wearing his uniform pants, but had on black ones and a white shirt. Well, things

377

were better than David had thought. Abbie had given Gage some of her husband's clothes.

Gage turned at the sound of the knock.

"Captain Morgan, I'm Corporal David Clark. Mind if I come in?"

"Not at all. Corporal?" Gage was puzzled. The man wore no uniform, and though he sounded like a Northerner, Gage wondered which side he'd really fought on.

"I rode with Sherman before I was mustered out," Clark offered.

"Then why are you back in the South?"

"I came to help my relatives in Georgia rebuild their plantation. But my horse went lame a few days ago, and Abbie is letting me stay on until he's healed. What about you? How'd you end up at Riverbend?"

Gage looked at the corporal and realized that the man must have ridden day and night from St. Louis after mustering out to have arrived so quickly in Tennessee. No wonder his horse had come up lame.

"My company was heading to St. Louis to muster out, but we ran into some Rebs who were probably on their way home, too. During the skirmish I was separated from my men and got lost. I stopped here for food and some rest."

Noticing that Clark looked well fed and rested, Gage asked, "Didn't Mrs. Randolph try to run you off?"

Clark grinned. "She didn't take a shot at me, if that's what you mean, but I know she wasn't happy to see me when I first arrived."

"That makes two of us." Gage was surprised that the woman had let a Yankee stay for any length of time.

"So, how's your head? You were bleeding pretty heavily," Clark said.

"It's still attached, but there have been a few times in the last twelve hours that I wished otherwise."

"You took a nasty fall, but it could have been a lot worse."

"I know. And with any luck, I should be strong enough to ride out tomorrow, or the day after at the latest."

"Well, I hope you recover quickly."

"Thanks, Corporal."

"Call me David, sir. The war's over."

"And I'm Gage. But you may be wrong about the war."

"What do you mean?"

"The generals may say the war is over, but for some people it never will be."

"It is difficult to forgive and forget," David said, "but we have to try."

"I know, but sometimes the pain is so terrible it's impossible to forget." Memories of Gage's men dying around him in battle returned. The war had been so long and so violent. How many families had been torn apart? How many children had been left without fathers? Wives with-

379

out husbands? Mothers without sons?

The ugly senselessness of it all angered Gage. His men—his trusted sergeant, his friends—were dead. He doubted he could ever forget their screams as they lay fatally wounded.

"We'll just have to work harder to create peace—within ourselves and others," David said.

Intrigued by his words, Gage glanced back at David, and for an instant, brilliant sunshine shone through the window and bathed the man in a radiant glow. Then, as quickly as it had come, the light was gone.

Gage frowned and looked outside to see if a cloud had overshadowed the sun, but the sky was clear. Strange, he thought, then dismissed it, deciding his injury had affected his vision more than he had realized. Everything had been slightly out of focus since his fall. "You're right," he said, "but sometimes creating peace is easier said than done."

"We have to at least try to show others by our example how good life can be once we forgive our enemies."

"I don't know how I'll be able to convince anyone else, when I can't forgive or forget myself." Why was he confiding his deepest feelings to this man who was a stranger, but who, for some reason, inspired his trust?

"Start by helping her," David said, looking out

the window. "She's lost so much—a husband and a son."

Gage followed the direction of David's gaze and watched the lovely young woman as she called for someone named Willy to come in for breakfast.

"Well, I have to go," David said. "I'm sure Micah's waiting for me to get back to work. Glad to see you're on the mend, Gage. I'll come see you again later."

"How did Captain Morgan seem to you?" Abbie asked David. They had finished breakfast and she had followed him outside to speak with him privately.

"He's still weak, but he'll be fine."

"How soon do you think he'll be able to leave?"

"Not for at least another day or two," David answered. "Are you worried about him being here? Has he done something I should know about?"

"No . . ." she admitted.

"I would have been surprised if he had. He seems like a good man, but if you need me, just send Willy to find me. I'll be working on the barn with Micah today."

It had been so long since she'd had anyone strong to rely on that Abbie smiled at him. Somehow, just talking to David made things seem better and lightened her spirit. "Thank you." She touched his arm.

He returned her smile. "I'm glad I can help you. After all, that's what really matters—that we care about each other. Now, I'd better catch up with Micah or I'll be hearing about it."

Abbie watched him walk away, feeling more peaceful than she had in a long time. She glanced back at the house, saw that no one was looking for her, and happy that she could slip off for a while, headed toward a grove a short distance away.

It was warm walking in the sunshine, but as soon as she reached the shade of the trees, she felt cool. There, sheltered in the center of the copse, was the family cemetery.

She walked to the newest headstone and knelt beside the grave of her son, the baby she had never had the chance to love or cherish. "Preston Randolph, Jr.," the marker read. She'd had it placed next to Preston's stone, which she'd erected when she'd been notified of his death.

She lingered, thinking of the past and remembering the dreams she'd had for the future. She had been young and innocent then. Now it seemed so long ago. Her dreams were lost to her forever, and there was nothing left of her former life.

Drawing a ragged breath, she touched the grave marker lightly, lovingly. Memories of the night of blood and pain, of that Yankee captain finding her where she'd fallen, of the loss of her son, and of the following morning when she had been alone . . . so very alone . . . were seared in her mind.

Slowly, almost painfully, as if weighed down by her past, she stood. All that matters is that we care about each other, David had said, and she knew it was true. But it was so hard to care about anything or anyone when the world was such an ugly place. The Yankees had killed her husband, invaded her home, and ravaged her land, and the pain of those losses had a stranglehold on her heart and soul. She wondered if she would ever be free of it.

Gage sat staring out the window, his conversation with David playing in his mind. David's words of having to work harder to create peace were all well and good. But David's suggestion that Gage start by helping Abbie wouldn't work. He wasn't wanted here. Abbie's shooting at him had been all the proof he'd needed.

Suddenly he realized he was thinking of her as Abbie now, and not as Mrs. Randolph. He would still address her as that when speaking to her, but in his mind she was Abbie—strong, courageous Abbie who, as David had said, had survived the loss of her husband and son.

Gage told himself that thinking of her that way was insane. She was courageous, all right. Courageous enough to run him off with a gun. She harbored no love for any Yankee.

That thought reminded him of seeing Abbie

coming out of the house earlier today with David. They had been too far away for him to hear them, but he could see them clearly. He noticed right away that Abbie acted differently toward the corporal than she did with Gage. When she looked up at David, she appeared awed, as if she were hanging on his every word. She smiled at him and even touched his arm in a gesture that indicated trust and intimacy. There was no trace of coldness or hostility. Rather, she seemed to like David. And he was a Yankee!

Angry, Gage scowled. She never smiled at him, spoke to him only when necessary, but he quickly realized he was being foolish. What did he care how Abbie treated David? She was nothing to Gage. And he would be gone from this house just as soon as he was physically able.

Late that afternoon, Gage still sat thinking about Abbie. Before he left, he should try at least to summon up some civility to thank her for tending to him.

When he looked up, he was startled to see a little black boy watching him from the doorway. Gage hadn't heard the child come into the room.

"Hello," Gage said, smiling.

"Hi, I'm Willy." The child moved easily toward the bed and jumped up on it as if he owned it, then bounced up and down a few times.

"Well, it's nice to meet you, Willy. I heard Mrs.

Randolph call you for breakfast this morning.
I'm Gage Morgan."

"I heard David and my grandpa say you is a
Yankee captain." Willy stared at him with open
interest.

"Yes, I am."

"So's David a Yankee, but he says he ain't no
captain. He's my friend. He saved me from
drownin' in the creek."

"How'd he do that?"

"I fell in when it was real high, and he jumped
in and got me out. He was real brave. Now even
Miz Abbie likes David. How come she don't like
you?"

Gage managed a slight smile at the child's
honesty. "I think it's because I'm a Yankee."

"That don't make no sense. I bet she'd like you
if you helped her like David does. He works
hard. Are you gonna help her when you feel better?"

"Are you sure Miz Abbie wants my help?"
Gage asked, an idea forming in his mind. It
might be a way of thanking her.

"Sure. She wants mine all the time. That's why
I'm up here," he said in an exaggerated whisper.
"I'm hidin' from Miz Abbie so I don't have to
work."

"Think she'll find you?"

Willy giggled conspiratorially. "I hope not.
You got a pretty horse. I petted him today. All
we got are two old nags. My gramma says that

before the war, Mr. Preston and Miz Abbie had lots of fine horses, but they don't anymore."

"I'm glad you like Rogue. I've had him for many years."

"Rogue's his name?" Willy asked. Gage nodded. "I like that name!"

"There you are!" Abbie stopped at the open bedroom door. "Your grandma and I have been looking all over the house for you, you rascal!" She entered the room and picked up Gage's luncheon tray from the table beside him. "I hope Willy hasn't been bothering you," she said coolly to Gage.

"Not at all. He's good company."

"Captain Gage gonna help us just as soon as he's better!" Willy said excitedly, and hopped down from the bed.

"Really? Well, you go on downstairs now." Abbie shot Gage a quick glance as the little boy left the room. Then she turned to leave.

Gage touched her hand to detain her. "I'd like to stay and help you out if you'll let me."

"Why?" The word was little more than a whisper, and he saw her hands tighten on the tray. "I shot at you. Why would you want to stay?"

"You didn't have to take care of me, but you did, and I'm indebted to you. I always pay my debts."

"That's not necessary, Captain. Besides, you're not strong enough to do anything yet, and you might reinjure yourself."

"I think I'm healed . . . though there are some wounds that never heal," he said softly, not letting go of her hand.

"I know, and there are some losses that can never be forgotten and shouldn't be."

Their gazes locked, his eyes searching hers, wary and cautious.

"You're right," he said solemnly, memories of what he'd seen and done in the war haunting him. "We can't change the past."

Silently, they stared at each other, and suddenly he wanted to caress her warm hand.

"Miz Abbie! Gramma says she needs you downstairs!"

Willy's call, followed by the sound of his footsteps as he charged back up the staircase, shattered the fragile moment between them.

Red-faced, Abbie snatched her hand from his and started to flee the room.

"Abbie? Is it all right if I call you that?"

She glanced back at him, her eyes wide, and slowly nodded.

"Good. Then how about a truce, Abbie?"

She left the room quickly without answering him. Gage wondered if she ever would.

Chapter Four

Abbie woke to Gage's harsh, pain-filled cry and bolted from her bed. Fearing something terrible had happened to him, she unlocked her bedroom door and, without putting on her dressing gown, hurried down the hall to the front bedroom.

She threw wide his bedroom door. "Captain Morgan! Are you all right?"

He sat up in the bed, staring wildly, his gaze traveling around the moonlit room. He appeared disoriented, confused. Sweat ran down his face and his body trembled.

"What . . ." he croaked.

He looked so tormented that she hurried to his bedside.

"Gage . . ." His name slipped from her lips in a hoarse whisper as she bent and touched his cheek to check for fever. "What is it? What's wrong?"

"There was nowhere to go . . . They had us pinned down . . . We had to fight . . . or die . . ." He shut his eyes, shook his head slightly, and shuddered.

She sat on the bed "Gage . . . It's over. It's finished. You're safe now." She spoke softly, soothingly, trying to break the grip of his terrifying nightmare.

"Abbie . . ." He stared at her as if seeing her for the first time. "Abbie . . ." He leaned toward her and his lips sought hers, gently, tentatively.

She did not move, surprised at the pleasurable sensation of his soft lips on hers, and when his kiss deepened, she reacted instinctively, returning his embrace with equal abandon. It had been so long since she'd known a man's touch, so long since she'd been held in the safety of a man's arms. But this man? Her enemy?

Confused, shocked by her willingness to surrender to him, she broke free and rose from the bed. He was watching her, his gaze unfathomable, making her nervous and uncertain. What had she been thinking of? How could she have kissed him so passionately?

"I'd better go," she managed, retreating a few steps. She felt her face flush hot with embarrassment and the realization of what could have happened between them. "I'm sorry."

"No, I'm sorry, and in more ways than one."
He smiled ruefully.

"I shouldn't have come in here, but when I
heard your cry—"

His expression darkened. "I didn't mean to
disturb you." His eyes filled with sudden pain.

"You were having a terrible dream. Would it
help you to talk about it?"

"War is horrible," he said harshly, "and my
men and I have seen a lot of it in the past few
years."

Then, like dammed-up water finally released,
his words rushed from him, and he spoke of his
last battle, of the horror of watching his men
mown down like blades of grass, dying all
around him, and of his powerlessness to stop the
carnage.

"Is that when you were wounded?" she asked,
staring at the scar on his side.

"Yes, and there have been times when I
wished I had died with my men that day. Nearly
half of us died."

"But you won."

"Did we? Does anyone win in war?" He raised
a tortured gaze to her. "And at what cost? For
what? There was no need for all those good men
on both sides to die."

She stared into the depths of eyes that were
filled with all the pain and sorrow he hid so well.
It had never occurred to her that he might bear

the scars of emotional wounds just as she did. Suddenly she saw clearly that he was not gloating over the South's defeat, but that he thought winning the war was an empty victory and grieved at the loss of Northern and Southern lives alike. She had seen him only as a much-hated conqueror and herself as the ill-fated conquered. But now she saw him as just a man, a man who felt pain, a man who knew the torture of losing people he cared about.

She wanted to erase the haunted desperation in his eyes, but she controlled the impulse. To touch him again would be a mistake.

"Gage," she said softly. "I wish we could say the last four years never happened, but we can't. We both have to find a way to go on with our lives."

"It's not going to be easy."

"No, it's not. It's going to take years, maybe generations, but we have to start."

"Do you think we can?" he asked, his gaze holding hers.

She felt uncomfortable. It seemed he was looking into the very depths of her soul and knew the insights she had gained. She shifted her gaze. "We have our truce, don't we? And that's a beginning. Now, get some sleep."

Gage watched her leave the room, her white nightgown a flowing caress on her slender body, clinging to her breasts, her small waist, her curvaceous hips. The heady scent of her fragrance still lingered in the room, heightening his sensual awareness of her. She had been soft and feminine and desirable, and kissing her had made him burn for her. Admitting that he wanted her unnerved him, as did the realization that she had been as aroused as he.

He got out of bed and began to pace, raking his hand through his hair. He went to the window. The night was clear and starry, the crescent moon lighting the lawn and distant fields. He stared out the window for a long time, waiting for his tension and desire to ease.

At least he had gotten one thing he had wanted. She had accepted their truce, though any false move on his part could break it. He knew what he had to do. He could not remain in this house. She was a widow and alone with him, and he would do nothing to compromise her reputation.

He put on the clothes she had given him, which he presumed had belonged to her dead husband, then gathered his uniform, hat, and saddlebag and quietly left the room. For a long moment he stood in the hall outside her bedroom. After one last longing look at the closed door, he left the house.

Considering last night's excitement, Abbie was surprised she'd slept so soundly and felt so rested . . . and, well, wonderful. As she bathed and then took extra time with her hair, she realized that Gage's grief and despair had forced her to face certain truths that had lightened her heart. She even hummed a tune she hadn't thought of in years as she emerged from her bedroom.

Moving down the hall, she saw that Gage's bedroom door was closed and assumed he was still asleep. She smiled and went downstairs to the kitchen, where Bess was fixing breakfast.

"Good morning," Abbie greeted her cheerfully.

The older woman shot her a puzzled look. "You sound mighty happy this mornin'."

Abbie gazed out the doorway at the cloudless blue sky and the sun shining clear and bright. "I *am* happy this beautiful morning. Have you checked on Gage?"

"Gage? You mean Captain Morgan?"

"Yes, is he better this morning?"

"I don't know, Miz Abbie, but I guess he was."

"Was? What do you mean?"

"He's gone. I went up to look in on him and the room was empty. He's gone and so are all of his things."

"He left?" Abbie stared at Bess. A multitude of conflicting emotions battled within her, but her anger won out.

How could he have gone, and in the middle of the night? That miserable hypocrite! That ungrateful wretch! All those high and noble words about the war, about his always paying his debts, had been just—words! Wasn't it just like a Yankee to take and give nothing in return! Was this his idea of a truce? To sneak off without so much as a thank-you or a good-bye? And he'd had the nerve to kiss her! Thank heaven she hadn't let things go any further!

"I don't know why he didn't wait until mornin'," Bess said. "Willy told us last night that Captain Morgan was plannin' on stayin' and helpin' out like David. I wonder why he changed his mind."

Abbie sat down at the table. "I don't know." She would never see that awful man again, and that was just fine with her.

The sound of Micah's voice came from outside. Abbie groaned. She was in no mood for making small talk. Right now, she just wanted to be left alone.

Micah came in, followed by David.

"We brung another hungry man to breakfast this mornin'," Micah announced, smiling broadly.

Abbie looked up, wondering what he was talking about. Behind Micah stood Gage, his hat in his hands. Her heart skipped a beat and her breath caught in her throat. She almost smiled brightly in welcome, but caught herself. How could she have been so angry when she thought he had gone, and be so excited now to find he was still here?

"Good morning, Abbie." Gage smiled.

Abbie saw Bess and Micah exchange glances at his use of her first name. She became infuriated at his casualness.

"Well, Captain Morgan, what a surprise," she said tightly. "Bess and I thought you had ridden off in the middle of the night."

Gage stared at her. "No, ma'am," he answered. "I told you I always pay my debts, so I'll be staying to help out for a while. Since I was feeling better, I thought it would be best if I moved into the barn. It isn't proper for me to stay in the house since you're a lady and alone."

"You mean you decided to act the gentleman?" she said sarcastically. His saying he'd moved out because he cared about her reputation angered her even more, because she didn't believe a word of it. Why hadn't he discussed it with her last night? She knew the answer to that. He'd moved out because after she left his room, he realized he'd made a mistake kissing her, that he couldn't stand to be around her. Hadn't he said he didn't want a Rebel touching him?

"Abbie?" He glanced at her, a puzzled look on his face. "I hope you don't mind my joining all of you for breakfast."

"You're welcome to breakfast, Captain Morgan, but frankly, I have no desire to sit at the same table with you."

"Miz Abbie, you don't mean that! Sit down, chile, and have somethin' to eat," Bess urged.

"Oh, I mean it all right," Abbie bit out. "Have you forgotten that men like him took over this house and all but ran us out of it? His army took our food and our livestock! We're lucky we're still alive. God knows Preston isn't . . . or my son!"

Unable to bear the rage and humiliation coursing through her, she turned and fled the kitchen.

Slowly, Gage rose from his chair, his face hot from his humiliation. His anger barely controlled, he excused himself and quickly headed for the main house. He was going to get to the bottom of her outburst now, damn it. After all, he had left the house last night for her sake, not his. He had tried to do the right thing and instead got blamed for everything the war had done to her. Well, she wasn't going to get away with it.

Angrily he stormed through the back door and marched down the hall. He heard movement in the sitting room and looked in. Abbie stood near the mantle, her back to him.

"Abbie?"

She spun around, her dark eyes flashing fire, and her hand tightened on the gun that lay on the mantle.

"How dare you enter my home uninvited, you pompous, arrogant miscreant!"

"So now we're going to insult each other, are

we? All right, then. You, madam, are nothing but a cosseted, spoiled Southern belle who can no longer depend on the servitude of others, like your slaves, to make you happy and wealthy. So you're miserable and blaming it on everyone else."

"Slaves? What on earth are you talking about?"

"Bess, and Micah, and Willy," he answered.

She glared at him, her eyes narrowed. "Why, you smug hypocrite! They are *not* my slaves. They and all our slaves were freed years ago. Micah, Bess, and Willy chose to stay with me. They are my family."

She had cornered him with that one, but he wasn't about to admit defeat yet. "Oh, and I suppose that before your slaves were freed, your husband never beat any of them, or broke up their families, or sold any of them?"

She stiffened. "What right do you have to speak of my husband that way? As a matter of fact, he did none of those things. Preston was a good man, a real Southern gentleman. But then, what would a Yankee know about being a gentleman?" She sneered and looked away from him.

Gage, his anger now turned to rage, strode across the room, grabbed her arm, and spun her around. "I'll tell you what I know about it. A gentleman repays his debts, which I intend to do, and he does not sleep in the same house with an unchaperoned, widowed lady. But I obviously made a mistake, for you, madam, are no lady."

He dropped her arm. He could see the hurt and humiliation in her startled gaze. Well, she'd had it coming. She had hurt and insulted him, too. And he wasn't through with her yet. She was going to face the truth about him and herself whether she liked it or not.

"Madam, the war is over. I can't bring your husband or your child back to life, and you can't return my dead friends to me or the years I lost with my family. The lives we led don't exist anymore. The sooner you realize things will never be the same, the sooner you can get on with your life. The choice is up to you, but I'll be damned if I'll take responsibility for every injustice and hardship you've suffered. I've suffered, too, but I'm not going to live the rest of my life blaming the entire South for it."

Abbie heard Gage stalk from the sitting room, and when the door slammed, she swayed, her fingers loosening around the gun. Tears streamed down her cheeks, and gripping the mantle, she shook with grief and anger. How dare he hurl those awful words at her, accuse her of being spoiled? Hadn't she gone without food, saving her portions for Willy? Hadn't she worked the fields with Micah, and tried to scratch out a vegetable garden, so they would have food? She had the calluses to prove it.

He'd said he'd suffered, too. Well, that much was true. She'd seen the evidence of that for herself last night. But what right did he have to speak to her about getting on with her life! How could she without her beloved Preston?

She moved from the fireplace and sat limply on the rose satin settee, her head against a pink fringed pillow. She closed her eyes, letting her anger slowly seep from her body.

As her tension eased, the memory of the intimate thoughts they had shared, of the opening of her heart, of the excitement of Gage's kiss, flooded her mind. She felt guilty, guilty that she had gone days without thinking of Preston, and that she had begun to accept and to forgive their enemy.

She wiped her wet face with the back of her hand. It was true she hadn't believed Gage's reason for moving out of the house, and once again had transferred her own prejudice to him. Grudgingly she realized that Gage was right. She couldn't continue to blame him for her suffering and pain, but she wasn't prepared to concede that to him yet. She needed more time to accept the painful changes that were creating such havoc inside her heart and soul.

But there was one thing she could do, and that was to allow him to stay, proving to him that she was a lady, a Southern lady, who would honor his desire to repay her.

Chapter Five

David gladly labored alone on the fence across
the field from the main house, for he had a lot
of thinking to do. In all his time of helping hu-
mans he had never met two more stubborn people than Abbie and Gage.

In the three weeks since Gage had recovered
and since his and Abbie's argument, the pair had
hardly spoken to each other. Their tentative attempts at civility and respect had deteriorated
to the point where Abbie avoided Gage as much
as possible and spoke to him, if at all, curtly and
coldly. Even so, several times David had caught
her watching Gage with troubled curiosity
rather than anger, and she hadn't asked him to
leave.

When David thought about Gage, he became even more frustrated. Obviously, Gage cared about Abbie, but why the man couldn't see it himself was a mystery. He barely spoke to her. Day after day he worked side-by-side with David and Micah to fix the place up for her, and night after night he quietly bedded down in the barn. He made no effort to seek her out or make amends. David was afraid that soon Gage would just ride off without a word, never realizing what he'd lost until it was too late.

Wearily, David stood and rubbed his neck. He wondered how much influence he could really have on two obstinate, proud people who were blind to the truth. He lifted his gaze heavenward.

I don't know which is more wearisome—hard physical labor or trying to do Your work with two of the most hard-headed people ever born.

A shimmer of light played over him, and he smiled.

"David!"

Willy's distant call interrupted his silent exchange, and he looked up and saw the boy running toward him.

"Hi, Willy." He was happy to see the youngster who had come to mean so much to him. "What brings you out here?"

"I was just watchin' the horses for a while, but then I saw you. . . . " His eyes were big and round with wonderment. "What were you doin'?"

"Thinking," he answered simply, not wanting to say too much.

"About what?"

"God and the war and things."

Willy looked thoughtful. "You looked kinda different. There was a light shinin' on you. Where'd it come from?"

"Inside me. You have it, too."

"I do?"

"Sure. Sometimes, when good things happen, don't you feel happy and want to laugh?"

Willy nodded earnestly.

"Well, when you feel that way, your happiness shines through you. Hey, you want to be the answer to one of my prayers? How about giving me a hand here?"

"Sure! What d'ya want me to do?"

David handed him a piece of wood, and Willy eagerly pitched in to mend the fence.

They worked together for the better part of an hour before Gage joined them.

"I'm glad you're here, Captain Gage," Willy said. "Now you can help David, and I can take a rest."

"Wait a minute. How come you get to rest, and I have to keep working?" David teased the boy.

" 'Cause I'm a little kid," Willy said, and dashed off across the field toward the house. "I'll bring you somethin' to drink!" he yelled.

David laughed as Willy disappeared in the direction of the house. "He's a good boy."

"Yes, he is. I'm going to miss him when I go."

"You're leaving?" David asked.

"Probably in a day or two. There's really no point in my staying now that I believe I've repaid Abbie for her hospitality. In fact, I've been wondering why I haven't left sooner. I really have to muster out and get home to my family. They're probably worried sick about me."

Though David could understand Gage's concern about his family, he couldn't believe how blind the captain was to his own feelings and needs.

"Gage." David laid down the piece of wood he had been trying to fit into a gap in the fence. He looked up, pinning the other man's gaze with his own. "You know exactly why you've stayed. Don't you think it's time you admitted it to yourself?"

Gage frowned. "I don't know what you're talking about."

"You could have left for St. Louis any time after your first week here, but you didn't. You wanted to help Abbie because you're grateful to her, true, but there's more to it than your gratitude. Abbie is a beautiful, kind, strong woman. It wouldn't be difficult to come to care for a woman like her."

Gage scowled. "Abbie's never going to be able to forget that her husband was killed by our troops. Somehow she blames me for all that's happened to her. When we argued that morning, we said some pretty ugly things to each other, things I'm afraid neither one of us will ever forget or forgive."

"We all say things we really don't mean in the heat of the moment. In a way it was good that you argued and cleared the air between you. You've both been surrounded by death and destruction for so long, neither one of you knows how to get on with your life. She's not the only one who has to learn to forgive and to love again.

"If you want to heal from the wounds you carry inside and out, begin with Abbie. In showing her how to live again, you'll be helping yourself. In reminding her how it feels to be young, you'll be renewing yourself. In making her feel like a woman, you'll feel like a man again."

Gage gave David a strange look. "You're very wise for one so young."

"Thanks."

"Don't get overconfident, though, I still outrank you."

"I wouldn't be so sure about that," David muttered under his breath, trying not to smile. When he looked up, Gage was looking at the house as if he were weighing his choices.

"What did you say?" Gage asked, turning to David.

"I said you'd better get going. You've wasted too much time already."

"Maybe you're right."

*   *   *

On his way to the barn, Gage decided he *had* wasted too much time since his argument with Abbie. David was right. Gage had gained great respect and admiration for Abbie since he arrived at Riverbend, but he hadn't realized how much he cared about her until he'd decided to leave.

The thought of never seeing her again, or hearing her seductive Southern drawl, or feeling her soft body in his arms, disturbed him more than he had wanted to admit. There was no denying that even while they had argued, she had stirred his desire.

He had also realized after their argument that she had been angry because he had moved out of the house, misinterpreting his reason for doing so. That had been a good sign. It showed that she did care about him and had taken their truce seriously. He was the idiot for waiting all this time to try to bridge this hellish gap of bitterness and hatred that separated them. But he was going to try now. He had to. He couldn't leave without making peace with her.

Gage entered the barn, found Micah, and enlisted his help. Micah looked at him as if he'd lost his mind, but hurried to do as Gage had asked.

Leaving the barn, Gage stopped at the pump to wash up. When he finished, he looked up at the house. As he had always done when going into battle, he prepared himself for the worst possible contingency. His commanders had considered him an expert strategist. He hoped their faith in him proved true this time, for he wanted badly to succeed with this campaign.

He shook his head. He had to stop thinking of Abbie as his enemy. She needed to be coaxed, not conquered.

As prepared as he would ever be for the upcoming skirmish, he passed the overgrown garden on his way to the house and stopped to pick some of the wildflowers. He knew they were probably weeds, but he didn't care. He was going calling, and this was the best he could do for now. He would have preferred roses. Roses would have suited her, but this was not Boston before the war. He would have to make do with what he had.

"Bess, where's Abbie?" he called as he passed the kitchen.

Bess stuck her head out the door. "Last time I saw her she was in the parlor."

Gage could feel her eyes on him as he continued toward the main house.

"Abbie?" he called.

"I'm in the front parlor," came her answer.

Worriedly, Abbie went into the hall. Gage had not been in the house since the morning they'd fought. She wondered if something was wrong. He walked toward her from the back of the house, and she feared he had hurt himself, for he held one hand behind his back and had the oddest expression on his face.

"What is it?" she asked. "Has something happened? Did you hurt yourself again?"

"No, but I have something for you." He stopped before her, and in a gallant motion reminiscent of a knight presenting a garter to his lady, offered her the bouquet.

She stared at him. "Flowers," she whispered, her gaze going from the colorful wild arrangement to his face. "You brought me flowers?"

He handed them to her, then bowed. "And your carriage awaits, milady," he announced, gesturing toward the front of the house where Micah had just driven up.

"My carriage? What are you up to?" she demanded warily.

He smiled broadly. "I'm kidnapping you and taking you for a carriage ride."

"But I have to . . ."

"When was the last time you had some fun, Abbie?"

"Well, I . . ." She clutched the flowers, gazing up at this darkly handsome man who wanted to carry her away.

"Allow me."

He took her arm and held the front door as they left the house, and he helped her into the open carriage.

"Thanks, Micah," he said as the old man handed him the reins.

Micah smiled and walked toward the kitchen. As she watched him go, Abbie's first impulse was to call him back. She couldn't believe she was actually sitting beside Gage—in her own carriage, no less. They'd barely spoken since their argument, and the terrible words they had flung at each other still hovered between them. Why had he sought her out now?

Gripping the flowers in her trembling hands, she felt anxious, skittish. She quickly glanced at him. Doubts assailed her, yet she couldn't help admiring the strength of his profile, his dark hair glinting almost black in the sunlight, his strong, competent hands.

He looked at her, grinning rakishly. "Where to, milady?"

She laughed heartily, then wondered at her own sanity. How could she be feeling so carefree when so much anger and bitterness existed between them, when she felt so keenly the heavy weight of her responsibility for Riverbend and for Micah's family on her twenty-two-year-old shoulders?

Though troubled, she tried not to question the craziness of her actions, but to enjoy the moment. After all, nothing would change during her brief absence. All her worries and the struggle for survival would still be waiting for her, and perhaps during her few hours of freedom she would find out what the unpredictable Gage was up to.

"I think, milord, that I'd like to drive to the pond," she pronounced, willing to suspend her anger at him and join in his game-playing. "Follow the drive and I'll show you where to turn off."

"My pleasure, milady," he said in the most courtly manner.

They drove at a leisurely pace, each enjoying the quiet, each very much aware of the other's presence.

"So tell me about the pond," Gage said.

"It's past the stream, a mile or two. My friends and I used to picnic there before I got married and before the war," she explained, feeling slightly sad as she thought of those long-ago days. "We had so much fun. Life was good then."

"Life can be good again."

"I don't know. Nothing will ever be the same."

"No. It won't. There's no bringing back the past. We have only the future."

"That's true, but I really shouldn't be doing this. And I shouldn't be here with you," she said, hoping to discover Gage's reason for this outing.

"Of course you should," he insisted. "You have to take time to enjoy each day."

"I suppose." So this carriage ride was just a break in their work-driven routine. But why had he chosen today to take a day off? And why hadn't he sought out her company before today? Maybe, she mused, because he planned to leave soon and this was his way of saying good-bye.

Upset by that thought, she gazed down at her bouquet. His bringing her the wildflowers meant so much to her. This reaction surprised her. What was wrong with her? She wanted him gone, didn't she?

"These are beautiful flowers. It was thoughtful of you to give them to me. Thank you, Gage."

He smiled at her. "You're welcome."

She showed him where the turn was then, and they started down a narrow dirt road.

"Tell me more about your picnics."

Putting aside her troubled thoughts, she told him about the beaux who'd courted her, her friends and the games they used to play.

"It used to be such a beautiful place." She sighed. "Preston proposed to me at the pond. He promised he would never leave me. He promised me, too, that we'd always be happy. If we'd been able to foretell the future, I doubt he'd have believed it. He thought he would live forever."

"Every man thinks that," Gage said.

They topped a low rise, and before them lay the pond, sparkling in the sunlight.

"Which way now?" he asked.

"To the right and stop there, by the grove." She pointed to a small clearing.

As soon as he'd reined in, she placed her flowers on the seat and climbed down without waiting for him to help her.

"It's so overgrown, it's hard to tell where

everything was." She looked around, trying to remember exactly how things had been. It had been so long since she'd ventured this way. There just had been no time, and even if there had been, it wasn't safe to wander the country-side alone anymore. "I think the boat was over here."

Suddenly, feeling young and free, she ran lightheartedly toward where they used to dock the boat. To her delight, the small craft was there, but it had been battered by the weather. She was so excited she was almost dancing.

"Look! I was right! Gage, help me put it in! We've even got the oars!"

"This doesn't look too sturdy," he remarked thoughtfully as he helped her drag the boat to the water's edge.

"Oh, please. Let's try it! It'll be fine. I'm sure."

"Well . . ."

"If you're afraid, I can take it out by myself and you can stay on shore," she dared him, laughing.

"Afraid? Me? Never. You wait on the dock, and I'll row over and pick you up there so you won't get wet."

The bank was marshy and she knew it would be difficult for her to get in the boat with her long skirts. "So, you are a true gentleman," she teased.

"It took you long enough to notice," he countered with a grin.

She flushed at his remark and turned toward the dock. She had difficulty walking up the path, overgrown with bushes and foliage, but she picked her way carefully, studiously trying not to watch Gage. Try as she might, though, she couldn't keep her eyes off him. His broad shoulders and long, lean build made her heart beat a little too quickly. She watched him climb into the small craft and push off from the bank with the oar. He seemed to know what he was doing as he maneuvered toward the dock.

She was unsure of her feelings as she watched him, but she smiled. Then he suddenly stood up in the boat, and her smile faltered.

"What the—" he shouted.

"What's wrong?"

"It's got a leak!"

He sat down and tried to row faster, but he was still more than six feet from the dock. She realized that the boat was taking on water too quickly.

As it sank, Gage stood again and jumped over the side, but the water was over his head, and he vanished beneath the surface.

Chapter Six

"Gage!"

Terror seized Abbie. She was about to plunge into the water when Gage surfaced.

"I'm all right," he yelled. "Stay there!"

He swam easily to shore and slogged up the bank.

As she watched him wade toward her, dripping wet, her fear evaporated. She burst into laughter, unable to stop.

"You think it's funny, do you?" he challenged, moving toward her.

She shrieked, laughing as she tried to evade him, but he was too quick for her. Before she knew it, his arms were around her waist and she was enfolded in his soggy embrace, tight against his muscular chest.

The shock of that contact held her perfectly still, and she felt the back of her dress grow wet. She knew she should try to free herself, but it felt so good being close to him. She seemed to fit perfectly into the curve of his body. He pressed a soft kiss on the side of her neck and a wave of excitement shot through her. She stifled a groan, shivering from the power of the emotions that simple kiss evoked in her.

She sighed, turning in his arms, lifting her lips to his. "Oh, Gage . . ."

His kiss trapped her in a whirlwind of desire that sent her spinning out of control. All at once she was young and desirable and alive again. This man . . . Gage . . . made her feel that way. She looped her arms around his neck and clung to him. Her breasts were pressed tightly against his chest and her hips nestled against him. It had been so long since she'd known such passion . . . too long. She moaned softly.

He ended the kiss and lifted her in his arms. "Gage!" she gasped.

He silenced her with another kiss as he carried her up the bank to the grove. He set her down on the soft grass and then lay down beside her.

"I want you, Abbie." His gaze held hers.

She raised her arms and drew him down to her. For just a fleeting instant she thought she saw a flash of pain in his eyes, but then it was gone. Her lips found his, and nothing existed but the sensual world of their kiss.

A web of passion spun around them. Abbie shifted closer, wanting to be near him, needing that closeness. He wanted her. The thought excited her, and she realized there was no denying that she wanted him, too.

When Gage began to caress her, she stiffened. It had been so long since she'd been intimate with a man. But he seemed to understand her resistance, and she relaxed. His kiss softened, coaxing her to respond to him, and emboldened, she caressed him and felt him shudder.

Her hands skimmed over his broad shoulders and back. Then, wanting to feel his skin, she began to unbutton his shirt. He drew away and stripped it off, then pulled her back into his arms. She rubbed her cheek against his bare chest, purring with delight.

When Gage unfastened her bodice and slipped down her chemise, she did not resist. At the touch of his mouth on her breasts, passion erupted inside her. She arched against him and he moved over her, fitting his body to hers. It was as if they had been made for each other. She wanted him, needed him . . . And then suddenly he was pulling away, withdrawing from her.

"Gage . . . What is it?" Breathless from his kisses, her eyes closed, she was still aroused, still wanting to feel the heat of his body. Nearly mindless with her newly awakened need, she reached up to bring him back down to her.

"Abbie, look at me." Gage's voice was hoarse with passion as he lowered her arms to her sides.

She opened her eyes and saw in his face his determination to master his desire for her. "Why did you stop?"

"Because you're not sure of how you feel about me, and I respect you too much to do anything that might cause you pain."

"I want you," she admitted, embarrassed to say such things. She had never spoken like this to Preston.

"Why do you want me, Abbie?"

She had no answer. She felt lost and disoriented and more confused than ever. "I . . . I don't know. . . . " She moved away from him, fumbling with her buttons to cover herself.

She stood, trembling, and to hide her confusion, she brushed her clothes and tried to straighten her skirts. Her dress was damp, though, and some of the stains would not brush out. She hoped the garment dried before they returned to the house.

"We'd better go," she suggested, trying not to look at him.

Sitting there in the sun without his shirt, Gage looked devastatingly handsome and desirable. It was all she could do not to go back into his arms. She thought about her life with Preston and tried to remember how she'd felt about him before they'd wed. She remembered enjoying his kisses, but she had never felt this driving passion that she experienced in Gage's arms.

"Not yet," Gage said, looking up at her, giving her a tender smile. "Let's take a walk."

She saw the kindness, the gentleness in his eyes and, pleased, smiled back. "I'd like that."

He stood, grabbed his still-wet shirt, and shrugged into it. He didn't button it, though, letting it hang open. His expression was amused as he reached for her hand. "I think Bess and Micah are going to give us some funny looks when we get back."

Abbie laughed conspiratorially as she took his hand. "I'm sure we look frightful, but we have a sunken boat to prove our story."

They circled the pond, stopping at different spots while Gage asked her about the area. As they walked, she asked him about his home and family, and he told her of his parents and brothers and sisters in Boston. It was more than an hour later when they returned to the carriage.

"I had a wonderful time, Gage."

"That's exactly what I hoped you'd say. I thought a day together would be good for both of us, Abbie." He leaned toward her and kissed her once more, a tender kiss that spoke less of passion than of devotion.

So he hadn't wanted to tell her he was leaving. All he had wanted to do was make her happy, bring some fun back into her life. Relief flooding through her, she knew now that it was time for her to give something to him.

"Gage . . ." At his questioning look, she said, "I'm sorry for the way I've treated you. I know I said some truly awful things the day we fought. And I regret them deeply. I also realize that some of what you said was true, and I know I can't blame you for my unhappiness. Can you forgive me?"

He touched her cheek tenderly and smiled. "The price of my forgiveness is high."

"How high?"

"One kiss . . ."

Their lips met softly.

"I'm sorry, too, Abbie. I know you're not any of those things I called you. You're strong, brave, and most of all, a lady."

Touching his hand, she smiled and felt a warm glow, as if the sun had burst inside her.

For a moment they gazed into each other's eyes. Then Gage helped her into the carriage and climbed in beside her.

During the return trip to Riverbend, Abbie felt peaceful and happy sitting next to Gage, as if it was where she belonged.

Abbie helped Bess clear the table, then started washing the dinner dishes. Usually, such a mindless task bored her, but tonight she was glad for the monotonous chore, for she needed the time to think.

Dinner had been most enjoyable, as enjoyable as her afternoon with Gage.

They had all said grace, shared the plain yet nourishing fare, and spent the next hour talking and laughing and simply enjoying one another's company.

Halfway through dinner, she had realized she no longer thought of Gage or David as Yankees or her enemies. They had helped her when she needed them most, and she would never forget their kindness. She was also glad she and Gage had apologized and made peace with each other.

Frowning, she methodically scrubbed the dishes in the hot sudsy water, handing each clean one to Bess to dry. But it was more than that. All through the meal, her gaze had been drawn to Gage. Several times when their eyes had met across the table, he'd smiled at her, and the intimacy of his smile made her catch her breath as if her heart were in her throat.

She had told herself it was because he was handsome and looked even more so in Preston's neat, stylish clothes, filling them out perfectly. When they had returned from the pond, she had seen that the shirt and pants she had given him when he'd first arrived were ruined. So she had retrieved more of Preston's clothes from the attic and asked Micah to give them to Gage. He had thanked her when he'd come to the house for dinner.

419

But it wasn't his good looks that had excited her. It was the memory of his kisses and his caresses, and to her shock, her longing for more. That realization had made her eager for the meal to end, and she had been somewhat relieved when the men left the dinner table to do the evening chores.

She didn't know or understand what was happening to her, and her confusion was leading to fear.

"Miz Abbie? What's troublin' you?" Bess asked, taking another wet dish from her and drying it. "You look like you got the weight of the world on you."

"I don't know, Bess." Abbie sighed.

"I think I do. Does it have to do with Gage?" Bess looked directly at Abbie and chuckled.

Abbie felt her face grow hot.

"There's nothin' to fret about," Bess said. "He's a good man."

"I know, and that's what scares me."

"Scares you? What's there to be scared of? You done everything you could to chase him off, yet he stayed. How many men do you think would act the way he done if you took a shot at them?"

Again Abbie flushed, remembering that day not so long ago. "He is kind."

"Very."

"And hard-working."

"Micah told me they just about finished off that fence today."

"And handsome . . . Bess, I'd like to take a walk. Would you mind . . . ?"

"Go on." Bess took the plate Abbie was holding and shooed her from the kitchen. "I'll do these last few dishes."

"Thank you."

Abbie escaped from the kitchen into the cool, quiet evening. She had to sort out her puzzling thoughts and feelings. She wandered through the garden, remembering all the times she'd walked there with Preston, memories that were gentle and beautiful. Her steps took her toward the peaceful grove sheltering the cemetery. As she neared Preston's marker, she began to cry softly.

Gage and David were splitting logs near the barn when they saw Abbie leave the house and pass the garden. David saw how Gage watched her as if transfixed, and quickly assured him he could finish the job alone.

He watched Gage follow Abbie in the direction of the cemetery and smiled. "Well, things are definitely looking better. Gage has been more lighthearted since this afternoon, and Abbie actually seemed happy and relaxed tonight at dinner. I hope all goes well for Gage right now. He's beginning to love her and needs to know they have a future together."

He waited.

"No comment?" He glanced upward. "Then I

guess I'm doing all right."

"Of course you are," Micah said from behind him. The old man gave David a curious look, then followed his gaze upward to the cloudless evening sky. "You worried it's gonna rain?"

"Never can tell."

"I know you doin' fine with them there logs, but you want some help?"

"Sure, then we'll be done in no time."

"Where did Gage go? I thought he was helpin'."

"He was. He just has a more important job to do."

Micah didn't question him, taking a log from the pile.

As Gage neared the cemetery, he could hear Abbie's voice. He'd thought she was alone, and not wanting to intrude, he paused to hear who was with her.

"Oh, Preston. I never thought I'd have to live without you."

Hearing the misery and sorrow in her voice, he felt frozen, rooted to the spot where he stood.

"I miss you and our life together, more than I ever thought possible. You were my reason for living. Why did the war have to take you away from me?"

Gage's chest tightened.

"I never loved anyone but you, Preston, in my whole life. From the time I was twelve, I dreamed of the day I would marry you. You were my hero . . . my knight in shining armor. You were perfect in every way, and I shall never love anyone the way I loved you. Nor will I forget the reason I lost everything."

Hearing her cry, Gage felt all the excitement and anticipation that had built all afternoon and during dinner die, and feeling cold and empty, he backed away from the graveyard, careful to make no noise. He realized he should have let her know he was there, but now he was painfully glad that he hadn't. He'd needed to hear the truth from her, and now he had.

He had thought that today had been a turning point in their lives, that they had found peace and perhaps the beginning of love growing between them. But obviously he had been wrong. They had no future together. He could not battle a ghost or their past. Abbie loved Preston—still. And no matter what she had said this afternoon, she would never forgive this Yankee for all she had lost.

Chapter Seven

Lost in thought, David put away his axe. It seemed his mission was almost completed. If all was going well, then at this moment Gage and Abbie were finally admitting they loved each other, and David could be on his way.

The thought gave him pause. His time at Riverbend, though frustrating, had been a welcome reprieve from the violence and misery he'd seen and dealt with during the war. The beauty and tranquility of the plantation had done much to ease his spirit, and he would miss its serenity. God only knew where he would be sent next!

He would also miss Abbie, Micah, Bess, Gage, and of course, Willy, but it always felt wonderful when people's lives fulfilled God's plan.

He started to leave the barn but then saw Gage enter and stopped. "That didn't take long. Did you talk to Abbie?" He had expected good news, hoping his mission had been a success. What had happened?

"There was no point," Gage said tersely. He stalked to his saddlebag and began stuffing the pants of his uniform and his few toiletries into it, leaving the rest of Preston's clothes on a bale of hay.

"What are you doing?"

"I've overstayed my welcome. So I'm heading out."

"What does Abbie have to say about this?"

"I didn't bother to ask."

"Why not?" David stared at him in exasperation and thought, Not again!

"Let's just say Abbie and I have too many memories between us. It was incredibly naive of me to think that anything would change because of some flowers, a walk by a pond, and some pretty words."

"But you can't leave! I know she cares about you."

Gage turned on him with a cold-eyed glare. "You didn't hear what I heard. I know exactly how she feels. No man is ever going to replace Preston in her heart, especially a Yankee, so there's no need for me to stick around."

His packing done, he quickly went outside and saddled his horse. David followed him.

"But, Gage, you do love her, don't you?"

Again the angry man pinned him with an icy look. "I can't force Abbie to love me. Love has to be freely given."

"You're willing to walk away from the woman you love without a fight?"

"David, believe me, Abbie and I are better off living our own lives, mine in the North where I belong and hers where her husband is buried. Just tell everyone in the morning that I'm long overdue in St. Louis and that it was time for me to go home."

"You know, sometimes in life you get only one chance at happiness. If you let it slip away, you may never have that chance again."

"I have to go." Gage slid his rifle into its sheath, threw his saddlebag over his horse's back, and swung up into the saddle. Taking up the reins, he looked down at David. "Trust me, it's better this way."

"Think about what I said," David said, offering Gage his hand.

They shook hands, and then Gage rode slowly off down the lane. David watched him go, wondering how things had managed to fall apart so quickly. He'd thought they'd realized they loved each other. Obviously, he'd been wrong.

When at last her tears were spent, Abbie sat quietly for a long time at Preston's grave, gazing at the countryside. There was serenity here, a peace that had helped her let go of her grief, resolve her troubled thoughts, and know the secret of her innermost desires. She looked up again at the marker.

She would never forget what she'd shared with Preston. Their love had been beautiful and precious, and she knew a part of her would love him forever. But she also faced the truth that she didn't want to spend the rest of her life alone. Preston was gone and the war was over. It was time to let go of the hate and anger and bitterness it had created. It was time to heal, to learn to live again, to forgive herself as well as Gage. At least she had taken a step in that direction this afternoon, and any doubts she'd had about her feelings for him had been washed away by her tears.

Images of Gage played in her mind. Gage as the forbidding Yankee captain who reminded her of those who had taken everything from her. Gage as the long-suffering patient after she'd shot at him. Gage wading out of the pond dripping wet. Gage as the man who'd brought her back to life with his kisses. She smiled.

She hadn't believed she could ever fall in love again, but she thought she might be falling in love with Gage. What she felt for him was different from the young, innocent love she'd had with Preston.

She fell silent for a minute as she imagined a future with Gage. She thought of making love to him, of sharing with him, of laughing with him and living with him. Excitement built within her as she pictured all these things in her mind.

She rested her cheek against the marker for a moment, in a last loving gesture for what was past. Then she rose and went to look for the man who was her future.

After Gage had left, David hadn't been quite sure what to do. He had asked for guidance, but there had been only silence, so he'd been pondering his dilemma for about a half-hour when Abbie entered the barn.

"Evening, David." She looked around, then frowned.

"Evening, Abbie. Anything I can do for you?"

"I was just looking for Gage. I thought he'd be getting ready to bed down. I wanted to talk to him. Do you know where he is?"

"No. He rode out a while ago. He said to tell you it was time for him to leave."

Abbie looked stricken. "He's gone." Her voice was a whisper. "Did he say why?"

"He followed you to the cemetery to talk to you, but then came right back. All he would say was that there wasn't any point in his staying."

"Did he say where he was going? I have to find him. I have to tell him—"

"To St. Louis to muster out and then home, so he's riding north. He couldn't have gone too far. He hasn't been gone that long."

"David." She gripped his arm. "Will you help me find him? Now? Tonight? I have to go after him. I can't let him leave this way."

"Do you love him?"

"Yes, I think I do. After this afternoon, I spent the rest of the day soul-searching. Now that I know he overheard me in the cemetery, I understand why he left. But I have no intention of letting him get away."

"All your mistrust and hatred is gone?" David took a deep breath and smiled, believing a miracle had happened.

"Yes. I've come to understand a lot these last few days. Not only because of Gage, but because of you, too. You've shown me there's no difference between Yankees and Southerners. That we are all alike. And your kindness and generosity have meant a lot to me. I'll never forget you."

"Well, now, since you put it that way, let me get Harmony and your horse, and we'll ride after Gage right now."

"Really? Oh, David, thank you! You're an angel!" She kissed him on the cheek, then ran toward the house, her hair flying behind her. "I'll change and tell Bess where we're going. Then I'll be ready."

David shook his head. Would wonders never cease!

* * *

As Abbie rode beside David down the drive, she felt sure that once they found Gage, everything would be all right.

Somehow, David had the ability to make her feel that way. Things certainly had been different with his presence at Riverbend, and she wasn't thinking only about the eggs that had mysteriously multiplied from three to five and then to six when Gage arrived. Or the fresh meat that had appeared quite often after the first time David had sent Willy home with two rabbits. Or the incredible number of repairs that had been accomplished. For example, the shutters—she still couldn't figure out when he had replaced the missing ones and fixed the rest.

All she knew was that more than the plantation had changed, and she would be forever grateful to the quiet man beside her.

Gage rode only for about an hour before deciding to make camp for the night. The ground was as hard and unforgiving as he remembered, and his sleeping bag offered little comfort. Not that it mattered. He figured he wasn't going to sleep much anyway, not the way he felt.

He had always prided himself that when he made up his mind to do something, he did it. As he lay there awake, thinking of all that had transpired that day, his heart told him to go back, to try again.

But his mind knew it was pointless. Her words

were branded into his soul. *I never loved anyone but you, Preston, in my whole life. Nor will I ever forget the reason I lost everything.* And he would never forget the tears she'd shed in her grief and loneliness.

When David had asked him if he loved her, he'd been unable to deny it to himself any longer, and knowing that he did, he had to leave. It would hurt too much to stay, knowing how she felt.

Accepting the decision he had made, and believing he'd had no other choice, he settled back and tried to sleep.

"I hope we find him soon," Abbie said as she and David made their way north on the road from Riverbend. They'd been traveling nearly an hour, yet had seen no sign of Gage. The road ahead curved to the left. As they neared the turn, gunshots rang out and three Confederate soldiers came running from the woods.

"Hold it right there!" one of the men ordered in a harsh voice.

Abbie screamed and pulled on the reins to keep her horse from bolting. Beside her, David reached out to calm her mount. When he grabbed the reins, the steed quieted, and the three Rebs, armed and deadly, surrounded them.

"What do you want?" David asked.

"Your horses," the man who had ordered them

431

to stop replied, his gaze hot on Abbie. He licked his thick lips as he ogled her. "Sam—you and Joe take their horses."

"Okay, Cal," Sam, a thin gaunt man, replied, and he and his heavyset cohort dragged Abbie and David off their horses to the ground.

David tried to go to Abbie, but the thin man grabbed him.

"She's Cal's now."

David swung at him, knocking his gun away, and they began to fight.

"David!" Abbie cried, fearing for his life, knowing he was outnumbered. But she had little time to think of him, for suddenly Cal gripped her arm and yanked her to him.

"I didn't know I was going to be rewarded this nicely tonight," he said, leering at her. "I thought we were only going to get some horses. Looks like I'm going to get a better ride than I ever dreamed of."

He fondled her breasts, and she panicked and struggled with him. "No!" she screamed.

Wildly twisting away from his pawing hands, she saw David knock the wiry man off him and stagger to his feet. But the other man was there waiting, and David wrestled him like an avenging angel.

Abbie could see he was valiantly holding his own, but then the thin Rebel came up from behind him, and before she could warn David, the man hit him on the back of his head. David slumped forward into the dirt.

"David!"

At that moment, Abbie knew deep, soul-wrenching terror. Had she survived the horrors of the war to die like this? And David . . . He was trying to rise, though still dazed.

"Looks like you're all mine now, sweetheart," Cal said with a triumphant laugh, and began dragging her toward the woods.

"You're not taking her anywhere, mister. Now, get your filthy hands off her before I put a bullet right between your eyes."

Gage's rifle was trained on the man holding Abbie, ready to shoot. He had been dozing off when he'd heard the gunshots and recognized Abbie's voice when she screamed. Quickly, he had mounted, ready to ride to her aid. He hadn't known what she was doing out in the country-side in the middle of the night, but he'd hurried to find out.

The Reb dropped his hands and stepped away from Abbie.

"Gage!" Abbie ran to him. "Thank God you're here!"

"Thank God, indeed," David managed as he finally stood.

"David, take their guns while I keep an eye on them. Then we'll tie them up and see how the law will deal with them in town."

Within minutes, David had bound and gagged

Bobbi Smith

the three men, and only then did Gage relax his vigilance and lower his rifle. He'd nearly lost control at the sight of the man's groping hands on Abbie.

Leaving David to guard their captives, he walked to where Abbie stood near the trees at the side of the road, a safe distance from their prisoners.

"Are you all right?" he asked, his gaze going over her lovely features in the moonlight, reassuring himself that she hadn't been harmed.

"Now that you're here," she said.

Unable to stop himself, Gage took her in his arms. "What were you and David doing out here at this time of night? Didn't you realize it could be dangerous?"

"I was coming after you! Why did you leave, Gage?" She nestled against his chest.

"I couldn't stay, Abbie," he began. Then, realizing she deserved to know everything, he took a deep breath and gathered his courage.

"I followed you to the cemetery to talk to you, but when I got there, I heard you declaring your love for Preston and your sorrow for all you'd lost. I love you, Abbie, but I can't compete with your husband, or make up for all the war has done, not just to you but to both of us. We have to accept that all that's over now, that Preston's gone. There's so much life yet to be lived—and I want to live it with you."

She drew slightly away to look up at him. "I

434

know Preston's dead." She looked him straight in the eye. "And I loved him and everything we had built together before the war. But I've finally realized there can be no future for me if I can't let go of the past. You don't have to compete with anyone, Gage, not now or ever, and I don't hold you responsible for what I've suffered. I had come to the barn to tell you that, but David told me you'd gone."

"Oh, sweetheart," he groaned, and bent to kiss her. "And to think I almost lost you tonight. . . . "

He clasped her to his heart, vowing to the heavens that he would never let her go.

"I love you, Gage Morgan."

"And I love you. Will you marry me?"

"Yes." Her eyes were aglow with happiness as he looked down at her. "I can think of no greater joy than being your wife."

Gage kissed her again, a passionate embrace. "I will never let anyone or anything hurt you ever again, Abbie. I promise."

"And I will never let you get away from me again," she told him with a gentle smile.

They kissed once more, then walked to where David guarded the Rebels.

"We're turning them in tonight, aren't we?" David asked.

"Yes. We'll take Abbie home first, then ride into town."

"Good. The sooner they're locked up, the better."

"David, thank you for bringing Abbie to me," Gage said, his arm around her waist.

David smiled, then looked at Abbie.

"We're going to be married," she said, her adoring gaze on Gage, who couldn't wait to make her his.

"Well, what a surprise!" David laughed.

They laughed, too, and Gage held Abbie tight as they headed their horses back to Riverbend.

Chapter Eight

"Do you, Abigail Randolph, take this man, Gage Morgan, to be your lawfully wedded husband?"

"I do."

"Do you, Gage Morgan, take this woman, Abigail Randolph, to be your lawfully wedded wife?"

"I do."

"I now pronounce you man and wife. What God has joined together let no man put asunder," the minister intoned, and closed the Bible.

"You may kiss your bride, Mr. Morgan."

Gage needed no encouragement. He took Abbie into his arms and kissed her.

Then the small celebration began, and after the minister left, Bess, Micah, Willy, and David gracefully excused themselves as quickly as they could.

Eagerly, Gage swept his bride into his arms and carried her up the stairs. He entered her bedroom and set her gently on the featherbed. He closed and locked the door, then sat down beside her.

"I'm sorry your family couldn't be here for the wedding," Abbie said.

"I didn't want to wait," he answered, seeing her love for him shining in her warm brown eyes. "I told them in my letter that we were marrying and then I was leaving for St. Louis to muster out. I promised we'd visit them soon after I got back to Riverbend."

"I'd like that."

"I love you, Abbie." He gazed down at her, thinking her the most beautiful woman in the world.

"I love you, too," she answered, drawing him to her.

He stretched out beside her and took her in his arms. The moment was ecstasy for him. He had often dreamed of a time when she would be his in all ways, and now that time had come.

He helped her remove her dress and under-garments and then gazed down at her lovely body. She was a goddess. Her full breasts invited his caress, and he laved them with sensual kisses that left them both breathless with desire. His hands traced erotic patterns on her smooth skin, and he felt her shiver.

Leaving her for only a moment, Gage turned down the lamp on the table and then undressed. She was waiting, her arms lifted up to him. He went to her, his body fitting hers, and they locked in love's most intimate embrace.

He began to move inside her, cherishing the glory of making her his own. When she matched his movements, urging him on, he was swept away by the beauty of their union.

Theirs was a perfect mating, a giving and taking of pleasure that left them both completely sated and yet excited for more. They loved through the night, finally creating new memories to replace the old, memories they would cherish forever.

Wrapped in each other's arms, Gage and Abbie woke at dawn, yet refused to relinquish the sweetness of their loving. They took their time, whispering endearments, exploring and kissing until their desire became unbearable. They made love once more, celebrating their first morning as husband and wife. It was almost nine o'clock before they even considered leaving their marriage bed.

"We'd better go downstairs," Abbie said, smiling a little guiltily. "Bess might think something's happened to us."

Gage grinned wickedly. "Something has happened to us."

She laughed and looped her arms around his neck. She pulled him to her, her lips seeking his. "And I loved every minute of it."

Nearly an hour later they entered the kitchen, and Abbie took in the scene of Bess, Micah, and Willy talking to David. She could see his horse saddled and tied up just outside.

"You're leaving?" she asked, taking Gage's arm and holding it tightly.

David's gaze met hers, his startlingly blue eyes filled with peace and joy. "I have to go."

Gage offered David his hand. "If you ever need anything, just let us know. Be sure to keep in touch."

"I will. I hope you two are always as happy as you are now." David went to Abbie and kissed her cheek. "Just remember he was heaven-sent."

She smiled. "I will . . . and so were you. Stay well and be careful on your way to Georgia."

"I will."

David kissed Bess and shook hands with Micah. He stopped before Willy and knelt down. "You take care."

Willy's eyes filled with tears. "I'm gonna miss you, David."

"I'll be as close as your call," he answered softly, and Abbie's eyes were wet as the man and child embraced.

After a long moment, David released Willy

and left the kitchen. He mounted Harmony and with one last wave started slowly down the drive.

Crying, Willy ran from the kitchen. "I wanna say good-bye again!" he yelled, running down the drive. Abbie and the others followed, watching as he stopped, his arms dropping at his sides, and ran back to them.

"He's gone!" he told his grandfather.

"He can't be. He was just there," Micah said.

Abbie gazed down the drive. It was true. There was no sign of David or of Harmony's hoofprints in the dirt. She looked at Gage and put her arm around his waist. "I never really knew much about David or his family. But I know one thing. He was an angel to me."

Gage smiled at her, hugging her close to his side. "I know. He was a gift from heaven."

She gazed up at her husband. "Yes, just like our love. I can think of no greater gift than to love you and to be loved by you."

Gage kissed her gently, poignantly, and then they followed the others to the main house.

About the Author

Bobbi Smith is a hopeless romantic and a firm believer in happily-ever-after endings. She was thrilled to be invited to contribute to this angel anthology, for she has a deep faith in the presence of our loving celestial guardians. She found the thought of creating an angel who was not only a guardian and a peacemaker but also a matchmaker delightful.

Bobbi believes that love is our reason for being. Unless we give love and receive love, we are not fully alive. Love does, indeed, make the world go around. Love is a gift from heaven.

Over the thirteen years of her writing career,

A Gift from Heaven

Bobbi has published twenty historical romances and four novellas. She lives in St. Charles, Missouri, with her husband, two sons, and four dogs.

An Angel's Touch

Heavenly Persuasion

LORRAINE HENDERSON

Lovely Jessica McAllister vows to honor her dying sister's final request. Determined to raise orphaned Maria as if she were her own daughter, Jessica never thinks she'll run into trouble in the form of the child's uncle, handsome winery-owner Benjamin Whittacker.

Benjamin is all man, and as headstrong as Jessica when it comes to deciding what is best for Maria. As sparks fly between the two, their fight for custody turns into a struggle to deny their own burning attraction.

Left to their own devices, the willful twosome may never discover their blossoming love. But Benjamin and Jessica are not alone. With one determined little girl—and her very special angelic helper—the stubborn duo just might be forced to acknowledge a love truly made in heaven.

_52069-9 $5.99 US/$7.99 CAN

Dorchester Publishing Co., Inc.
65 Commerce Road
Stamford, CT 06902

Please add $1.75 for shipping and handling for the first book and $.50 for each book thereafter. NY, NYC, PA and CT residents, please add appropriate sales tax. No cash, stamps, or C.O.D.s. All orders shipped within 6 weeks via postal service book rate. Canadian orders require $2.00 extra postage and must be paid in U.S. dollars through a U.S. banking facility.

Name_____
Address_____
City _____ State _____Zip_____
I have enclosed $_____in payment for the checked book(s).
Payment must accompany all orders.□ Please send a free catalog.

An Angel's Touch

Heaven's Gift

Janelle Denison

The last thing J.T. Rafferty expects when he awakes from a concussion is to find a beautiful stranger tending to his wounds. She saved his life, but the lovely Caitlan Daniels has some serious explaining to do—like how she ended up on his isolated ranch lands, miles from civilization. Despite his wariness, J.T. finds himself increasingly drawn to Caitlan, whose gentle touch promises sweet satisfaction. She is passionate and independent and utterly enchanting—but Caitlan also has a secret. And when J.T. finally discovers the shocking truth, he'll have to defy heaven and earth to keep her close to his heart.

_52059-1 $5.99 US/$7.99 CAN

Dorchester Publishing Co., Inc.
65 Commerce Road
Stamford, CT 06902

Please add $1.75 for shipping and handling for the first book and $.50 for each book thereafter. NY, NYC, PA and CT residents, please add appropriate sales tax. No cash, stamps, or C.O.D.s. All orders shipped within 6 weeks via postal service book rate. Canadian orders require $2.00 extra postage and must be paid in U.S. dollars through a U.S. banking facility.

Name_____

Address_____

City _____ State_____Zip_____

I have enclosed $_____in payment for the checked book(s).
Payment <u>must</u> accompany all orders.□ Please send a free catalog.

An Angel's Touch

D.J.'s Angel

LORI HANDELAND

D.J. Halloran doesn't believe in love. She's just seen too much heartache—in her work as a police officer and in her own life. And she vowed a long time ago never to let anyone get close enough to hurt her, even if that someone is the very captivating, very handsome Chris McCall.

But D.J. also has an angel—a special guardian determined, at any cost, to teach D.J. the magic of love. So try as she might to resist Chris's many charms, D.J. knows she is in for an even tougher battle because of her exasperating heavenly companion's persistent faith in the power of love.

_52050-8 $5.99 US/$7.99 CAN

Dorchester Publishing Co., Inc.
65 Commerce Road
Stamford, CT 06902

Please add $1.75 for shipping and handling for the first book and $.50 for each book thereafter. NY, NYC, PA and CT residents, please add appropriate sales tax. No cash, stamps, or C.O.D.s. All orders shipped within 6 weeks via postal service book rate. Canadian orders require $2.00 extra postage and must be paid in U.S. dollars through a U.S. banking facility.

Name_____

Address_____

City _____ State_____ Zip_____

I have enclosed $_____in payment for the checked book(s).
Payment <u>must</u> accompany all orders.□ Please send a free catalog.

An Angel's Touch

Longer Than Forever

BRONWYN WOLFE

"A wonderful, magical love story that transcends
time and space. Definitely a keeper!"
—Madeline Baker

Patrick is in trouble, alone in turn-of-the-century Chicago,
and unjustly jailed with little hope for survival. Then the
honey-haired beauty comes to him, as if she has heard his
prayers.

Lauren has all but given up on finding true love when she
feels the green-eyed stranger's call—summoning her across
boundaries of time and space to join him in a struggle against
all odds; uniting them in a love that will last longer than
forever.

_52042-7 $5.99 US/$7.99 CAN

Dorchester Publishing Co., Inc.
65 Commerce Road
Stamford, CT 06902

Please add $1.75 for shipping and handling for the first book and
$.50 for each book thereafter. NY, NYC, PA and CT residents,
please add appropriate sales tax. No cash, stamps, or C.O.D.s. All
orders shipped within 6 weeks via postal service book rate.
Canadian orders require $2.00 extra postage and must be paid in
U.S. dollars through a U.S. banking facility.

Name_____
Address_____
City _____ State_____ Zip_____
I have enclosed $_____in payment for the checked book(s).
Payment <u>must</u> accompany all orders.□ Please send a free catalog.

ATTENTION PREFERRED CUSTOMERS!

SPECIAL TOLL-FREE NUMBER
1-800-481-9191

Call Monday through Friday
12 noon to 10 p.m.
Eastern Time
Get a free catalogue
and order books using your
Visa, MasterCard,
or Discover®

Leisure
Books

LOVE
SPELL